Praise for (

"An author who has a unique voice and a magical plotting ability"

Frost Magazine

"Carver gives us strong heroines battling against the odds, fast-moving plots and a strong sense of place. She deservedly won the CWA Debut Dagger for Blood Junction"

Publishing News

"Gorgeously written... dazzlingly well-realised"

St. Petersburg Times

"Fans of action thrillers with an international flavour will find Carver's suspenseful, high-stakes, high-octane adventure a page-turning must read"

Booklist

"Powerful writing, a gripping plot and a unique setting... outstanding"

The Mystery and Thriller Club

"Stunning. Highly recommended."

Library Journal (starred review)

"One of the most riveting thrillers of recent years"

New Zealand Times

"A shocking, complex and beautifully written thriller and another cracker from the pen of bestseller CJ Carver"

Reader's Retreat

Also by CJ Carver

THE SNOW
THIEF

CJ Carver

FIGHT NUISANCE
PUBLISHING

First published in Great Britain by Right Nuisance Publishing in 2020
This paperback edition published by Right Nuisance Publishing in 2020
Right Nuisance Publishing website address is
www.rightnuisancepublishing.com

Copyright © 2020 C. J. Carver

A CIP catalogue record for this book is available from the
British Library

ISBN paperback 978-1-9164468-4-7

ISBN ebook 978-1-9164468-5-4

Printed and bound by CPI Group (UK) Ltd, Croydon, CR0 4YY

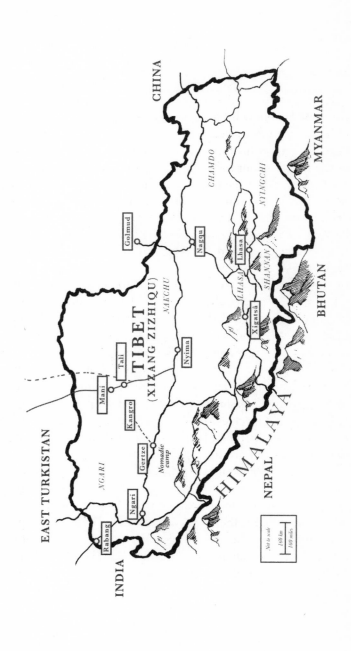

1

THE BOY KNELT IN the snow and peered through the gap in the tent. He knew he shouldn't be here – he'd been warned off by his parents as well as the Abbot – but how could he not keep an eye on his brother? Pemba wasn't very clever and needed looking out for or he'd get into trouble.

Tashi couldn't see much, just the edge of a monk's robe, so he parted the canvas a little further. A waft of incense drifted out; juniper and wild thyme. He rolled the scents over his tongue, revelling in the heady sensation that followed. He felt as though he could fly, soar into the sky and reel like an eagle above the spiky snow-capped mountains. For some reason incense had always had that effect on him, he didn't know why. Pemba could stick his head in a bonfire of juniper, breathe as deeply as he liked and experience nothing but a blackened face and smoke-choked lungs. His brother was about as spiritual as a pile of yak droppings.

You'd never think they were twins. Where Pemba was broad and strong for his age with a ruddy complexion and an open expression, Tashi was small and had a narrow, intelligent face and bright black eyes. When people were told they were twins, they sucked their teeth and shook their heads, amazed that nature could produce such an anomaly.

Their mother likened Pemba to a sturdy buffalo, Tashi a busily hopping sparrow, and, despite their differences, they were the best of friends, the closest of brothers, and even when they fought, they made up quickly. They hadn't spent a day apart since they were born. Well, aside from the time when Tashi had fallen ill last spring, but even then Pemba found a way to sneak into the monastery's medical ward each evening.

Where was Pemba? Anxiety nipped Tashi's belly as he swept his gaze around the interior of the tent, taking in the silent, formal atmosphere, the heavy rugs of yak wool on the floor, the wall hangings and the bronze cups smoking with juniper and rosemary twigs. The village had spent all day yesterday preparing for the lamas' visit, dragging carpets from the attic of the monastery and beating them, dust flying, until even the dogs were sneezing. Bowls had to be polished, chairs cleaned, and plentiful cauldrons of yak-butter tea set to brew.

There were five lamas, all wearing maroon robes and huge yellow discs like half-suns on their heads. Tashi scanned their serious, unsmiling faces, and although some were thinner and more angular than others, they all shared the same brown, minutely lined skin, like the leather of his father's shoes where the laces joined. They all looked the same age – ancient – and while part of him hated them for separating him from Pemba, the other felt a reluctant admiration that they'd made the journey from Lhasa in winter.

'Special times require special deeds,' Lama Sonam had told Tashi when he'd asked why they'd travelled at such a danger-ous time. Snow drifts were deep enough to swallow a truck, avalanches were common, and the temperatures at a point where your cup of tea froze solid within minutes if left outside. Pemba and Tashi's favourite game was throwing cups of boiling water into the air and watching the liquid freeze into minuscule crystals before it hit the ground.

'But what if you'd all died?' he'd asked, wide-eyed.

To his surprise, Lama Sonam chuckled. 'We'd still be here,' he said with a wink. 'You just wouldn't see us.'

'All of you?' Tashi was agog. 'Like Lobsang Norbu?'

Although the lama's expression didn't change, Tashi got the feeling he'd said something important.

'Are you talking about your Abbot?' he asked. 'Lobsang Norbu, who died two years ago?'

'Yes. I dream about him a lot. He nags me about studying.

2

He says I'm very bright but very lazy.' Tashi pulled a face. 'As if I didn't know that already.'

*

Now, Tashi could see Lama Sonam sitting cross-legged on the floor to one side of the tent. He was looking intently at something just out of Tashi's vision. All the monks from the monastery were here, squashed inside like a flock of sheep in a sheering pen, and although Tashi tried to peer past the bulk of one of the village monks he still couldn't see what everyone was staring at.

'This is the final test,' said a crisp voice. It belonged to Dawa Rinpoche, the High Abbot, a venerable figure clad in a faded tattered robe that appeared as old as he was. His skin was thin over his bones, his shoulders stooped, but despite his fragile appearance, he had an aura not just of serenity, but of immense power. 'Relax and take your time, my son. You have done well so far.'

Briefly, there was a swell of voices, excited and animated, but when the lama lifted his chin and looked around, everyone fell silent. Before he could change his mind, Tashi quickly slipped inside, closing the gap behind him and praying no one would notice the sudden draught of freezing air. On his hands and knees, he scurried around the edge of the crowd until he could see what everyone was looking at.

For a moment, he thought he was seeing things.

In front of the lamas, looking anxious and not a little scared, sat Pemba. He was poking some smooth grey river stones with a finger. Tashi frowned. He had poked those same stones the day before with Lama Sonam. Would Pemba remember which one to choose? He'd told him all about the games he'd played with the lama, but Pemba's memory wasn't great and he was bound to forget.

Just as he was about to drop on his belly and try and signal to Pemba, Lama Sonam raised his hand slightly and gestured *No*.

3

Tashi blinked. The lama hadn't glanced once in his direction. Had he really seen him?

The lama extended his fingers a fraction. Made the faintest of shoo-ing motions. Go away.

With a shiver inside, he realised Lama Sonam had been aware of him all this time.

Another unmistakable gesture. *Now. Before you get caught.*

Tashi dithered briefly before deciding to play it safe and crawl back outside. Pemba was fine, he reassured himself. He just had to hope his brother passed whatever test it was. Everyone appeared to be willing him to pick the right stone, as they'd will their horse to win a race.

'Do I sense an intruder?'

Tashi's skin shrank at the voice. He didn't know which lama had spoken, but it sent shivers through his soul. The tone sounded outwardly calm but Tashi could hear an enormous rage reverberating. The lama knew he was spying. *They could sense him just as he sensed they weren't what they were supposed to be.*

He reacted purely on instinct, without thought. As fast as he could, he wriggled out of the tent, got to his feet and ran. He raced past his uncle's house, startling the huge black mastiff into hysterical barks. Dodging around a row of little dwarf apple trees he swung right into the main street and away from the ceremonial tent. His breath was hot and raw in his throat as he approached his cottage, and although he wanted to run inside and bury his head in his mother's lap, tell her how scared he'd been, his instinct warned against it.

Instead, Tashi paused at the stone wall and doubled over, panting until he'd caught his breath. Only then did he saunter inside and settle himself in the kitchen with his mother and grandmother. He tried to appear relaxed, as though nothing was worrying him, and it was only during the afternoon that he realised the women were doing the same. They were all biding their time, waiting for Pemba to return.

Finally the sun set behind the peaks of the Himalaya. From the monastery came the sound of trumpets. The streets became crowded with chattering villagers. Hundreds of butter lights were lit, cooking pots put on fires, butter tea to heat.

When Pemba finally came home, he was exhausted. Their father was half-carrying him, but he didn't look unhappy about it. Immediately their mother began to busy herself preparing supper.

'What were you doing in the tent?' Tashi asked Pemba, his voice hushed. 'Why was everyone looking at you?'

'I don't know,' Pemba mumbled. 'But it was worse than school. They never stopped asking questions.'

'Like what?'

'How I'd describe creation and dissolution.'

'What did you say?'

'That it was like striking a match and then blowing it out.' He ducked his head, ashamed. 'I know it was your answer, Tashi, but I couldn't help it. I couldn't think of anything else. Will you forgive me?'

'Of course.' Tashi smiled, glad to have helped.

'They seemed happy with me.' Pemba tucked hungrily into a bowl of stew. 'I can't think why. I'm not clever or anything. I'm just glad it's over.'

They slept together as they usually did, curled closely like animals to keep warm inside a nest of blankets and sheepskins, and fell asleep with the sound of the wind moaning around the stone walls. Tashi woke once during the night, senses alert. Unsure what had disturbed him, he lay still, blinking in the dark. The fire had gone out but embers still glowed, reminding him of demon's eyes. He felt a little frightened, but he couldn't say why. He thought he saw the shadow of a maroon robe out of the corner of his eye but when he looked, nobody was there.

After a while, his eyes grew heavy and his senses dulled. Everything darkened, as if someone had dashed water over the coals, dimming the light. He tried to fight the closing of his eyes, sure there was someone in the room. He felt a brush of cold malignance against his mind and wanted to shout for help but his mouth wouldn't work. He experienced a terrifying surge of fear and tried to move but couldn't. He was losing the battle for his consciousness. Everything was fading to black. His senses were forced into a darkened silence.

When he awoke in the morning, Pemba was gone.

2

'WHO FOUND THE BOY'S body?' Supervisor Shan Lia Bao Third Class asked.

'His twin brother.'

'Poor kid,' she murmured. 'He's only six.'

The pathologist scratched his belly and Lia had to force herself not to stare at the rolls of fat spilling over his belt. Hua Ming was borderline obese and how he'd managed to cram his massive bulk onto the grey government-issue chair without it collapsing had to be a miracle.

'How did Pemba break his neck?' Lia continued. 'Any ideas?'

'Not really.' Hua Ming looked as though he didn't care, and for some reason, this stung her.

'I'd like the autopsy reports of the other boys,' she said crisply. 'There are four who died the same way, if I recall correctly.'

Hua Ming looked startled. 'They're not connected.'

'I'd like them *now*.' Her voice was sharp. 'Not next week.'

'How much vinegar did you eat this morning? Good grief, woman, don't you think I've got better things to be doing than running errands for you?' Despite his grumbling, Hua Ming rose to his feet and ambled out of the office. For such a big man he moved remarkably nimbly, but his breathing rasped. Too many cigarettes, probably. It wasn't often she saw him without one.

She moved to the window. She didn't recognise herself in the reflection – the face was unfamiliar, thin and haunted, the eyes unnaturally large. They were empty, as if the life behind them had been erased. She looked like a ghost, ephemeral. The woman who'd just snapped at Hua Ming was who she used to be – energetic, impatient, animated; where had she gone? Lia couldn't remember when she'd lost her. She'd been numb, unfeeling, almost paralysed. She had trouble sleeping, but could barely drag herself out of bed in the morning. Some days she felt nauseous, others as though she had flu, but a doctor could do nothing to help. It wasn't her body that was sick.

She rested her forehead on the glass. Below, armed military details were stationed at each corner of the square, six-troop patrols marching up and down the centre in synchronised step. In the distance loomed the Potala Palace, its sheer white walls seemingly being forced skywards by the rock below. People waddled through the square hunched over, bulked up with layers of fleeces, sheepskin and nylon, anything to keep warm.

Had she really been transferred to Tibet? It could be a dream for all she knew, or a living nightmare. Or was it her previous life that had been the dream? She closed her eyes and pictured where she used to live, the chic Shenzhen apartment, the smooth tiled floors and chrome and glass furniture. She visualised Jian coming home with the shopping, bags over-laden, in too much of a hurry, spilling mangoes and strawber-ries everywhere. His strong figure coming to kiss her on the lips, jeans dusty, boot laces flapping. The joy of seeing him every day. Waking with him in the morning and sharing a mango, sucking the stone and the skin, the juice dripping down their chins. Sometimes friends would stay over from Fuling, Beijing, Hong Kong and Australia. They'd bring their kids and cram into the apartment like sausages squeezed into a frying pan. Her home had vibrated with joy and laughter. Her home had been *alive*.

For the first time, she noticed the emptiness of her office. The echoing silence. There were no charts or posters on the walls, no books, no colour. Just two chairs and a metal desk covered in stacks of files. And a telephone, several notebooks and a penholder stuffed with a variety of pens and pencils. To one side was a white filing cabinet, but otherwise the room was bare. It was the size of a broom cupboard and the air had no energy and felt inert, almost dead. What had she been doing for the past six months? She frowned, unable to remember any specifics. She'd gone through her induction, meeting everyone in the building, in a daze. What now? She knew her old life was over, but the future held nothing. What to do with it?

She turned back to the photograph of the dead boy. The heating rumbled and clanked behind the walls. She sat at her desk and stared at the photograph for a long time.

*

Hua Ming returned within the hour. This time, Lia couldn't help but watch the plastic legs of the chair bow out as he lowered himself but once again, it held. The pathologist's breathing was laboured, his forehead beaded with sweat from having to climb the stairs thanks to the lift breaking down earlier that morning. A heavy waft of nicotine drifted her way and she had to force herself not to grimace. She didn't want to offend him. She wanted him on side, open to share the information he held.

'Well?' she prompted.

He was staring over her shoulder at the map she'd stuck on the wall, the four coloured pins scattered west to east.

'*Ai Yo!* They're not connected!' He flung up his hands. 'How can they be? Tibet's a third the size of India, remember? Fucking huge. If someone's undertaking to travel thousands of kilometres across some of the most hostile country in the world and in the middle of fucking winter, then I'm the Emperor of China.'

'Five boys dead in five weeks.' Her tone was hard as she went to the map and stuck a fifth coloured pin in the Xigazê Prefecture, on a village called Rabang. There were two

9

villages of the same name in Tibet, one in the east of Ngari Prefecture, the other – where Pemba Dolma had died – in the far west, a hairsbreadth from the Indian border and slap bang in the middle of nowhere, surrounded by nothing but the jagged peaks of the Himalayas and endless stretches of rocks and stunted grasses.

She studied the map again, but couldn't discern any pattern. The deaths stretched from the capital Lhasa and west into Xigazê and Ngari Prefectures. No boys had broken their necks in the four other prefectures. She wondered if this was pertinent.

'Kids die out here all the time,' he said.

'All the time?' she repeated. 'Like this?' She returned to her desk where the photographs of the children's bodies lay. She fanned them before Hua Ming, tapping them individually as she spoke. 'Drukpa Kunlek, found with his neck broken. Dawa Tandu found with his neck broken. Karma Delek...'

'Yeah, yeah, I know what they died of. I did their autopsies, remember?' Hua Ming looked away, but Lia knew it wasn't out of embarrassment or discomfort at the sight of the dead children.

She said, 'Do we still have the bodies?'

'No way.' He looked appalled. 'The families went insane when the rural police stepped in and insisted their kids be sent here. We had to release the bodies within twenty-four hours to avoid a riot.'

Lia flicked through the autopsy reports to see the same police officer's name at the bottom of each except for the one in Lhasa, which was her responsibility, and the one in Xigatsê, which her boss had covered. She considered where three of the boys had come from, the remote high plateaus and valleys, and wondered about Supervisor Chen Tao. Because of religious beliefs, Tibetan people wouldn't usually allow an investigator to conduct a post-mortem diagnosis on their dogs, let alone one of their children. She wondered how Chen had managed to get permission from the families or, more likely, whether he'd simply seized the bodies, uncaring of the family's feelings.

Hua Ming cleared his throat. 'Supervisor, I hate to be pedantic, but haven't you considered they might have had accidents?'

'Of course.' Lia returned to her desk. 'But we're still faced with the same problem: five kids dying of the same injuries, none of them near a crevasse or a ravine or anything that could explain such an accident. It doesn't add up.'

Hua Ming sent her a sly look. 'Perhaps kids don't have accidental deaths in Shenzhen. Or Beijing, for that matter.'

She ignored his dig about her past. 'If I could get to see one of the sites where a child died, it might help.'

'The committee won't agree.'

'I'll persuade them.'

He gestured at the photographs. 'Do you honestly think they'll care?'

An odd tightness constricted her breathing and for a moment she was confused at the sensation. She'd forgotten what anger felt like. Her voice was quiet as she said, 'I didn't take you to be racist, Hua Ming.'

A flush crept up his neck. 'I'm not. But the committee…'

Lia gathered the photographs as if she could protect the children from hearing any more. 'Does this mean you won't back me?'

'I didn't say that.'

She regarded him coolly. 'Well, what do you say?'

Hua Ming heaved himself upright. He still wouldn't meet her eyes. 'I suggest you don't take them head on. You've barely been here two seconds. Obedience always goes down well.'

Along with submission and compliance, she thought, two characteristics her old self had had trouble with. She wondered how her new self was going to behave. It couldn't remain the same, not after what had happened.

*

After Hua Ming had left, she took up position by the window once again. Even though it was winter, there were still dozens of pilgrims making their tortuous way to the Jokhang. Wherever they came from, fifty k's away or fifteen hundred, they walked the entire distance, prostrating themselves to the ground every few steps. She'd known they were there every time she crossed the square en route to the police station, but she hadn't *seen* them. Now, she looked at one of them, a woman. She wore a leather apron to protect her clothes, and had wooden blocks on her hands, also for protection. Her lips moved as she chanted a mantra, and her hair was matted and filthy, her skin a coarse brown and heavily wrinkled. She looked to be in her fifties but Lia knew she was probably much younger and that hardship had aged her.

She struggled to understand what made the woman undertake such a physically demanding journey, and she was baffled, unable to comprehend having a religious belief so strong that you would suffer so for it. The woman looked just about dead.

Lia sighed, clouding the glass with her breath and causing the woman to briefly disappear. It was going to be difficult to persuade the committee to give her dispensation to travel to the villages where the boys had died. Budgets were tight, but more relevant was the fact she hadn't yet proven herself. Would they feel they could trust her? A woman who had been demoted from Supervisor First Class in the investigative section of one of the busiest city police forces in the country to Supervisor Third Class, and transferred here as punishment?

The only way she might get what she wanted would be if she managed to make the committee think it was their idea. How could she give them big face, she wondered? Was it possible? They weren't stupid – especially Commissioner Zhi – and would probably see straight through her. She wasn't sure if she was brave enough to try and manipulate them.

She nibbled the inside of her lip. If she didn't interview the boys' families, how could she find out how they had broken their necks? She had nothing to work with but photographs of the bodies — shipped in from the provinces using frozen food trucks — and a reluctant pathologist.

Lia struggled to remember interviewing the family of the first boy, Drukpa Kunlek, who'd died in Lhasa. His body had been found by a street sweeper who immediately alerted the police. Normally they wouldn't be bothered by a small boy's death, but Commissioner Zhi had instructed the body to be autopsied, authorised an interpreter, and ordered Lia to 'get on with it'.

What had made Zhi request an autopsy?

*

Back at her desk, Lia brought out Drukpa's file and read through her notes. She couldn't remember writing them. Her memory might be shot to pieces but her notes were neat and precise. If she was a stranger, she wouldn't know the author was barely functioning. She'd think they were doing a pretty good job. Carefully, she read every word. Leaned back and closed her eyes.

She remembered Drupka's mother had been distraught, almost incoherent, the father openly rude. She'd known the man was suffering, but even in her deadened state she'd blinked at his remarks. He'd called her scum, a Chinese whore who wanted to breed the Tibetans out of existence, destroy them from the inside out, and when he spat at her, cursing her and all her race, his brother had dragged him off, almost fainting with terror that she might report them.

Constable Deshi, twenty-four years old and four ranks below Lia, had wanted to arrest the whole family for subversion, but she'd restrained him, preferring to be lenient. Should the father act the same way in a month's time, then she'd consider a firmer response, but not on the day his little boy had died. Deshi had given her a narrowed look that warned her to tread carefully, and not overly favour the Tibetans or she'd get arrested herself.

How had the boy broken his neck? The street sweeper had found him just after dawn at the end of their street, sprawled untidily on the ground as though he'd fainted. No other marks were on his body. There appeared no evidence of a struggle. He was wearing a woollen jumper over his pyjamas and a pair of shoes but no socks.

'It was as though a friend had called him out to play,' said the mother, speaking between sobs. 'He was in a hurry, I could see, so he wasn't scared or anything. But none of his friends were out that night. It was snowing. Too cold.'

Lia's thoughts turned to the Snow Thief who lured children from their homes. He was the soul of a child who'd died years ago, suffocated in the snow. Legend had it he'd been punished for arguing with his parents and ever since that time, if a child misbehaved, it was said the Snow Thief would fill his pockets with treats and, singing as sweetly as any bird, sing all the naughty children away into the forest, never to be seen again. It was one of the nursery stories her father used to read to her and she'd found it frightening, scared she might be enticed away from her parents without knowing.

She gazed unseeingly at the map, the coloured pins scattered across its barren space like M&M's in a field of snow. What should she do? Pretend these kids weren't dying? Would this hasten her return to civilisation, or hinder it? Did she care? She turned and looked at her computer. Finally, she switched the machine on and hooked up to the Internet and began searching for profilers linked to boy murders. She didn't get very far against China's ferocious Internet censorship. Access to permitted blogs and websites was tortuously slow thanks to congestion on China's backbone network and the time it took for communications to travel via overland and undersea cables to the USA and Europe. Overseas news channels were banned, as were religious sites, and any mention of the FBI or Scotland Yard, or any overseas police forces, made her computer freeze.

Refusing to give up, Lia kept trying, and she was hastily reading a recent news report of a profiler in the USA when someone knocked on the door and at the same time, her computer blacked out.

'Yes?' she barked.

Constable Deshi stuck his head inside. 'The committee's ready for you.'

3

LIA SWALLOWED. Checked her reflection in the window. Did up the top button of her tunic and straightened her skirt. Made sure not a single stray hair had slipped from her plait. She dithered over whether to wear her cap or not, and settled for carrying it beneath her arm, like a soldier. She was grateful for her official armour. It made her look less feminine. The jacket flattened her chest and the skirt took away any curves so she resembled an ironing board.

As she walked down the overheated corridor, she lifted her chin, reminding herself that although she'd been demoted, it wasn't because she'd failed in her police work. It had been a disciplinary action to re-educate and make an example of her. Being part of the system, she'd never been scared of the security services before, but since she'd borne the brunt of their mindless brutality every meeting she attended made her mouth go dry, her palms damp.

When she entered the room she took two steps forward, stopped, and saluted. She didn't look left or right, but dead ahead, aiming her gaze twelve inches above her boss's head and its balding crown.

'You're not on parade,' Commissioner Zhi said. 'Sit, sit.' He sounded irritable, but she knew he was pleased at her formality, and that she'd shown him the appropriate respect. It had been Zhi who, when she'd first arrived, had commanded she had her own office. Most Supervisors shared with another of the same rank but he'd moved her upstairs to her miniature office saying that although it was cramped, he was sure she'd appreciate her own space. She hadn't thanked him at the time, as she hadn't cared. Now, she was glad she could show him some recognition.

She kept her expression neutral as she took the single chair facing the table. The Commissioner introduced her to the six people that made up the committee: two women and four men. Three were with the PSB – Public Security Bureau – and three were from the MPS, the Ministry of Public Security. Unlike the MPS, which was a national police force and handled day-to-day law enforcement, the PSB dealt with public security and social order. Both the MPS and PSB were police, but they were as different as rock and sand. The MPS were cops, the PSB not unlike the old Russian secret service, the KGB.

Commissioner Zhi headed the MPS in Lhasa and ran the committee with the head of the PSB, Tan Dao. Both men were sharp-eyed, dedicated officers, but there the resemblance ended. Zhi was fifty-four and a broad man with a round face and dimples in his cheeks. Officer Tan was twenty years younger, and as sleek and sinuous as a leopard. He wore a black polo-necked sweater beneath a sharply tailored jacket. His face was all hard planes and angles. He didn't seem to have the double eyelid most Chinese were born with, making her wonder if he was mixed race. Or had he undergone plastic surgery? More and more Chinese were having blepharoplasty to make their eyes appear wider, more Western. Tan looked as though he'd be vain enough to go under the knife. When his eyes met hers, she felt a tingle of anxiety in case he'd read her thoughts. She quickly looked away.

She knew the other MPS officers, and how Superintendent Zhang and Constable Deshi had managed to crawl onto the supposedly elite committee was anyone's guess, but Lia guessed they'd been voted on due to connections, or *guanxi*. Unlike police forces elsewhere in the world, you rarely got anywhere in the Chinese police due to your ability. It was always who you knew, and what debt was owed, who had influence with who, that oiled the promotional wheels.

Deshi was on her team – which comprised just five of them – and reported directly to her as Head of the Criminal

Investigation Department. She didn't like the fact she was being forced to face a subordinate in the committee, but since there was little she could do about it, she kept her chin high and tried to hide her unease.

Zhang smiled, showing faintly yellow teeth. She couldn't think what he might be smiling about. Zhang oversaw the twenty-two patrolmen in Lhasa, who regulated everything from hotels and ID cards to holding random household checks to confirm births, marriages, deaths and divorces. Zhang was twenty-nine, ambitious and, if office rumours were to be believed, ruthless in pursuit of promotion. He said, 'The Commissioner tells us you think you might have a serial killer on the loose.'

'I never said that.' She wasn't stupid. She had studiously avoided using those very words to avoid any rumours surging through the police station.

'But that's what you're intimating, isn't it?'

'I won't know until I start a proper investigation and—'

'Tibetan kids die all the time.' Zhang cut her off. She was glad his smile had vanished. She'd found it disconcerting. 'They live in shit, eat shit, and breathe shit. Their parents can't be bothered to vaccinate them against the most common diseases, so what do you expect?'

'All these boys died because their necks snapped, not because of the environment,' she replied. She was pleased her tone remained calmly neutral.

'You're from Shenzhen, aren't you?'

This was from one of the PSB women, the prim one with the tight chignon and hard cold eyes. Myra Kwok Chun.

'I'm originally from Fuling,' Lia prevaricated. She didn't like Wok's intimation that because Lia used to live in Shenzhen, she was in any way different to them. Carefully avoiding Kwok's eyes, she wondered at the woman's Western first name. In China the surname came first, the given name next – her name switched from being Shan Lia to Lia Shan whenever she spoke to a Westerner – but it was becoming common for Chinese people to swap their names round and add a Western Christian name not only to make their dealings with Westerners easier, but to make them appear more cosmopolitan.

'But you've spent seven years policing in Shenzhen,' Kwok continued smoothly.

'And the last eighteen months policing Beijing.'

'You think we don't know that? Or the reasons why?'

It took an immense effort for Lia not to respond and remain silent, dignified.

Kwok glanced down at her papers. 'Tell me, Supervisor. Do you get many serial killers in Shenzhen?'

'There was only one that we knew of.'

Kwok blinked and Lia felt a kick of satisfaction that she'd surprised her.

'One?' Kwok repeated.

'He was Australian. He killed young Asian girls. He moved between countries, confounding local police until some smart guy in Hong Kong put together a profile and sent it to every PD in every major city, including Beijing and Shenzen. When we began to collaborate, we realised we had a serial killer on our hands.'

'I never heard about this.' Kwok looked as though she wasn't sure whether to be outraged or disbelieving.

'It never reached the media, if that's what you mean.'

'Why not?'

'The man died before it got that far. Hit and run in Macau. It's not uncommon.' She wasn't going to add that her contact in the HKAPF, the Hong Kong Auxiliary Police Force, suspected the driver of the car who'd killed the murderer was the father of one of the dead girls. That was something his department had been happy to sweep under the carpet.

*

There was a long silence while Kwok pursed her lips, making a note on the pad in front of her. Superintendent Zhang sucked phlegm noisily before swallowing. Jenny Wang, PSB officer and the same rank as Myra Kwok, fiddled with her pen. Like Myra Kwok, she'd chosen an English name. Quietly, seemingly to nobody in particular, Jenny said, 'I heard about the case. It was an exemplary example of national and international co-operation.' She lifted her soft brown eyes to Lia's. 'You must have been very pleased with the result.'

It was an unconcealed compliment that affected everyone at the table. Kwok glowered. Zhi and Deshi nodded thought-fully. Zhang looked disgruntled. Tan, however, turned to study his subordinate with open surprise.

'When did you hear about this?' he asked Jenny.

'Two years ago.' Jenny brushed a lock of hair from her pretty heart-shaped face. 'I was in Bejing, at a conference on Implementing the Strategy of Community and—'

'Rural Policing,' Tan interrupted rudely. 'Yes, I was there too. But I don't recall hearing about an Australian serial killer.'

'I'm sorry, sir.' Jenny ducked her head deferentially, as though it was entirely her fault her boss had missed the story.

'I was obviously at the wrong talk,' he remarked, surpris-ingly magnanimous. Most superior officers hated being shown up by their inferiors and even Jenny blinked. Wisely, Jenny didn't say any more but kept silent, a good move as far as Lia was concerned. Tan was known throughout the police station for his volatile disposition.

Tan shuffled through some photographs, picked one up. It was of the fifth child, six-year-old Pemba Dolma. He'd been found in the chicken shed apparently, lying on a bed of straw. How anyone could think he'd broken his neck by accident was beyond Lia.

'What makes you think it might be a serial killer?' Tan asked.

Everyone stiffened in surprise. Her mind skittered. Was the PSB officer going to take her seriously? Nobody wanted a serial killer on their books. It meant a doubled work schedule, public hysteria and a mountain of official pressure. Why had he asked her almost the same question as Zhang if he didn't want to know the answer?

Deciding to take a risk, Lia leaned forward. 'None of the boys were found in a place that leads me to believe their broken necks could have been caused by an accident, like a fall down a flight of stairs. There was no bruising on any of the bodies to indicate they'd been hit say, by a car, or thrown across a room. The victims were all between five and six years old, and all died during the night...'

'During the night?' Tan repeated, eyebrows raised. 'I didn't know that.'

'Maybe the boys couldn't see where they were going,' Zhang remarked.

Lia met Zhang's eye. 'Are you seriously suggesting all five children tripped in the dark and broke their necks?'

Zhang flushed.

'Look,' she continued. 'It's winter. Nobody wants to get up in the middle of the night. Kids have strong bladders. What made them get up and go outside? Who persuaded them to leave the sanctuary of their home?'

'They went to play with a friend,' Tan said dismissively. 'There is nothing to suggest they've been murdered, let alone by the same person. According to the reports, the bodies weren't even placed in any particular position—'

'How do we know that for certain?' Lia jumped in. 'Just because the provincial authorities haven't made specific mention of how the bodies were found doesn't mean there wasn't something significant at the scene.' She took a breath. 'This is why I'm asking for permission to go to Rabang. To talk to the boy's brother, who found the body. I want to interview his family, and conduct a proper investigation into his death. I'd also like to travel to the other three sites—'

'Impossible,' snapped Myra Kwok, bristling. Even her chignon looked affronted. 'We can't have you swanning

21

around the country scaring the locals just to make you feel useful.' She turned to Tan and Commissioner Zhi. 'Do we have to sit here listening to any more of this drivel? After her high-life in the bright lights the Supervisor is obviously trying to alleviate her boredom. If there's a serial killer out there murdering little boys then I'm the Queen of England.'

Lia tried to ignore the heat crawling up her neck at the reference to England, which was a direct reference to her Western – *gwailo* – looks. Refusing to be cowed she said, 'We have to tell the public what's going on. Once word gets out, every parent will be on the lookout. We'll prevent more deaths.'

'Impossible.' Kwok began stuffing her notepad, pens and photographs into her briefcase. 'You'll just create a panic.' She looked at her fellow committee members. 'Am I right?'

Zhang and Deshi looked to the Commissioner as to how they should respond but Zhi was watching Tan, who was in turn studying Lia. Tan said, 'Supervisor Shan, how much do you know about serial killers?'

'As much as the next police officer,' she admitted. 'Maybe a little more. I read a lot.'

'Then you'll know they're a Western phenomenon, like your Australian murdering young girls throughout South East Asia. Serial killers are invariably white males in their twenties and thirties. You'd think if a Westerner had been present in any of the villages where these children died, it would have been mentioned. Foreigners aren't just rare at this time of year, they're virtually non-existent.'

This fact hadn't passed Lia by but she wasn't going to let it bury her. 'Perhaps we have an ethnic serial killer. It's not impossible.'

A stony silence fell.

*

Lia felt a wave of hopelessness wash over her. Was there any point in continuing? If she still had Jian it would be a different matter. He'd always encouraged her to push boundaries.

What would he tell her to do? Immediately she could hear his voice in her mind as clear as day.

Never give up.

Staring past Tan's head, her hands clenched in her lap, instinct told her that if she slid back into the pit of numb grey where she'd been living since she lost Jian, she'd never climb out of it.

She licked her lips. Dragged her courage up from the bottom of her shoes, and forged on. 'As Head of the Criminal Investigation Department, I'd like to start communications with experts in this area. We need to make sure we know what we're dealing with. We need to confirm or refute the fact we may have a serial killer on our hands. And if we have, we need to be prepared to know the social and psychological forces that might have produced such a killer, and whether they are of ethnic origin or not. We need to learn how to predict their behaviour, where they might go next. Above all, we need to know how they reveal themselves through their crimes. We need their profile.' She took a breath. 'The experts in this area are, as you're no doubt aware, the FBI in Quantico.'

You could have heard a pin drop.

Lia swallowed and kept going. 'The Hong Kong police worked with the FBI on the Australian serial killer case. I received copies of the FBI's comments. Without the FBI, it's doubtful he would have been caught.'

Nobody moved. Nobody said a word.

'Supervisor.' Tan's voice was gentle. 'We are all very aware of the circumstances that brought you to Lhasa. The pressure you have been under has been...immense.'

Lia's skin prickled. She didn't like his tone or the change of subject.

'The mind is a delicate instrument.' He laced his fingers on the desk in front of him. His face was a study of kindness. 'Dealing with the past can be hard. Traumatic. Grief can play tricks. Sometimes we see things that aren't there. Sometimes we fight ghosts…' He gave a theatrical little sigh. Intensified his look into one of compassion. 'Perhaps you would benefit from seeing a psychiatrist who is an expert in these matters. Medication might be helpful.'

Jenny turned her head aside but Lia didn't miss the tiny fluttering gesture she made with her fingers, directed at her. *I'm sorry.*

With heavy heart, Lia took in the rest of the committee's expressions. Zhang and Deshi were parodies of pity. Myra Kwok had pasted what she probably thought was a kindly, concerned look on her face, but it merely made her look as though she had indigestion. Even the Commissioner was looking sorrowful at his Supervisor's fragile mental state and although she knew he was going along with the others because he didn't dare go head to head against the PSB, it was still as painful as a jackal's bite.

'There's nothing wrong with me.' Her voice was tight.

'If you say so,' Tan said slowly.

Lia swallowed an urge to shout an obscenity at him.

'Supervisor,' Tan continued in the same soft tone, 'there is no serial killer. Do you hear me? We are not in Shenzhen, or Bejing for that matter. We're in Tibet. Now, I suggest you take the remainder of the day off and get some rest, and return refreshed tomorrow and able to see that you have been imagining things.'

He may have presented it in a roundabout, seemingly kind and benevolent manner, but Tan had warned her off and everyone knew it.

4

NIMA CHODEN WATCHED THE police officer through his miniature Leica binoculars. He'd bought them from a tourist last year and had been astonished how something so small could be as powerful. They had cost a fortune but it had been money well spent. He could virtually count the officer's nose hairs through the eyepieces.

He'd left the others setting up camp to walk back and check to see if anyone was following them. For a moment he'd honestly thought he was seeing things. He'd been lulled into a sense of false security by thinking that because it was mid-winter, nobody would come looking for them, but he was wrong. The police were here. They were on their trail. His heartbeat picked up as he studied the Chinese police officer – a wiry man wearing spectacles – who was rummaging in the rear of his Land Cruiser. He was so *close*!

He put down the binoculars briefly. Even though it was cold, he was sweating heavily and he longed to curse out loud, use a really foul word, but he held his tongue. Even though he couldn't be overheard, he knew it was better to keep the mask on at all times so he wouldn't slip up accidentally another time. Some days he wondered how he managed to keep his temper. He'd wanted to leave Rabang the day the dead boy was found, but the weather turned against them and they were forced to wait another two days before they got moving. *Two days!* This had to be the most frustrating, maddening of missions, being forced to travel between villages following such an elderly crew.

Did the lamas know he was behind them, dogging their every move? Picking up intelligence on every ceremony, every formal procedure held?

Somehow, he doubted it. He'd been trained in the art of camouflage, as had Sharmar and Rinzen, the two men who had joined him on this mission. Nobody who met them thought they were anything but monks. All three of them had shaven heads and wore maroon robes. They spoke fluent Tibetan, and were cognisant with every inch of monastic life. Wherever they went they were welcomed with open generosity and humble approbation. If the Tibetans knew the truth...

He quickly turned his mind aside from that particular thought. No point in attracting the wrong energy to what might never happen.

Nima studied the rude little village once again, the police Land Cruiser. How much did the police officer know? It couldn't be a lot, he reassured himself. If the officer had an inkling as to what was going on there would be helicopters in the sky, aircraft criss-crossing the expanses of Himalaya searching for them. As long as the villagers kept quiet as the lamas journeyed, they'd be safe.

He refused to think they might be betrayed.

He watched the police officer walking around the outskirts of the village, looking for tracks, and smiled grimly, glad it had snowed last night and that there would be no trace of them, or the lamas. His attention switched to a movement on the west side of the monastery. A small boy was looking his way. As he adjusted the focus on his binoculars, the boy's narrow face sprang into sharp relief, his eyes bright as a blackbird's. It was the same child who had given him a packet of herbs to use in his tea yesterday, to help ease his heartburn.

Nima gave a shiver. It was as though the boy was looking straight at him and into his soul.

5

LIA KICKED HER SHOES free of snow outside her apartment, which had been created out of the second floor of a traditional Tibetan house. She hadn't cared where she lived when she'd arrived in Lhasa, but now she looked around, oddly taken aback as she registered she was living in the Tibetan quarter, an area of ancient narrow thoroughfares that surrounded the Jokhang Temple.

As she looked down the street, she saw no Chinese shops. Not a single one. All of them were Tibetan. Traditional antique and handicraft stores, a dry goods store, two Tibetan tea houses. Watching a pilgrim step blithely around a prostrating monk, she wondered if it had been such a good idea to shun the shiny pink and white government block where the other cops lived. Sure, this place could be called quaint and charming, and it had its own front door, but you had to go to the side of the building and climb a set of treacherously steep wooden steps to get to it. She was used to sleek modernity, elevators and electric doors, not a stone cottage held together with ancient, rotting timbers that looked as though they might crumble any second.

One bonus, however, was not having to share the entrance with a hundred others, their bicycles and stacks of junk mail. There was even a tiny balcony offering a spectacular view of the mountains. Had she taken in the vista before? She couldn't remember seeing the angled roofs of the Jokhang Palace, black against the night sky, or the clarity of the stars rising behind it. She could just make out the silhouettes of two soldiers standing sentry on a rooftop.

Despite the oppressive policing, the atmosphere was lively. A smattering of people chatted cheerfully as they walked home, dogs barking at bicycles, barking at anything. Lia breathed in scents of wood smoke and juniper, feeling as though she was waking from a deep sleep. But as she awoke, the pain inside her increased, rising to a steady shriek. Would it ever stop? Shuddering, she turned and opened the door. Dropped her day pack inside. Kicking off her shoes, Lia shook out her socks. She stepped past her bedroom and across the living room, flicking on a couple more lights. A fire burned in the grate and the air was slightly steamy, indicating rice was on the boil. She thought she could smell lamb cooking, maybe with garlic.

As she always did, she touched Jian's photograph where it stood on a table in the living room. She'd taken it two years ago, when they'd spent a weekend in Guilin to celebrate their sixth wedding anniversary. They'd been having a long, lazy lunch in the sunshine and he'd been smiling directly at her, and not the camera. He'd just finished telling her a joke – a pretty awful one, she remembered, but at least it had been clean – and his face was alight, his dark brown eyes gleaming with laughter. Not long afterwards they were in their hotel room, hands pulling at each other's clothes, the heat between them igniting and making her gasp. When he put his hands on her waist and kissed her, she lost her focus, aware of nothing but the smell of him, the sight of him above her, inside her, and when she came, she gripped the small of his back with her fingers and cried out his name.

Whenever she remembered that moment – the last time they made love – a hollow opened up inside her, so dark, so endless, that it threatened to swallow her.

In the kitchen, she peered into the pots on the hob. Normally she didn't care what was for supper – she couldn't remember when she last had an appetite – but for some reason today, she was curious. She'd been right about the lamb, but not about the rice. Instead, the pan bubbled with noodles. The kitchen was in the centre of the apartment, with a door at the far end leading to another bedroom. The door was firmly shut and for a moment Lia was tempted not to announce her arrival. She wasn't in the mood for an argument, but if she slipped off to her room without eating it would cause more friction than if she simply sat down and ate her meal. Sighing, Lia rapped on the door to say, *I'm home.* She didn't expect a response.

As she considered her meeting with the committee earlier, she wondered if her father had ever been mocked by his work colleagues. He'd been an engineer based in Beijing, a burly man with a mop of unruly black hair and an infectious laugh. He'd met Lia's mother in Fuling where he'd been working on the Five Gorges Dam. It had, apparently, been love at first sight, and when he'd died in a building accident three years ago – crushed by falling masonry in Shanghai – Lia's mother had returned to Fuling. At first Lia thought it was because that was where the memories were strongest, but when she visited her mother three months later, it was to find her dishevelled and confused, barely able to recognise her daughter. Lia had immediately brought her back to Shenzhen. After a while, she had recovered enough to look after herself, and she moved back to Fuling to share an apartment with her two elderly sisters, where she still lived, in relative contentment.

What had her mother said? Lia frowned as she remembered.

I went a little crazy when your father died.

Lia hadn't understood what she meant. She hadn't experienced the immense power of grief, how it undid you, unravelled your very being, until now.

*

Changing out of her uniform into a baggy sweater and sweatpants, she switched on the TV and half-watched the news, gazing around as though seeing her home for the first time. She hadn't realised how small it was. You could fit the entire apartment into her Shenzhen kitchen twice over. What had she been thinking? She loved her space and now she felt cooped up, claustrophobic.

Noises came from the kitchen. It sounded as though the noodles were being drained. Hoping for a convivial supper without the usual accusations flying around, Lia made her way to the kitchen where a bent, twisted old woman dressed head-to-toe in black was mumbling under her breath. The day they'd moved in, the first thing the woman had done was hang a mirror over the wall, so when she was cooking she could see behind her. *Eyes in the back of her head.* Faultless feng shui, Lia thought, so nobody could sneak up on her.

'Hi, Fang Dongmei,' Lia greeted her.

The woman didn't glance around or acknowledge her presence. Just thumped two steaming plates on the table, along with some chopsticks, before submerging the pots in the sink.

'Oh, come on,' Lia said. 'You're not still angry at what I said yesterday, are you?'

Fang Dongmei returned to the table without a word.

Lia rolled her eyes to the ceiling. 'What if I said sorry? Would that help?'

No response.

Lia sighed and picked up her chopsticks. Both of them were to blame for last night's row, but someone had to make amends, and since it obviously wasn't going to be the stubborn old mule sitting opposite her, Lia decided she'd better wave the white flag.

'Look, I'm sorry.' Lia leaned forward. 'I shouldn't have said what I said. Blamed you for our being here, but when you accused me—'

'You are a police officer,' Fang Dongmei snapped. 'You should have done something.'

'I did!' Lia protested. 'And look where it got me! And who was it who started it all? Not me, not Jian—'

'Ai Ya!' Fang Dongmei made a noise of disgust and plunged

30

her face deeper into her bowl. 'We fight for no reason. Neither of us is at fault.'

Wasn't that the truth, Lia sighed. Taking a bite of lamb, to her surprise, her appetite kicked in. 'This is delicious,' she remarked, but if she'd thought complimenting the woman on her cooking would soften her, she was wrong.

'Of course it is,' Fang Dongmei muttered. 'You think I would feed you rubbish?'

Determined not to be drawn into a cloud of resentment all over again, Lia forced herself to try and make conversation. 'Well, it's great. Thank you. How was your day?'

No response.

Lia wondered how to take things forward. They came from such different worlds; how to forge a bridge? Lia, as one of the younger generation, had received enormous support from the state to ensure she pursued a higher education, but Fang Dongmei had lost her youth and opportunity in the Cultural Revolution. She came from Henan, one of China's poorest provinces, and when her parents moved to Beijing, she'd been pushed into working in a factory before getting a job on a construction site – both positions that were usually occupied by men. She'd met her husband, a site manager, soon after starting at the construction site, and although Fang Dongmei bore a child, she continued working on the site, rising at five thirty every morning and getting home after six.

Women were regarded as equal according to the revolutionary rubrics but the traditional roles of women after work in the domestic scene never changed. Like nearly all women of her time, Fang Dongmei carried the burden in housework and child care but she didn't consider herself a 'housewife' because she had full-time work. 'Housewife' became a term for uneducated or less knowledgeable women with no sense of civilisation.

At least Fang Dongmei approved of Lia working full-time. She looked at other women, those who stayed at home, with contempt, telling them they should be ashamed of their irresponsibility for not making a greater payback to society.

Taking another mouthful of lamb, Lia thought if she shared some of her experiences in the office, it might help create a dialogue between them. Anything but this continual scratching against one another, like a rough-edged nail catching on silk.

'Another little boy died,' she said. 'The same as the others. I'm not sure if I told you about them?'

Silence.

Lia ran through each boy's death. Her tone was conversational but her words were all police jargon: perpetrator, crime scene, non-accidental death.

'The fifth victim died in Rabang. I want to travel to his village and interview his family, but Officer Tan stepped in and warned me off. I know that none of us want a serial killer on our hands, but even so, I harboured a hope that he wouldn't dismiss me quite so out of hand...'

As she spoke, she was reminded of how she used to chat to Jian over their evening meal, decompressing from her day and helping her clear her mental desk in preparation for the next morning. Jian occasionally asked a question but Fang Dongmei gave no indication she heard a word as she gobbled her food, seemingly oblivious to Lia's monologue.

*

As in a lot of families, Fang Dongmei and Lia had been thrown together thanks to strings of misfortune. They were related only by marriage, but family honour dictated that when Fang Dongmei was made homeless, family would take her in. The trouble was, she had no family to help her, aside from Lia.

Lia hadn't wanted to take on the responsibility of Jian's grandmother, but she'd had no choice. Without her, Fang Dongmei would either be homeless, living on the streets of Beijng, or rotting away in jail. Even Lia had been shocked when she'd heard the old woman had been forcibly evicted from her home – bulldozed by the government to make way for an urban redevelopment project – but she was even more shocked when Fang Dongmei insisted on applying for a permit to protest. Anyone in the security services, from Hunan to Hong Kong, would have bet a year's wages that any person who applied to protest would either be refused permission, or carted off to a labour reform camp. China couldn't afford open criticism that might spiral out of control. China had to keep control of the masses or all hell could break loose.

Lia was still living in Shenzhen with Jian when the news came through that Fang Dongmei was under arrest for *Disturbing Social Order*. Fang Dongmei wasn't allowed to be furious at losing her marital home. She'd been widowed the previous year and was supposed to swallow what the government dished out, either taking the derisory amount of money offered, or moving into a grotty government apartment block eighty kilometres away from everyone she knew, everything she was familiar with, and be grateful she was alive. It was, Lia now admitted, a miracle the authorities finally let her free. But the cost of her freedom was beyond any price. The state had taken each of Fang Dongmei's family and jailed them, including Jian and his mother, and now it was just Fang Dongmei and Lia, banished to Tibet.

Lia ate the last of her lamb and pushed her plate away. She didn't want to think about that time. She'd already cried enough tears to fill the Yangtse twice over and she didn't want to cry any more.

She wanted to find out how five little boys had broken their necks in the last five weeks.

6

OFFICER TAN LET HIMSELF out of the block early, to make sure his driver didn't spot him, and quickly ducked around the corner to work his way to the back of the building and the shabby strip of land filled with boulders and low shrubs. Everything was coated with snow and a sudden drop in temperature had frozen a layer of ice on top. It was so cold that for a moment he wondered if she'd be here, or if she'd been forced to stay away somewhere warmer.

'Here, girl,' he called softly. 'Here, sweetie, here.'

The bitch immediately appeared in a rush, tail wagging. She'd been waiting for him, a scruffy mongrel with bright eyes and a thick, rusty coat that hid a set of ribs that resembled a coat rack.

A door slammed somewhere and Tan jerked his head round, senses alert. He couldn't afford for anyone to see him, but nobody was there. All was still and quiet in the snowy gloom.

'Hey, girl,' he murmured. With his gloved hand – he didn't want to catch fleas – he scratched the dog behind her ears and was rewarded when she turned her head to lick his knee. He smiled inside as he reached into his pocket and withdrew the leftovers from his meal. Diced beef and vegetables, some rice. The dog ate delicately, unhurried. She knew he wouldn't rush her. Tan bent his head to see her nipples were still engorged, the hair around them whorled. He hadn't seen her pups, and wondered where she kept them. He'd increased her food when he realised she was pregnant and she'd briefly held a slim layer of flesh over her bones before she'd given birth but now she was as skinny as a rake again.

She finished the food and stood with him for a while, letting him stroke her head and neck, her shoulders. Her tail waved companionably. And then she deemed the niceties were over and, after a quick glance to check he wasn't going to offer her any more food, she trotted away.

As usual, he felt a stab of sorrow at her leaving. He wished he could keep a pet, but he couldn't let anyone witness he was sentimental about such things. When he'd arrived in Tibet, he'd been amazed – and also strangely touched – at how Tibetans loved and looked after their dogs. In northern China soup was made out of dogs, especially black ones and especially in winter as dog meat was considered 'hot' food in Chinese medicine. Dogs also needed feeding, which meant less food for the family. This, in people's eyes, meant that those who had dogs as pets were either very rich or very stupid. Tan was, he supposed, both, which is why the dog was his secret.

His mother had had a pet dog, a pug-like creature who'd been Tan's companion when he was little. He still had a photograph of it, sitting on his knee with one ear up and one ear down, eyes like black buttons in its brown whiskery face. He'd cried when it died. He couldn't recall if he'd cried since. Did that mean there was something wrong with him? He'd overheard a rookie talking about him once, saying he didn't have any emotions, but it wasn't true. He felt as much as the next person, and a stab of self-pity ran through him when he realised the most affection he'd received since he'd been posted to this godforsaken region was from this dog.

*

A car horn sounded briefly, alerting him that his driver had arrived. He walked away, but just before he reached the corner of the building, a movement caught his eye. A child had appeared – a ragged, disgustingly filthy Tibetan child – and was shovelling snow into its mouth. The snow where Tan had put the food for the dog. Dear God. Even with pups the dog hadn't been hungry enough to eat the snow, but this child was obviously feral, and obviously starving.

Before he could change his mind, Tan rang his driver.

'Come back in ten minutes,' he told him. 'Go around the block, drive up the highway, I don't care. I don't want to see hide nor hair of you until oh-nine-forty.'

Tan jogged to his apartment and grabbed some cans of food; sweetcorn, shitake, red kidney beans, tuna. Opened them. Brought them to the rear of the building. The child — he hadn't been able to tell what sex it was with its matted hair and dirt-encrusted face — was nowhere to be seen. Tan left the open cans on the snow. He called, 'Help yourself, little one. I'll be back tomorrow.'

He left without looking over his shoulder, just as he used to with the dog.

'Where to, boss?' his driver asked.

Tan gave Xhu the address and leaned back in his seat, gazing outside, unable to shake off the vision of the child desperately gobbling the snow. Bringing out his mobile phone he made some calls, but was thwarted at almost every turn. He continued to persist until finally, just after 2 p.m., he got hold of the person he wanted.

'How can I help?' Betty Lu, the director of the CWI — Children's Welfare Institute — sounded cautious, with good reason considering she was talking to one of the most powerful people in Tibet.

'There's a feral child lurking at the back of my private apartment block. I want it removed.'

He could have added he wanted the child bathed, fed, clothed in clean clothes and sent to school, but since the institute would do this anyway, there seemed little point.

'Oh.' The woman sounded taken aback. 'Is it a girl or a boy?'

'I couldn't tell, it was so filthy.'

'How old, do you think?'

Tan considered the fact that the child was probably under-sized due to a lack of nutrients and said, 'It looks as though it's four, but it's probably closer to six years old.'

'And you saw the child, where?'

He gave the woman directions, who said she'd go there personally, and straight away.

'Keep me informed,' he told her.

'But of course.'

With the child taken care of, Tan could at last turn his concentration to sorting through the catch cradle of intelligence that had landed on his desk earlier. It was difficult work, and by the time he'd untangled it and sent his report to the Ministry of Public Security, it was past 7 p.m. and he felt he needed a break. Ordering Xhu to drop him outside Lia's house in the Barkhor — the old town — he then instructed him to wait for him to return.

'Yes, boss.'

*

Before he committed himself to the set of lethal-looking steps, covered in ice, Tan studied the house and the surrounding area, the rats slinking in the shadows, the rotting remnants of the weekly vegetable market slowly freezing on the cobblestones. *Ai Ya!* Was that human excrement? It wouldn't surprise him. He'd never met such a dirty, disgusting race as the Tibetans.

After the peaceful liberation of Tibet in 1965, one would think that the following social stability would have improved people's living standards, but many Tibetans continued to resist. He couldn't understand why. Tibet was enjoying sustained and rapid economic growth on an unprecedented level. And what about Lhasa? It was almost unrecognisable from the city it had been even twenty years ago. It now had asphalt-paved roads, street lamps which burned all night, and what about the cultural facilities? Various ancient structures like the Potala Palace had been repaired and dilapidated buildings in the old city renovated. Over a hundred new residential quarters had been built around the city, and the new water works ensured everyone drank clean water.

Old Tibet hadn't had a single highway. No power supply. No postal or telecommunications services. The traditional Tibetan system was feudal serfdom, with a handful of aristocratic families and monasteries which kept the people in filthy poverty – hell on earth as far as he was concerned. Tan was proud to be part of the state which had brought great changes to Lhasa and Tibet – *'projects of happiness'* – but he still found it puzzling that many ethnic Tibetans resented this. Personally, he would have embraced every change with open arms.

He looked up at the second floor of the stone and wood house, the windows spilling yellow light on to the snow outside. A spiral of smoke drifted into the chill night air. You had to be kidding. An open fire? Didn't they have electricity? What on earth had made the Supervisor live here? He couldn't understand why she had turned down the apartment in the modern block across town. He'd orchestrated it specifically so that it would meet her requirements: spacious, warm, modern. It even had a washing machine and dryer, and was superior in every way to the smaller, more cramped apartment normally offered to someone of her rank. He'd expected her to move in, delighted, and eventually when she discovered it was thanks to him she was living in a Commissioner's apartment, she'd be in his debt.

He liked people knowing they owed him something before they met. It made life easier all round when they knew their place. But Supervisor Shan hadn't moved into the apartment, so he had nothing on her. He didn't like that. It made him feel insubstantial and oddly frail.

He began his careful ascent up the stairs, one gloved hand

on the rail, the other on the ancient pitted wall. He didn't want to slip, make himself look stupid. Standing on the tiny balcony, he took in the potted red plastic flowers to the left of the front door, placed specifically to bring prosperity and good luck. Then he spotted the snow-covered bronze Buddha to one side of the doorstep, and frowned. Religious practice was severely controlled – people in the service weren't allowed to take part in religious or superstitious ceremonies, and for a police officer to have such a thing was indefensible. Taking off his glove – by all the gods it was cold – he rapped on the door.

'Who is it?' Lia called.

'Tan Dao.' He shoved his hand back inside the glove. Already his fingers were tingling.

'One minute.'

*

The door opened and for the second time that day, Tan's breath caught in his throat. He'd heard the rumours – that she was beautiful, exotic, ugly, strange – and had no idea what to expect, but when she'd walked into the room with her hair fiercely tied back, her ramrod-straight posture, her hideous oversized police-issue shoes, her femininity was inescapable. Her uniform couldn't hide her curves, just as her salute couldn't hide the slide of fear at the back of her eyes. He felt a kick of satisfaction that he scared her. It meant she knew her position. Having her would be much easier than he'd initially thought.

'Is something wrong?' she said.

He was disappointed that she was wearing a shapeless sweater that covered every inch from her chin to her knees. She was, he realised with a shock, the same height as him. He'd never been with a woman so tall and the thought of lying on top of her with his fist in her hair, thrusting into her, looking straight into those strange, honey-coloured eyes rather than the top of her head – which is what he had to do with normal Chinese women – kindled a flame in his groin.

'Nothing's wrong,' he assured her, well aware it was past ten o'clock and beyond a polite time for a social visit. She obviously assumed it was to do with work. He tried to peer past her shoulder into her apartment, intrigued at the vivid orange and yellow colours, and was frustrated when she moved to block his view.

'How can I help?' she asked. He caught a hint of something that reminded him of spring flowers, perfume perhaps, noticed her poise, her elegance, and was reminded of a ballet dancer.

He stamped his feet and clapped his gloved hands together hoping she'd get the hint and invite him in, but she didn't. He wondered whether she was hiding something, or if she was being obtuse. You didn't treat the head of the PSB with anything but deference. He gestured at the bronze Buddha on the balcony. 'Yours?' he said.

He felt a surge of satisfaction at the spark of fear he'd ignited. She knew he had the power to do what he liked with her. If he doubted her integrity in any way, he only had to say the word and a platoon of official busybodies would descend, cooking things up until they'd got some story together that would send Lia to a reform camp, perhaps one of the gulags on the borders. She had no friends in Lhasa, no colleagues willing to defend her, nobody to call for help. She was his for the plucking.

'No,' she said. He didn't miss her nervous swallow. 'It's my landlord's. Would you like me to remove it?'

'Don't bother,' he said with a shrug.

She had started to shiver as the cold air got to her, but she still refused to let him in. She was more stubborn than most, he must remember that. His eyes went to her hair gleaming in the light behind her. She wore it loose, curling and flowing around her shoulders like a glossy cape of mahogany. He wondered if it would feel as soft and fine as it looked.

'You said you wanted to go to Rabang?' Tan said. 'Where the last boy died?'

She blinked. 'Yes.'

He said, 'I'm headed there tomorrow. On official business. I thought you might like to join me.'

If he'd expected her to jump at his offer, he was mistaken. Shan simply stared at him as though she was unable to process what he'd said. A scraping noise, like a chair being moved, sounded from within the apartment and she flinched, showing her nerves were strung tight.

Tan narrowed his eyes. 'You have company?'

She gave a nod.

'I apologise for disturbing you.'

Lia gave another nod but didn't offer any information about who it might be. He knew it couldn't be her husband, so who was it? He hoped it wasn't a boyfriend. He could do without that sort of complication.

He saw her take a breath.

'Sir, I would very much like to join you on your visit to Rabang,' she said stiffly. 'Thank you for the opportunity.'

'It will be my pleasure,' he said. A warm coil of gratification eased through his belly.

'Will I have time to meet with Commissioner Zhi before we leave? We have a meeting at nine.'

He didn't know she had a meeting with her boss first thing and wondered why Zhi hadn't mentioned it. Deciding to keep things simple, he said, 'I'll pick you up at daybreak. Eight, sharp. And you needn't worry, Myra Kwok will let your office know you're accompanying me.'

A frown furrowed her brow indicating she didn't like this arrangement, but was wary of refusing him. He studied her face. Her nose, he noticed, was long and slender. Her mouth small and soft. She was strong but there was a fragility that intrigued him. He was baffled how people could call her ugly.

'Eight, here?' she said.

'Yes,' he said.

'How long will we be away for?'

He smiled. 'As long as it takes.'

As he made a cautious descent to the street, he could have sworn he heard someone hawk and spit behind him but when he turned, no one was there. He must have imagined it.

7

LIA WATCHED FANG DONGMEI close the door behind Tan. She'd been eavesdropping but Lia wasn't going to take her to task over it. She had every right to know why a PSB officer had called at their home.

Why had Tan changed his tune? Why humiliate and threaten her in one breath, then offer an olive branch the next? What was going on? It was clear he had an agenda, but she had no clue what it was. She couldn't read him. His eyes were emotionless and his body language gave nothing away. All she had were his words.

You said you wanted to go to Rabang...I thought you might like to join me.

You might *like* to join me? That wasn't cop talk. And it certainly wasn't PSB talk. The next thought made her bile rise. Please God, he's not looking for a mistress. She'd heard he was married, but apparently his wife hadn't liked the thought of living in Lhasa and had stayed behind in Xian. *Gāisǐ!* Curse all men and their libidos, she thought, recalling the displeasure he'd displayed when Fang Dongmei had accidentally shifted the chair. She bet he'd thought she had a man in her apartment and didn't like the competition.

Lia thought over the fact he wanted to leave so early. Was he trying to prevent her from visiting the office? Or was he trying to prevent her from meeting Zhi before they left? Was he really going to Rabang? Could it be a ruse to get her alone? Rabang was at least fifteen hundred kilometres away, involving a two-hour flight to Ngari before they requisitioned a vehicle and headed into the snowy wastelands. What official business would the head of the PSB be conducting in a remote and isolated Tibetan village? What if it was a lie?

'Granddaughter.'

Lia jumped. She hadn't realised she'd moved to the sofa and was huddled in one corner. 'Yes, Fang Dongmei?'

'I want to borrow your telephone.'

If she'd asked for a return ticket to the moon Lia couldn't have been more surprised. 'My phone?' she repeated. She couldn't think who the old woman was going to ring. All her former friends and neighbours from Beijing were, like herself, scattered and living who-knew-where.

Fang Dongmei rolled her eyes. 'If you'd like me to pay for the call, I will.'

'Of course not.' Lia reached for her bag and fished out her mobile phone, passed it across. She was going to show Fang Dongmei how to use it but the old woman had it in her claw and was already scuttling through the living room and across the kitchen, heading for her room. Lia couldn't help herself. 'Who are you calling?' she asked.

Fang Dongmei opened her door and vanished inside without a word. When the old woman returned, she passed back the phone with a curt nod. Lia checked the calls list but the last call recorded was the one she'd made across town to the forensics department just after 6 p.m. Had Fang Dongmei actually made a call? Perhaps she'd sent a text and then deleted it? She flicked a glance at Jian's grandmother from beneath her eyelashes.

'Fang Dongmei,' she said.

The woman gave a grunt.

'Why won't you tell me who you called?'

Fang Dongmei rose, gave the tiniest inclination of her head that Lia knew meant *goodnight*, and disappeared.

Lia rolled her eyes at her departure. Talk about stubborn, but at least they'd managed to remain relatively civil. Perhaps they'd finally vented the worst of their anger at one another? She hoped it might mean they could begin forging a new relationship without the past rearing its hideous head and making Lia blame Fang Dongmei for Jian's death while Fang Dongmei blamed Lia – omnipotent police officer – for not saving everyone.

*

The remainder of the evening was spent packing the warmest items she could find while trying to work out how to fend off a potentially dangerous situation developing between her and the head of the PSB. It wasn't as though she could report Tan. If she did, the next stop would be...where? She'd already been punished by being sent to Tibet; what could be worse? Urumqi? Turpan?

She wished she could go home. To Shenzhen, where she'd fallen in love with Jian. Where she'd married him. Her throat thickened as memories crowded her mind. She'd never met anyone like him, a man who couldn't bear to see any child looking sombre. He had run alongside a bus crawling in traffic one day, yelling and whooping and windmilling his arms to make the children laugh. The bus driver had shouted at him to *bugger off, you madman!* but the kids pressed against the windows, eyes alight, shrieking, encouraging him further.

It was easy to imagine what he'd have been like as a father. How he'd have greeted his children by scooping them up and twirling them in the air, laughing his infectious laugh and making strangers smile. It wasn't just his exuberance, his joy that attracted her, but his wanting to live life to the full.

When they first met, they'd slip off after work, catch a bus away from the crowded noisy streets to the corner of Shenzhen Bay they thought of as their own. Jian would make himself comfortable against the trunk of a coconut tree, nestling Lia between his knees, his chin on her shoulder, his arms around her, both of them staring out to sea. Behind them sprawled sandy dunes with scrubby trees, before them was Hong Kong, separated by a harbour that some days was blue, but more often a flat pewter.

She'd trace the veins in his hands, blue worms beneath his

cashew-coloured skin, and feel the rise and fall of his chest against her spine. His hands were rarely still, always moving, sketching ideas in the air, accentuating his thoughts. She loved his hands. Their square tips, the strength in them, their tenderness. She'd press a palm against her cheek to feel their heat, then she'd kiss the tips. Sometimes she would turn and take his index finger in her mouth and tease it with her tongue, watching his eyes darken, his mouth part.

With Jian she could be herself. She could be as feminine as she liked, wear pretty underwear and cry at a sad movie, and there was never any need to try and hide her tougher side, the self-sufficient, independent police officer. Jian came to her graduation, and applauded her promotions. He was proud of her. He called her his Supervisor, his fantasy in uniform.

She'd never laughed as much as when she'd met Jian.

And when he'd asked her about her heritage, her *gwailo* looks, she hadn't been embarrassed. Jian made her feel as though she could confess to anything and it would be all right. Nobody knew for sure where her unusual appearance came from, but her mother suspected that *her* mother – Lia's grandmother – had had an English lover, a handsome and wealthy Londoner called Hugo Laird who had done business with Lia's grandfather.

When her grandmother died and Lia saw a faded sepia photograph of the man hidden among her grandmother's papers, she knew she carried his blood. She couldn't deny their likeness. She had the same sharp chin and pointed nose, the same wavy mahogany hair.

Lia had tried to contact this man's family to no effect. Like most Chinese, she would have worked any Western connection to death to get out of China, visit relatives and not come back, anything to leave the country for a better future. But she never heard anything in return. Officially, she was one hundred per cent Chinese, but there was a portion of her – maybe five per cent, maybe ten – which some days didn't feel

Chinese at all, and she wondered if blood could have this effect on you, or if it was her imagination.

She remembered talking about this with Jian, and how he didn't laugh or mock, but took her seriously.

'Yes, of course it's had an effect,' he said. 'You saw that photograph when you were, what? Five years old? Even if Hugo Laird wasn't your grandfather, he may as well have been. You saw yourself in him, and since then, you've considered yourself to be part-English. You take pride in the fact you speak fluent English. You read English newspapers when you can, English books.'

He'd put his arms around her and nuzzled her neck. 'Hello, my little *gwailo*,' he'd murmured. 'Care to show me how an Englishwoman makes love?'

*

Now, Lia lay in bed staring at the shadows on the ceiling, the thick rope of grief tight around her neck. A part of her asked the question: what if she let Tan fuck her? What then? Did it matter? Without Jian, she had nothing. No future. Why was she bothered by it?

She got up once to drink some water, returning to lie down. Occasionally a dog barked, but otherwise it was silent. She stared into the darkness, waiting for the night to pass.

At 7 a.m. it was still pitch dark, the air icy. Feeling sluggish and tired, Lia clambered out of bed. Her skin puckered into goose bumps as she hurriedly lit a lamp. Shivering, groaning under her breath, she dressed as fast as she could, lots of layers, her fingers fumbling, unco-ordinated. To her surprise, when she struggled into the kitchen, Fang Dongmei was already there, preparing bowls of warm congee, rice gruel. She wore a padded, quilted red robe trimmed with yellow satin and a pair of sheepskin booties.

'You didn't have to get up,' Lia told her.

Grunt.

'But thanks anyway.' She accepted the cup of green tea already brewed, mellow and bitter all at once, and just how she liked it.

Come eight o'clock she was standing on the pavement, ankle-deep in snow, her breath pluming in the icy air. She wasn't sure why but she didn't want Tan coming up her apartment steps and knocking on her door again. But if she didn't care what happened to her, why was she troubled by him?

She stamped her feet and tucked her gloved hands under her armpits, trying to keep warm. Light was creeping into a sky the colour and texture of grey silk. Her suitcase stood beside her, her ID card and papers rested in her breast pocket. Nothing moved, not even a rat. It was too cold. She'd been told Lhasa's winters were mild, rarely below -10°C, but Lia struggled with this supposedly 'mild' temperature thanks to having lived most of her life in the tropics. Smoke trailed from the chimney opposite and she could see two people moving downstairs. She didn't know who lived there. She didn't know anyone on the street.

The sound of an engine made her turn her head. A white Toyota Land Cruiser appeared, clouds of steam trailing from its exhaust. Instantly, her nerves wound themselves into knots.

When it slowed to a stop, she saw Tan was in the passenger seat. She hadn't seen the driver before, a chunky Chinese man with a thick neck and pits of acne on his cheekbones. As the driver climbed out to fetch her suitcase – Tan obviously had no intention of leaving the warmth of the car for something as trivial as good manners – another car appeared. For a moment Lia thought it was a back-up vehicle – the PSB were renowned for never travelling alone if they could help it – until its driver climbed out and stamped his way over.

Her mouth opened in surprise. 'Commissioner?'

'I wanted to catch you before you went to Rabang,' Zhi said. He didn't look at Tan or his driver, who was wheeling her suitcase to the rear of the Land Cruiser. He was concentrating on Lia.

'Word travels fast,' she said, trying not to appear surprised. It seemed she'd read Tan wrong and that their trip to Rabang was official after all.

'Here, you'll need this.' He handed her a dark blue folder, which she immediately recognised. Yesterday, she'd brought together the photographs of the dead boys, copies of their autopsies and her notes, and collated them in the one folder, which she'd left on her desk.

She stood quietly, one thought chasing around and around her brain with astonishment: *she had an ally*.

'Thank you,' she managed.

Both of them looked around at the sound of an electric window buzzing down. This was followed by a blast of the horn.

Zhi turned around. 'In a hurry, Tan?'

Tan looked at Zhi, his expression perfectly bland. 'Always, Commissioner,' he called.

'I won't keep you, then. It's a long journey you're undertaking.' He sucked his teeth as he shook his head. 'I'm impressed you're driving. Personally, I would have waited for Ngari Airport to re-open.'

'It's shut?' Lia was startled.

'Snow storm. Don't forget it's over four thousand metres above sea level. The fourth highest airport in the world...' Zhi shrugged his shoulders as if to say, *what do you expect?* 'But business is business.' He clapped his hands together as he finally looked at Tan. 'Have a safe journey.'

Lia clambered into the back of the Land Cruiser to see her suitcase was four times the size of Tan's, and that the driver's luggage consisted of a single plastic carrier bag. There were no emergency supplies, not even a spare blanket in case the weather turned and they got stuck.

'Are you sleeping with him?' Tan asked. He was watching the Commissioner's car drive past.

'If I was,' she responded with a flare of her old nature, 'you'd be the last to know.'

'He's *go pi*.' He's shit.

Lia clutched the folder to her chest and, feeling braver than she had in months, nearly said, *and you're not?* but managed to bite her tongue.

'Get out,' Tan said.

Ai Ya! Had she spoken aloud without realising?

'I'm sorry?' she stammered.

'Leave your stuff, and get out. I've forgotten something. I'll be back –' he pulled up the sleeve of his fleece to check his watch '– in forty minutes. Maybe an hour.'

Baffled, Lia climbed outside.

'You can leave the folder too,' he called.

Her fingers tightened on the cardboard. 'I need to read it.'

He gazed at her briefly, face expressionless. Then he turned to his driver. 'Go,' he said.

*

An hour later, Lia stood on the pavement feeling a weird sense of *déjà vu* as Tan's Land Cruiser approached the second time. Behind it was an identical vehicle with a driver and in the passenger seat, a young woman dressed in casual jeans and fleece. Lia's spirits lifted when she recognised Jenny Wang. Perhaps the journey wouldn't be so bad after all. Jenny gave her a smile. She smiled back. Jenny was obviously presiding over the back-up vehicle Lia had expected earlier.

She climbed into the back seat of Tan's Land Cruiser. In the rear were two suitcases, a leather holdall, two crates of mineral water and a box stuffed with an array of high-energy food bars, instant noodles and soups. There were tow ropes and a twenty-litre jerry can of diesel, a high-lift jack and a tool box. Facing forward, she saw a satellite phone plugged into the dashboard. Everything needed for a perilous journey into a harsh winter wilderness.

Her instinct had been right. Tan had never intended to go to Rabang. He'd used the promise of taking her there as a ruse to get her on her own, and after he'd done whatever he wanted with her, they would have returned to the office with their stories rehearsed and accordant: Lia's one of failure to find a serial killer, no doubt — she could hear the sniggers already — and Tan's triumphant in some way.

Everyone would have known the truth, of course.

Everyone would have known he'd fucked her.

But the tables had been turned. Without knowing quite how, Lia had managed to force him on a hazardous journey he'd had no intention of undertaking. As the car accelerated, spraying snow over a woman setting up her cabbage stall, Tan turned in his seat. His eyes were perfectly expressionless, like black stones at the bottom of a clear-running stream. He said, 'If you're not sleeping with shit-face, then how did he know about this little trip?'

She'd already worked it out but she wasn't going to share the information. She gave him a perfectly blank look and said, 'I have no idea.'

8

LAMA SONAM FINISHED HIS meditation with difficulty. He found it almost impossible to empty his mind of worry – for their mission, for the future of his country – and find freedom from his mental anguish. He felt like a novice, restless and agitated, and about as likely to attain enlightenment as an elephant might grow wings and fly to the moon. He slowly opened his eyes to see his spiritual teacher and *zawé lama*, root guru, Dawa Rinpoche, regarding him steadily.

'You are struggling today,' the High Abbot said.

'Yes,' Lama Sonam sighed.

'I also,' Dawa Rinpoche admitted. 'We would have to be the Buddha himself not to be affected by what is going on.'

Lama Sonam rose and went to the fire, and put on a pot of water to boil for tea. It was warm inside the tent, and slightly fetid from the smell of unwashed bodies and last night's cooking. Although it was a bright day outside, crisp and clear, he was glad they weren't travelling today. The last few days had exhausted him. Although he was fit for his age, carried no spare fat and had no physical infirmities, the fact he was sixty-four was taking its toll.

But what about Dawa Rinpoche? He was over eighty, and how he managed to cling on to his horse all day yesterday through the knee-high snow was anyone's guess. This journey was meant to take many months and they were being forced to undertake it in weeks. Sometimes a mile a day was the most they could travel, a mile of floundering through snow, scrambling over boulders with the mountain wind howling around them and snatching at their robes, making their eyes water, their skin blister.

When they could, they caught lifts in passing lorries or

cars to the next town. However, there were no roads to many habitations, forcing them to walk. They'd bought two yaks in Rabang to carry their supplies, and two horses to carry anyone who was failing. Sometimes deep crevasses barred their way, enforcing a long and arduous detour. Three days ago, they had to remain in their sealed yak-hide tent while a storm raged around them. When they came out in the morning, they were as blind as moles emerging from below ground. The yaks survived the storm relatively well, but the horses suffered. He felt sorry for the horses. They didn't have thick coats like yaks, and did poorly on the thin vegetation. The horse the High Abbot rode was sturdy, but it still laboured.

Tenzin paced around the tent. The only Dob-dob, fighting monk, in their midst, he was obviously restless at the unscheduled delay.

'We leave first thing tomorrow?' Tenzin asked for what felt like the hundredth time.

'Yes, Tenzin.' Lama Sonam patted the monk's shoulder affectionately. 'First thing.'

'Sorry.' Tenzin gave a rueful smile.

'Go and check the equipment,' Lama Sonam said. 'Double check the tack. Mend anything that looks remotely in need of repair.'

He knew Tenzin would already have done this, but sending him on an official task would help settle him for a while. Tenzin was a big man, strong and fit, and he found it hard to sit around doing nothing. He'd known Tenzin a long time, since he was a child. A monk had found him wandering in a snow storm near the Tashilhunpo Monastery. Nobody knew where he'd come from. He couldn't speak. The monks had to teach him everything. He didn't even know what tsampa was: a staple foodstuff of barley flour blended with yak butter tea to produce dumplings or porridge. It was as though his memory had been erased, but when Lama Sonam took him under his wing as his spiritual guide, his personality began to shine through. Clearly not academic, Tenzin hated studying, but on the other hand, he was tough and resourceful and bursting with energy. It had been Lama Sonam's idea for him to become a Dob-dob, a fighting monk, and the instant he'd mentioned it, Tenzin's eyes had blazed with delight.

In old Tibet, Lama Sonam mused, there had been no police force, so the job of overseeing law and order in the great monastic universities – where there were often thousands of monks – was given to the Dob-dobs. They were less academic monks who weren't inclined towards study and spiritual practice, but attracted to more physical matters like sport and fighting. Dob-dobs still existed in some monasteries and, just like their ancient counterparts, were usually big men, heavily muscled and as strong as bulls.

Lama Sonam watched over Tenzin as he grew into a forthright, honest, hard-working and extremely loyal monk. He was known for his generosity and sense of fairness, and he was well-liked throughout the Tashilhunpo Monastery. Lama Sonam couldn't have been more proud of him if he'd been his son.

Not for the first time, he wondered about Tenzin's rebirth, and who he'd been before. His previous incarnation. Rebirth in Buddhism was the doctrine that the actions of a person would lead to a new existence after death, in endless cycles. When a person died, they were reborn into another body, and not necessarily as another human being. Change from one life to the next – *punarbhava* – literally meant 'becoming again'.

It was like a flame being transferred from one candle to the next. One life to the next. Neither was identical, neither was completely distinct.

Every time the Dalai Lama died, he was reincarnated.

Every time the Panchen Lama died – the second most important Tibetan spiritual leader after the Dalai Lama – he was also reincarnated.

The same applied to himself and Dawa Rinpoche and the three other lamas. Every person in the world, every animal, reincarnated.

Eternal flames between one life and the next.

And Tenzin? Lama Sonam had been surveying the fighting monk recently, his ability to read the stars, his talent for making a comfortable camp just about anywhere, and wondered if he'd been a soldier in his previous life. If so, then Tenzin had been sent to them all those years ago with a purpose: to help guide and protect them on their hazardous journey.

9

THE JOURNEY TO RABANG was one of the hardest Lia had undertaken and not just because of the conditions. Tan was meticulously polite, almost brittle in his actions towards her, creating a tense atmosphere that had their driver Xhu sweating and George Shi — the driver of Jenny's back-up vehicle — watching them both warily.

After her reckless outburst — *you'd be the last to know* — Lia made sure she thought before she spoke and offered nothing but measured, deferential responses. Whenever she talked to the drivers or Jenny, Tan soon interrupted, making it clear that all conversation should be conducted through him. He refused to have the radio on, or let the driver play a CD. He wouldn't allow a rest stop unless it was on the hour. At the end of their first day, he insisted they stay at the first village they came to rather than continue another ten kilometres to the next, which was a tourist destination and would have had more comfortable amenities. He made it abundantly clear that the trip wasn't to be pleasurable in any way.

On their second day and after they'd swung off the main route, away from Ngari, the road deteriorated to a snow-filled track that had the big Land Cruisers struggling to cope. Twice, their vehicle got bogged down and had to be towed free. The third time it happened, Tan told her and Jenny's driver, George, to get out and push. As usual, he refused to get out himself and sat in the passenger seat, seemingly oblivious of their discomfort.

Shin-deep in snow, Lia put her shoulder to the rear of the bogged-down Land Cruiser alongside George. The two vehicles were roped together and now Jenny yelled, 'Push!'

Lia and George strained and heaved. Nothing seemed to

be happening and then with a rush, the vehicle's wheels spun, spraying wet muddy snow in a rooster's tail, right into their faces, and when she turned to look at George, she was blinking through a pancake of mud.

Wiping her eyes, Lia said, 'Remind me not to order the mud pie next time.'

George grinned at her, his teeth bright white against the filth dripping down his face. 'Why, don't you like mud?' He pretended to lick his lips. 'Hmm,' he said. 'A pinch of coriander might help. Or do you think coriander's too faint-hearted? Chilli might be better.'

Lia could see Tan watching them in the side mirror, his sunglasses smooth black and reflective, hiding his expression, but she could see the hard set of his mouth. Turning her back on George's banter she scurried to the Land Cruiser. After the sub-zero temperature outside, the car felt overly hot, stuffy and claustrophobic, but she knew it was deceptive and that once she'd warmed up, it would feel perfectly comfortable.

'Were you eating beancurd with George?' Tan accused her of flirting, his tone deceptively silky.

Xhu caught her eye in the rear-view mirror and they both shied from the contact. He didn't want to lose his job and she didn't want to get him into trouble. At least they knew their place. Tan had seen to that.

'How could I flirt looking like I do?'

Tan twisted in his seat and looked at her. He started to laugh. 'You're right! You look like shit!'

*

Lia sank back in her seat, staring outside. How had it come to this? Two years ago, if she'd been told she'd be transferred to Tibet, she would have laughed so hard she'd have broken a rib. But that was before Fang Dongmei's protest, before Jian was flung into jail, his parents and his siblings, aunts, uncles and cousins put on trial for supposedly practising Falun Gong.

A gentle style of living with Taoist and Buddhist principles, Falung Gong was immensely popular throughout China. Unfortunately, it was also illegal. Religion was restricted to five government-sanctioned organisations and if anyone was found praying or meditating outside these five, or outside a registered place of worship, they were arrested.

However, Falun Gong held a special place in the state's heart, where it was comprehensively hated. Since it was banned in 1999, Falun Gong followers had been branded as belonging to an *evil cult*, its members persecuted, tortured and killed. As Lia fought to free Jian, she tried to work out why the government loathed such a kind and placid way of thinking. Since the only ideology the government could offer its people was 'make money' and 'prosperity', Lia eventually surmised the hatred sprang from fear. Fear of not having control. Fear of its people – from the deserts in the west to the cities in the east – finding something they all related to and banding together and rising, turning against the state. Fear, fear, fear...

Jian didn't practise Falun Gong but his parents did. The police only found this out when Fang Dongmei began protesting at being evicted from her home. Wanting to find something to get her off their back, the PSB dug around and so started the witch hunt until every living relative of Fang Dongmei's was in jail. Except for Lia, who was a police officer.

Jian had flown to Beijing to help try and release Fang Dongmei and his parents only to end up arrested himself. He wasn't granted bail. Nobody was. It took on average six months to a year before a case was put before a court, and should the case then go to appeal, the appellant could wait in jail another year. Lia heard of people waiting for three years before they went to trial and there was no guarantee this wouldn't happen to Jian, especially since his parents had already been waiting nearly a year for their case to be heard.

The day Jian was arrested, Lia flew to Beijing. She wanted to be near him and although she could only visit him once a month – bringing him vital necessities such as warm clothing and food – knowing she was in the same city helped her sleep at night. To her horror, his jail had to be the worst she'd seen and she could feel the shock on her face when she first visited. Not only was the place filthy, infested with fleas, lice and snakes, but the inmates stank – they were only allowed to shower once a fortnight. Eleven men shared a cell with six beds. Two bare bulbs lit the cell twenty-four hours a day. Jian looked cold and wet, as if he'd been hosed, and his face was bruised and cut, along with his arms. The hands she so loved were split across the knuckles and weeping blood. He denied he'd been beaten, but Lia knew he was lying.

Her boss in Shenzhen was sympathetic and supportive, allowing her to take compassionate leave, fully paid for the first few weeks, but when she hadn't returned after two months, he put the pressure on for her return to her job.

Jian begged her to go back, resume her life without him, but when she pictured herself walking through their apartment with its power shower, stainless steel fridge-freezer, widescreen TV and luxuriously soft bed, a wave of nausea overcame her. She'd never be able to sleep there, let alone eat or breathe while he remained in Beijing's Number 2 Prison.

And so she joined the Beijing police. After several months, she thought she knew who to talk to, who to flatter and who to bribe, but she was naïve, a child at walking the corrupt negotiating fields of authority, and her plan backfired. Her boss took her kickback and for reasons she never knew, reported her. The next day she was told that both she and Fang Dongmei would be transferred to Lhasa at the end of the week.

Jian was executed two days later.

She hadn't known this, because Fang Dongmei didn't tell her until it was over. She'd kept it a secret and at the time Lia had hated her with venom she didn't know she possessed. She'd wanted to be there for Jian when he died, be the last thing he saw, the last thing he heard. She would have shouted to him that she loved him, over and over...

I love you! I love you!

Instead, it had been Fang Dongmei who had witnessed Jian's execution. It was, she told Lia, what Jian wanted. She didn't say any more, except that it was *mercifully quick*.

Lia could have resigned from the police, but she was beyond caring what happened to her. Numb, unable to think what else to do, she'd taken her orders silently. Part of her didn't understand why she'd remained part of a system that appeared to destroy with every step it took, but what else was she supposed to do?

She was a police officer.

It was part of her fabric, the way she was made, and even as she sat in the back of a PSB Land Cruiser, banished to a strange country she had yet to know, she knew she couldn't have acted any differently.

*

Later that day the clouds lifted and they emerged onto a vast plain flooded with light. They were on the edge of a sea of gleaming white snow stretching in every direction. In the distance stood a spine of mountains, black ribs of rocks jutting against a vivid blue sky. Lia had never seen such distances before. The clarity of the air was astonishing. Everything was in sharp focus. Behind them lay Lhasa, filled with bustle and noise, ahead was an immense space empty of humans. As the Land Cruiser ventured across the plateau, she felt they were as exposed as a beetle trundling across a freshly laundered bed sheet.

They travelled as fast as they could, stopping only to relieve themselves at the side of the road or allow the drivers a brief rest. They ate on the move. Lia passed snacks forward. Xhu appeared addicted to prawn crackers. Tan, vacuum-packed Surimi, crab-stick imitations. The car reeked of fish. Lia would have been happy to drive for a while, but she didn't offer as she knew it wasn't acceptable. Drivers were drivers and police, police. They didn't swap roles, not unless it was an emergency.

The villages they passed through were small and ram-shackle, the buildings built of stone and mud, but they always received a warm welcome. Butter tea was offered along with tsampa and a place by the fireside, but Tan shunned every hospitality. He sneered at the Tibetans. He thought they were below him, an inferior race, and every move, every gesture he made, made his contempt clear. Jenny Wang, on the other hand, was well-mannered and courteous. Lia hadn't realised she spoke Tibetan until their second day, when they were forced to ask directions. When Lia looked surprised, Tan had rolled his eyes as though stunned at her stupidity. 'Why else would she be here?' he said.

Few people travelled out here and there were no hotels, no guest houses – visitors were at the mercy of the village's hospitality – and while Lia and Jenny bedded down in people's back rooms, Tan steadfastly refused any contact with the locals and stayed in the car. Lia knew he'd be so cold he couldn't sleep, and while part of her admired his fortitude, the other part of her became smaller, even more frightened. He was the type of man who would happily injure himself in an effort to punish someone else, and that made him doubly dangerous.

*

It took just under four days to get to Rabang, during which Tan grew more steely with every hour, more acerbic. When the village finally came into view, even Lia felt a rush of relief. The sun was out, lighting the monastery roof a rich red, its walls ochre. Blue smoke drifted through the streets, blurring outlines and giving the village a mystical air. A pack of dogs raced out as they approached, biting at the wheels and barking. Some were as big as wolves with shaggy coats and long tails held high and curving over their backs.

The Supervisor who oversaw Xigazê and Ngari Prefectures came out to greet them. He had, apparently, been driving just ahead of them from Ngari, where he'd been giving evidence in court.

In charge of an area the size of France, Supervisor Chen — a lean man with an angular face and rimless spectacles — had a dozen police posts and barely twice as many men. Which appeared pretty paltry until you took in the fact that when Chen reported some unrest at one of the monasteries in the year of the Beijing Olympics, over a thousand soldiers were immediately deployed to quell a possible uprising. Twenty monks were arrested, Tan told Lia. Twelve were still in prison. Despite the remoteness of the area, Chen had power. He made a call, and the authorities responded fast.

It had been Chen who'd sent Pemba Dolma's body to Lhasa. Pemba had been the third boy to die with a broken neck on Chen's patch — the fifth child, as far as they knew, in total — and, like Lia, he was puzzled. Lia studied Chen surreptitiously. He obviously wasn't stupid, because he appraised their little group in seconds and immediately directed his energy towards Tan. After they were introduced he ignored Lia and Jenny. He didn't once glance at the drivers.

First, Chen settled them in their quarters. Tan and Jenny stayed with one family, the drivers another. Lia felt a knot of tension loosen when Chen drove her to the outskirts of the village, a good quarter of a mile from the PSB officers.

'Sorry there was no room near your colleagues,' Chen apologised.

'Please, it's no problem,' she told him, and when she saw her room, the bare earth tamped down by years of footsteps and covered with yak-wool rugs, the huge bed a raised platform smothered in sheepskins and blankets, she smiled inside. It may not have a bathroom, heating or any running water, but it was far nicer than the PSB officers' accommodation – a spartan outhouse with sheep droppings in the corners. Lia glanced at Chen, wondering if he'd engineered this or if it was just the way things had fallen.

'It's great,' she said. Gratitude and relief threaded her voice. 'Thank you.'

He gave a nod but there was no expression on his face. 'I hope you will be comfortable.'

*

Chen introduced her to her hosts, a robust couple with ruddy cheeks, and their four children. The children were all under six years old and as playful and noisy as puppies. They had holes in their shoes, their sweaters and gloves were threadbare and worn, but they looked healthy. Like most villagers, they were farmers. They had a handful of sheep, several yaks and a few chickens. There were some rough fields carved out of the tundra that in summer would yield a meagre crop of barley, but Lia gauged they had enough resources to keep them warm and feed them throughout the year.

She knew Chen would pay the family for their trouble, but she still asked him to thank them for having her stay. Chen translated for her. The couple beamed. Lia smiled back, her lips feeling stiff and uncomfortable, reminding her how little she smiled these days.

'Do they know anything about Pemba's death?' she asked Chen.

'Not specifically, but they knew the boy. It is a small village. Everyone knows everyone.'

'What do they think happened?'

Chen posed the question to the couple and translated the husband's answer. 'I'm not sure,' the husband said. 'They say he broke his neck, but how could he have done such a thing?

He was found in the hen house. There isn't anywhere to jump from, or fall. It's a real puzzle.'

Lia looked at Chen. 'Could he have died somewhere else and been moved there?'

'It's possible.'

Chen explained he hadn't seen the body where it was found because it was already en route to the funeral when he arrived. 'I managed to persuade them that the boy's body should go to Lhasa. That by doing so we could prevent more boys dying.' His gaze turned slightly inward. 'It wasn't easy. As soon as someone dies, no one is allowed to move or touch the body until the funeral takes place. Then the body is carried by a family member to a professional body carrier...that's when I interrupted them. The body mustn't touch the earth, because they believe the soul of the dead will then wander there for eternity. I took the boy to Lhasa myself, with the boy's father. It was the only way they'd let him go. Once Hua Ming had done the autopsy, I drove the body back for the burial.'

Lia found herself reassessing the Supervisor. This wasn't some clone pumped out of the BPPC – Beijing People's Police College. This was an intelligent, resourceful man who saw beyond the law.

Chen continued, telling her it had been Pemba's brother Tashi who'd described the body's position to him. *It looked as though he'd tripped over and hadn't got up.*

'It was the same for the other two boys,' he said.

'Same story for all five,' she agreed. 'May I meet Tashi?'

Chen pushed his spectacles further up the bridge of his nose. 'Shall we collect Officer Tan on the way?'

Lia dipped her head. 'Of course.'

10

TASHI WAS A SHARP-EYED little boy with a thatch of scruffy black hair. His clothes were filthy, caked in dust and dried mud, his fingernails rimmed with grime. Despite his small size, he looked strong and hardy. Like Chen, he seemed to get the measure of their group quickly, and deferred directly to Tan.

Yes, he said. He'd found his brother's body. Yes, in the chicken house. Yes, Pemba was lying on straw. Yes, it looked as though he'd simply tripped over and hadn't got up.

The boy fidgeted anxiously, pulling pieces of stray cotton from his fraying cuffs.

Tan questioned the boy with surprising gentleness, taking Lia aback. She'd expected him to be ham-fisted and rude, but instead he hunkered down so he was at eye-level with the boy and spoke to him quietly and calmly, as one equal to another. Watching him, she wondered about his abidingly foul mood in the car. He'd made sure the journey was as awkward and unpleasant as possible. Was it his way of letting everyone know how furious he was at being forced all the way out here? His way of demonstrating his absolute power?

While Tan ran Tashi through timings – when the boys had gone to bed, what time Tashi had woken in the morning, when he'd found his brother's body – Lia glanced at Tashi's mother, who was sitting in the corner quietly smoking a pipe. She hadn't said a word since they arrived, just taken up position on the floor with her back against the wall. Like everyone else in the village she wore a chuba, a traditional coat with fur at the throat and lined with sheepskin. Where the men's chubas stopped at the knees, the women's reached to their ankles. They looked windproof and as warm as sleeping bags.

As though she'd felt Lia's gaze on her, Tashi's mother looked across, straight into Lia's eyes. Her gaze was bold and didn't fall away. Lia's eyes dropped first. The woman appeared remarkably composed considering she'd just lost a child, but Lia didn't take this at face value. She recalled visiting Jian in jail, and one of the inmates praising her poise. Externally she walked and talked and breathed, seemingly unaffected by her husband's arrest and the charges trumped up against him – inciting social disorder by practising Falun Gong – but inside her was an unceasing high-pitched never-ending scream of agony.

'Describe how he looked when you found him,' Tan asked Tashi. 'Every detail, mind. Don't leave anything out. It might be important.'

'He was sprawled on the straw,' Tashi said. His face screwed up with concentration. 'For a moment I thought he'd tripped over. I couldn't tell he'd broken his neck, not until the police officer moved him. His head went all floppy, like a rabbit that's been killed.'

'Was there anything else?'

The boy shook his head.

'Did anything stand out to you the day your brother died? Did you have any visitors to the village, for instance?' He turned an amused gaze on Lia, letting her know he was humouring her, but Lia was watching Tashi's mother. Although she didn't change her position, didn't blink, Lia sensed a tightening in her posture.

Tashi looked puzzled. 'Like who?'

'I don't know,' Tan shrugged. 'A tourist, perhaps? Someone wanting to sell something? A farmer from another village looking to buy a sheep?'

Tan had just shown his complete lack of knowledge of rural life out here, she thought. It was winter. Tourists and travelling salesmen were as likely as a visit from the President of America. Or was he being disingenuous? It wouldn't surprise her if he was pretending to be stupid in order to trip the boy.

'No,' said the boy. 'Nobody came.'

Tashi didn't look at his mother, nor she at him, but Lia discerned an unspoken communication between them. As she watched, wondering whether she should step in with a few questions of her own, Tashi looked straight at her.

The word, *bù,* formed on his lips. No.

Lia stared at him. He spoke Mandarin?

Tashi mouthed another word and brushed his palm to one side. The gesture and the word were unmistakable. *Guòhòu.* Later.

Unnerved and not a little startled, she was opening her mouth to ask a question, when Tashi's mother, in one swift movement, rose to her feet. 'May I get you something to eat?' Jenny quickly translated when the woman spoke.

'If it's more of that disgusting tsampa,' Tan said, 'no thank you.' He raised his eyebrows at his PSB officer. 'Has she got anything better on offer?'

Obediently Jenny spoke to the woman, who shook her head.

'Tea, then?' Tan said. 'Not that sickly pig's urine they dish out but something drinkable.'

While Jenny trotted obediently to Tan's Land Cruiser to fetch some green tea, Tashi melted away. Lia didn't see him go. One second he was there, looking at her bright-eyed and alert, the next he'd gone.

*

Supper was provided by Tan's hosts. Boiled yak – lots of grey fat and gristle – and spoonfuls of noodles cooked with onions and green peppers. Considering the meal wasn't particularly flavoursome, Lia was surprised at how much she ate. She put it down to the freezing mountain air and her body demanding copious calories, uncaring where they came from in an attempt to keep warm.

Lia stifled a yawn, running her mind over the day. They'd spent the remainder of the morning interviewing villagers and, come the afternoon, Tan had become irritable and bored.

'You question them,' he told her. 'Chen and I will observe.' A sly smile crept onto his face. 'We'll give you marks out of ten at the end of the day.'

Having Tan alongside her hampered Lia's questions. He shook his head a lot with an expression of dismay, and whenever she wanted to follow an avenue of questioning that interested her – like a domestic violence issue between a married couple two doors from Pemba – he'd raise his eyes heavenwards and sigh, disconcerting not only Lia, but who-ever she was questioning at the time. She knew he was doing it on purpose, to unsettle her and show his dominance, but instead of putting her off, it simply made her more determined.

In the monastery, Jenny patiently continued to translate. Chen could also speak Tibetan but he remained silent as Tan had requested, observing. Jenny had an easy way about her and was obviously polite, because nobody seemed offended at her questions and people answered easily, without any sign of stress. However, each time Lia asked whether the village had received any visitors recently, there was an almost imperceptible contraction in the atmosphere. It didn't matter who she asked, tea boy or senior monk, she elicited the same guarded response. Tan appeared oblivious, but she wasn't so sure about Chen.

On their way back, Jenny fell into step with Lia. She was frowning. 'Do you really think there's a serial killer at work here?'

'I don't know what to think. But they're hiding something, that's for sure.'

'Hmm. I'm not sure it's anything to do with the dead boy. I think it's something else.'

'Like what?' Lia's interest was piqued.

'I did a few head counts. I think they have too many monks.'

By law, numbers of monks in each temple were limited.

'I guess it's possible,' Lia said neutrally. She wasn't going to say she believed the village had had visitors recently, because she didn't want the information filtered to Tan, who would sneer at her.

'Shall I look into it?' Jenny appeared keen.

'If Tan thinks it's relevant.'

They ran over the interviews, debriefing informally before Lia said, 'Thanks for your support in the committee meeting.'

'Not that it made any difference.' Jenny pulled a face. 'But if I can help any further, let me know. I have access to intel that might be useful.'

Lia sent her a sideways glance. 'Nobody wants me investigating this.'

'I'm aware of that.' The PSB officer's expression turned tight. 'But what if there really is a serial killer? What will happen if it gets out? The entire region will become even more volatile. Can we risk it?'

Lia extended her stride to miss a pile of frozen yak dung. 'Tan and Kwok seem to think so.'

'Tan and Kwok won't have to know we are looking into it.'

Although she would have loved to take Jenny up on her offer, Lia was only too aware it was a double-edged sword. If the case was successful, Jenny would take mutual – if not all – credit and further her career. If Lia failed, however, Jenny could deny her involvement. Jenny's input could be vital, but could she be trusted? She might gain more by informing on Lia down the line. Lia studied the young PSB officer. She knew little about her aside from the fact she'd been married for three years and had a two-year-old son.

Lia blew into her gloves to try and warm her fingers. 'Let's see what we've come up with by the time we leave,' she said, not wanting to commit either way.

Jenny nodded. 'Nothing, I hope. Then we won't have to worry about it.'

*

Lia joined Jenny, Chen and Tan for supper. Tan's hosts kept the fire stoked as well as their bowls of tea refreshed. They lit candles and oil lamps when darkness fell – there was no electricity – and draped rugs over the windows to keep in the heat. Dogs curled in the corners of the room, one eye opening whenever someone moved. A tabby cat came and lay on Lia's lap and purred when she absently stroked it.

'How do you think our little Supervisor did today, Chen?' asked Tan around a mouthful of stew. 'What marks shall we give her?'

Chen gestured apologetically that his mouth was full and couldn't answer.

'Very diplomatic,' said Tan. His eyes were glittering in the candlelight. 'How about you, Jenny? Any suggestions?'

Jenny mumbled something unintelligible before absorbing herself in her tea.

'I'd give her a two for effort, how about that?'

Nobody said anything and kept their gazes averted.

Tan turned to Lia. 'Tell me, Supervisor, are you still convinced there's someone going around the prefectures snapping little boys' necks?'

Lia cupped her hands around her tea bowl, trying to warm the chill in her bones. She said nothing. She didn't want to admit she'd learned nothing new by coming out here but at least she knew why he was being so unrepentingly unpleasant. He was making it clear it was her fault he was here, on what he believed to be a wild goose chase.

'It's a mystery.' Chen spoke up. 'In the three years I've been working the area, I haven't seen any children with broken necks, and then I have three, all in the last fortnight.'

Tan put his spoon down and fished in his pocket for a cigarette, lit up. 'Are you saying that if it wasn't for you,' he said, casually exhaling blue smoke, 'we wouldn't be here?'

'I suppose so.' Chen looked discomfited, but unlike Lia,

he wasn't cowed. 'There's something funny going on, but we just haven't found out what it is yet.'

'Another believer in fairy tales,' Tan scoffed. 'Honestly, you two should get married. Supervisor Shan's free to marry again, aren't you? Remind us what happened to your husband?'

Lia eased the cat from her lap and rose to her feet. She kept her eyes cast down. 'I'm tired,' she said. 'If you'll excuse me...'

Chen leaped to his feet. 'I'll drive you.'

'That would be kind.'

She pulled on her down coat and turned up the collar as she walked to the door. Slid on her hat and gloves. Just before they stepped outside, Tan called out, 'Don't forget to set your alarms, my little love birds, so we leave on time tomorrow. I don't want to spend a minute longer in this shit-hole than I have to.'

*

After the smoky atmosphere inside, the icy air caught Lia's throat, making her cough. Frost glittered beneath a moonless sky, bright with stars. Ahead of her, Himalayan peaks stretched their sharp white fingers skywards. There was no breeze. A rush of amazement filled her as she looked upwards. She'd never seen a sky like it before and for a moment she forgot about the cold in her bones, the dead boys, Tan and her recent hardships. There were so many stars! Thousands, millions, *trillions* of them, scattered from one end of the inky horizon to the other. She felt as though she was standing in the centre of the Milky Way. She had an urge to reach up and pluck a star, right from its centre.

'It's beautiful,' she murmured.

'Yes,' Chen agreed.

She was grateful he didn't say any more but let her enjoy the wonder, until her feet began to grow numb. She couldn't believe the cold. She was wearing three pairs of long-sleeved silk vests and leggings beneath her first layer of clothing.

They were lighter than thermal underwear and just as effective, trapping warm air in their layers and keeping her core temperature just above freezing. She had sheepskin insoles in her boots, double-lined sheepskin gloves and a fur hat with padded ear flaps, but she couldn't remember buying them. It must have been Fang Dongmei, and at the same time she realised her grandmother-in-law had done more than just make sure she had the right things to wear. She had made a good home for them in the most harsh and difficult conditions.

Finally, Lia crunched her way to Chen's car. 'Thank you,' she said after they were settled inside, heating on full blast.

'It was a joy to witness your appreciation,' he said. 'It reminded me when I first saw such a sky. I was almost overcome.'

He put the car into gear and drove carefully down the street, tyres crunching on frost. Nobody was around. They were all tucked up with their families, sitting beside fires and bubbling pots of noodle stew.

Lia turned the air vent on the dashboard so it blew hot air onto her lap. Chen said, 'How does the killer lure the children out of bed? You wouldn't get my boy up in the middle of the night. He sleeps like the dead.'

'I don't know. It's almost as though he has some power over them, like the Snow Thief.'

'Who?'

Lia told Chen the legend of the haunted soul of a child who'd suffocated in the snow, and how they enticed all the naughty children out of their homes and into the forest.

'The Snow Thief, huh? Scary stuff.' He turned off the main street. He was driving slowly, barely ten k's an hour, but Lia guessed it wasn't so much to avoid skidding on the frozen ground as because he wanted to talk.

'Supervisor,' Chen said. 'May I ask you something about these boys?'

'Of course.'

'Did any of them show signs of sexual abuse?'

Lia shook her head. 'Nothing, according to Hua Ming. None of them suffered any trauma to the bodies, aside from their broken necks.' The car tilted and bounced as they drove over a pothole. They remained quiet, lost in their own thoughts for a minute. Finally, Lia said, 'There is one thing that mystifies me.'

'Yes?'

'Everyone's caution when I asked about recent visitors.'

Chen nodded. 'That puzzled me too. Somebody's visited, but they're not saying who. My guess is they're protecting them.'

'Could you follow that up for me? Ask around other villages, maybe try and catch someone off guard. Pretend you already know who visited, maybe. Lull them into thinking they're not telling you anything you don't already know.' She caught him flicking a quick glance at her. 'Sorry. I shouldn't tell you how to do your job.'

He gave his head a brief shake. 'I appreciate your input. Truly. Look, there is something –' he faltered briefly '– sorry, it is nothing.'

Chen swung his car right, the off-front tyre bumping over a pile of frozen yak dung. Lia slid her eyes to the side of his face, wondering what was on his mind. She knew better than to bring attention to the fact he'd been about to say something, but had thought better of it. When she was a rookie she'd put off several witness's attempts to confide by being too eager to gain their trust.

They reached the end of the street. A string of prayer flags between two cottages hung motionless, frozen in the still air. As Chen turned left, she could make out the lettering stamped on the flags. If she hadn't known the light came from the stars, she'd have thought it was a full moon.

It wasn't until he pulled up outside her lodgings that he spoke. 'There is something,' he said again.

Lia remained silent.

'I only sent the boy – Karma Delek – to Lhasa because another two boys died the same way the previous week.'

She let his statement settle for a few seconds. No wonder he'd been reticent. He didn't want the wrath of Tan's disapproval for producing two more victims. Or Tan's wrath for not reporting them. Whichever way the PSB officer reacted, Chen would get it in the neck.

'Let me get this straight,' she said in a level tone. 'You mean that, in the area that is your responsibility in these two prefectures, there are five boys who died with broken necks, not three?'

Chen turned his head to look at her straight. He said, 'Yes.'

'You thought the first deaths were accidents.' It wasn't a question, but a statement.

'Yes.'

She looked away first, her thoughts racing. 'What happened to the bodies?'

'The families buried them.'

Lia stared at the frosty ground. 'How?'

'Water burial. It's a derivative of the celestial burial.'

Lia had heard of the sky burial, where a body was dismembered and fed to the vultures, which were considered flying deities, but not its water equivalent. 'How does it differ?'

'Very little. The body is carried to the waterside, disemboweled and dismembered and thrown into the water where the fish consume it. That's why the locals don't eat fish around here.'

They both stared ahead at the buildings coloured blue-grey in the starlight and sprinkled with shards of frost.

'Did Commissioner Zhi send you out here?' he asked.

She pictured Zhi turning up out of the blue with her folder. 'Yes.'

Chen gave a nod, almost in approval. 'How many other similar deaths are you aware of?'

'Just two. One in Lhasa, the other in Xigatsê Prefecture.'

'Commissioner Zhi knows about these?'

'He investigated the one in Xigatsê. I covered the one in Lhasa.'

Neither spoke for a few seconds.

'You weren't always a Supervisor Third Class,' Chen remarked.

'No.'

He took off his spectacles, studied them briefly, and put them back on. He said quietly, 'Our greatest glory is not in never falling, but in getting up every time we do.'

He'd quoted Confucius. He was letting her know he was aware of her demotion, and probably the reason why she'd been sent to Lhasa. She wondered if he'd got his information from Zhi, or someone else, and then realised it didn't matter. He could think whatever he liked.

She reached for the door handle. 'Thank you for telling me about the first two boys. I will use what you said with care.'

'Thank you.' He ducked his head to show his gratitude. 'I would also be grateful if you could keep me informed of your ongoing investigation.'

She found herself dipping her head to him for the second time. 'Of course.'

11

TAN SAT AT THE table, smoking another cigarette more for something to do than because he really wanted one. He exhaled a stream of smoke, still unable to believe how he'd been manoeuvred into coming to this godforsaken dump. One day, he'd make the Commissioner pay. He hadn't realised Zhi and Shan were in cahoots, and although Shan said she wasn't sleeping with Zhi, he wasn't sure he believed her. When he returned to Lhasa, he'd put a couple of men to watch her place, see if the Commissioner visited.

A vision of Zhi stripping Supervisor Shan of her bra and panties filled his mind and he threw down his cigarette, stamping it out on the floor with more force than necessary. Surely she wouldn't go for an old man, he thought. She was only thirty-one and although Zhi was pretty fit, he was already going bald. Tan gave a sigh. Could she really be fucking Zhi? The Commissioner had said she'd been a zombie when she'd arrived, sunk in a quicksand of grief and depression, which Tan knew would have made her easy prey.

He didn't understand her withdrawal. His wife had died two months ago of a brain haemorrhage, and all he'd felt was relief. He hadn't told anyone at work of Mei's death. He hadn't wanted to be forced to take time off, or have to put up with everyone's two-faced sympathy. Mei had been a fair wife – houseproud, a good cook, quite a decent fuck – but so dull he could have screamed. He hadn't realised he'd find her worthiness an irritant. He'd honestly thought that all he wanted was someone to do his washing, shop and keep the house clean, but after six months of marriage he was already seeing another woman. Anything to alleviate the boredom at home.

He'd been relieved when Mei had balked at moving to Tibet, insisting she stay at home near her friends. Both sets of parents had been shocked when he'd left her behind, but he pretended it was all Mei's doing, and that he didn't want to make her unhappy.

Tan glanced down to see the tabby cat that Shan had been stroking earlier was preparing to jump up. He lit another cigarette and let the animal settle in his lap. He was about to run his palm along its spine – it was already purring in anticipation – when he took in Jenny's surprise and hurriedly put his hand on the table. He said dismissively, 'I only let it up to help keep me warm.'

Which was only half a lie. By all the gods it was cold. Almost as cold as his wedding day, when it had snowed.

It had been his mother who'd suggested he marry Mei, and thus join the two families. Mei's father ran a used-car supermarket, Tan's father a workshop and breaker's yard. For both their businesses, it was a marriage made in heaven and Tan hadn't thought of any reason why he shouldn't marry Mei. She was pretty enough, and keen to please. Tan remembered meeting her and thinking she would do very well. Which she had, he supposed, but her addiction to TV soap operas, her insistence on buying things only in the colour pink, soon drove him to distraction.

Now he was free.

But a shadow of guilt lay over him, mingled with a strange sense of shame. He hadn't grieved for Mei. Not like Shan, who was mired in mourning for her husband. He'd never lost anyone he'd loved. He wondered what it was like, to love someone so much you barely functioned when they disappeared, and decided he was better off not knowing.

Absently, without realising it, he began stroking the cat. He wondered how the dog was doing without her nightly meals, and whether she'd still be there waiting for him when he returned. And what about the child? He'd called the

Children's Welfare Institute earlier on the sat phone – making sure he wasn't overheard – who told him they still hadn't found them, despite searching the area. When he'd returned from Shan's that night the cans of food had been licked clean, and not by an animal from the footprints in the snow. When he got back, he decided, he would put food out for both creatures. The dog now trusted him and let him pet her, but it could take weeks for the child to overcome its mistrust of him. The day it did, he'd be able to help. Maybe house it in one of the orphanages. Sponsor it through school, anonymously, of course.

He turned his mind to Shan's police work earlier. She seemed to be on the ball, asking the right questions of the right people. Curious to see her perform under pressure, he'd pushed her hard, trying to sabotage her, but she'd ignored him. He gave her top marks for tenacity. He'd enjoyed watching her today, and listening to her voice, firm but surprisingly melodious. He liked the straight line of her jaw, the fine point of her chin. She made graceful gestures to punctuate her words. Her hands were small and delicate, her fingernails pale pink and not long, but not too short either. He was glad she didn't bite her nails. He couldn't abide people who did.

People seemed to warm to her when she talked to them, which was invaluable for a police officer. She had empathy, but there was a steeliness too, commanding respect. Picking a piece of tobacco from his lips, he considered the monks. He didn't like the fact they seemed to be covering something up. He'd pretended not to notice, to see if Shan picked it up. She hadn't mentioned it, but instinct told him she had, and so had Chen.

He flicked his cigarette to the floor and watched the stub burn. Three kids dead in just this area, all of broken necks. Five, total. Even he had to admit it was peculiar, and normally he'd be keen to find out the truth. But not with the words *serial killer* being bandied about. His job was to keep social order, keep the lid on the tinderbox that was Tibet, and if that meant a few more kids dying, then so be it. No way was he going to have the entire country go up in flames on his watch.

12

LIA CLIMBED OUT OF the car, wondering how a man as bright as Chen had ended up policing one of the harshest, most remote areas of the world. What was his story? Had he been banished here? Or was he here to prove himself? She was grateful to have a steadfast man like Chen on side, but what use was he, so far away from her office? She crunched her way carefully to the mud-brick cottage, wary of slipping over. She liked Chen, and she liked him even more when he didn't drive off immediately, but waited until she was safely inside. A decent man with principles, she thought, as well as good manners.

Her hosts had left an oil lamp burning on their front doorstep, and Lia took it with her to light her way to her room. In the corner of the kitchen she saw a huge pile of cushions, bodies and blankets where the family were heaped together for warmth.

Lia tiptoed past and pushed open the door to what she now realised was their bedroom. At least she knew why they had such an enormous bed — it had to accommodate all six of them. She wondered vaguely what would happen when the kids grew, and supposed they'd build another bed. It was bitterly cold and she shivered. She decided to go to bed fully dressed or she'd freeze. She put the lamp down on the floor, about to take off her boots, and nearly shrieked when she saw the figure hovering in the corner of the room.

'Sorry,' said Tashi. He held out his palms. 'I didn't mean to frighten you.'

'You speak Mandarin?'

'Lobsang Norbu said it was important.' He came and hopped onto her bed, dangling his legs over the side. 'He made our school teach us English also.'

Her jaw dropped. 'You speak *English*?'

'Not very well,' he said, in heavily accented but unmistakable English. 'I don't like it much.' He screwed up his face. 'Neither do any of the other kids, but he insisted.'

In her mind, she thought: why? She considered the remote area, the wilderness, and although she hated to suggest there was no point in him learning such things, she wondered when the children would use their languages. Perhaps they would somehow get themselves to Lhasa and enter the tourist industry?

He fiddled with his fraying cuffs, kicking his feet back and forth. 'Will you find my brother's killer?'

Startled, she said, 'How do you know he was murdered?'

'He didn't break his own neck, did he?'

Lia couldn't think what to say next. She sat on the bed next to him. The lamp flickered gently, making their shadows distort into giants, then midgets.

'I miss him,' Tashi whispered.

Tears rose in his eyes.

'I'm sorry,' she said.

'He wasn't very clever,' Tashi said. He wiped his eyes, blew his nose on his sleeve. 'But he was kind. He liked animals. His favourite was a little white dog called Cherry. Cherry keeps looking for him. I do too, even though I know he's dead. He was born five minutes after me, which makes me the eldest, but he's still my twin.'

Lia tentatively put her arm around his shoulder. He leaned into her embrace, snuffling. 'You'll find the killer?' Tashi insisted. 'Put him in prison?'

'I'll do my best.'

'It'll be hard,' he said. 'He's not like a normal man.'

A chill washed down her spine.

'What do you mean?'

'You can't tell anyone this.' He wriggled from her embrace to look into her face. 'It's secret. Promise you won't tell?'

'I'm not sure.' She decided to be honest. 'I'm a police officer. If it's important information that might help us catch your brother's killer then I'm bound to share it. Holding information back can sometimes hinder an investigation.'

'But if you can't promise, then I can't tell you.' He looked dismayed.

'Oh.' Lia pretended to think this over. As a cop she made and broke promises all the time, and today was no different. Besides, should she break this promise, she'd probably be hundreds of kilometres away and the boy would never find out.

'OK,' she said. 'I promise.'

'Look at me while you say it,' he told her.

She did as he said and as she said the words, 'I promise,' she felt as though something dark was being drawn from inside her chest and brought into the room where it hung briefly, like mist, before dissolving. She felt dizzy and off-balance. The tongue of flame in the lamp fluttered wildly for a moment, causing their shadows to twist and dance together.

'He put me to sleep,' Tashi said.

She dragged her mind into focus. 'Who did?'

'The monk. I don't know which one because I couldn't see his face. The moment I saw him, he realised I was awake and sent the darkness to me.'

As Tashi told her the story of his creeping into the ceremonial tent to watch his brother and five high lamas, how Lama Sonam had spotted him and without looking at him once, warned him away, Lia wondered how much of it was true. But when he spoke about the malevolence of some kind of spirit that could sense him and read his mind, despite telling herself the boy was making it up, something elemental inside her trembled.

'So you see why we must keep it secret.' He was looking at her earnestly. 'If he finds out that I know a monk killed Pemba, he'll come back and kill me too.'

Lia couldn't fault his logic. No wonder he was scared. But a monk? Why on earth would one of them murder a little boy?

'Tell me,' she said. 'Where did the monks come from?'

'All over Tibet.' He thought further. 'But they congregated in Lhasa first. Before beginning their travels.'

'Why were they here?'

'I don't know. Nobody would say. We spent all day preparing for them. It was hard work, but it was fun.' Briefly, his face lit up. 'Pemba and I pinched a block of sugar each. He ate his all in one go. He was nearly sick afterwards.' His lips quivered, and Lia saw the effort it took not to give in to tears. 'I gave mine back the next day, after I found him dead. I thought we were being punished for stealing, but Lobsang Norbu says Pemba's death had nothing to do with the sugar.'

Lia had no idea who Lobsang Norbu was, but wanting to comfort the boy she said, 'I'm sure he's right.'

'There was a ceremony when they arrived, of course, with all of us in the temple. There was incense and hot butter tea. The walls of the temple always seem to breathe in time with the chanting.' His expression turned dreamy. 'Lobsang Norbu came and visited me. He was quite anxious, but it wasn't until later that I realised why.'

'Who's Lobsang Norbu?'

'He was the Abbot of the monastery.'

Lia frowned. 'Was?'

'He died two years ago. He was eighty-two. He's my spiritual leader.'

'Ah,' she said as though she knew what he was talking about, but inside she was wondering if losing his twin brother hadn't unhinged him. She remembered the depth of her mother's grief, how she'd admitted to going *a little crazy*. How losing Jian had also consumed Lia, and laid her waste.

'Lobsang Norbu told me to trust you. I didn't want to,' he added with a child's customary frankness, 'but he says that you have…' He squeezed his eyes shut as he searched for the word and when he said it, it was in a rush of what Lia took as relief that he'd remembered it. 'Integrity.'

A part of her smiled at this. She said, 'Next time you talk, tell him thanks.'

'You can tell him yourself,' Tashi said. 'He's here at the moment.'

Discomfited, Lia looked quickly around the room. 'I thought you said he was dead.'

'You can't see him,' Tashi said. He seemed amused.

'Right,' she said faintly. She could almost feel her mind bend at the possibility of a six-year-old boy having conversations with an eighty-two-year-old dead Abbot. Out of nowhere she felt exhaustion ride through her. She suddenly wanted to go to bed, bury herself in the pile of smelly sheepskins and forget where she was.

'You're tired,' he said gently. The softness of his tone made her want to cry. She couldn't remember when someone last spoke to her as kindly.

Lia watched Tashi slide off the edge of the bed and go to the door. She had a vague sensation that she should be walking him home, making sure he got there safely, but she didn't move. Her veins were filled with lassitude.

'Goodnight,' he said.

And then he was gone.

13

LAMA SONAM TUCKED HIMSELF into his bed roll next to the fire. His legs ached from walking through snow all day, and his eyes were sore from the glare of sun on ice. He had two blisters forming on his heels and although the medical monk, Lama Nawang, had lanced them, he worried they would get worse and slow him down.

OM MANI PADME HUM.

The mantra chanted steadily through his head, suffusing him with calm.

OM MANI PADME HUM.

He brought out a battered, faded photograph of the Dalai Lama and studied it in the firelight. His Holiness had his palms together in a prayerful gesture, but he was smiling and behind his large round spectacles his eyes were alight with good humour. Lama Sonam longed to meet him and hear his voice, listen to him speak. The Dalai Lama was a part of his soul and the fabric of his spirituality. Without him, he would be rudderless, set adrift on a sea of disillusionment.

And he wouldn't be the only one.

Most Tibetans revered the Dalai Lama, they adored him. He gave them hope and love, and lifted their spirits to another, higher, plain. He gave them belief in themselves, that they might attain a better life in their rebirth. He was the bedrock of their beliefs, their culture and religion.

He dreaded to think what was going to happen when Tenzin Gyatso, the current and fourteenth Dalai Lama, died.

The Dalai Lama had stated that there was a chance that he wouldn't be reborn, and if he *was* reborn it might not be in a country possessed by the People's Republic of China. He stated that after he died it was possible that his people might no longer want a Dalai Lama, but Lama Sonam knew this wasn't true. Every Tibetan man, woman and child would atrophy spiritually without the Dalai Lama. It was vital that when he died, he was reborn.

Carefully, Lama Sonam tucked the photograph inside his robe. Photographs of the Dalai Lama were forbidden except inside temples. You could get arrested for carrying one. He sighed and rolled onto his side and gazed into the flames. How were his countrymen going to survive the ongoing onslaught? Not only was Tibetan Buddhism under threat, but Tibetan language schools had been banned, and the use of the Tibetan language banned in post-secondary institutions.

Recent history had been brutal. In 1965 there had been nearly six thousand monasteries in Tibet but nearly all were ransacked and destroyed by Red Guards during the Cultural Revolution. Barely ten remained. The most well-known, the most revered, the magnificent Potala in Lhasa – built on a rocky point sacred to the Bodhisattva of compassion – and the chief residence of the Dalai Lama until the current Dalai Lama fled to India after the Chinese invaded in 1951, had been converted into a museum by the Chinese government. Over 100,000 volumes of scriptures, historical documents and works of art had been removed, damaged or destroyed. If this wasn't proof that the Chinese government wanted to obliterate Tibetan Buddhism, wipe out an ancient civilisation that had survived unchanged for hundreds of years, then Lama Sonam couldn't think what was.

He struggled to understand why the Chinese government was so hostile to Tibetan culture, which was based on the goal of spiritual enlightenment – Buddhahood – and to help all other sentient beings to Buddhahood. A love of nature and animals was part of its teachings, where every animal became a person and every person had once been an animal. All life was connected; every leaf, every ant, every human being. Every creature depended on another – the lion its prey, the whale the krill it fed upon – and eventually became another. It was a peaceful, kind and compassionate religion and its destruction seemed at best ignorant, and at worst, cruel and evil.

Why had the Chinese government swamped Tibet with Han Chinese, forcing two opposite social systems to live together, face-to-face? Surely, it was asking for trouble? When Dawa Rinpoche came to him and proposed this journey, showed him what was at stake, Lama Sonam had seen the final plan. Tibetans, their culture, their beliefs and spiritualism, were about to be annihilated.

But not if he could help it.

He fell asleep with the mantra in his mind and a vision of the Dalai Lama in his heart.

14

WHEN THEY RETURNED TO Lhasa, it was just before midday and the streets were covered in ice. Lia didn't say goodbye to Tan or Xhu, his driver. She didn't acknowledge Jenny either. She simply grabbed her bags from the rear of the vehicle and lugged them into the office. It was a relief to be in the warm again.

Even though it was a weekend, the place was busy. Lia couldn't remember when she'd last had a weekend off, and realised she'd come to work every day since she'd been sent here and would probably continue to do so. She couldn't think what she might do with a rest day and it seemed that a lot of officers felt the same way. Or were they attempting to please their superiors by working every hour of every day, so they could be rewarded by being returned to China sooner?

Constable Deshi brought her up to speed over a box of freshly steamed, soft and fluffy pork *bao*, buns. Lia tucked in hungrily. 'Where did you get these?' she asked around a mouthful. 'They're delicious.'

'Lily Pond Moonlight.'

The name meant nothing to Lia. She turned back to Deshi's reports. Nothing appeared out of the ordinary, with the usual arrests for shoplifting, theft and drunkenness. A couple of Tibetan thugs had beaten up a Han shop owner. Some students had been fined for illegally downloading music from the Internet. A Tibetan dissenter was arrested for shouting anti-China slogans in the market earlier in the day. Same old, same old. Lia was about to dismiss Deshi when he said, 'Did you find anything in Rabang?'

Lia cooled her gaze. 'Why?'

'I...er.' He ducked his head. 'Can I speak freely?'

She was instantly reminded of Chen, his caution. She remained silent.

Deshi twisted his hands. His fingers were long and slender, as fine as a surgeon's. Finally, he made eye contact. His eyes were large, with unusually luxurious eyelashes. He was almost a decade younger than her, with unruly black hair that contrasted with his eyebrows, which were as neat and straight as two black rulers.

He said, 'I only brought Drukpa Kunlek's death to the attention of the Commissioner because I'd heard of another boy dying the same way.'

Lia felt her eyes widen. She hadn't realised Deshi had been involved from the start. 'Where?'

'Also in the Barkhor.'

She stared at him. She'd investigated Drukpa's death with Deshi last month but he'd made no mention of another boy dying in the same area with a broken neck.

'When?' she asked.

'Three days before Drukpa.'

'They both died in the same week?' Her spine was tingling.

He gave a nod. His fingers continued to twist. He was obviously waiting to be reprimanded for withholding information and she wanted to reduce his apprehension by telling him that the same thing had happened to Chen —two boys dying before he'd taken notice – but held her tongue. She'd promised to protect Chen, but now the total of deaths appeared to be eight, not five, should she continue to do so?

'Does Commissioner Zhi know about this?'

'Yes. I thought my connecting the two deaths was good police work.' He sank lower in his chair. 'I thought it was what a good investigator would do. I've been here for two years and still haven't been promoted...'

She waited.

'I thought he'd be pleased with me, but when I told him about the other boy, he wasn't –' he took a deep breath as though about to dive into a bottomless pool '– exactly enamoured. He thought my investigating Drukpa's death was a waste of time.'

'But he ordered an autopsy.'

'Yes.'

Lia wondered why the Commissioner hadn't mentioned this other boy's death at the committee meeting, giving her more credence. Deshi, she recalled, had also remained silent during the proceedings. They were, no doubt, being self-protective, lying low to avoid drawing the displeasure of the PSB. It wouldn't be the first time that had happened.

'I will put your comments on file.' She turned her attention to her notepad, effectively dismissing him, but just before he stepped through the door she said, 'Wait.'

He turned. The anxious look remained.

'I'd like you to interview the family of this other dead boy. Find out what you can.'

His face cleared. 'I already have. Shall I send you a copy of my report?'

'Thank you.'

*

Deshi's report came as an email attachment and, as she suspected, held no new clues. The boy had been five years old. He had been found at the end of his street in the morning, with his neck broken. Nobody knew why he'd got up in the middle of the night and let himself out of the house.

What did the killer get out of it? she wondered. There had to be something. People didn't kill for no reason. It didn't appear to be sexual in any way. Or did the killer simply hate little boys? Had they lost their own child and resented others for living? And how did they lure them out of their homes? Tashi had mentioned a malevolent spirit of some kind and once again, she was reminded of the Snow Thief.

After clearing her emails and trudging through her in-tray, Lia began to draft her report on her visit to Rabang. Come 6 p.m. sleet began splattering against the window. Traipsing home was going to be a real joy without an umbrella, and she was glad she didn't have far to walk. Reluctant to head home just yet, she read the news on the *People's Daily* online to see heavy snow storms were predicted for northern China. Did this mean Tibet would be affected?

She read on to see that the fourteenth Dalai Lama, Tibet's exiled spiritual leader, was undergoing yet another medical procedure in hospital. What would happen when the man died, she dreaded to think. After the riots in 2008, the government responded to any behaviour it deemed unacceptable with vigour. Lia had no doubt the numbers of paramilitary police and the army already drafted into Tibet would double overnight to crush any unrest. Which was a good thing, as far as she was concerned. The last thing she wanted was the Tibetans to have an excuse to rampage through the city, waving their swords and terrorising Chinese residents, beating shopkeepers and setting cars and houses on fire.

She yawned and stretched before leaning back in her seat. She closed her eyes, thinking she'd go home in a minute. Unpack, have a shower and change, give Fang Dongmei a monologue about her trip. She wondered what Jian would have thought of Tibet and decided he'd have rather liked it and all its challenges. He'd travelled quite a bit before they'd met – he was an architect and had worked on projects in Hong Kong, Malaysia and Singapore. She remembered them curling in bed together, the sound of car horns honking below, and telling each other about their future. Jian saw them moving to Sydney, living in Chatswood first, where he'd set up his architectural practice, and Lia would become a New South Wales police officer. They both spoke English. She could work with the growing Chinese community.

If they were careful, they would put aside enough to buy a boat, so they could explore the harbour and its tributaries with their children, teach them how to fish. Jian would get his captain's licence and they would sit on the deck at the end of the day, watching the sun set. Lia could see herself with their children, beach-combing, finding pretty shells and collecting driftwood. Sydney represented freedom with its acres of space and blue air to breathe.

She didn't realise she'd fallen asleep until someone knocked on her door. She glanced at her watch. *Wo te ma!* My mother! She'd been out for almost half an hour!

'Yes?' she called. Her voice was thick with sleep.

'Supervisor?' It was her boss.

Immediately she closed down her web page, not wanting to be caught reading about the Dalai Lama even if it was on an official site. 'Sir,' she called, 'come in.'

She hoped he wouldn't stay long. Her head was woolly, her thoughts like mush.

'Shouldn't you be at home?' Commissioner Zhi said, stepping inside. 'You had a long trip. You must be tired.'

'I'm leaving now.' She began shutting down her computer.

He walked to the window, looked out at the blackness peppered with weaving bicycle lamps and strings of street lights. He held his hands behind his back. 'How did it go?'

Lia tried to get her brain activated. How much or how little to say? Zhi may have appeared to be her ally earlier but things could change with a click of the fingers, especially with Tan around. 'On balance, I'm not sure,' she hedged. She quickly rubbed her eyes. 'I'll have my report ready for you tomorrow.'

Still staring outside, he said, 'If another boy is found with the same injury, I want you to go to them immediately. Take Hua Ming with you.'

Lia's back straightened. Hope lifted inside. 'Yes, sir.'

'Chen is calling the killer the Snow Thief. He told me why.' He turned to face her, resting his shoulders against the window and crossing his arms. 'I must be frank. I gave the cases to you in the hope your past experience might help. I want to catch this Snow Thief, and before the public get wind of him.'

'Yes,' she said neutrally, and after a pause added, 'May I speak freely, sir?'

He lifted his eyebrows but gave a nod.

'Did Chen mention anything about more boys dying?'

'What do you mean?' His gaze sharpened.

Pause. Beat. She took a breath. Decided to take the plunge.

'Two boys died from broken necks before Supervisor Chen got suspicious.' The flare of surprise in her boss's eyes confirmed this was news to him. She hoped her openness wouldn't backfire on her or Chen.

'Chen is one of our best officers outside Lhasa,' Zhi said. By praising Chen and not remarking on the two unreported deaths, he was letting her know she could continue to speak candidly.

She said, 'Constable Deshi reports there was another boy who died in the Barkhor the same week that Drukpa Kunlek died.'

'Yes. He told me.'

'What if other police have ignored other boys' deaths? Believed they were accidental?'

He mulled this over briefly. 'I hope not, but it appears likely, doesn't it? Which is why, should there be another victim, I want you and Hua Ming on the case. We need a lead. Did you find anything in Rabang?'

She flicked through a variety of issues in her mind. She pictured Tashi creeping into the tent to watch his brother and five high lamas, how Lama Sonam had spotted him and warned him away. The monks were important. If Tashi was correct, they'd come from all over Tibet, congregating in Lhasa before beginning their travels.

Forgetting her promise to Tashi, Lia opened her mouth to tell Zhi that the boy suspected a monk of murdering his brother, but at the same time a dense shadow plunged into her chest, freezing her words on her lips.

She couldn't breathe.

Lia slapped a hand to her chest, working her mouth.

'Supervisor?' Commissioner Zhi moved swiftly to her side. 'What's wrong? Are you all right?'

Immediately her lungs filled with air. She gripped the edge of her desk with both hands, taking comfort in its solidity as a wave of nausea washed over her.

'Supervisor...' Zhi looked concerned.

The nausea passed. She said, 'I'm OK.' She felt oddly bewildered and off-balance.

'Can I fetch you some water?'

'No. Thank you.'

'If you're sure you're all right?'

'I'm just tired. I'll be fine after a good night's rest.'

'In that case, I won't keep you.' He stood before her, his broad shoulders making her office appear even smaller. The concerned expression on his face hadn't gone away. 'May I ask you a personal question?'

She wanted to say no, but didn't dare go against a superior officer. 'Of course.'

'What made you live in the Barkhor area?'

'I'm not sure,' she answered honestly.

'We security personnel live together, except for you. Why have you set yourself apart?'

Lia tried not to squirm beneath his gaze which was both enquiring and assessing. 'It wasn't intentional,' she said. Which was true; she couldn't even remember moving into the apartment, let alone the reasons why.

'I would have thought you'd need your own kind around you.'

Her own kind? Tan wasn't her own kind, and nor were Myra Kwok and Superintendent Zhang. She supposed she could say she'd moved to the Tibetan district because she liked the area, but didn't have the nerve because it could be deemed an insult not liking where her colleagues lived.

When she didn't reply he raised a hand vaguely, let it fall. 'Well,' he said. 'I shall leave you to it. Goodnight.'

*

As she headed home, dragging her suitcase behind her, vapour pouring from her mouth in the freezing air, Lia suddenly spotted Deshi's *bao* vendor. She walked over and met the owner of the stall, Mrs Lily, a cheerful middle-aged woman with rebellious red streaks in her hair.

'Your pork *bao* are fantastic,' she told Mrs Lily, who beamed, and before Lia could protest, packed a box with half a dozen complimentary buns to take home and try.

She let herself into the apartment to be greeted by the sound of dishes clattering in the kitchen. Kicking off her boots, she padded across the room to find the table already laid, vegetables put to steam.

'Hi,' she said. She put the box of *bao* on the counter. 'From Lily Pond Moonlight.'

Fang Dongmei opened the box and gave an approving grunt.

In silence, they took their seats at the kitchen table. Through the bedroom door, she saw the head of Fang Dongmei's bed faced south-east, to preserve her energy and not drain her strength. Her own bed faced the other way. Perhaps she should move it? She needed all the energy she could get. She felt exhausted.

Fang Dongmei conveyed vegetables and assorted *bao* from her bowl to her mouth with her usual dexterity. Lia sighed, bit into a fluffy bun.

'Commissioner Zhi came to my office today,' Lia said.

Jian's grandmother didn't look up or give any indication she'd heard Lia speak.

'You rang the Commissioner after Officer Tan had been here,' Lia went on. 'You told Zhi about Tan's offer, and the next morning, Zhi stepped in.'

No response.

'Thank you.'

Slurp. Munch.

'How do you know him? I mean, he's a pretty important person and —'

'You're saying someone like me can't know someone like him?'

'Of course not.' Lia hastily backtracked. 'I was just curious, that's all.'

Fang Dongmei raised her eyes to the ceiling as if it was obvious. 'I know his grandmother. We met in the market one day. I helped her with her shopping. We have tea from time to time.'

She didn't need to say any more. *Guanxi*. That good old network of who-knew-who and who did favours for who. Fang Dongmei would no doubt be in debt to the Commissioner's grandmother now, but Lia couldn't criticise her for it. She was, in fact, incredibly grateful for having been rescued from Tan's clutches.

'Thank her for me, please.'

Fang Dongmei gave a curt nod.

Lia ate another *bao* – they really were delicious – as she pondered.

'The Commissioner,' Lia mused after a while, 'was curious why we live here. I couldn't tell him what made us choose this place. Why didn't we move into the new building on the other side of town? Why the Tibetan district?'

Fang Dongmei smacked her hairy lips together before spooning some rice into her bowl.

'He accused me of setting myself apart.' Lia looked down at her hands, the long fingers and what she thought were oversized knuckles. 'I don't just look different,' she said, 'but I don't even live in the same area.'

'You want to live with them?' The old woman was glaring at her. Startled, Lia fell quiet.

Fang Dongmei gave a snort. 'You want to eat and breathe their shit, feel free, but you can leave me out of it.' She lumbered to her feet and without another word, took her bowl into her bedroom and shut the door behind her.

Lia put her head in her hands. She couldn't blame Fang Dongmei for reacting angrily. After her experiences at the hands of the authorities, she loathed the police, and although Lia wanted to say not all police were corrupt, she couldn't with any degree of honesty. No wonder so many Chinese citizens were getting fed up. There were hundreds of thousands of people like Fang Dongmei who'd suffered severe injustices against which they had no recourse thanks to having no independent legal system. They weren't the only family to have been brutalised, ruined by a heartless system that didn't care a jot for the individual as long as the whole ticked along relatively smoothly.

If she was a fatalist, she might think she'd been put into this position to bring some decency into the system, some honour and respect. A lot of the police seemed to think they were above helping the common person, aligning themselves with the moneyed classes, the urban entrepreneurs and businessmen. And what about the farmers, the rural people? They were looked down on with contempt. What happened to the equal system their parents used to know? It wasn't dog eat dog any more, but *ren chi ren*: man eat man.

*

Lia put her bowl next to the sink and began washing up the vegetable pot. Her mind turned to consider what would happen if she moved into the government block, let herself be absorbed into police culture. She imagined moving across town in order to blend in, hanging out with fellow officers, dining with them, chatting, socialising. How easy would it be to pretend she belonged? To fake contentment with her posting? To laugh at all the right jokes, whisper all the right gossip and suck up to the right officials?

She'd tried pretending to be someone else when her parents had moved from Fuling to Shenzhen just before her fourteenth birthday — her father had won a government project to build a hotel — and it hadn't worked. Desperate to fit in at school, she'd worn what the other kids wore, cut her hair the same, listened to the same music, and although she was eventually accepted — some of the older girls were fearsomely jealous of her *gwailo* looks — she was always an outsider because she thought differently. She was unusually independent and self-sufficient for a Chinese, and didn't need to rely on a group to make a decision.

Her closest friends weren't the most popular kids in school, but they were the most interesting, especially Ting. Ting was a boy the same age as her, who'd spent the first ten years of his life in the UK and, like her, spoke English well. His parents worked tirelessly with Amnesty International, which garnered them unwelcome interest from the authorities, but the fact they seemed to court danger in order to try and stop human rights abuses made them nothing short of heroic in Lia's eyes.

She hadn't spoken to Ting since she'd been banished to Tibet. On impulse she rang, catching him just before he was about to sit down for supper with his wife and two-year-old son.

'So, you're still alive,' he said.

'Just.'

'And you're still a cop?'

'What else would I do?'

'I can think of a dozen alternative careers, starting with banana boat captain.'

'Ai,' she said, rolling her eyes. 'Don't remind me. I hated that ride.'

'Jian loved it.'

'He loved anything ridiculous.'

'Including you?'

She said, 'I'd forgotten how rude you were.'

'It's why you love me, right? Fill me in while I eat. Don't leave anything out.'

She hadn't realised the tension she'd been holding until she started to talk. She told him a little about her work but she didn't mention the dead boys. She didn't know who might be listening. She did, however, tell him about her doubts living in the Barkhor, and as she described the area, the old woman on their street who sat behind a wooden table, cutting prayer flags from a brightly coloured bolt of cloth, Lia felt a swell of affection for the place.

It was also at that moment when she saw the incongruity of having a Tibetan district in Lhasa. The Hui and Han populations in the city were now far greater than the Tibetan population. It was like having a Chinatown in Shanghai or Beijing. Lia tried to imagine what it would be like if the roles were reversed, if China was suddenly overrun with Tibetans, the local temples knocked down and Tibetan shops put in their places. She was pretty sure she wouldn't be too happy about it and for the first time she could see why some Tibetans hated the Chinese so much.

'The air smells of herbs,' she told Ting. 'Fang Dongmei buys fresh yogurt on the corner, along with vegetables. The yoghurt's really strong. I can't eat it raw but Fang Dongmei loves it.'

'If you move into one of those new-build blocks,' he said, 'I won't be coming to stay with you. I hate them. Too hot in winter, over-airconditioned in summer. Shall I bring a tent?'

Lia looked around at the thick rugs on the floors and local artwork on the walls. She was beginning to like the vibrant colours as well as the twisted, ancient beams criss-crossing the ceiling.

'No tent,' she told him. 'You can sleep on the sofa here.'

After she'd caught up with Ting's news – his son's first words, his first steps – she hung up. Immediately her phone beeped, telling her she had a missed call. She checked the list to see it was from Commissioner Zhi. She called him straight back. He didn't wait for her to announce herself. He said, 'There's been another one. Ngari Prefecture. Chen's with the body. I told him you'd get there as soon as you could.'

15

NIMA CHODEN COULDN'T BELIEVE it. The same police officer who had been in Rabang, poking around asking questions about the death of the boy, Pemba Dolma, was here.

Here! In the camp!

Anxiety twisted his belly and immediately he felt his bowels clench. They had to leave immediately. They couldn't afford to be seen by this man.

He sped across the tamped-down snow. Dived into the tent where his men were sleepily drinking tea.

'We have to go,' he told them. *'Now!'*

Sharmar and Rinzen didn't need telling twice. His tone said it all. They packed their backpacks swiftly and without a word. Their host, a middle-aged man with a face shaped like a spade, rushed inside, expression panicky.

'The police,' he panted.

'We know. We must go. We mustn't be seen.'

'Of course.' The man thrust his head through the tent's opening and called out. A young woman rushed inside. 'Go and distract the police officer. Talk to him. Shout or scream, gather a crowd, do anything you like, but make sure he doesn't see our esteemed guests leaving.'

The woman nodded, and hurried away.

'Thank you.' Nima tried to give the man a handful of notes, enough money to feed his family for a month, but the man wouldn't take it.

'We'd do anything for the Dalai Lama,' he said, shaking his head fiercely. 'Except be paid for helping him. Now, go!'

With his rifle strapped across his back, Nima led the way around the periphery of the camp. The officer's Land Cruiser stood between the camp's entrance and the road. It was empty. He glanced over his shoulder to see a crowd had formed where the boy's body had been found this morning. He assumed the police officer was buried in the milling throng and hastened past the Land Cruiser and turned east, heading for town and keeping an eye open for a vehicle that might give them a lift, and get them out of the area fast.

The sound of wailing reached him, genuine howls of grief from the boy's parents. For a moment he felt a stab of guilt, of sorrow, but this was overridden by a feeling of relief that the nomads believed the boy had died accidentally. As did all the other villages and their inhabitants behind him. But what about this cop? He was on their trail. He obviously didn't believe the boys were dying by accident.

Nervous sweat trickled down his spine.

How many boys to go? He had no idea. The only people who knew the answer to that were ahead of him, trundling along at a snail's pace and thankfully oblivious of the mayhem being caused in their wake.

Would they complete their mission? They had to. Anything else was unthinkable.

Nima picked up his pace and at the same time, heard an engine approaching. He turned and held out a hand. A battered truck slowed to a halt beside them. The Tibetan driver jerked a thumb at the trailer, half-filled with rusty engine parts. The three of them climbed on board.

Nima watched the nomad camp dwindle into the distance. He wondered how long it would take the Chinese police officer to work out what was going on, and whether he'd do anything about it when he knew the whole story. As a precaution, Nima reached into his robe and withdrew a satellite phone. Time to let his boss know the next set of developments.

16

LIA HAD WANTED TO get moving right away until Zhi told her she'd be flying to the prefecture of Ngari by helicopter, and that it wouldn't be taking off until dawn. He told her he'd already alerted the forensic team, and that he was going to send Constable Deshi with her, along with Superintendent Zhang.

'Who's coming from the PSB?' she asked, praying it wouldn't be Tan or Myra Kwok.

'Jenny Wang and...' She could hear him shuffling some papers. 'I'm not sure yet. They'll meet us at the airport. I'll organise a car to collect us from the office at seven thirty. Get some rest, Lia. You're going to need it.'

After she'd packed, Lia wrote a note to Fang Dongmei and left it on the kitchen table where she wouldn't miss it. Back in her bedroom, Lia set her alarm for 5 a.m., leaving her plenty of time to drop into the office to collect her files as well as call Chen and get the lowdown before heading to the aerodrome. She was so wired she didn't think she'd get any sleep. She lay in bed trying to relax for what felt like half the night until, quite suddenly, she awoke to the sound of her alarm beeping to find she'd slept a solid seven hours.

Everything was quiet, the sky dark as she walked across town, her footsteps crunching on frost, her suitcase rattling on the cobblestones behind her. It kept twisting off course, forcing her to pause and wrestle it back on track, and by the time she reached the office she was warm enough to shed her coat. Despite her being the first person in, the place still reeked of cigarettes, making her long to open a window, but they were all locked. Heaven knew what would happen if there was a fire and the stairs were inaccessible. No doubt they'd all die. What a cheerful thought to start the day.

The heating clanked and groaned as she made herself some tea and fetched the files on the boys. She rang Chen several times, but didn't get through. Zhi had told her the town of Gertse – the nearest town to the nomad's village – had cell-phone reception but the mast was either down or her boss had been misinformed. Lia spent the hour before Zhi's car turned up rereading every scrap of information on the boys' deaths and trying to open up new avenues of thought as to how to catch the Snow Thief.

*

The Commissioner briefed them inside the hangar while the military helicopter was loaded. One end of the hangar was open to the elements and despite the giant electric fan blasting hot air inside it still felt cold. The sky was only just beginning to lighten, the stars losing their glimmer to a collar of pearl on the horizon.

Aside from everyone's personal bags and holdalls there were piles of forensic kit: aluminium cases, protective clothing, lighting equipment and stacks of plastic boxes and crates containing who-knew-what. There were three police officers including Lia, three forensic personnel plus Hua Ming and one PSB officer – Jenny Wang – who greeted her with a wave.

'No mud pancakes today,' she said cheerfully, reminding Lia of her and George's dousing en route to Rabang.

Lia surveyed the ancient aircraft. Much of China's fleet of helicopters were invariably overworked and, she suspected, under-serviced.

'I hope not,' she replied. She'd only flown twice in her life, once to Beijing after Jian's arrest, and then from Beijing to Lhasa. She could remember little about either journey thanks to being emotionally traumatised at the time, and hoped this third journey would be as unremarkable.

'Listen up,' Zhi called.

Everyone crowded around the Commissioner, expressions expectant.

'The reason why we're going to Ngari is to see whether we have a serial killer on our hands or not. I want you to collate every particle of evidence to support or discount this possibility. As you know, Supervisor Shan is working this case, so please report directly to her. If you have a hunch about something, you tell the Supervisor. If you see something that you're unsure about and are tempted to discount it, you tell the Supervisor. Shan comes to us with a wealth of experience from Shenzhen and she knows how to conduct a case like this, OK? You'll be safe in her capable and competent hands.'

He paused while everyone glanced her way before continuing. 'As you're aware, five boys have died the same way in the past seven weeks. This is officially the sixth, but you must remember that the figure could be eight, perhaps even higher. All of them are between five and six years old. None of them came from the same village. They all died near their homes during the night, with no witnesses that we know of. They were all partially dressed, as though they had left their beds in haste.'

Lia shivered inside. And the Snow Thief sang his sweetest song and the children followed...

'Although we can speculate about motives, there seems little point until we know what we have on our hands. Are these children dying by accident, or by more sinister means? It's up to you to find out. Over to you, Supervisor,' Zhi finished crisply.

She glanced at the helicopter outside to see their kit had been loaded and stored and that the pilot was watching her — she'd met him and the co-pilot earlier to study the flight plan and forge a workable itinerary — and when their eyes met he saluted her with a forefinger before holding both hands in fists with his index fingers pointing out. His face was questioning.

He was asking her how long he had to wait for. He was waiting for her orders.

She felt a rush of pride that she was leading this expedition. Skin hot with pleasure, she copied his gesture then crossed her index fingers to make a plus sign. The hand signal for 'ten'. Because of so many dialects in China, this was a good way of communicating, especially in markets. Ten minutes, she told the pilot. He nodded.

'OK.' She turned back to the group. 'The bad news is that the boy's body is fifty k's from the nearest town, in a nomadic camp. Our man on the ground – Supervisor Chen – has told us it's safe to land nearby, so we'll fly straight there and get set up. I don't want to risk losing any time in case the weather turns. At the end of the day we'll be flown to Gertse where there's a government guest house. The next day – and any days thereafter – we'll take cars that will be locally requisitioned to the site. The helicopter will be needed elsewhere while we work. When we're finished the pilot will collect us and return to Lhasa.' As she spoke she felt more like a travel agent than the leader of a police investigation, but after Zhi's speech, there seemed little point repeating the same things.

'Any questions?' she asked.

'What's the good news?' Zhang muttered in an undertone.

'The good news,' Lia said calmly, 'is that if these children are being murdered, then this is our first crime scene. We have the opportunity to make sure we process it absolutely correctly and gather every clue possible. The work we do today may well define the start of an extensive murder investigation. The work we do today may well make sure we'll catch the killer.'

Lia saw Jenny, Hua Ming and his forensic trio nod. Superintendent Zhang just stared at her without expression.

'Anyone else have any questions?' Lia looked around the group.

'Have any Hui or Han children died?' one of the forensic

team asked, a woman in her twenties with acne scars on her cheeks and sheets of glossy blue-black hair cut into a bob. Ivy Peng. Another woman who had chosen an English first name.

'No,' Lia said. 'They're all Tibetan.'

Hua Ming clicked his tongue against the roof of his mouth. 'There's no sexual abuse,' he said. 'No trauma, not even a single bruise. It's a real mystery.'

'Which is one we're going to solve,' Lia said briskly. 'Anything else?'

When everyone shook their heads, she walked onto the apron to a man in camouflage overalls and asked if he was ready for them to board.

'Sure,' he said. 'I'll get my list.'

As her team clambered up the rungs bolted onto the fuselage, he ticked their names off his clipboard. The turbine began to whine, the rotors moving, gradually increasing speed with each revolution. Lia was last to board and despite her plait being tucked beneath her cap, her hair began to unravel in the downdraught.

Zhi shook her hand. 'Good luck,' he said. He had to shout above the sound of the engine.

'Thanks for the vote of confidence back there,' she said. 'For a moment I wondered who you were talking about.'

He smiled. 'Do a good job and prove me right, OK?'

As Zhi walked back to the hangar, heading for his car and the office, the ground officer next to Lia tapped his clipboard. 'Where's Officer Tan?'

'Oh,' she said, without missing a beat. 'He's not coming. Didn't anyone tell you?'

'Nobody tells me anything,' he grumbled. 'Some days I wonder if they think I'm a mushroom.'

Lia gave him a sympathetic grimace before shimmying up the rungs, suddenly in a hurry to take off. 'Let's go!' she called out. 'Get this show on the road!'

She took the seat behind the pilot and strapped herself in.

As the rotors lifted into a clattering roar, the machine began to tremble, everything shaking and juddering in the din. The runners lifted, and then they were airborne, rising slowly, lifting into a sky lightening into pink. As the pilot banked west, Lia saw a car come to a fierce halt next to the hangar, four wheels locked and skidding, snow spraying.

Lia didn't think she'd seen anything as gratifying as Officer Tan Dao standing with his hands on his hips watching them fly away.

*

The journey was noisy and mind-numbing, the monotony of the countryside matched only by the monotony of the flight itself. There was nothing to do, no in-flight magazine or movie, and it was too noisy for conversation. Everyone was cold and cramped. The doors weren't snug and there were cracks in the metal along the floor. Lia hugged her arms to her chest and stared at nothing but endless carpets of snow rolling to far-off mountains. Towns were almost non-existent and those that did exist were situated on the single road north and appeared uniformly dismal.

They flew over a high pass which descended to a bridge, where a tiny dwelling sat on the north side. Lia wondered who lived there, and how they scratched a living. They had to be hundreds of kilometres from the nearest town. Then they were flying alongside a snow-covered range of mountains, crossing glacial outwashes streaked with rocks and boulders.

She looked for the scores of Chinese mines that were apparently ravaging the wilderness and accelerating climate change thanks to spewing millions of tons of pollution into the crystalline air, but saw nothing, making her wonder if all the rumours were true.

Eventually Gertse came into view, a depressing strip of what looked to be warehouses and junkyards, and as the pilot eased the aircraft to a lower altitude, Lia spotted a long wall of chŏrtens – Buddhist shrines – and prayer flags on the south side of town.

Before they landed, Lia got the pilot to fly over the nomadic camp. He dropped to around a hundred feet and cruised across. Lia saw each of her team peer through the windows, including Zhang. Good, she thought. At least he was curious. She looked out herself to see a rough circle of a dozen black yak-hair tents and people rushing outside, all wearing chobas, and all with their faces upturned, watching the aircraft.

'I want to see if there are any tracks outside the camp,' she said to the pilot. Then she turned to her team. 'Everyone,' she called out, 'I need you to look for tracks. Anything leading to or from the camp, wheel tracks, footprints or animal prints, we need to check them out.'

Carefully, the pilot circled the area. There were a few yak and sheep tracks, and marks where they'd pawed the ground to get at the grass below, but nothing else. The only visible footprints as well as tyre tracks led from the camp directly to the main road. Lia made the pilot circle the camp again, and then twice more in the opposite direction; she thought she'd seen a circular shadow to the south-east of the camp, with a diameter of about five or six metres, and on the fourth rotation she was sure she wasn't mistaken. It looked as though the snow was slightly shallower within the circle. She pointed it out to the team. Ivy opened her mouth as though she was going to say something, but when Zhang glanced at her, she shut it. Lia made a mental note to remember the moment, and that the two officers obviously had a history, and not a particularly pleasant one from the way Ivy's mouth was now puckered.

Lia directed the pilot to land away from the camp. He banked steeply east, heading for the other side of the road. As he descended, the rotors whipped the snow into a thick white storm, and although visibility was nil, he set the helicopter onto the ground as softly as a feather. Gradually the snow settled, and as he switched off the engine, two Land Cruisers and three army jeeps arrived. Supervisor Chen Tao and associates.

'How was your trip?' Chen asked, shaking Lia's hand. She was first out of the helicopter and she could see that although Chen appeared to have his attention on her, he was looking for Tan.

'Cold,' she said. 'Please, Chen, tell me there's heating in the government guest house in Gertse?'

'I'll bring you a hot water bottle,' he said.

Lia introduced him to each of the team as they descended. When Tan didn't appear, Chen glanced at Jenny then back at Lia. A question stood in his eyes but she pretended she hadn't seen it.

'OK,' she called, waiting until she had everyone's attention. 'Let's unload the aircraft...work stuff only. Remember we'll be flown to Gertse with our personal belongings at the end of the day.'

'Anyone know where we can buy some coffee?' Zhang muttered.

'If you're after the nearest Starbucks, I suggest you start walking now,' said Lia. 'You might get to Lanzhou in time for breakfast this time next month.'

Deshi gave a chuckle which he swallowed when Zhang glared at him.

While the team helped the pilot and co-pilot unload the helicopter, Lia caught up with Chen.

'How did you know the boy had died?' she asked.

'I told all my officers to start spreading the word and to talk to as many ethnic people as possible, including nomads. This particular boy died two days after one of my constables from Gertse had spoken to these people.' He gestured at the camp. 'One of the nomads came into town to report it.'

'Good work,' she said.

He gazed past her at Hua Ming, who was battling to lift a large aluminium case into the back of Chen's Land Cruiser. 'I also ordered my officers throughout the two prefectures to ask if any boys had died recently from having their necks broken.'

'And?'

He turned to face her. A dark shadow moved deep in his eyes, like a distressed fish. 'Another eight. This brings the total count to sixteen.'

17

OFFICER TAN DAO'S FOUL mood stayed with him for the rest of the day. If he could have requisitioned another helicopter to take him to Gertse he wouldn't have hesitated, but Supervisor Shan had taken the only one available. He had no choice but to wait for its return.

Commissioner Zhi had given him a flight time of 10 a.m., briefing at nine, but the chopper had taken off an hour early. *An hour!* Zhi had apologised profusely, but Tan sensed the Commissioner wasn't entirely displeased at Shan being in charge.

'You don't want her to actually *find* evidence of a serial killer, do you?' Tan asked Zhi in disbelief.

'No,' Zhi agreed. 'But the station is already swarming with rumours and my concern is that if the public get wind of it, they'll demand to know what we're doing. If we're perceived to be sitting on our backsides doing nothing, it could be a disaster. This way, we can at least show we're on top of it.'

It was a neat response which Tan agreed with wholeheartedly, but he was still furious at being left behind. 'It looks as though you're encouraging her,' he remarked stiffly. 'Is that really the impression you want to be giving?'

'I would prefer it if we saw eye to eye on this.' Zhi spread his hands appeasingly. 'Like you, my prime concern is to retain stability. Please rest assured that I will keep a lid on anything she finds. I will contain it. You have my word.'

Tan returned to his office unconvinced. If Shan found anything to affirm there was a serial killer, the Commissioner wouldn't be able to suppress it. By all the gods, how to keep it quiet? He could just imagine the panic and hysteria rolling through the country like an out-of-control bush fire and

112

reigniting the simmering resentment between the Tibetans and the Chinese. The last thing they needed was another riot. He could remember the last one as though it was yesterday. What an unholy mess. He pinched the bridge of his nose with his fingers at the memory.

Ai Ya! How had it got out of control so quickly? Even now, he found it hard to believe. It had all started when protests broke out at three monasteries, the date coinciding with the anniversary of the failed Tibetan uprising in 1959 which forced the Dalai Lama – the lying, CIA-backed charlatan – to flee to India. Tan immediately ordered sixty monks to be arrested and confined the rest in their monasteries. But no, that wasn't the end of it. Rumours of his officers beating monks and killing Buddhist nuns began swirling among Tibetans. What a joke. As if his men would be stupid enough to kill a nun in public!

When monks left the Ramoche Temple in Lhasa, Tan made sure they were met by police officers. A large crowd formed and the atmosphere quickly turned ugly. To his disbelief, someone threw a rock at one of his men, hitting his face and splitting open his cheek. It was as though the Tibetans had been waiting for blood to flow. The crowd charged the police. Tan immediately ordered his men to withdraw. His orders had been clear: to avoid engaging the Tibetans until high-level approval was granted.

While Tan desperately tried to get hold of the right officials, the Tibetans galloped through the city's old quarter, burning and looting Chinese shops. They dragged clothes, souvenirs and tourist trinkets outside and torched them. They toppled fire trucks and beat Chinese shopkeepers. But what made him cringe inside was the memory of seeing his officers flee and not reappear for almost twenty-four hours.

He should have ignored his orders and told his men to stay where they were and, if necessary, open fire on the rioters. Gain control of the city from the start. High-level approval be damned! What did they know? The top officials had been strutting about at the National People's Congress when the violence erupted and they'd dithered like a bunch of old women, terrified of taking a firm line, terrified of how the Western world would react. Terrified of doing anything that might threaten their precious overseas trade.

Tan spat a glob of spittle into a metal bowl by his feet. Why did China have to bow and scrape to the world media? What business was it of theirs what China did? He'd bet his last yuan that if the southern part of the US declared independence, the Americans wouldn't stand back and let it happen. Westerners had a Tibet complex, holding deep-rooted bias against China, and he hated them and their intolerance, their blinkered vision.

'Sir?'

A constable with a mole the size of a mouse on her chin was peering nervously around his door. He'd forgotten her name.

'What?' he snapped.

'Officer Kwok wishes to see you.'

Tan hesitated. He didn't trust Myra Kwok, not since she'd adopted a Western name, and although Kwok insisted she wasn't pro-Western, that she used the name Myra to make her dealings with Westerners easier, Tan saw it as nothing but pro-Western grovelling. He didn't see anyone from America swapping their names around when they visited China.

'Send her in.'

He picked up a pen and began scribbling some nonsense on the pad in front of him, ignoring Kwok when she slid inside.

'Sir,' she said.

He continued to scribble. *Make her wait.*

After he'd finished the page, turned it over and scribbled a few more characters at the top, he raised his head. She wore a pale grey skirt and black-belted jacket. She had a neat waist and a pair of surprisingly shapely legs, but no tits. Compared to Shan, Kwok had all the appeal of a dead frog. He couldn't believe he'd once found her attractive.

'What is it?' he said. He didn't offer her a seat.

'About this serial killer. Supervisor Shan's conviction they exist.'

He put down his pen. 'Go on.'

'It concerns me that if she continues her dabbling she may destabilise the currently peaceful situation in the prefecture.'

He wasn't going to tell Kwok he'd spoken with the Commissioner. He wanted to hear what she said first. He wondered what Shan was doing at this moment. Was she questioning more monks, more kids, more snotty, stinking Tibetans? He gazed past Kwok, still unable to believe how he'd been manoeuvred into going to Rabang.

What was it between the Commissioner and Shan? If they weren't screwing, why did Zhi take such an interest in her? Tan had put a couple of men to watch Shan's place, but the Commissioner had never been spotted. Just an old hag of a woman who was, apparently, Shan's relative. How Fang Dongmei had slipped past his initial check was anyone's guess. He'd thought Shan had come out here alone, and here she was sharing her apartment with an ancient babysitter. No chance of him seducing Shan at her place with that wizened old hag looming over them.

'Sir?'

He glanced at Kwok. He'd almost forgotten she was there. 'Yes?'

'You may find it useful to know the Supervisor spoke to someone called Mao Ting last week. He's an old school friend of hers from Shenzhen. He's a human rights lawyer. He is currently representing two Falun Gong practitioners, one of whom is his sister.'

Tan felt a flare of admiration for Kwok. How clever of her to find a lever to use against Shan. Shan's husband had been executed for being Falun Gong. It would be easy to inform the Shenzhen authorities of this, who would take the opportunity to tar Mao Ting with the same brush. Mao Ting's personal contact with a convicted member of the criminal cult would be deemed unacceptable. Tan wondered how important the man was to Shan, and what she'd do to keep her old school friend safe.

'Is that it?' he said.

Kwok flushed. 'Yes, sir.'

He picked up his pen and turned his attention purposely back to his pad of paper. Kwok took this, rightly, as her dismissal, and left. Putting down his pen, Tan's mind drifted to the last time he'd seen Shan. The PSB didn't share the same building as the police so he'd had to make an excuse to visit the station. He'd dropped in to see her with the purpose of inviting her to dinner. It was time for him to switch roles, turn on the charm and show her he could be good company. However, the second he ducked his head around her office door – ye gods, her office was tiny – she was already out of her chair and moving to the door.

'Sorry, sir.' She'd been polite enough. 'I can't stop. I'm late for a meeting...'

He had kept his disappointment from showing. 'Don't let me hold you up,' he'd replied, feeling magnanimous, but she didn't respond. Simply strode past him and down the corridor, her plait dancing like a gleaming brown snake between her shoulder blades.

That evening, Tan went home to an empty flat. He fed the dog and, later, left a plastic plate of food out for the child. Despite his absence when he'd been in Rabang, both dog and child kept returning and devouring whatever food he left out. He found it hard to believe the Children's Welfare Institute hadn't captured the child yet. Either the CWI weren't doing their job properly, or the child was clever and didn't want to be caught.

He fell asleep dreaming that he was making love to Supervisor Shan. He was drowning in honey, his hands buried in waves of silken mahogany hair. Shan's mouth was small and sweet, her breasts warm and soft, her nipples puckered excitedly between his fingers. He was like an engorged rock inside her – he didn't think he'd been so big before – stroking every inch of her pussy, and as he built to a roaring climax, he dreamed that despite Shan's reluctance, she came so hard, her juices drenched him.

18

THE DEAD BOY'S NAME was Mingmar, and he was five and a half years old. He didn't have a surname. The Tibetans, like the Chinese, had their own quirks about naming their children, and a lot of Tibetans didn't have family names. In a Tibetan family, all of the first and last names of each member might be different, which wasn't going to help the police. Lia did a rough head count to see the camp held a total of around fifty people, two thirds of whom were adults. She gave Jenny the job of working out who was related to who before it could give her a headache.

Mingmar's body lay behind one of the tents, diametrically opposite his own dwelling. Each tent was shared by one family, although there could be one subsidiary tent when a son had married and had his own children. Mingmar wore tattered trousers rolled up at the knees and a red sweater. Items he'd gone to bed in, his mother told them. He looked as though he'd fallen over and was about to get up and go running off, but then Lia took in the fact his feet were bare, and had lost their healthy brown colour to a waxy grey. He looked so small and defenceless, she felt her throat contract.

A piece of white cloth covered his face, a traditional gesture, which would only be removed when the funeral was to take place some four to five days later. Lia was grateful for the religious practice forbidding anybody to move or touch the body – not even the boy's parents – which meant that aside from the trodden-down area around the boy, the body was pristine for the forensic team.

Lia left Hua Ming lumbering to process the area. She asked Jenny to help translate for Zhang and Deshi once they knew the dynamics of the relationships within the camp. 'I want you to find out if anyone visited the camp recently,' she told them. 'I want you to try and be polite, make them relax. Be nice to the kids. Be respectful.'

Zhang looked at her blankly, as though he didn't understand.

'If you're nice to them,' she said, deciding to appeal to his baser nature, 'they'll feed you, give you hot drinks.'

'You're joking,' said Zhang. 'I wouldn't touch anything they offered. The place is disgusting.'

As if to prove his point, a woman emerged from a tent, pulling a wailing child behind her. The girl's face was caked in grime and snot, her hands engrained with dirt. Despite the filth, she looked healthy enough. The instant she saw them she fell silent, her eyes rounding into the size of soup-plates.

'Jenny,' Lia commanded. 'Introduce yourself. Zhang and Deshi, do the same.'

Jenny immediately dropped to her haunches to talk to the little girl, and Lia moved away. Chen followed. Dogs trotted around the camp, tails jaunty as they inspected the new arrivals, hopeful of a titbit but always cautious against a well-aimed kick. They'd obviously learned not all strangers were tolerant towards them.

'I assume you'll want to talk to Mingmar's parents,' said Chen. 'Can I translate for you?'

'Yes, please.' Lia wanted to do more than just talk, she wanted to get to know them because she was sure they knew the killer. As soon as Chen had said *the count is sixteen*, she'd felt a strange mixture of horror and satisfaction. Horror at the high number, satisfaction that her instinct had been right.

Mingmar's parents lived with his maternal grandparents in the largest tent in the camp. Inside, clothes hung from the wooden ribs and the floor was covered with items from nylon shoulder bags, sacks of flour and sugar to tea cups, blackened pots and pans, and although it looked messy, Lia got the feeling everything had its place and was more organised that it appeared.

Weatherbeaten, their skin red and coarse, the couple looked to be in their twenties but were, in fact, in their late teens. The mother could barely speak with grief, so Lia turned her attention to the father, a sweet-faced young man called Anil who had laughter lines at the corners of his eyes and mouth that were now drawn tight with grief.

Mingmar was so named because he was born on a Tuesday, Anil told them. He had never harmed anything and, as their first-born, was the apple of their eye. No, they'd had no visitors to the camp lately. Not a single one for at least three months, except the police officer from Gertse, of course, who dropped by last week, asking them to report any boys' deaths.

Lia let Chen talk to Anil. Occasionally she asked a question of her own, not always relevant to the case, but to give her an insight of some sort, like what happened to the massive stove when they moved camp? Waist-high, made from mud and bricks, it stood in the middle of the tent, dominating the space like a hulking pregnant sow. Fuelled by dried yak dung, it was kept burning all day but the temperature inside the tent couldn't be called warm. Not by Lia's standards, anyway. She wore three layers of thermal undergarments beneath her uniform and knee-length down coat and the marrow of her bones was still chilled.

The stove, Anil explained, was left behind in the spring. It only took a day to build and would last for five years or so before having to be rebuilt. If it didn't get re-used it would be weathered by storms over the years and – if he didn't invest in a metal stove next year which was easier to pack on the back of a yak – would eventually become rubble and return to the earth.

Anil gradually relaxed until Lia thought it was time to increase the pressure. She said, 'When did your visitors leave?'

'We haven't had any visitors,' Anil said, but she couldn't

mistake the sudden tension in his shoulders, or the shiver through his wife's body.

Lia decided against pressing further and went and rejoined Hua Ming's team.

*

On the horizon, jagged peaks jutted through the clouds, piercing the delicate fabric like needles through cotton wool.

'How's it going?' she asked Hua Ming.

The fat man rubbed a hand across his round, pink face. 'I'll let you know at the end of the day.'

'Can I borrow Ivy?'

'Help yourself.'

Lia walked Ivy out of the camp and to what she gauged to be the edge of the circular depression she'd spotted from the air. She gestured at the area. 'What do you think?'

'Give me ten minutes.'

Lia watched Ivy fetch a spade and dig through the snow to expose the ground below. She made a dozen such holes before returning to Lia. 'A tent was pitched here recently. Before the last big dump of snow. The grass has been flattened and there are holes from the tent pegs.'

Just as Lia had suspected. 'How many people?'

'Half a dozen? Could be more, could be less. I won't know much until we've cleared the area and given it a proper going over.'

'You suspected this when we flew overhead,' Lia said.

Ivy ducked her head. 'I wasn't certain.'

'I don't care how uncertain you were,' Lia said. 'You should have told me. You heard what the Commissioner said. You see something that might be relevant, you tell me. Got it?'

'Sorry.'

'And whatever's between you and Zhang, don't let it hamper your work.'

Ivy flushed. 'Sorry,' she said again.

'Keep going. I want to know who was in that tent.'

Lia and Ivy employed four of the stronger-looking male nomads to help shift the snow and expose the ground below. They kept a close eye on the men in case they pocketed anything that might be a clue of some kind, but neither of them saw anything untoward. It wasn't until late afternoon that the work was finished. The grass was brown and moist and whorled in places where the tent had rested and despite Ivy poring over the area, she didn't find many clues. There were no cigarette butts, used tissues or any sort of useful debris. Instead, there were fibres from a black yak-hair tent, horse hairs, dog hairs and perhaps some human hairs, all of which could have come from the nomads themselves.

'I'll bag as much as I can,' Ivy told Lia, looking dispirited. 'But unless we get a suspect...' She trailed off as a broad-shouldered Tibetan man arrived in the camp. He was shouting and waving his arms, looking around him much like a bewildered bullock. Mingmar's parents rushed up to him and he disappeared from view, swallowed by a crowd of nomads. The man began to wail. Lia walked over to Chen, who was standing near the crowd with a bland expression, trying to look as though he wasn't eavesdropping.

'Who is he?' Lia asked.

'Mingmar's uncle.' He pulsed his thumb over his shoulder at a truck parked by the roadside. 'He lives in Gertse. He was returning from a trip delivering some telecoms equipment in the north-west of the prefecture...'

There was a sudden commotion and voices began to rise. The crowd surged in the direction of Mingmar's body. Anxious that the crime scene shouldn't be disturbed, Lia followed, shouldering her way to Hua Ming, but the crowd respected the tape surrounding the body and stood back, forming a half circle around Mingmar's uncle who'd fallen to his knees and was rocking back and forth, weeping noisily.

His uncontrolled, broken sobs reminded her of her own

grief at hearing Jian was dead and she had to swallow hard to dispel the tears threatening to rise in sympathy. Lia turned her back, leaving him to mourn in peace.

*

They were all exhausted by the time they were flown to the guest house in Gertse at the end of the day. There were three accommodation blocks, one favoured by truck drivers and which Lia had no intention of going near – she'd already seen the urine streaks on the walls and some lumps in the truck park that looked suspiciously like human excrement – and she chose the block furthest away. Thanks to the fact that the bathrooms were locked due to a lack of water, and had been for months, the entire place stank of body odour and stale sweat.

Lia took a so-called deluxe room, but if she expected any kind of luxury, she was in for a disappointment. No toilet. A stained sink in the corner. A thin blue towel with a burn mark in its centre. A single wrought-iron bed with four blankets. A rickety bedside table. At least it appeared to be relatively clean and she had a TV. She switched it on to find it didn't work. Great. Dumping her suitcase on the bed, she headed straight outside, wondering what on earth she was supposed to do if she needed to use the toilet in the middle of the night. Do what everyone else did, she supposed, and go in the car park. Talk about revolting.

She gathered the team in a shabby Chinese restaurant along the main road and, after they'd ordered, began swapping notes. Jenny had questioned Mingmar's uncle and now she said, 'Yeshe's a bit simple in the head. Nice enough, and strong – always useful when loading and unloading the truck – but I wouldn't give him much of an IQ. He was in Golmud, apparently, when his nephew died. The guest house Yeshi stayed in confirms it, along with a couple of truck drivers I managed to track down.'

'You got a signal?' she asked, surprised. Her phone had remained resolutely silent all day.

'No. I used a public phone.'

Lia then listened to what Zhang had to say. 'One of the kids mentioned some monks passing through, but the second I asked him when, his parents hushed him.'

Ivy brightened slightly. 'I found some maroon thread where the tent stood. Perhaps it came from their robes. I'll check.'

Lia's pulse picked up. Visiting monks? Was Tashi right? Was the killer a monk? Her excitement abruptly turned to dismay at the realisation that if he was, it would cause a mess that would reverberate beyond Tibet's borders. She could picture it now, the Chinese government taking the opportunity to persecute every Tibetan Buddhist in the name of justice, of wanting to find the killer. No lama would be safe. No monk, no nun. Lia might not support Tibet's fight for independence, nor did she sympathise with the TPUM, Tibet People's Uprising Movement, but the thought of what might happen if it became public that a Buddhist monk was killing little boys made her blood run cold. Abruptly she remembered Tashi's conviction that it was a monk who'd killed his brother.

He's not like a normal man.

Please, all gods, she prayed, let Tashi be wrong.

Zhang dug in his jacket pocket and pulled out an odd assortment of magazine clippings and postcards and chucked them on the table. 'Look at that lot. Honestly, you'd think they'd know better by now.' Lia flicked through them to see all the pictures were of the Dalai Lama – one of him beaming so hard you thought his spectacles might crack, the others showing him walking, praying, chatting to people. Lia tucked them into her pocket.

'Don't you want to know who had them?' Zhang said. He brought out a notebook and began flipping pages.

'It's not relevant,' she replied.

'But we could arrest them.' He looked baffled.

'We're not here on a religious witch hunt,' she said. 'We're here to see whether we have a serial killer on our hands. Please remember that when we return to the camp tomorrow. I don't want to get sidetracked.'

A tinge of pink crept up his throat. She ignored it and turned to Hua Ming, who was stuffing his face with strings of greasy fried onions.

'How did the boy die?' she asked.

He put down his chopsticks and wiped his mouth.

'And don't say "of a broken neck".'

'I wasn't going to.' He gave a muted belch. 'I was going to say that someone caught the boy's head between their hands and twisted it –' he clicked his fingers, making a sharp snapping sound '– severing the spine by cervical dislocation as the head was forced to face backwards. It reminds me of someone wringing a chicken's neck.'

A hush fell over the table.

Lia said, 'Is this what happened to the other boys?'

A brief silence where Hua Ming shifted his bulk uncomfortably on his chair. Lia guessed he was remembering their meeting all those days ago, and his insistence the deaths weren't connected.

'Yes,' he finally said, barely a murmur. He took a breath as though to say something more, and then hesitated. He reminded her of someone scared of heights preparing to jump off a diving board.

'What is it?' Lia asked.

'Nothing,' he said immediately, and she cursed for being too impatient. He'd closed up like a clam. She would have to ask him another time, when there weren't so many people around, perhaps.

Instead, she asked, 'Would you have to be particularly strong?'

Hua Ming put his head on one side. 'It's more about technique than strength.'

'Could a woman have done it?'

'I suppose so.'

She started when Hua Ming's mobile phone beeped.

'Looks like I've got a signal,' he said, checking his screen. 'Excuse me. I need to make a call.'

Immediately everyone dived for their mobile phones and began ringing home or texting. Since Lia had nobody to call, she sat watching Hua Ming amble outside, her mind still on the killings. The broad connection between the children was straightforward. All small boys, all lured from their beds in the middle of the night. Each had had his neck wrung. How did the killer select his victims? Did he walk through villages and camps until he spotted the right boy? And then what? He befriended them. Maybe he even hinted he'd show them something special, or bribed them with sweets. There was no sign of any of the children struggling. The boys trusted their killer. The killer had to be reasonably strong. And fast. He wouldn't be an old man, but someone younger, in reasonable shape.

Lia had no doubt it was a man.

*

'Everything OK?'

Jenny was watching her. Recalling the woman's offer of support in Rabang, Lia sighed. 'I can't work out the killer's motive,' she confessed. 'What makes him tick? Most serial killers don't start with murder, they build up to it from smaller offences, like torturing animals, arson, rape. But this clean way of killing feels odd, out of step with what I know.'

'You still think it's a serial killer?' Jenny's expression was narrowed.

'What else do you suggest?'

The young woman pursed her lips. 'Perhaps the children overheard something they shouldn't.'

Startled, Lia said, 'Like what?'

'I don't know.' Jenny's expression grew thoughtful. 'Maybe the Tibetans are planning something.'

Lia studied the PSB officer's face but it gave nothing away.

'Is there something I should know about?' Lia asked.

Jenny's pensive air remained. 'I think we should remain vigilant for any subversion.'

Nothing new there, Lia thought with a mental shrug.

An elderly Tibetan man came and began clearing away their plates. His hands were twisted with arthritis and as he raised Jenny's dish his grip slipped. Remnants of watery slop spilled onto Jenny's lap and he sprang back, dismayed, an apology already on his lips.

'Fong go pi!' Shit on you! Jenny leaped to her feet, her face filled with fury. 'You worthless piece of scum, can't you be more careful?'

The man cowered, mumbling his regret but Jenny seemed oblivious. The stream of invective continued.

'You clumsy oaf! All you had to do was clear the fucking table! What's wrong with you people? We give you every-thing and you treat us like garbage!'

'Hey.' Lia rose. 'Who put too many chillies in your rice bowl?'

Jenny swung round, eyes blazing. 'Don't you fucking dare take his side. For all I know he did it on purpose. They're always creeping around eavesdropping, trying to undermine us...'

'It was an accident,' Lia said quietly.

With an obvious effort, Jenny took a shuddering breath, fought to bring her temper under control. The man scurried away without looking back.

'Yes,' Jenny managed. 'An accident.' She passed a hand over her face. 'I'm sorry. It's this place...it's really getting to me. Everything I touch is filthy. Disgusting. How can they live like this? I don't understand them. There's no water to wash with in the guest house. My towel is infested with lice.' She took another breath. 'Sorry,' she said again.

'It's OK,' Lia said. 'We all get stressed from time to time.'

'It won't happen again,' Jenny said stiffly.

Lia watched Jenny walk outside, her back rigid, as though she had a broom handle thrust down the back of her shirt. Yin and yang, Lia thought. Dark and light. Even the seemingly even-tempered Jenny wasn't immune to a disturbance in the universal balance.

Lia walked back to her room. She decided to talk to Mingmar's parents again. See if she could discount the monk theory. But when she turned up the next morning, it was to find the helicopter by the side of the road, and a team of PSB swarming in and around the camp.

Tan was here.

19

TAN GATHERED EVERYONE ON the north side of the camp. He
crackled with energy, his eyes bright, skin clear and gleaming
with health. He didn't look at Lia once and nor, she noticed
with a feeling of apprehension, did Chen.

'I got a phone call from Hua Ming last night,' he said,
'telling me we have a killer of young boys on the loose.'

Lia didn't look at the pathologist. She didn't dare in case
she let slip how angry she felt with him. Why had he betrayed
her? And why did he want Tan here?

'We're here to help you catch the perpetrator,' Tan
continued. 'With both our teams working together, we
should solve this case quickly. As the superior officer, you
will understand it is appropriate for you all to report directly
to me.'

Lia felt a few glances slide her way but she kept her
expression absolutely cool, absolutely smooth.

'First, I would like to talk to the forensic team. Then I will
brief you. Please, wait here.'

Lia had no intention of hanging around. The second Tan
turned his back, she slipped away. To her surprise, she was
joined by Chen. He said, 'Would you like some help translating?'

'I'd love some, but I don't want you to get into trouble.'

He took off his spectacles, gave them a cursory inspection
and put them back on. 'Tan is going to ship the boy's body
back to Lhasa tonight.'

'Tonight?' she said, dismayed. 'Is that all the time we have?
Just today?'

'Yes.'

'Let's get moving, then.'

Mingmar's mother poured both Lia and Chen some sweet black tea. Her eyes were red from weeping, her lips pressed together as though to stop herself from shouting out her grief. She held her prayer wheel in her right hand, prayer beads in her left. Anil, Mingmar's father, appeared more stoic, but his brother Yeshe, the truck driver, sat hunched by the stove, tears running down his chubby face.

Delving in her jacket pocket, Lia withdrew the pictures of the Dalai Lama, passed them to Anil.

'These were taken in error from around your camp yesterday,' she said. 'My apologies.'

She watched him tenderly stroke one of the postcards before hiding them in his choba.

'I will return them to the right people,' he said. 'Thank you.'

Lia sipped her tea, watching the smoke from the stove pour skywards through a flap in the roof of the tent. An old woman with sunken cheeks sat in the corner, rolling out small dough balls with a narrow rolling pin. Her grey hair was greasy but neatly pinned at the nape of her neck. Chen took some tea to her and she nodded at him, patting his forearm like an affectionate aunt.

'She's deaf,' Chen told Lia. 'But she's not stupid. She can lip read and I'm pretty sure she knows more than she lets on.'

Lia asked Anil gentle questions, like where he'd met his wife, where he'd been born, where they'd head in the spring. After a while, she turned to Yeshe, and learned he was twenty-five years old, and had been a truck driver for the past four years. He liked moving from place to place, and usually travelled in a convoy for company and a regular supply of Tibetan tea. He was distraught over his nephew's death and ceaselessly worried his prayer beads over his wrist and around his knuckles.

'Do you ever give people lifts?' she asked him.

'Sure. I get bored sometimes. It's nice to have the company.'

'Did you give any monks a lift this week?'

'No.' The answer came easily. He was looking at his prayer beads and didn't see his brother's tension.

'Do you know who did?'

'No, sorry. But someone would have. We wouldn't let them walk if we could help it. Not in winter...'

'Yeshe, enough,' his brother snapped.

The big man jerked his head up at his brother's tone. Immediately his expression crumpled. 'Sorry,' he said. He passed a hand over his face. 'I wasn't thinking...'

'We need some more fuel for the fire,' his brother said, still curt. 'Fetch some.'

Yeshe stood up and stumbled outside.

Lia fixed Anil with a narrowed gaze. 'When did the monks arrive?'

He shook his head. His skin had turned waxy.

'They were here,' she told him. 'We have forensic proof they set up camp next to yours.' Which was pushing it a bit, but she hoped eliciting a bit of fear might encourage him to talk.

Long silence. Nobody moved. The old woman had stopped rolling out her dough balls and was watching them through rheumy eyes.

Lia held Anil's gaze. 'I think one of the monks killed Mingmar,' she said.

'No, no.' He doubled over as though he felt ill. His wife was staring at Lia as though she'd just sprouted horns and a tail. 'You're wrong. It's not possible. It can't be, because...' He licked his lips. 'It just can't.'

'Why were they here?'

'They weren't.' His wife moved to stand between her husband and Lia. Her expression was fierce. 'No monks were here. Yeshe is confused. He loved his nephew. We have lost our son, please leave us to grieve. Why do you have to take him away? That other police officer said he must take

Mingmar's body to Lhasa for tests. We just want to bury our boy properly, make sure his spirit rests in peace. Why do you torment us?'

Lia's voice was gentle as she spoke. 'The body has to go to Lhasa because that's where the specialist equipment is. Your son's body will help us find his killer.'

Silence.

'We want to stop whoever killed Mingmar from killing more little boys,' she added.

'What do you mean, *more*?' asked Mingmar's mother. Her fingers had stopped their ceaseless roving over her prayer wheel.

'I've already said too much.' Lia spread her hands, wishing she could tell them the truth but knowing she daren't.

'Are you saying Mingmar's not the first?' Anil looked horrified. His wife swayed as though she was going to faint.

A long silence fell.

Eventually, Mingmar's mother took a long breath. 'That's awful. But I don't understand…how can Mingmar's body help catch the killer?'

Lia let Chen explain as best he could the forensic process. He finished by saying that they hoped they'd find some traces of the killer on Mingmar's body which would confirm their suspect.

Eventually, the mother glanced at Anil, who nodded. 'When will we get him back?'

'As soon as possible,' Lia said. 'I know how important it is for him to be buried.' She rose to her feet. She wanted to offer them her sympathy, to let them know she could see their devastation, but she knew from her own experience words didn't help. Ducking her head, she took a formal stance, saying simply, 'I'm sorry.'

*

Outside, she vainly looked for Yeshe. A small boy, his face caked in green snot, ran up to her begging for money. She gave him a boiled sweet and, through Chen, asked him where Yeshe was. The boy ran off, beckoning for them to follow.

Yeshe stood next to a knee-high stack of dried manure. His shoulders were bowed, his head dropped low on his chest. He said, 'I bought Mingmar a toy truck. It's not very big, but he would have loved to play with it. It's in my glove box. He won't ever see it.' He wasn't speaking to anyone in particular. He was just talking out the beginning of his sorrow.

Lia said softly, 'We want to find who killed Mingmar, do you understand?'

Chen translated for her in the same gentle tone.

Yeshe raised his head. 'I understand.'

'The monks who stayed here, where did they go afterwards? Where were they headed?'

He took a step back. 'There were no monks.'

'We have to talk to them,' Lia persisted. 'They may know something about Mingmar's killer.'

Yeshe shook his head. He walked away. Lia watched him go. She said, 'He's protecting them. Everyone's protecting them.'

Chen was also watching Yeshe. 'I don't understand why they're travelling in winter. Perhaps...' He paused, pushing his spectacles further up his nose. 'No, I couldn't say.'

Lia waited quietly, inhaling smells of wood smoke, feeling the cold air bite her lungs.

'Perhaps,' Chen ventured, 'they're planning something.'

She could feel her senses sharpen. He'd voiced the same concern as Jenny. 'I'm not sure I want to hear this.'

He spread his palms. 'I could be wrong.'

'Not monks, surely,' she said.

'What better cover?'

'They're pacifists. They preach love and acceptance, tolerance. Charity. Forbearance.'

'Things change,' Chen said. He was staring into the distance, towards the jagged backbone of mountains pluming snow into a sky the colour of sapphires. 'How much do you know about Tibet's history?'

'I'm no expert. I just know what most Chinese on the street know, that the government has tried to keep a lid on Tibet since their failed uprising in 1959. That the Tibetans want independence from China. That the Dalai Lama has advocated peaceful protest.'

'All correct,' he said. 'But never forget that Tibet is an extension of China, and independence is never going to happen. Many Tibetans don't agree, however. Take the recent violent anti-Chinese protests. They're becoming more common, which in turn meant more arrests. It's a tinderbox, and China's way of responding was to build a railway from Beijing to Lhasa…'

'And swamp Tibet with Chinese.' She gazed into the distance, the peerless blue sky. 'Cultural genocide.' Whether you liked it or not, everybody knew it was happening.

'Yes.'

'What about Tashi, the little boy we met? He said he thought the killer was a…'

As she tried to form the word *monk*, her lungs contracted.

'Supervisor? Are you all right?'

Abruptly her breathing resumed. She ran a hand down her face. It had to be the altitude getting to her. Lhasa was over three and a half thousand metres high, and here on the plateau, it was even higher. She'd thought she'd acclimitised, her body getting used to the reduced oxygen levels, but now she realised she may be suffering mild altitude sickness.

'Yes. Sorry.'

'What did Tashi say?'

She licked her lips. 'This is to remain between just us, OK?'

He nodded.

'He said that a group of monks visited his village the week his brother Pemba died.' She spoke softly, not wanting to be overheard. 'Five were lamas, at the top of the spiritual pole. He never mentioned terrorists.'

Chen gave a snort. 'Lamas or not, more and more Tibetans are calling for the right to use violence. They hate us, Supervisor. Hate us for trying to destroy their culture, their belief system. Some say if they sit back and hope independence is going to be delivered on a plate, nothing's going to happen.'

'But *monks*?'

Chen's voice turned soft. 'Who says they're monks?'

A chill swept through her. 'If they're not, then who are they?'

He turned to stare into the distance once more. 'Do I have to spell it out?'

He's talking about terrorists, she thought. Tibetan terrorists who are going around the countryside to gain support to...what? Overthrow the Chinese? Burn all the Chinese shops down, stone their owners, kill their kids, and force their invaders to leave? They'd never win. The government would activate its troops already inside Tibet, and then deploy tens of thousands more from Bejing and beyond. The Tibetans would be massacred.

'I can see why the Tibetans could turn to terrorism,' Lia said. 'It's a way of regaining control. Making yourself heard. But do you honestly think our killer is one of them?'

'It's a possibility.'

'Have you discussed this theory with anyone?' she asked.

He shook his head. 'Not yet. But if we can find the Snow Thief, then we'll know what we're dealing with. We need to find him fast in order to prevent an uprising and all its consequences.'

'What if they're just monks?'

Chen's gaze was flat. 'Do you really believe that?'

She didn't know what she believed. She turned her mind to Jenny, who only last night had said they should remain watchful for subversives. What intel did the PSB officer have?

'Perhaps we should inform Tan of your thoughts?' Lia suggested. 'He could authorise an air search—'

'Yes, he could, but we'd need a lot of luck. The area's enormous. It'll be like searching for a grain of rice.'

Lia frowned, wondering why, if he truly believed a group of terrorists were travelling through his prefectures, he was reluctant to take it any further. She was about to ask the question but he pre-empted her.

'Let's find the Snow Thief first,' Chen said. 'I don't want to start a war unnecessarily.'

She arched her eyebrows. 'You admit they could be just monks?'

He looked away. 'I wanted to air my thoughts. Will you tell anyone?'

'I might.' She was thinking of Commissioner Zhi.

Chen nodded. 'I trust you will do the right thing.'

*

The remainder of the day passed too quickly for Lia. Although she managed to interview the people closest to Mingmar, she was no nearer to understanding why a monk might kill the boy. If he was a monk, of course, and not a terrorist with a twisted mind.

She watched Tan talking to Yeshe at some point, and she could tell the big man was distressed by the way he twisted his prayer beads, pulling and tugging them so fiercely she expected them to break. Tan asked Yeshe to show him the toy truck he'd bought for his nephew. Bright red, it had oversized wheels and a horn that honked. The children flocked around Yeshe, clamouring to play with it, but Tan ordered them away and then gave it to one of his officers. 'Evidence,' he announced. The children fell silent, their faces dropping with disappointment when the truck vanished inside a plastic bag and was sealed from view.

Tan's callous attitude sat at odds with how he'd behaved

when questioning Tashi, and she looked at him askance, wondering what made the man tick. Cold and hard on the one hand, but oddly temperate the next.

'He's a strange one, eh?' Jenny joined her in her inspection of Tan. Her expression was calm and held no evidence of her loss of temper the night before.

'Heartless,' Lia said as one little boy burst into tears.

'I wouldn't say that.' Jenny flicked some hair off her shoulder. 'I caught him feeding his breakfast to a cat in Rabang. He talked to it like he would a child.'

'He obviously prefers animals to humans,' said Lia drily.

'Féihuà.' No kidding. Jenny's face was wry.

At four o'clock Tan ordered them to pack up. 'Supervisor Shan's team flies back tonight,' he announced. 'My team will fly back tomorrow.'

Lia and the team boarded the helicopter. She watched Mingmar's body as it was strapped onto a stretcher and loaded inside. His parents looked on in anguish as the helicopter rose into the air, tilted its nose forward and accelerated. Their brown faces were upturned, their eyes creased against the helicopter's downdraught. Lia watched them until they finally vanished from sight.

20

LAMA SONAM WAS TOO far away to see the helicopter, but he knew it was there because a shopkeeper in Gertse had told them all about the police flying in to investigate a dead boy found at the nomad's camp. Apparently, the boy had broken his neck, an accident, but the lama's heart had just about stopped when he'd heard it was the same boy that they had talked to four days ago.

Was it a coincidence?

No time to ponder the fact. They had to get moving. Immediately he instructed Tenzin to force their little caravan hard over the next few days, working their way to the next prefecture border. They stopped at two villages en route before taking refuge with another band of nomads, tucked in a fold of the mountains. He had to hope the prefectures remained independent of one another and didn't compare notes or they could be in trouble.

He watched as Tenzin began looking to prepare camp. Millions of years ago this area had been alive with erupting volcanoes, and when the flames died down, it left networks of tunnels and caves. For centuries, monks had used these for shelter as they travelled. The cave Tenzin found was intact, its walls streaked with copper. From the far wall trickled a mountain spring and there was a stone circle from a previous fire beneath a natural chimney.

As they unloaded the yaks, the medical monk, Lama Nawang, came over. Like the rest of them, his movements were weary, his footsteps slow.

'Dawa Rinpoche is ill,' he said. 'It's a good place to rest. Well done, Tenzin.' Nawang's face crinkled into a smile. 'Your talents appear to be boundless.'

Tenzin nodded, not saying a word, but Lama Sonam could tell that although the Dob-dob was frustrated with the delay, he was also pleased at the praise. He watched as Tenzin moved away to help settle the fatigued travellers into their temporary home. They'd hoped to cross the border tomorrow but now, they'd have to wait another day, possibly two. At least they were well-hidden here, where the authorities would never find them. It would be along the border when they'd be exposed. He'd have to instruct Tenzin to make sure they were well away from any roads and thus, any military patrols. Which again would take time, trudging across kilometres of rough open ground rather than hitching a ride.

A fire was lit and as smoke began to fill the cave, he moved outside. The sun slowly sank, outlining the high peaks, the plumes of snow streaming from each pinnacle. Deep purple shadows crept out of the hollows, climbing higher and higher until only the white peaks blazed white. He watched the last gold curve of the sun vanish behind a rocky pass. Night plunged around them, but inside the cave candles flickered, the fire burning brightly with Dawa Rinpoche huddled alongside. The High Abbot was the oldest of their group, and possibly the toughest. Lama Nawang was mixing potions for him to drink and burning herbs to ease his laboured breathing. Nobody knew if he'd find the strength to continue or not.

Lama Sonam was grateful there were no lights indicating any pursuers, no sound of any helicopter. He spent the remainder of the evening by the fire, praying for Dawa Rinpoche's quick recovery.

*

Fang Dongmei was out when Lia arrived back at the apartment, but there was fresh *man tou*, steamed, plain bread shaped in buns the size of her fist, and a pot of soup ready to be reheated on the stove. Lia assumed Fang Dongmei had gone shopping, or was maybe visiting a herbalist for potions to keep her in good health. She was particularly spry for her age and, like many Chinese, believed in the power of alternative medicine, avoiding the Chinese public health system which – it was widely stated – would 'kill you'.

Lia ate at the kitchen table, pad and pen to hand, writing up the past two days. Tired and travel-weary, her head muzzy after hours of suffering the thundering roar of the helicopter's engines, she went to bed early. Fang Dongmei still hadn't returned and Lia couldn't think where she might be. Perhaps she was having tea with the Commissioner's grandmother? Or had the old woman actually made another friend and gone visiting?

It wasn't until after midnight that she heard heavy footsteps on the stairs outside, then the apartment door opened. She listened to Fang Dongmei's grunt as she took off her boots. Lia rolled over. She didn't know it, but the cells in her body finally relaxed at the sound of Jian's grandmother's return and her breathing slowed. She fell asleep seconds later.

*

Fang Dongmei made congee for Lia in the morning and sprinkled it with sugar, just how she liked it.

'Where were you last night?' Lia asked.

The old woman didn't respond. Didn't look at Lia.

'Were you out visiting?'

Nothing. She may as well have been talking to the wall. Abruptly, her anger flared. 'Come on, Grandmother. I've suffered enough of your silences. Talk to me, dammit! Or do you want to punish me for ever?'

The old woman rounded on her. Her eyes blazed with fury.

'You think it's about you?'

Lia took a step back. Here we go again, she thought. Why didn't I keep my mouth shut?

'You think I feel no guilt for what's happened?' Fang

Dongmei's voice rose. 'You think I don't lie awake every night berating myself for protesting when I did? You think I don't picture your husband, my grandson, dying in front of my own eyes? Every time I begin to open my mouth to say something civil, something trivial, I think my soul will fly out, black and stinking and reeking of evil. That's why I keep it shut. To keep the evil I have done inside.'

Lia stared at Fang Dongmei, shocked.

'My penance is seeing you every day. Mourning for Jian. Miserable. Your life torn apart because of me!' She thumped her chest with a gnarled hand. 'Me! It was my actions that brought you here. My actions that brought death to everyone we loved. You are the only one left and I keep my mouth shut because I dare not lose you as well.'

Fang Dongmei spun on her heel and marched for her room, slammed the door shut behind her.

Lia stared at the door. How could she have been so stupid? Of course Fang Dongmei would blame herself for her part in their family's arrests and deaths. She tried to remember what had been said in their earlier fights, but could only recall herself screaming at Fang Dongmei that it was her fault Jian was dead.

Could she forgive Fang Dongmei? Not today. Not tomorrow either. The resentment was still too strong. But maybe in the future when time had passed and dulled her grief into something more manageable, it might be possible. And then they could...what? Finally be civil to one another? Able to make conversation like normal relatives, and squabble over petty things without falling into the endless pit of blame? It would make a change, if nothing else.

Lia walked to the front door and pulled on her boots. 'See you later,' she called, and she wasn't surprised there was no response.

The first thing she did when she arrived in the office was type up her report. She was mainly concerned about the ethnicity of the Snow Thief, and didn't discount the fact that it could be possible for him to be Tibetan or Chinese. *Unlikely,* she wrote, *but I've learned over the years that human nature can always surprise us.* She cited the two Indian serial killers who murdered more than twenty-five children between 2005 and 2006.

Twenty-five. They had to catch the killer soon.

Lia printed off four copies of her report and spent the remainder of the morning catching up on two days' worth of paperwork generated in her absence, and when Commissioner Zhi stuck his head around her door, the last thing she expected was for him to say, 'Tan's arrested the killer. He's bringing him in now.'

'What?'

'He's got a full confession. Good work, eh?' Zhi looked pleased. 'It didn't take long to solve the case after all. It's a relief, I have to say.'

'Who is it?' She was up and around her desk in a flash.

'A man called Yeshe.'

21

LIA WASN'T ALLOWED TO see Yeshe until the following day, and when she did she had to lock her emotions into a small black box inside her, and double-lock the lid. He was supposed to be in solitary – no visitors – but thankfully Commissioner Zhi had stepped in and pulled some strings. She'd brought Jenny with her, to translate, and the young PSB officer walked down the bare-brick corridor as jumpy as a cat. Both of them knew Tan would give them hell for being here, even if Zhi had approved it.

Yeshi's cell was approximately two metres by three and lit by a bare bulb dangling from the ceiling. It had no windows, no bed, no blankets. The walls were bare brick, the floor concrete. It was ice cold, like walking into a refrigerator. A bucket already half full of effluent sat in the corner, stinking the air.

Yeshe lay crumpled in the corner of his cell. He didn't look up when she entered. Instead he brought his arms over his head, cowering. He mumbled, 'No, please...'

'It's me, Yeshe,' she said. She squatted down and gestured for Jenny to do the same. 'Supervisor Shan. I returned the pictures of the Dalai Lama to your brother. Do you remember?'

He kept his arms in place. His clothes were ripped and torn. He wore no shoes. Lia's stomach clenched at the state of his feet. They'd been beaten – probably with a piece of wood, maybe even a baseball bat – and were black with bruises. The soles looked spongy and soft with congealed blood. All his toes had been broken and sat at odd angles, their joints swollen and blue.

When she spoke, her voice was soft. 'I've brought you some food and water.'

She put the bottles and high-energy bars on the floor, where

143

he could see them. She'd also smuggled in some nuts and dried seeds – the most calorific and nutritious foods she could think of. A lot of the time, prisoners weren't fed or given water.

Slowly, he lowered his arms to reveal the bloody pulp that used to be his face. One eye was completely swollen shut, the other a mere slit. His lips were split and still weeping blood. He had a deep cut on his forehead that gaped wide like a sea anemone, and another above his right eye. His left cheekbone had been shattered, and splinters of bone showed through the wound.

She couldn't help herself. She said, 'Oh, Yeshe.'

He started to sob.

'You poor love.'

He toppled into her arms. Immediately she began to wriggle back, uncomfortable with such physical closeness from a man, but then she remembered how simple he was and that mentally, he was little more than a child. Despite Jenny's look of disapproval, she gently embraced him. He reeked of blood and vomit and shit, but she held him, careful of his wounds, surprised when he gripped her hard, burying his damaged face into her shoulder. 'They say I killed Mingmar,' he sobbed. 'I didn't, I'm sure I didn't, but they say I just can't remember. I didn't, did I? I love Mingmar, I wouldn't hurt him, I swear…'

Lia rubbed his back in gentle circular motions. 'Poor Yeshe,' she murmured. 'I know you loved Mingmar very much. I'm going to try and get you out of here, OK? I'll do everything I can, I promise.' She rested her cheek against his head and rocked him gently, still murmuring, Jenny softly translating. Gradually, Yeshe's sobs turned to hiccoughs, and his muscles relaxed.

Lia let him sleep in her arms until her feet and legs were numb and she could hold him no longer.

*

The first person she rang was Chen.

'Yeshe's in jail here. What happened?'

'I couldn't stop him.' Chen sounded exhausted. 'I tried, but he wouldn't listen. He wanted it solved within twenty-four hours. He didn't care how.'

'We have to find the real killer. Yeshe won't last long.'

'Lia...' He paused, then said, 'Sorry, I'm tired—'

'Please. Lia's fine.'

'I've more bad news.'

'Go on.'

'Another boy...'

He ran her through the details. Dhamo Sopa, five years old, found with his neck snapped at a village fifty k's north-east of Gertse.

Lia went to her map and stuck a pin roughly where she estimated the body was and stood back and surveyed the seventeen pins, the pattern they made. 'It's almost as though he's working in a circle. He started in Lhasa, and so far has done the bottom part of the loop...'

'My guess is he's working his way around Tibet,' Chen said. 'Or rather his colleagues are and he's just moving with them.'

'You still think they're...' She paused while she considered who might be listening in. She wanted to say, you still think they're terrorists?

Chen caught her wariness. 'Yes, I do.'

Her mind sharpened. 'We must warn the other prefectures. What if they cross the border into Nagqu? Who do you know who you can talk to?'

'I only know the people in my prefectures, sorry. But I'll contact the Chief Supervisor and tell him to tighten up his border controls, keep an eye out for them.'

'You do realise he's only got two more prefectures to go? What then? Will he keep going, do you think?'

'Let's worry about the present,' Chen said. 'Can you get to the village? Work the scene?'

'I'll have to get permission from the committee. But yes, I think I can.'

'Will you keep me informed?'

'Dāngrán.' Certainly.

*

It took two days of fierce badgering to bring the committee together to see her. She wasn't allowed to see Yeshe again, and although she knew she risked severe disciplinary action if caught, managed to bribe a guard to bring Yeshe fresh food and water daily. She tried to arrange a doctor to visit, but the guard wouldn't have it. He stonily refused a further bribe, obviously not wanting to incur Tan's wrath should Tan find out.

This time when she faced the committee, she didn't salute Zhi. She didn't salute at all, just took her seat opposite them, spine ramrod straight, her hands folded in her lap, her knees and feet locked together. Today it was just Myra Kwok, Tan, a skinny middle-aged man called Tao Cong from the PSB, and Commissioner Zhi from the police.

'I hear you have a problem with the person I arrested,' Tan said. His nostrils were flared, his lower lip jutting.

'Yeshe didn't do it.' She held his gaze.

'Who did?' This was from Myra Kwok.

'We don't know yet—'

'Yeshe's a truck driver.' Tan leaned forward, his eyes glittering. 'He was driving through the Xigazê and Ngari Prefectures during the past seven weeks. He confessed to being in Rabang, Gertse and Kangro the nights when the boys died – in fact he confessed to all the killings. What more do you want?'

'I want the real killer,' snapped Lia. 'Yeshe was in Golmud when his nephew was killed.'

'He lied,' Tan said smoothly, leaning back. He picked up a pen and spun it between his thumb and index finger.

'There were witnesses.'

'He bribed them. Just as he bribed the boys with his toys. You saw the look on those kids' faces when they saw his toy truck. They would have done anything to get their grimy little paws on it. Even get up in the middle of the night and go outside.'

Briefly, she gritted her teeth to quell her rising anger. She had to remain calm, appear cool-headed and dispassionate. If she appeared even remotely emotionally involved, he'd get her removed from the case. Any excuse.

'What about the latest little boy?' she asked. 'His neck was snapped in a village north-east of Gertse. Kangro. You heard about this? Chen called me an hour ago...'

'Yes, we heard.'

'Who killed him? It obviously wasn't Yeshe since he was in custody at the time of the boy's death.'

'It's a gang.' Tan shrugged. 'Yeshe's truck-driving friends. They work together.'

She stared at him, wondering if she'd heard correctly. 'You're saying there's more than one killer?'

'Well, what would you suggest?'

He had, without realising it, given her the perfect opening.

'I agree,' she said.

Tan blinked.

'Which is why I'd like more police. Perhaps we could bring in some troops to help. We know one of the killers was in Kangro on Wednesday, and if we had troops at our disposal, we could cordon off the area and search it properly. We could set up road blocks and checkpoints. We could patrol the roads. We could trap the members of this gang.

'I'd like to publicise the case, make the public aware of what's going on. If it's on the news, on TV and radio, word will soon get out. Parents will watch their boys, and protect them, especially at night.'

As she spoke, her mind raced ahead, evaluating the risk of mentioning the monks now or not. It would certainly guarantee the safety of future boys should a band of travelling monks turn up in a village or township — all parents would be on her guard. However, what if the committee refused to go public? The PSB would go after the monks and probably not even the right ones. What had Chen said? No point in starting a war unnecessarily.

If she and Chen found the monks they were halfway there. However, without military back-up, the little group would be almost impossible to find.

Like searching for a grain of rice.

Even if they caught the monks, how would they know which of them was the Snow Thief without a profile? How would they know how to question him in order to break him?

Keeping her inner discourse to herself, Lia ploughed on. 'Without troops, without going public, more boys will die. So far, we have a total of seventeen. This could double in the next month. Do you really want their deaths on your watch, and risk losing face?'

Tan continued twirling his pen. 'Kwok?' he prompted. 'What do you think of our little Supervisor's request?'

'Impossible,' she said. Her chin was raised and she looked along her nose at Lia, creating an unmistakable air of arrogance.

'To ask for more men to help us is to admit to Beijing that we cannot cope. And to publicise the case...' She gave a bark of sarcastic laughter. 'Where do I start?'

Again, Lia felt the bite of anger in her chest. 'You'd rather more boys died than admit that a serial killer is roaming Tibet?'

'I think I've made myself clear.' Kwok turned to Tan. 'Am I right? We cannot have a whiff of this Snow Thief to reach the public. And what a name to give the killer! If it gets out the whole province will be in terror of a ridiculous fairy tale.' She glared at Lia. 'It's unforgivable.'

'I agree.' Tan put down his pen. 'We have the Snow Thief in custody. The case is closed. Agreed?'

Lia's stomach swooped when everyone nodded, including Commissioner Zhi.

'Supervisor,' Tan said. 'You are aware that it will be impossible for you to continue working this case without my knowing?'

She gave a nod.

'Everyone will be made aware the case is closed. They will report anything untoward to me immediately. This includes Hua Ming, as well as Deshi and Zhang.'

Her stomach gave another roll at the thought of her own team spying on her.

'Yeshe will go before the court at the end of the week.' Tan checked his diary. 'I have no doubt he'll be sentenced to death.'

Lia concentrated on keeping her face muscles perfectly smooth. *I am an alabaster doll*, she told herself. *I will not give him the satisfaction of seeing my horror.*

Tan's eyes fixed on her. 'One more thing, Supervisor. If I hear of you supplying the prisoner with any luxuries in future, it won't just be him on trial. You will join him. Do I make myself clear?'

The shock of his threat took all speech away.

'That's all.' He put his hands flat on the table. 'You may go.'

Lia walked outside with her back rigid, her arms stiff at her sides. Terror sat in her stomach like a sack of stones. Did she have the courage to continue? Was she prepared to put herself on the line to find the Snow Thief? Was she prepared to *die*? Because that was what Tan had threatened. To throw her into jail alongside Yeshe and have her executed, probably as his accomplice.

Back in her office, she tried to take control of her fear but it continued to swell. She was shuddering and shaking beneath a thunderbolt of self-realisation.

I never thought I'd be here. I never thought it was possible.

Last month, I wanted to die.

But now, I want to live.

22

Lia photocopied the file on the boys' murders and took
the copy home. She'd nearly shredded the entire file earlier,
not wanting to keep it around in case Deshi or Zhang found
it and presented it to Tan, who could then use it an excuse to
arrest her, but at the last moment, she found herself stuffing
the copies into her briefcase.

She put them on the table in front of the TV. Went and
made herself some tea but she didn't drink it. She couldn't
stop thinking of Yeshe, his round, simple face. His sobs. His
shattered cheekbones, his broken feet, the way his toes had
been snapped. She'd seen innocent people being framed in
Shenzhen but she'd turned a blind eye; it was part of police
life. But that was before Fang Dongmei's protest and Jian's
execution.

Now she knew what it was like to be a victim, and
everything she'd believed in had fallen away. Curled on the
sofa – no sound from Fang Dongmei, was she out again? – Lia
wondered if this was what the Tibetans meant about facing
your karma. Or was it about being reincarnated so you could
see someone else's point of view?

Three years ago, she'd arrested a young man called Wesley
Qin, who had appealed for political liberalisation on his blog.
At the time, she'd been convinced he should be silenced,
brought to justice for undermining the system, but now she
wondered if she'd done the right thing. Wesley was a student,
only nineteen. His life was just starting. He'd been expressing
an interest in the government and although she'd found his
views unpalatable, many young people in China started on the
route of dissidence, but very few completed it. Wesley had
been jailed for five years. She had, effectively, ruined his life.

Would she be reincarnated as Wesley in her next life, so she could understand what he'd gone through? She frowned, unable to comprehend how reincarnation worked when the reincarnated person didn't know who they'd been in the past. And what about animals? Where did they fit into it all? Soon, she gave up trying to work it out and switched on the TV to see that northern China was frozen solid beneath a cape of snow two metres thick. That the Dalai Lama was still in hospital with some complication or other. She took a sip of tea but it tasted overly bitter, so she pushed it away.

Could she continue the investigation? Was it possible? What were her chances of finding the Snow Thief? Would Chen support her? Commissioner Zhi? She considered Jenny, but decided she couldn't risk it. Lia took the top copy of her report and added some notes. Things she wanted to record for her own personal use, like Chen's concern that the monks might be terrorists and Tashi's belief he could talk to his dead Abbot. She eventually went to bed still thinking of Chen and Tashi, and before she left for work the next morning, she grabbed the copied file and secured it beneath a loose ceiling tile. The hidey-hole also held a copy of her ID card and birth certificate, as well as a copy of Fang Dongmei's ID card. Nothing like living with paranoia, but it helped her sleep better at night should Tan or anyone else confiscate their documents.

Going into the kitchen, she caught Fang Dongmei pushing a small parcel of food inside the back of her trousers. She hurriedly pulled down her tunic, hiding it, looking embarrassed. She said, 'Beggars. It is cold.'

Lia hadn't taken Fang Dongmei to be so charitable, but then she hadn't realised how eaten up by guilt the woman was. The old woman's recent experiences had probably helped change her, made her want to share what little good fortune she enjoyed. Beggars populated Lhasa's streets in unprecedented numbers. In Tibet, begging wasn't stigmatised. When Lia had asked a fit-looking young man why he was begging he'd drawn himself tall and said, *the Buddha was himself a beggar. Besides,* he added slyly, *if I can make a better living begging than by farming, why not?*

'It's a good thing to do,' Lia said.

'Yes.'

Fang Dongmei nodded. She shuffled her feet, looking uncomfortable, which Lia put it down to the fact they'd exchanged a couple of sentences without fighting. After a bowl of congee and some tea, Lia thanked her, wished her a good day, and headed to her shoebox office, where she took the original file from her desk and shredded it.

*

Lia struggled through the week. When she learned Yeshe had been sentenced to death, his execution to be held in four weeks' time, she wanted to visit him but didn't dare. She wanted to ring Chen but again, didn't dare. The same went for Jenny. Finally, she told herself not to think about the dead boys, and pushed them aside and concentrated on the piles of grey investigative files which regulated her life. For a while this seemed to work, until she received a phone call from reception.

'I have Palden Oshoe here to see you.'

'Who?'

The receptionist repeated the name, adding, 'He's a monk. He says it's important.'

'He speaks Mandarin?'

'Fluently.'

'Did he say what it's about?' Lia was frowning.

'No.'

Nothing else was forthcoming. Finally, Lia's curiosity got the better of her.

'OK.' She relented. 'I'll come down.'

Palden Oshoe was in his mid-thirties, a fair bit taller than her, with the usual shaven head. Past the bulk of his robe, she saw he was lean and muscular. His hands looked strong. The muscles on his neck were well-defined. She saw a self-awareness that sat oddly with his calm demeanour. She was reminded of an attack dog dressed up as a family-friendly Labrador.

'Supervisor Shan,' he said. His gaze was piercing, seeming to spear through her uniform and to her soul. She resisted the impulse to cross her arms. Instead, she pushed back her shoulders, lifting her chin and meeting his gaze head-on. He smiled. As the crinkles at the corners of his eyes radiated outwards, she hurriedly reassessed his age to mid-forties.

'How can I help you?' she said.

'It is regarding a mutual friend.' He glanced around. His gaze reached Constable Deshi, who'd walked into reception and had stopped, watching them. 'May we talk privately?'

'What about?'

He dropped his voice to a whisper. 'Our friend in jail. Yeshe.'

'I'm sorry.' Her tone turned stiff. 'But I can't discuss this with you. If you need to talk to someone, try the officer over there. Now, if you'll excuse me...'

'I know who is killing the boys,' he said in the same low tone. 'Please. Just a minute of your time. That's all I ask.'

She stared at him for a long moment. 'Who's the killer?'

'Not here.' He closed his eyes. For a moment, Lia thought he'd fallen into a trance. The sound of a radio squawk brought him back. He blinked and looked at her, expression calm and untroubled. 'Please,' he said.

'I can't help you,' Lia said. 'Now, if you'll excuse me...'

'Do you know the Meru Nyingba Monastery?'

It wasn't far from her apartment, but she didn't give any indication she recognised the name.

'I will wait for you there.'

As Palden Oshoe walked towards the exit, she called out,

'I won't come,' but he didn't turn or hesitate in any way. He simply stepped outside.

*

Lia headed for the lifts. She could feel Deshi watching her curiously. She didn't look at the constable. She didn't want him to misread anything on her face and give him an excuse to call Tan and tell him she'd been consorting with Tibetan monks. Back in her office, Lia tried to concentrate on her work – she had two shoplifting charges to process – but Palden Oshoe kept intruding.

I know who is killing the boys.

How did he know? Had he been a witness to one of the earlier murders, here in Lhasa? Or was it something else, something more sinister? Were more monks involved? Was it a conspiracy of some sort, stretching across the country, as Chen suggested?

She put down her pen and went to the window. Looked at the city anew. She saw the video cameras tucked into the rooftops above the square. The armed military details stationed at every corner. She took in the neon-lit fast-food restaurants spreading like a virus around the square. She considered the billboards advertising Japanese and American luxury vehicles creeping from the west side of town. The six-lane highways, flyovers, and the futuristic bridge leading to the new Special Economic Zone, feeding the area to grow and swell into another Shenzhen.

When the Chinese had poured into Lhasa they'd brought medicines, hospitals, schools, roads, supermarkets, hotels, restaurants and bars, but at what cost? Most of these were set up and run by Chinese for Chinese, and the majority of tourists to be found queuing for the Potala Palace were Chinese.

Chen's voice slipped into her mind. *They hate us, Supervisor. Hate us for trying to destroy their culture, their belief system.*

Before she could change her mind, she pulled on her coat,

hat and gloves, and left the office. As she crossed the square, Mrs Lily gave her a wave from behind her steaming stacks of bamboo containers. Lia waved back.

It was late afternoon, the sun hidden behind a thin cloud layer, but despite the cold, the Barkhor was busy with pilgrims and market shoppers. Monks sat cross-legged on the paving stones with their alms bowls, murmuring mantras. She followed the flow of pilgrims past sellers of jewelled daggers and religious photos before heading south. She continued down an alley, following the prayer wheels, and not long afterwards she paused at a doorway outside the Meru Nyingba Monastery. She looked around but couldn't see Palden Oshoe anywhere. She extended her gaze back up the alley.

At the far end, near a stall selling incense sticks, she saw him. He was walking towards her, his stride measured. His eyes were locked onto her.

As he neared, he gestured for her to enter the monastery ahead of him. The second she crossed the threshold she was enveloped in the smell of juniper incense, the low murmur of Tibetan chanting. The place was crowded with Tibetans thumbing prayer beads and swinging prayer wheels. Butter lamps created a warm glow.

She glanced over her shoulder at Palden Oshoe.

His expression turned cold, as though he'd purposely switched off his emotions.

He lunged for her.

His attack was so unexpected she didn't have time to dodge or block him. He grabbed her and jammed her against the wall. Clapped a hand over her mouth.

'Who are you working for?' he asked.

She jerked and lashed out, trying to kick him, but he was as solid and ungiving as the wall against her back, his strength unerring.

'Who?' He raised his right hand. It held a dagger with a thin blade that shone yellow under the lamps.

She tried to see past his bulk.

Hadn't anyone noticed what was happening?

'I'm going to take my hand away. If you scream, I will plunge this dagger into your throat and leave you to die. Do you understand?'

She nodded her head.

As he took his hand from her mouth, she felt the cold steel press against her throat. She couldn't move without him sticking her like a pig. She'd bleed out in seconds.

'Why are you smuggling food to the prisoner, Yeshe?'

'I'm not.' Her voice was scratchy with fear.

'Don't deny it,' he snapped. 'He told me himself.'

'I only did it for a few days...'

'You've arranged for someone to do it for you. An old woman. Why?'

'What?' Her mind was blank, her heart thundering like an express train. Keep calm. Keep breathing.

Anger rolled across his face. 'Stop pretending you know nothing about it! Why are you insisting Yeshe is innocent? Why are you being so unpatriotic?'

Her mind caught up with his previous words. *An old woman.* She abruptly recalled catching Fang Dongmei hiding a food parcel in her waistband. Her mind jumped to her report on the murders, sitting in front of the TV. Had Jian's grandmother read it? Had she decided to take things into her own hands?

'If you don't leave Goldhawk to finish his job, I will come and slit your throat.'

'I don't understand.'

The blade pressed against her skin. She tried not to yelp.

Come on, pilgrims! Anyone! Can't you see I'm being held hostage?!

He put his face close to hers. 'Leave the lamas alone.'

'The boy killer,' she gasped. 'Who...'

She felt the blade pierce her skin. Warm liquid trickled down her neck. 'Please, don't,' she begged.

He held her gaze, his eyes night-dark in the shadows. His body was so close to hers, his lips so near, they could be mistaken for lovers. Except he was a monk, and held a knife to her throat. His breath mingled with hers. It smelled slightly sweet, like buttered rice.

'Leave them alone.' His tone was fierce. 'I know where you live...'

'Supervisor?'

Palden Oshoe froze.

'Are you all right?'

It was Constable Deshi's voice, tentative, concerned. Lia didn't dare move.

'Supervisor?'

Palden Oshoe turned from Lia and ran.

She put a hand on the wall. Her whole body felt weak.

No time to stop! Go after him!

She pushed away from the wall and forced her legs into a shambling run, yelling to Deshi. 'Get him!'

As she shouted, her strength returned in a rush and she increased her speed, ducking around visitors, swerving past a small knot of startled-looking Western tourists. She rocketed onto the street, Deshi hot on her heels. The daylight seemed harsh and bright after the gloom of the monastery. She looked up and down the alley.

There!

A monk's figure was racing back toward the Jokhang. She tore after it, but she wasn't as fast as Deshi. He accelerated past her, his lithe figure dodging the countless pilgrims, but when he reached the next crossroads he stopped and looked wildly around him. Lia galloped to stand next to him. Together, they scanned the crowds.

There were maroon robes everywhere, but nobody was running. He could be any one of the monks moving along the streets.

Lia cursed.

'Who was he?' Deshi panted. 'What did he want?'

Her breathing began to level but her head was buzzing. She felt a wave of euphoria that she'd survived. 'He warned me off pursuing the Snow Thief. Which seems pretty odd, considering I'm not on the case any more.'

'You're not?' He looked surprised.

'It's closed, remember?'

He looked unconvinced.

'Do you really think I'd risk my life to find the killer of those boys?' Disbelief layered her tone.

He shrugged. 'You're not one to give up. You're a bit like a dog with a bone. Stubborn.'

'I'm not stupid.'

'No,' he agreed. His face was tight. He was still looking around, still searching for her attacker.

'I'm going back to the monastery,' she told him. 'See if anyone knows him.'

'I'll come with you.'

*

She wasn't sure if she wanted Deshi dogging her heels, but she didn't feel she could order him away. Without his intervention, she might be lying on the monastery floor with her throat cut. They began to retrace their steps. He gestured at her throat. When she put her hand there, it came away with a smear of blood. She brought out a tissue and blotted it.

She said, 'What made you follow me?'

He turned his head away. She couldn't read his face. 'I thought that you were still investigating the Snow Thief. I wanted to see what you did next.'

Her heart sank. 'Are you going to report this to Tan?'

'Why should I? I didn't see anything untoward.' This time he met her gaze. 'We were just keeping an eye out for protesters, weren't we?'

She bit her lip. Deshi wasn't her idea of an accomplice. He may have put two of the boys' murders together but he was thick with Zhang and had only got into the police force because – so Commissioner Zhi had told her – a senior officer had owed his father a favour. *Guanxi.*

They approached the monastery door. She paused before they crossed the threshold. 'Why, Deshi?'

The question covered asking why he'd followed her, why he'd rescued her, and why he suddenly appeared to be on her side and approving of her following the case against their superior officer's commands.

He met her gaze straight. 'Because of who you used to be. You used to be a Supervisor *First Class*. You worked on murders all the time. You've worked in Shenzhen and Beijing. You've loads of experience. I want to learn to be a really good cop, like you.'

It was a flattering speech but she didn't trust it, or the man behind it. Tan would have told him to keep an eye on her. Which, she supposed, could be useful if she wanted to send any disinformation back to Tan.

'OK. Follow me. And don't say a word.'

Inside the monastery, everything appeared the same. Same pilgrims, same monks. She walked up to one monk who appeared to have finished his prayers, and introduced herself. He stared at her, unblinking. She said, 'Do you know a monk called Palden Oshoe?'

He looked at her and spread his hands in apology.

She asked the same question in English, but he shook his head. He could speak only Tibetan. He beckoned another monk over. Lia posed her question again, in English.

The monk glanced at Deshi, then back at Lia. He looked baffled. 'Palden Oshoe?'

'Yes. Where can I find him?'

More puzzlement. 'What is it concerning?' His accent was thick, but she could understand him clearly.

'I met him earlier. I'd like to see him again.'

The monk blinked. 'You met him?'

'Yes.'

The monk hesitated before seeming to come to a decision. 'Please.' He inclined his head briefly. 'Wait here. I will fetch him.'

Lia couldn't believe it was going to be so easy, and when the monk returned it was with a man who looked about two hundred years old and was as thin and wizened as a dried vanilla stick.

'This isn't Palden Oshoe,' she said. 'At least, it's not the man I met earlier.'

'I used to be called Palden Oshoe,' the elderly monk told her in passable Mandarin. His eyes were bright with curiosity. 'Until I fell ill.'

At Lia's blank look, he went on. 'In Tibetan culture people sometimes change their names. For example, when someone becomes a monk or nun, they are given a new monastic name. Then there are occasions such as when someone becomes sick and medical treatments do not cure the person. At that time, according to a lama's advice, the sick person may have a name change in order to keep away obstacles and harm. This is what happened to me. My name is now Tsering Passang. I am the Abbot of this monastery. I haven't used my old name in a very long time, perhaps ten years.'

'But someone knew your old name,' she said.

'And borrowed it,' he agreed.

She briefly squeezed her eyes shut. Finding her attacker was going to be almost impossible.

23

'BUT WHY WOULD THIS monk attack a police officer?' The Abbot looked between Deshi and Lia, obviously baffled. They were in his rooms at the top of the monastery, tucked beneath the roof. Bare wooden floors, low beams, simple furnishings. Butter lamps flickered and glowed in every corner.

'It was a warning,' Lia said. 'He wanted me to stop investigating something.'

The Abbot's bright eyes fixed on Lia expectantly.

She glanced at Deshi, knowing she shouldn't say any more. The Snow Thief was still under wraps. What had Myra Kwok said all those weeks ago?

You'll just create a panic.

Deshi cleared his throat. He said, 'It's to do with the unexplained deaths of several Tibetan boys.'

Lia stared at the side of the constable's face. She said, 'Are you sure about this?'

'Boys have died?' The Abbot's face became alarmed. 'What boys? Where? How many?'

'Seventeen that we know of,' Deshi told the Abbot. 'All around the country. The last body was found north-east of Gertse.'

The Abbot's face paled to the colour of mashed rice. He stared at them, expression horrified. He turned to the monk who had accompanied them from the temple and said something. His tone was sharp. The monk raced off.

Lia wasn't sure what to do next. Neither was Deshi. The constable shifted from foot to foot, looking vaguely around the room. The Abbot held up a hand, indicating it wouldn't be long. He had regained his air of calm, but his eyes were crackling with agitation.

Lia took Deshi to one side. 'Do you know what you're doing?' she hissed. She didn't trust him not to be setting her up.

'I want to find the Snow Thief,' he hissed back.

'But Tan's already got Yeshe in custody.'

'Everybody knows Yeshe's innocent.' Deshi's eyes flamed. 'Come on, Supervisor. Don't you want to solve the case?'

'I don't want to die for it,' she snapped. 'It's all right for you, you can switch sides any time by saying you were just keeping an eye on me. It's my head on the block.'

Immediately he backed off. 'Sorry,' he mumbled.

She surveyed him cautiously. Was he really following her to hang on her coat-tails to try and advance his career? Recent experience had taught her not to trust anyone. Least of all a fellow police officer.

The door swung open and a flood of monks entered, about a dozen, aged between thirty and eighty. They settled around the room, restless and fretful, like a group of corralled sheep.

'Please,' the Abbot said, looking at Deshi. 'Repeat what you just said to me. Most of us speak English.'

Deshi looked at Lia, as though he wanted her approval. Lia tried to look into the future and see what effect the information would have. News of the child killer would rip through the community like a tsunami. How long would it take before it broke through to the rest of the country? When would Tan find out the Tibetans knew about the Snow Thief and that he was still at large? That Yeshe was innocent?

Her fingertips tingled. *Ai Ya!* This could be the one thing that would bring the country to the edge of the chasm. Tibetans protesting at Yeshe's execution, the army mowing the protesters down with machine guns, killing monks, nuns and children...

She could see it now and she wanted no part of it.

'No,' she said to Deshi. 'We can't do this.'

His stare seemed to pulse, as though he were begging her to change her mind.

'Let's go.' She jerked her head at the door and, without waiting for him, stalked outside, down the stairs and into the chill evening air.

Deshi caught up with her a minute later. 'Will you make a report of your attack?'

'No.'

'Why not?'

'I'm sure you're intelligent enough to work it out.'

He didn't say any more, just accompanied her back to the station. She wasn't sure what he was thinking when they parted, but she couldn't mistake the look in his eyes, the curl of his lip. Contempt was written all over him.

'Deshi!' she barked.

'What?' Sulky, sullen.

She went up to him and stood close. 'You want to be an investigator?'

He gave a nod.

'A really good investigator?'

Another nod.

'Then think about what and try and work out *why*. What my motivations are. When you think you have the answers, please come and see me. We will sit and have a frank discussion. OK?'

She could almost see the cog turning in his brain. 'I don't understand.'

'And that,' she said, turning on her heel, 'is why you haven't been promoted.'

*

She didn't expect to see Deshi for a while, so she was surprised when he knocked on her office door the next morning. His body language was deferential, his expression abashed. He said, 'I thought you'd want to warn the Tibetans about the killer.'

'I do. But...?'

'The Tibetans will go nuts if they suspect Yeshe is inno-

163

cent. And if he's executed in the sports stadium, they'll riot...We need to have the real Snow Thief behind bars before we make the case general knowledge.'

'Ten out of ten,' she said.

He flushed with pleasure and tried to cover it by scrubbing his hand back and forth over his head, making his hair stick upright like porcupine quills. 'What can I do to help?'

She thought his offer over. He was obviously keen. What harm would it do if she gave him an errand or two?

'The man who attacked me mentioned someone called Goldhawk. It has to be a code name. See if you can track him down. He might be in the Tibetan services. Find out what he does. Where he's based.'

Her attacker had also asked why she was being so unpatriotic. What did that mean? Patriotic to whom? Tibet? China? Or was it an outlandish reference to her *gwailo* appearance?

'If you have time,' she added, 'perhaps you could ask around about my attacker. You saw him. You can describe him. If you could find him, then...' She paused when her phone rang. 'Shan,' she barked.

It was Chen. No hello, no small talk, he didn't even announce himself. He simply said, 'I've found them.'

Her stomach lurched. She turned away from Deshi so the constable couldn't read her face. She bit her lip. She knew she should tell Chen she was no longer on the case, and hang up, but curiosity bit her.

'Where?'

'Mani, Nagqu.'

'Hold on a second.' Lia looked at Deshi. She said, 'If you wouldn't mind, Deshi...'

'Sure.' The constable ducked his head and scuttled outside.

She opened a drawer and pulled out her map. She'd taken it off the wall the day Tan had told her the case was closed. Her eyes widened when she spotted where the village was situated. 'How on earth did you—'

'The officer who reported Mingmar's death heard a rumour and followed it up. His cousin works in Mani. Can you get there?'

'Can't you?'

'Impossible. It's not my prefecture.'

Lia stared at the map, the spread of coloured pins. Could she pretend to take some sick leave and go there? Did she have the guts to do this on her own? And what about the monk and his knife? Would he follow her, and slit her throat like he promised?

Leave the lamas alone.

'I'm off the case,' she said. Her voice was brittle. 'Commissioner Zhi told me.'

'So why call me?' she snapped.

'Because you have integrity.'

A rush of goose bumps chased over her skin. *Integrity*. It was the same word the boy Tashi had used.

'I can't,' she said.

A long silence followed.

'Do you understand?' she added.

'Of course.' His voice was polite, but she sensed the disappointment beneath. He hung up without another word.

24

AT THE END OF the day, Tan dropped into Shan's office. He'd had a word with Deshi and Zhang and was pleased that she appeared to have dropped the Snow Thief case. He hadn't enjoyed bludgeoning her at the committee meeting, but he felt he had no choice but to force her to comply with the simpleton's arrest, especially with Tao Cong there. Tao Cong was from Beijing and had been sent to Lhasa to check up on a rumour that a group of terrorists were going around Tibet enlisting support. Tan had almost felt the blood drain from his head when Tao Cong had told him the reason for his visit.

'You have intel on these subversives?' Tao Cong asked, picking his teeth with a fingernail. 'They're calling themselves the TFG. The Tibet Freedom Group.'

Not wanting to admit he'd never heard of the TFG, Tan said, 'We have intelligence on all known subversives.'

'So where's this lot now?'

He wanted to say, *I haven't got a fucking clue*, but held his tongue. 'I'm not sure we have an exact position for them. I'll check with my team.'

Tao Cong withdrew his fingernail, inspected the piece of debris he'd picked free, and popped it back in his mouth. 'You do that.'

Like Tao Cong, both Jenny Wang and Myra Kwok had heard a vague rumour about the TFG, but that was all.

'Tao Cong says they're travelling around Tibet gathering supporters.' Tan felt like tearing his hair. 'Where did he get his information from?'

'No idea.' This was from Myra Kwok. 'But if it's true, we'd better start looking for them.'

'Agreed.' Tan turned to Jenny, who was fiddling with her pen. 'And you? What do you think?'

'That we'd better increase our surveillance on the subversives we already know about. They're bound to slip up and give something away.'

Tan gave orders for extra officers to be drafted in to help with the extra work. Three days later and to Tan's eternal relief, Tao Cong headed back to Beijing. Before he left for the airport, however, the skinny little piece of excrement had dropped into Tan's office. He said, 'Good work on finding the serial killer, by the way. I wouldn't have wanted that one to have been made public on my watch. I'll let Beijing know that you are doing an exemplary job out here. Well done.'

Tan glowed for the rest of the day, which was why he was headed to see Shan. He wanted to share his good fortune as well as make amends, and ensure she understood that he had no intention of flinging her in jail with the idiot Yeshe, and that he'd been purposely heavy-handed to show Tao Cong he wasn't going to stand for defiance within the ranks.

For no reason he could think of, his stomach gave a twist as he approached her office, which he put down to the bowl of noodles he'd eaten for lunch. Her door was open, but he knocked anyway. His breathing tightened when she called for him to enter.

The second he stepped inside, she rose from behind her steel desk. 'Sir?' she said.

'A little bird tells me you gave Chen the bum's rush today.'

'Yes.' Her voice was cool.

'Very wise,' he said, nodding. 'How about I take you out for dinner? There are some things I'd like to discuss. There's a new restaurant just opened in the Sheraton Hotel I'd like to try.'

'I'm sorry but I'm busy.' She began to close her folders, shut down her computer.

'Come on, Supervisor.' He smiled. 'Even the police need a little time out.'

She paused and looked up, meeting his gaze squarely. Once again, his stomach squeezed.

She said, 'Do you think so?'

'Oh, yes.' Her hair was in a ponytail today, and hung in a long wave down her back. Her small mouth was tense. His gaze travelled to her slender neck. It was the colour of almonds, unblemished and smooth. He longed to stroke it.

'In that case,' she said. 'I'd like to apply for leave.'

Tan blinked. 'But you've barely worked here half a year.'

'I'm tired from working the Snow Thief case.' She continued holding his gaze. Her delicate chin was raised. 'I'm sure you understand.'

She wanted to be rewarded for not pursuing the Snow Thief. If he gave her what she wanted, would she soften towards him?

'You may have a week, starting tomorrow.' He felt magnanimous. He'd earned *mian tzi*. Face.

Something flashed in her eyes. He wasn't sure what it was. Pleasure? Triumph? He found her so hard to read it was beginning to drive him crazy.

'Thank you,' she said.

'I will tell Commissioner Zhi this evening,' Tan said. 'Perhaps you will have dinner with me when you return?'

'Perhaps,' she agreed.

He was filled with satisfaction, anticipation. At last, he was getting somewhere.

He said, 'Enjoy your vacation.'

Oddly, the twisting sensation in his gut didn't ease until he'd gone home and downed two whiskies.

25

IT DIDN'T TAKE LIA long to find a car and driver. Nearly all travel agencies had a variety of guides on offer and after interviewing three, she settled on a young Tibetan fixer-cum-interpreter called Pete. Pete had high cheekbones and was as slim as a bamboo shoot. His eyes were jet black and sparkled with life, making Lia feel every one of her thirty-one years.

'Where do you want to go?' he asked.

Lia stuck her finger on the map pinned to the back of the office door.

He looked bemused. 'Why there?'

'I'm curious to see the countryside.'

She hadn't told him she was a police officer. Just said she was new in town and wanted to play tourist for a while. He gave her an odd look but didn't demur any further, just asked what she needed for the journey. 'Water? Snacks? *Suan mei?* Dried plums? I've got bottles of cola, even managed to get some granola bars off some American tourists. You like granola?'

Not wanting to appear unworldly, Lia said sure, she didn't mind granola, even though she'd never heard of it.

'We've a long way to go,' Pete reminded her. 'We'll need supplies.'

Lia was grateful for these during the three-day journey as the few shops they came across were poorly stocked. It didn't take long before she began to long for Mrs Lily's fabulous steamed *bao*, which she now bought every morning on her way to work, releasing Fang Dongmei from making her breakfast. What to do with Fang Dongmei? When she'd returned home after Tan had given her permission for a vacation, Jian's grandmother had been in the kitchen chopping vegetables. Lia went to stand next to her. She said, 'You've been helping Yeshe.'

The old woman kept chopping as though she hadn't heard.

'Who else knows?' Lia prodded.

Fang Dongmei pushed the cabbage and onions to one side and began on the carrots. 'The guard,' she grunted.

'Anyone else?'

'Anyone who can bribe the guard into telling them.' Fang Dongmei raised her head. 'I read your notes.'

'I guessed.'

'You can't let them kill him.'

It was what she'd said when Jian had been sentenced to death and last week, Lia would have launched an attack. But that was before she realised Fang Dongmei was being eaten by guilt and remorse, and now she let the comment go.

'I'm doing my best.' She reached for a stick of carrot but Fang Dongmei batted away her hand as though she was five years old.

'I read what that police officer said. Supervisor Chen.' Fang Dongmei's eyes were narrowed. 'Do you really think the Snow Thief is a terrorist?'

Lia sank onto the kitchen chair. 'I don't know.' She sighed. 'I just don't know.'

They hadn't said any more, but when Lia came to leave the next morning, Fang Dongmei handed her a small bag filled with goodies, from a packet of sliced candy to a box of dried raisins and another of lotus seeds. There was a pocket notebook and a pen, and a pretty velvet clip for her hair. Each item had been chosen carefully and she smiled when, right at the bottom, she found a furry pink toy mouse with a little label that said it was called *xiǎo*, Tiny.

Now, she yawned and stretched in the Land Cruiser's seat, grateful Pete didn't say much as he drove, but listened to a variety of Western pop music. He seemed to like Abba best, and knew all the words. Tinsel tassels swung from his rear-view mirror. The air was clear and bright, the sky vivid blue. They drove along a gorge, an ice-grey river tumbling below. Lia saw yaks, small flocks of straggly sheep and tiny fields lining the river bank.

In the distance, she caught sight of a monastery clinging to the side of a snowy hillside. A cluster of buildings tumbled from the monastery to the side of a lake. The water was a deep blue beneath the sun, the grasses poking through the snow the colour and texture of straw.

'Nearly there,' Pete said, pointing at the monastery with one hand while negotiating a set of slushy potholes with the other.

As they approached the village, Lia saw a large white tent set near the lake. Gold, blue and red stripes lined its roof and blue designs decorated its walls. 'Who lives there?' she asked Pete.

'It's ceremonial,' he responded. 'Perhaps someone's getting married.'

Aside from the pack of dogs running out to greet them, barking and trying to bite the wheels, the village was empty. No kids playing on the streets, no women gossiping. Just a handful of chickens pecking beneath a stunted shrub.

'Where is everyone?' she said. The place felt oddly deserted.

Pete parked the car next to a low wall. A yak with coloured braids adorning its horns slowly chewed on some straw.

'Wait here.' Pete hopped out and strode towards the nearest cottage, a one-storey stone building with a tin roof covered in rocks to prevent it blowing away. Smoke drifted from a rough chimney in the centre and as she looked further, she saw more smoke spiralling. The village wasn't deserted after all. She watched the dogs disperse, most of them trotting back the way they'd come, for the ceremonial tent.

*

Pete returned in under five minutes, expression anxious. 'Are you OK here for a bit?' he asked. 'I just want to check something, then we'll find somewhere to stay. It won't be here, but at the next village. Is that all right?'

'Sure,' she lied, keeping her expression bland. She had no intention of being palmed off but she didn't want to antagonise him. Not yet, anyway.

A flicker of relief crossed his face. 'Great. I'll be back in a minute.'

Lia turned her head and watched him break into a jog for the ceremonial tent. After he'd vanished inside, she waited a minute or two before deciding to follow him. He'd left the keys in the ignition and although she was a hundred per cent certain nobody was going to steal the Land Cruiser, she couldn't help but pocket the keys, the police officer in her always fastidious.

As she walked, a small black and grey dog tagged along at her heels, tail wagging. She stooped to pet it briefly, scratching it behind the ears. The dog's ears went back, its eyes dreamy. Despite her tension, she smiled. The English apparently loved dogs and she never knew whether her vague affection for them was because she'd taken on being mixed race from a young child as Jian had suggested, or if it was the tiny proportion of her English blood genuinely making itself known.

She paused outside the tent, listening. Three or four male voices were talking animatedly, including Pete's. Not for the first time, Lia wished she spoke Tibetan and as she listened uncomprehendingly, she resolved to start taking lessons. Better late than never, she told herself.

Carefully, she edged around the tent, searching for a fissure to peek through, but the seams were in good order and looked watertight. She ended up where she'd started, at the tent's front door flap, with the little black and grey dog wagging at her feet.

Pete's voice rose, and then another man joined in. A man with an unsteady, frail voice.

Cautiously, she put her hand on the canvas and inched it open, praying nobody would notice. A waft of incense greeted her, and she had to hold her breath, swallowing the sneeze that followed. There was an altar upon which stood burning incense sticks and four photographs of the Dalai Lama. Rows of benches. She counted maybe sixty people. Most were villagers. Two monks and a nun, dressed in maroon robes, sat to one side. A little boy sat in the lap of one of the women, sucking his thumb. He was about five years old and had ruddy cheeks. He was staring at Lia. She put her finger to her lips, *shhh*, but to her dismay, one of the monks turned to see what the boy was staring at and looked directly at her.

Bluff it out.

She smiled and gave a little wave.

The monk barked something angrily. Everyone leaped to their feet and spun round, faces startled.

'Hi,' she said. She kept her smile in place.

Pete was at her side in a flash. 'It's not a good idea, your being here,' he said. 'You must go.'

'What's going on?' she asked. 'What's the ceremony? Can't I watch?'

'No ceremony. They're just...' He took a breath. 'Look, one of their children died. Please, if you wouldn't mind...'

'Where's the body?' she asked.

'Please, go back to the car.'

Lia delved into her jacket's breast pocket and withdrew her police ID card. 'I'm a police officer,' she snapped. 'Now, take me to the body.'

Pete's eyes almost popped from his head. 'What?'

'Just do it.'

'Oh, shit,' he said. He looked faint. 'Shit, *shit*.'

One of the villagers stepped close, expression narrowed. He asked Pete something. Pete gestured at Lia as he replied. The temperature in the tent seemed to drop ten degrees as everyone switched their gaze to her.

'The body,' she said. 'Where is it?'

'There isn't one.' His voice trembled. 'They buried it this morning. Water burial.'

'How did the boy die?'

'How did you know it was a boy?'

'Just tell me.'

Pete ran a hand over his head. 'His neck was broken. Nobody knows how it happened. An accident.'

'What's the boy's name?'

'Chogyal.'

She ran her eyes over the crowd. 'Ask them if they've had any visitors recently.'

She watched them carefully as Pete posed the question. All of them shook their heads. Every single one. Nobody hesitated. Nobody had to think about it. It was an instant, instinctive denial that she didn't trust an inch.

'Tell them I know about the monks.'

'What monks?' His voice was suddenly high-pitched with nerves.

'The monks who stayed here recently.'

He swallowed. 'Nobody's mentioned any monks.'

She stepped close to him, forcing him to look at her. 'That's because they're protecting them. And I want to know why.'

'They've had no visitors. No monks.' He took a step back. 'I swear it.'

'I'm a police officer, Pete.' She held his gaze unwaveringly. Put steel into her tone. 'Please, don't forget it.'

His skin turned pale.

'Where are they? The monks that were here?'

'I don't know what you're talking about.' He was sweating and fearful, much easier to read than the stone faces of the monks and villagers. Although part of her felt sorry for him – he'd obviously been dragged into something he couldn't get out of – she was determined to break him down.

First things first.

'Chogyal isn't the first child to die like this,' she told him, and at the same time – finally – she decided the moment had come to be more open about the situation. Keeping quiet had done nothing to help catch the killer. Perhaps if the villagers knew how serious the situation was, one of them might give her some information she could use.

'Other children have been killed the same way. Initially we thought their deaths were accidental, but we now know this isn't true. They've been murdered.'

Pete swayed and for a moment she thought he might faint.

'Tell them,' she said harshly.

He worked his mouth briefly before he spoke. One of the monks – she didn't see who – gave a little cry but was immediately hushed. There was a burst of chatter, high-pitched, almost hysterical, and then a man barked an order. Everyone fell silent.

'Who spoke just then?' she asked Pete.

'I don't know.' He wouldn't meet her eye.

'Please, continue translating for me.'

'OK.'

'Since this is a murder enquiry, anyone who withholds information will be prosecuted for obstructing justice. Are we clear?'

Nobody moved, but Pete said quietly, 'They understand.'

Lia brought out her notebook. She wrote down the name of the boy, how old he was – six – but each time she asked about the monks, where they might be travelling to next, she was met with a stony silence. She wanted to ring Chen, but there was no signal. She'd have to wait until she neared a mast, although where that might be was anyone's guess.

Lia trawled the village with Pete. She studied Chogyal's home and interviewed his parents. She scoured the area where his body had been discovered, but found no clues. She searched the area for tracks, trying to see any evidence of a party of monks having visited, but it was impossible thanks to a recent snow fall.

Back in the tent, the villagers were animated and noisy, almost frenzied. 'What's going on?' she asked Pete.

He didn't answer but went to one of the monks and asked a question. The monk answered, jerking his chin at Lia as he spoke. Pete nodded. He came back to Lia and said, 'They won't tell me anything because I'm with you. They don't trust me.'

She watched the throng quietly. After half an hour of discussion, arguments and finally, what appeared to be complete agreement, one monk left the tent. Lia followed at a distance. He walked up the hill to the monastery where he climbed into an old Mitsubishi four-wheel-drive, started it, and without once looking at her, drove back down the hill and parked outside the tent where everyone now stood, milling around. The remaining monk and nun, both young, in their twenties or so, jumped into the car and before Lia could find Pete to ask what was going on, drove off.

*

Lia finally tracked Pete down to the rear of the tent. He was standing alone, picking at his fingernails, expression disconsolate.

'Where did the two monks and nun go?' she asked.

'Nobody will tell me.'

They left two hours later, and as the village receded into the distance, the Land Cruiser entered an icy plain with no visible horizon, stretching endlessly. Through the acres of light, Lia felt as though the Snow Thief could scent her trail. She imagined facing him and for a moment she was filled with a calm sense that where she was right now, at this time, was her destiny. As she surrendered to the sensation, the car lurched through muddy potholes, slowly hastening across the vast, empty plateau.

26

'LOOK, I'M SORRY I didn't tell you I was with the police.' Lia decided to play the nice cop role. 'I didn't want to spook you.'

Pete grimaced. 'Was the boy really murdered?'

'Yes.'

'You said he wasn't the first.'

'Sadly, that is true.'

He licked his lips. 'How many?'

'I can't tell you that. But let's just say too many.' She rested her head against the window and watched her breath steam the glass. 'The villagers have information, don't they?'

Pete remained silent.

'I want to interview the monks that visited the village. They might know something that could help.'

More silence.

'Will you help me?'

He swallowed. 'I'm sorry.'

She let it go for the moment and turned her attention to study the map, trying to work out where the monks would be if they were travelling as she thought, in a roughly clockwise direction. She made two calculations. One should they be walking, the second in case they had a car. Eventually, she asked Pete to head for Tali, a town which appeared roughly situated between her two estimates.

Lia spent the journey alternately dreaming of returning to Shenzhen and her old job and chatting to Pete. Initially it had been to try and put him at ease but as they talked, she realised she'd fallen on not just a good driver, but a fountain of knowledge on Tibet and its culture. Knowledge was power, and never more than when hunting a killer, so she started narrowing down her questions. Pete had a degree in foreign languages – he spoke French and German as well as English – but more importantly two of his brothers were monks.

'It used to be good to be a monk,' Pete told her. 'It meant you were looked after, educated, and always had something to eat.'

'And now?'

'They're barely tolerated...' He trailed off, his expression turning anxious.

'Please speak freely with me,' Lia said. 'I swear anything you say will remain between us, OK? I'm not on a religious witch hunt. I'm after a murderer and without your help, we may never catch him.'

Pete swallowed. 'OK.'

'You were saying?' Lia prompted.

He gave her a potted history of Tibetan Buddhism, the Dalai Lama's escape to India, the Chinese government's intolerance of him. Nothing she didn't already know. It was only when he began to appear uncomfortable with the conversation that she came alert.

'Er...well, the Chinese...I mean, your government...' He coughed uncomfortably.

'Go on,' she encouraged him.

'Um...they don't care for Tibetan Buddhism.' He paused and she glanced at him. He was holding his breath.

'I'm aware of that,' she said neutrally. 'And?'

'They, er...would like to see it gone. I mean *really* gone. Destroyed.'

'I see.'

He exhaled in a rush. 'You've heard about the Panchen Lama?'

She had, but shook her head, wanting to hear what Pete would say.

'He's the second-highest-ranking lama after the Dalai Lama and the only person who can proclaim the next Dalai Lama...'

'Proclaim?'

'When the Dalai Lama dies,' Pete explained, 'he is reincarnated. The Panchen Lama is the only person who knows who he has been reincarnated as.'

Lia turned her head to look at a chorten, hanging with colourful prayer flags. 'An important role,' she remarked.

'Yes. The trouble is that the Panchen Lama no longer exists.'

Lia fell silent. She already knew about the controversy, how when the Dalai Lama recognised the new Panchen Lama in the six-year-old boy Gedhun Choekyi Nyima over twenty years ago, the authorities immediately kidnapped him. Nothing had been heard of Gedhun or his family since and most people assumed he'd been murdered. Later the same year, the Office of Religious Affairs in Beijing chose another six-year-old boy, Gyaincain Norbu, as the Panchen Lama, claiming special ritual reasons. But everyone in Tibet knew Gyaincain wasn't the real Panchen Lama and to them he was nothing but a puppet, chosen by the Chinese government.

'What happens when the current Dalai Lama dies?' Lia asked.

Pete pulled a face. 'Since the real Panchen Lama is dead...who knows?'

Getting rid of the Panchen Lama had been a stroke of genius by a government that wanted to destroy Tibetan Buddhism from the inside out, Lia saw. Without him, the certainty of the next Dalai Lama was in doubt, along with Tibet's spiritual culture and way of life.

*

Tali was a shabby place with potholes in its streets and packed dirt for pavements. Not a single building had glass in its windows, just cardboard or sacking hammered into place. Despite its air of poverty, people were busy, their faces animated. Aside from two soldiers on the town's boundaries, she hadn't seen any Chinese. Everyone appeared to be Tibetan. She guessed the Han and Hui immigrants preferred the cities and the luxuries that came with them, like running water and central heating.

Pete pulled in at a petrol station and asked the attendant to fill their tank. Lia joined Pete and the attendant who were chatting. 'Could you ask him if he's heard of a group of monks travelling through the area?'

Pete posed the question for her. The petrol attendant didn't say yes, but he didn't say no either. He sucked his teeth and shrugged his shoulders and studied Lia.

'Tell him I mean no harm,' she added. 'I just want to talk to them, that's all. I have a message of vital importance.'

Pete's tone turned more urgent. He gesticulated fervently. The attendant gave a nod, but remained silent. He finished filling up the car. Lia brought out a roll of notes and paid the man. Finally, he walked away.

'He doesn't want to get involved,' Pete said. 'Never mind. I'll keep asking. Are you OK to spend the night here? I'll find us a decent guest house somewhere.'

'Fine,' she agreed. She checked her phone but she still didn't have a signal. It was like being in the dark ages out here. She typed a message to Chen anyway, in readiness. She was so absorbed that she didn't notice the police car driving past, or one of the men grabbing a radio off the dash when he sighted her.

*

Lama Sonam listened to the news with increasing concern. A Chinese police officer was trying to find them?

'We should see her,' said Dawa Rinpoche.

Although the High Lama's voice was weak, he was recovering remarkably quickly. His chest infection had cleared and his breathing was now steady and free of phlegm. He was now only hampered by old age. They had departed the last village two days ago, with Dawa Rinpoche clinging onto one of the ponies. The police officer was, apparently, in Tali, where Tenzin had picked up supplies that afternoon.

Questions pounded Lama Sonam's brain. How did the police officer know about them? She was alone, apparently, aside from a Tibetan driver. What did she want? How had she known where to find them? Had they been spotted from the air? He felt dizzy, all of a sudden, and he realised immediately they had to see her in order to find out what was going on, and how much danger they were in.

'She says she means no harm,' Dawa Rinpoche continued. 'She says her message is of vital importance.'

They were in their tent, ponies tied outside, camped in the shadow of a steep and rocky hillside. One lama was lighting a fire with flint and tinder, using dried yak dung, while another was mixing tea and tsampa. A third monk was preparing their sleeping pallets. No matter how busy they appeared, Lama Sonam knew everyone was listening.

'We can't afford to delay,' Tenzin said anxiously. 'Every day counts.'

'Why are we here?' Dawa Rinpoche's voice cracked like a whip.

Tenzin flinched, looked at the ground. 'Because the Karmapa sent us.'

'Precisely. Let me remind you how important this is. Since the Karmapa is emerging as favourite to front the Tibetan freedom movement...'

Feeling sorry for Tenzin – the monk only wanted to complete the mission successfully – Lama Sonam tuned out the lecture. He'd heard it all before, how the Karmapa – the third-highest-ranking lama in Tibetan Buddhism – was recognised not just inside Tibet, but was the only high lama acceptable both to Tibetans and to Beijing. Despite this fact, however, the Karmapa had shocked everyone by fleeing on horseback to India, where he still resided.

'We must trust His Holiness,' Dawa Rinpoche said. 'We must keep faith. Lama Sonam?'

Immediately he straightened. 'Yes, brother?'

'I want you to find this police officer and bring her to me.'

Tenzin scrunched up his face. He made to say something, then obviously thought better of it.

'Tenzin?' Lama Sonam. 'What is it?'

'What if it's a trap?' the monk said fretfully. 'What if she brings more police behind her? Army troops?'

'You see nothing but conspiracies,' Dawa Rinpoche said with a smile. 'But you're right. You will drive Lama Sonam to Tali, and you will both take every precaution.'

Tenzin leaned back but the apprehension didn't leave his face. Lama Sonam felt the same way. His heart was filled with fear.

27

NIMA CHODEN HAD STRUCK camp five kilometres from where the monks were settled. He'd erected the tent below a tall fissure of rock where Rinzen had lit a fire. Sharmar was now making tea and the same old dull and dreary tsampa. Nourishing, sustaining, and as inspiring as eating a plate of boiled stones. It wouldn't be long now before he was home, and able to eat what he wanted, when he liked.

Trying to ignore his groaning, starving stomach, Nima brought out his satellite phone and made his daily call, his daily report. As usual, his controller didn't say hello, or give any greeting. Just barked, 'Go ahead.'

'We had some trouble earlier today,' he said. 'But it's contained.'

'What kind of trouble?'

'Two monks and a nun from Mani,' he said. 'In a Mitsubishi four-wheel-drive. They had to be eliminated.'

'Why?' The voice turned tight.

'They were going to warn the group.'

'Ah. In that case, good work.'

The sat phone crackled and Nima glanced up, hoping the satellite wasn't going to vanish out of range. 'Look, I'd better—'

'We have another problem.' The voice cut across him. 'A police officer has arrived in Tali. She is looking for the group. She wants to talk to them. We cannot afford for her to meet them. Deal with her.'

'A police officer?' He didn't like that. It might backfire horribly on them later.

'Yes. She's a troublemaker. Her removal is vital to our cause.'

'But if she's with the police, isn't she——'

'If you argue one more time,' the voice hissed, 'I will make sure you spend the rest of your wretched life in one of the gulags on the Mongolian border. Your family will never make the journey to visit you because they won't know you're there and you will die alone and unwanted and in total misery.'

Fuck, he thought. How much snake bile did you ingest today?

'Call me when the job's done.'

Click.

His controller was gone.

Nima turned the sat phone around in his hand. He didn't want to kill a police officer, but it didn't look as though he had any choice. Anxious, uncertain, he decided to call Goldhawk. He'd know what to do. Nima checked his watch. He couldn't call Goldhawk for another hour. He tucked the sat phone into his backpack. Then he turned to his rifle and although he'd already cleaned it thoroughly after the previous shooting, he cleaned it again. A soldier couldn't afford not to look after his kit.

28

LIA WAS DREAMING SHE was a child again. She'd been running around, playing with her friends all day, and was hungry. Out of nowhere, a man appeared. He had a kind face, and gentle eyes. He looked nice. He offered to share his chocolate with her. Although her parents had told her never to accept sweets from strangers, Lia began to follow him towards the park...

She awoke with a start. It was dark. Not a pinprick of light. Not a sound. Where was she? She could be in a tomb for all the sensory information she was receiving. Cautiously, she moved her hands and feet to discover she was in a bed, alone. But where? She lay there, heart thudding, trying to work it out. Then she took in the chill, the roughness of the blanket and her memory came back in a rush. She was in a guest house, in Tali.

'Don't be scared,' someone whispered softly. A man. In her room. 'I mean you no harm.'

Lia sat bolt upright in bed. 'Who are you?' Her voice echoed and at the same time, her mind filled with a picture of the guest house room; bare of anything except the single iron bed and chipboard bedside table.

'My name is Lama Sonam. Please don't be frightened.'

Lia fumbled to find her torch on the bedside table but simply managed to knock everything onto the floor with a clatter. A sharp scratching sounded and suddenly a yellow light flared. Standing in the corner of her room was a tall man in a maroon robe. He was holding a match.

'I don't want to turn on the light,' he whispered. 'I didn't want to wake anyone.'

As the match began to splutter, Lia slid out of bed and picked up her phone, switched on the torch. It cast a strong white beam across the room. They stood looking at each other, the monk with a domed, shaven head and sombre robes, and Lia in a baggy fleece, tracksuit pants and socks.

'Why are you here?' the lama said.

She looked at him squarely. 'I want to speak to a group of monks travelling around Tibet. They started in Lhasa, moved west to Xigatsê Prefecture before turning north-west into Ngari. They are continuing clockwise from Lhasa.'

Lia felt the lama's attention sharpen. 'How many people know this?'

She thought of Commissioner Zhi, Supervisor Chen and Constable Deshi. The Abbot and his band of merry monks at the Meru Nyingba Monastery. She said, 'Quite a few.'

'I see.' He raised a hand briefly to cover his face. 'And why is it you want to speak to us?'

Her pulse jumped. He'd said *us*. He was one of the monks she wanted. Pushing her feet into her boots she went and stood in front of him, so she could watch his face, study every flicker of expression when she spoke.

'Wherever your group has been over the past weeks,' she said carefully, 'little boys have been murdered. So far seventeen have died but there may be more. Their necks have been broken, much like someone wringing a chicken's neck.'

She saw the blood leave the lama's face so fast she thought he might faint.

She put out a hand. 'Are you all right?'

'No,' he whispered. He closed his eyes. A tear leaked down his leathery cheek. 'Oh, no.'

'I'm sorry.'

He remained still for another minute. Finally, he opened his eyes. Brushed aside his tears and looked into her face. His expression was ineffably sad. 'I had a suspicion... but I had no idea he was killing all those boys.'

'You know who it is?' Lia was suddenly electrified. 'Who? Why? What makes him kill them?'

'Do you know why we are travelling around Tibet?'

Lia shook her head.

'The Dalai Lama——' he began and then stopped. He swallowed audibly. Again, he looked at her, then away. Softly, he said, as though to himself, 'Can I trust you?'

She wasn't sure how to answer. She was about to open her mouth to say, *absolutely*, but he seemed to come to an inner decision because he said, 'I think I have to.' He gave a sad smile. 'You see, His Holiness is coming to the end of his age. When he dies, he will be reincarnated. The Panchen Lama is the only person who can proclaim his successor...'

'But the Panchen Lama is dead,' said Lia, impatient to get back to the subject of the killer. 'He was kidnapped in 1995, probably murdered.'

The lama gave a twisted smile. 'The Panchen Lama,' he said, 'is very much alive.'

Lia blinked.

'Gedhun Choekyi Nyima was held in jail after his kidnapping, at a secret location. Unknown to us, he died of septicaemia of the heart roughly five years ago. We only found this out recently, thanks to a spy who has just returned home, to Lhasa.'

'So when you say he's alive...'

'I mean his reincarnation has already been born. We don't know when this happened, we just know he's a small boy between five and six years old, and although he doesn't know it yet, he is waiting for us to find him. Which is why we are touring Tibet. The Karmapa wants us to find him and keep him protected, so when the Dalai Lama dies, he can announce his successor.'

Suōyōu de shén. By all the gods. No wonder the monks wanted their journey kept secret. They weren't just protecting a small boy, but their entire culture.

'So,' he said softly. 'One of us is killing every boy we test to make sure that when we return to Lhasa in order to make our decision, not one will be alive.'

'You haven't found the Panchen Lama yet?'

'I didn't say that.'

'He's not one of the dead boys, is he?'

'No. As I said before, he's very much alive. I would know it —' he tapped his heart with his knuckles '— if he died.'

Lia was stunned. 'You know who he is?'

'Yes.'

'Who?'

He ignored her question, saying, 'Please, speak to no one of this. Not until we see Dawa Rinpoche. He is one of our highest lamas. He needs to hear what you have to say. Then we can decide what to do.'

Lia frowned. 'If you know who the next Panchen Lama is, why are you continuing your search? Why didn't you proclaim him when you found him?'

'I thought it a wise move to keep him hidden until I knew for certain he would be safe. But that was before you told me about the boys' deaths.' He straightened, stood tall. 'Now, we must go and see Dawa Rinpoche.'

Lia grabbed her down coat and scarf, gloves and woollen hat. 'Where is he?'

'Not far away, but we must be quick and we must be quiet. It is vital we do this in secret. After your meeting, I will bring you back here. Before we go, may I suggest you leave a note for your driver, in case he sees you're gone and is worried.'

Tearing a piece of paper from her pocket notebook, Lia did as he said before following the lama out of the room, and down the corridor. Where she needed the torch to find her way, the lama seemed to do it by instinct. It was as though he had internal radar — like a bat — that enabled him to unerringly identify objects, walls and doors in the dark.

Outside, the buildings were lit a ghostly grey by a single street lamp. It was cloudy, no stars, and cold. Lia shivered, zipping her down jacket up to her chin and slipping on her sheepskin-lined gloves. Lama Sonam strode out, managing to barely make a whisper of noise while Lia tripped and stumbled over stones behind him. They didn't walk for long, covering less than a quarter of a mile, when the lama paused beside what looked like an old army jeep. Another monk sat in the driver's seat.

'This is Tenzin,' Lama Sonam said. 'He will drive us.'

The monk wasn't particularly tall but he was muscular, his fists large and his wrists strong. Like Lama Sonam, he wore a maroon robe and his head was shaven. Tenzin gave her a nod and she nodded back. Tenzin said something in Tibetan to Lama Sonam which the lama ignored. Tenzin repeated it. The lama didn't respond. The atmosphere became peculiarly tense and Lia looked between them.

'Problem?' she said.

'No problem,' Lama Sonam said blithely. 'Tenzin wants to continue a discussion we were having earlier, about what he was going to be in his next life. It could be anything from a humble worker bee to a mosquito, who knows?' He beamed at Tenzin. 'I know he'd prefer to be something big and brave, like a bear, but reincarnation doesn't work like that, as he well knows.'

A strange look went over the monk's face as though he'd eaten something rotten and he jerked his head aside, fixing his gaze dead ahead.

Still smiling, Lama Sonam climbed into the rear of the vehicle, letting Lia take the passenger seat. She turned to buckle up, but there was no seatbelt. With a clattering roar, the jeep started, and Tenzin rammed the stick into first with a loud crunch, and pulled away. It didn't take long to get to the outskirts of town with no traffic, no chickens or children to slow them. Lia tried to keep her sense of direction once they were in open country, but when the monk turned the jeep off the road and onto dirt trails, switching course as they climbed into the mountains, without any stars or a moon Lia found it impossible. Which was, she supposed, the point. The monks were travelling clandestinely after all. They wouldn't want a stranger knowing their precise whereabouts.

*

They drove for an hour before Lia turned to look at Lama Sonam. 'I thought you said it wasn't far?'

'It isn't.'

He obviously had a different time clock than her, Lia thought sourly. The jeep had no heating and she was freezing. The lama didn't seem to notice the cold and was chanting something monotonous but soothing beneath his breath. Gradually, Lia nodded off, coming to with a jerk whenever they hit a particularly large pothole or Tenzin veered around a rock. At one point, Lia thought she could see a sliver of silver on the horizon, but then it vanished. The next time she awoke, the sliver was a streak of pale blue and the sun began to rise.

She glanced at the lama. They'd practically driven through the night and he thought it wasn't far?

'Nearly there,' said Lama Sonam as though he'd heard her thoughts. He spoke something in Tibetan to Tenzin, who slowed the car to a stop and switched off the engine. 'We'll walk the rest of the way.'

Lia clambered outside. Her limbs were stiff and cold and she stamped the ground, trying to get the blood moving through her muscles.

'Where are we?'

'No matter,' the lama responded. 'But we must get going. We have much walking to do.'

Alarmed, Lia said, 'How much?' If *not far* meant driving a hundred kilometres or so, what would *much walking* mean?

'Perhaps two hours.'

She glanced at her watch. If he was going to return her to Tali today, she'd wouldn't be back until late. She was glad the lama had suggested she leave a note for Pete. Stretching her arms skywards, she yawned. It was a beautiful day, the air crisp and as clear as crystal. Dropping her arms, she crunched her way to the front of the jeep. 'Is this your vehicle?' she asked Lama Sonam.

'I borrowed it.'

Lia looked around. She couldn't see any habitation, just acres of undulating hillsides, covered in rocks, ice and snow. 'From where?'

'Not far.'

Another query popped into her mind. 'How come you speak such good Mandarin?'

'I was taught by one of your people when I was a child. It was considered important, vital even.' He sighed. 'Now, I know why.'

'Do you all speak Mandarin?' She was eyeing Tenzin who was staring past them.

'Some of us, but not as well as me.'

'And Tenzin?'

'I taught him myself.'

The lama began to pick his way along a narrow, stony path, putting a halt to further conversation. Tenzin fell in behind, with Lia bringing up the rear. She looked over the valley below, littered with great boulders, poking through the snow like mountain tops through cloud. She felt oddly removed from reality and had to remind herself why she was there. Remind herself of Yeshe, broken and battered and sitting in jail, and of the boys who had died. She slid a sideways glance at the lama. Could he be the Snow Thief? Her instinct said no. What about Tenzin? The silent monk with the big hands and thick neck muscles? He'd certainly be strong enough. Lia forged on, climbing after the monks deep into the mountains. Soon she was warm enough to shed her hat and gloves, and open her jacket wide.

A stone clattered, rolled over the edge and bounced wildly before plunging down. She didn't hear it hit the bottom.

*

They walked for over an hour before Tenzin called a halt, needing to relieve himself. He stalked away and Lia took the opportunity to urinate behind a gigantic boulder, and although she knew it was natural she couldn't help her intense feeling of embarrassment that the monks knew what she was doing.

She switched on her phone. No signal. The nearest mast had to be dozens of kilometres away but she couldn't help checking.

As they walked, Lia asked Lama Sonam how they chose which boys to test.

'To start the search, High Lamas may have a vision or dream,' he told her. 'They often meditate, and wait for a sign to show where to search. If the Panchen Lama had been cremated here, for example, we would watch the direction of the smoke to show us the direction of rebirth. However, the visions this time have been muddled, because we don't know where the Panchen Lama died. Lamas throughout Tibet have been searching for his reincarnation and you could say we are working off a shortlist.' He gave a dry chuckle.

'How do you test them?'

'There is a secret set of criteria. But the main test consists of presenting the boy with a number of items to see if he can select those which belonged to the previous Panchen Lama.'

They continued to walk until at last, they broached a mighty rock face, and started walking downhill. The path narrowed into little more than a goat track. Lia put her hand on the rock face on her left, to steady herself. She didn't dare look at the dizzying drop on her right. She was skirting a boulder carefully, petrified of losing her footing, when she heard a distinctive *crack*, like a slate tile being splintered. To her disbelief, she saw the rock above her hand had chipped. Distantly, she heard an echo. The report of a rifle.

'Shooting!' she yelled. 'Someone's shooting...'

Crack. Another report.

She didn't see where the next bullet went. She was diving for the path, skidding onto her hip, scraping her wrists as she flattened herself, trying to make herself as small as possible while clinging onto the rock face.

Tenzin shouted, 'Lama Sonam! Get down!'

Ahead there was a blur of maroon robes. She saw Tenzin trying to shield the lama, who was already on the ground. She couldn't see if he was hurt or just trying to protect himself.

Crack.

Lia felt something tug her coat. She spun aside. Panic seared her. Had she been shot? She grabbed her upper arm and at the same time realised she was still moving – *towards the edge* – her boots slipping and skidding on the loose shale.

Arms and legs flailing in fright she tried to scramble back up the path but the stones and gravel rolled and shifted beneath her body, carrying her straight for the edge as though she was on an assembly line.

Mā de. Oh, shit.

Desperately she tried to scramble backwards. Stones clattered around her, bouncing past, dropping into thin air.

Lama Sonam was on his feet. Tenzin was hurrying him away, around the corner.

'Tenzin!' she yelled.

He didn't seem to hear her.

'Tenzin! Help!'

Both monks vanished around the rock face.

She continued sliding towards the edge.

She scrabbled desperately for a hold, but the stones were loose. She kicked her feet but there were no footholds.

Her feet slid over the edge, flippered thin air.

'Help!' she screamed.

She was going to die. She was going to plunge over the edge and her body was going to break on the boulders below, her bones shatter into a thousand pieces.

'Supervisor!' Tenzin shouted.

The monk burst into view. Robe flapping, he reached down for her.

'Your hand!'

She couldn't reach. She clawed at a rock. It came away beneath her fingers.

Tenzin bent over and grabbed Lia's collar. Immediately she stopped moving towards the edge. She kicked the air, trying to find the path. Tenzin pulled her upwards. He grunted with the effort.

Lia's foot caught on a rock. She pushed against it but it crumbled. She slid back.

She could hear the monk's breath rasping in his throat. The rustle of his robe. The scratch of stones.

Tenzin heaved, got a hand beneath her armpit. Inch by inch, he dragged her to the centre of the path. She wriggled away from the edge, clutched the wall. She was trembling head to toe.

'Shit,' she said. 'Shit.'

Tenzin didn't wait to see if she was OK. He got to his feet and charged back down the path.

She looked at the sheer fall in front of her, the thousands of feet plunging into the valley. She felt a knot of nausea rise into her throat. She realised she was in the grip of pure fear.

Mustn't remain here like a sitting duck, she told herself.

Sweating, whimpering beneath her breath, Lia forced herself to move.

She didn't have the courage, let alone the strength, to get to her feet, and eased herself down the path on her hands and knees, making sure her centre of gravity was low, clinging to every notch, every cranny of rock, terrified she might start slipping again.

She hadn't heard any more shots.

Had the gunman gone?

Her mouth was dry, her heart galloping as she cautiously

eased herself around the corner. To her relief the path broadened and flattened out, turning away from the cliff edge. She found Tenzin and Lama Sonam twenty metres on, sheltered behind a jumble of boulders.

Lama Sonam lay crumpled on the ground. He lay facing Lia, eyes wide. Tenzin was crouched over him. His dark eyes were brimming with pain and bewilderment.

Shock whipped through her when she saw the blood coming from the lama's mouth and trickling down his chin.

Tenzin's entire body was trembling, his face white. 'He's been shot.'

Lama Sonam's breathing was laboured. More blood bubbled from his lips.

Lia clenched her teeth together but they wouldn't stop chattering. She couldn't believe this was happening.

Tenzin reached for Lama Sonam, then snatched his hand away. 'I don't know what to do.' He sent a desperate look at Lia. 'Do you?'

Lia quickly knelt beside the lama. She tried to see where he'd been shot. From the blood in his mouth, it could be a gut shot, but then she took in the bubbles. His lungs...

She bent close, her fingers busily running over his robe, trying to find where he'd been wounded. If she could put enough pressure on the wound, maybe she could stop the bleeding, but if he'd been injured internally...

'Lia,' Lama Sonam's voice was so faint, she thought she'd imagined it.

She hadn't realised he knew her name. 'Yes?'

Laboriously, he reached up as though to touch her face.

'Closer,' he whispered. 'I must tell you...'

Lia put her ear next to his lips.

'Lobsang Jampo.' The name was like a breath of wind against her cheek, crystal clear. 'The boy's name is...Lobsang Jampo.'

She reared back, startled.

'What's he saying?' Tenzin said.

Lia ignored the monk. She was transfixed by the expression in Lama Sonam's eyes; fierce and urgent. She pushed her ear to his lips once more to hear his next words. 'Tell no one. Protect him. I beg you.'

'He's dying, isn't he? Can't you save him? He's my teacher. He's like my *father*.' A sound of pain erupted from Tenzin's throat. Sweat formed on his forehead.

Lama Sonam's body suddenly stiffened. His brown eyes were burning into Lia's but she could see the colour begin to dim, turn cloudy.

Ai Ya! she thought in horror. He's going to die!

The clouds in his eyes increased but he didn't drop his gaze from Lia's until at last his body slumped, went limp.

Tenzin's facial muscles contorted. He raised his face and a terrible, black animal roar of rage and grief tore from his chest. Crumpling to his knees, he cradled the lama's head as he wept.

Lia cautiously returned to the corner of the cliff face and dropped to her stomach, peering around the mountainside, looking for any evidence of the gunman. Nothing moved. Not even a bird.

She returned to where Lama Sonam lay and remained on one side, leaving Tenzin alone. When he began to gather himself, she said, 'What shall we do?'

Without warning, the monk rose and picked up the lama's body, hefting it over one shoulder. He made it look effortless, which Lia later put down to shock and adrenaline.

'We go to camp. You see Dawa Rinpoche,' said Tenzin.

Tenzin didn't look at Lia or say another word until he'd gently laid the body of his teacher beside the fire in the lama's tent almost as though he hoped it might warm him.

29

As Lia understood it, 'lama' was an honorific title conferred on a monk or nun who had reached a level of spiritual attainment and authority to teach — they were the pinnacle of enlightenment. There were five in the tent that she was introduced to, and how they'd travelled so far in such tough conditions was testament to their belief as well as their determination. Aside from Tenzin and three further monks, they were all in their sixties and seventies and although the eldest, Dawa Rinpoche, was over eighty, he was a stringy old bird with a grip like iron and eyes as bright and enquiring as a cockerel's.

'Lama Sonam was shot?' Dawa Rinpoche didn't sound surprised or disbelieving. His tone was impressively neutral considering what had happened.

'Yes.'

Lia sat with Tenzin in front of the High Lama. They spoke in Mandarin and although the remainder of the group appeared to be listening, there was virtually no reaction to the conversation, making her wonder if any of them could understand what was being said.

'Do you have any idea who by?' Again, he showed nothing but a seemingly genuine sense of puzzled curiosity.

Lia was tired and confused. She'd been shot at and nearly plunged to her death. A man had died looking into her eyes. He'd honoured her immeasurably by speaking his last words to her. She hadn't known him long, but she'd liked Lama Sonam. She'd joined him unerringly in the 'borrowed' jeep. She'd felt safe with him. Protected. She was sad he was dead.

'No.' She spoke honestly.

Dawa Rinpoche nodded. 'I see.' He turned his gaze upon

Tenzin. 'You said Lama Sonam spoke to the Supervisor before he died?'

'Yes.'

Lia's skin grew taut. She had already explained about the boy murders, that it seemed that someone was killing every boy the lamas had tested in order to destroy the new Panchen Lama, but she hadn't told anyone about Lobsang Jampo and Lama Sonam saying *tell no one*. She needed time on her own to absorb what had happened before she decided what to do with the lama's final words. He'd begged her to protect the boy. If he thought Lobsang Jampo was the next Panchen Lama, then shouldn't she tell these monks? After all, they were looking for him.

Tell no one.

She studied the lamas and monks. Was one of them the boy killer? Was that why Lama Sonam had kept Lobsang Jampo secret? Who was the shooter? Why had they killed Lama Sonam? Her head began to ache. She didn't understand any of it.

'What did Lama Sonam say?' Dawa Rinpoche looked at Lia.

'I didn't understand what he said,' she lied. 'He was dying. His words were unintelligible. Sorry.'

Dawa Rinpoche sighed. He resettled his robe in his lap, his gaze distant. He said, 'What will you do now?'

'Report his death to the police. Try and find who shot him, and why. Everything appears to be connected. The boys' murders, Lama Sonam's death...' She told him about Yeshe, suffering in jail and accused of the boys' murder. 'He's going to be executed in three weeks' time.'

Dawa Rinpoche sucked in his breath. 'How will you find the killer? They must be stopped.'

'Do you think whoever killed Lama Sonam, killed the boys?'

'It's possible.'

'Did any of your group –' she gestured at the monks and lamas around them '– leave camp this morning?'

'Just Lama Sonam and Tenzin. Everyone was here, waiting for you.'

'Nobody went out for an hour? Or for longer?'

'No.' He shook his head. 'We were all here, all day.'

'Do any of you carry arms? A rifle?'

'No.'

Lia had slipped easily into investigative mode but all she learned by questioning Dawa Rinpoche was that the group was tired of travelling and longing to return to their various monasteries when they'd completed their mission. Finally, she wound up by saying, 'I will come back tomorrow with a team of experts. We'll try and find traces of the gunman, maybe track him down. I'll need to take Lama Sonam's body to be autopsied.'

Dawa Rinpoche shook his head. 'I cannot allow that.'

'It's the law.'

He mulled this over for a while then gave a sigh. 'We really cannot waste time. You understand how important this search is to us?'

'Yes.' She nodded.

'Then I will trust you to do your job and you will leave us to continue travelling.'

'I will return with a team tomorrow.' She was firm. She wasn't going to let them go wandering off without a full investigation into the lama's murder.

For a moment his wrinkles deepened. 'I see.'

There was an awkward pause.

'Can I ask you to keep our mission secret?' Dawa Rinpoche asked. 'Not tell the authorities about our mission?'

'I'm not sure I can do that.'

'Just for a few weeks. Three at best.'

'But Yeshe's due to be exected in three weeks!' Lia's exasperation rose. 'I need to find the killer before then.'

'Yes, I understand.' His gaze turned inward. He remained silent for a while. Finally, he sighed. 'Tenzin will drive you to Tali tomorrow. We will wait here for your return.' Dawa Rinpoche clapped his hands. Two monks who had been tucked in the corner, playing some sort of game with pebbles, sprang to their feet and came over. 'Prepare a bed for our guest.'

'I'm sorry, but I must get back,' she protested.

'It is now dark.' He looked shocked. 'You will never find your way.'

Dark? She hadn't been here that long, surely? Lia rose to her feet and stepped to the tent's front door flap to see night had indeed fallen. Stars shone coldly in an inky sky. Although she didn't want to spend the night here, crammed in a tent with eight men even if they were monks, she didn't see she had a choice. At least Lama Sonam's body was now outside. There was no way she would have slept in the same tent as a corpse.

'Make sure the Supervisor is warm,' he commanded. 'And ensure she doesn't go hungry.'

*

The evening was subdued. After a meal of watery stew and tsampa, during which nobody said a word, everyone went to bed. To her relief, nobody undressed but climbed into their nests of blankets fully clothed. She didn't think she'd sleep, not with two of the men snoring as loudly as chainsaws, but the next thing she knew a hand was shaking her awake.

'Come.' It was Tenzin. 'I will take you to Tali.'

Monks were crawling out of their beds, yawning, setting the fire, putting tea on to boil. She struggled up, feeling stiff and achy, to see it wasn't even 5 a.m. Tenzin offered her a cup of buttered tea which she refused when she saw the yellow blobs of fat floating on the surface.

Dawa Rinpoche came to the tent flap. 'We are grateful to you, Supervisor, for coming to us.' He held her hands briefly, his skin warm, paper-dry. 'Thanks to you we can be on our guard and protect the boys we test in future.'

In turn she thanked him for his hospitality. 'I'll be back this afternoon. Can I bring anything from town for you?'

'We have plenty of supplies.' He inclined his head. 'But thank you. It was a kind thought.'

Lia followed Tenzin through the mountains. Stars lit their way, turning everything ghostly grey. The monk was impressively light on his feet and Lia found herself struggling to keep up on the rocky paths. The jeep was where they'd left it that morning, keys still in the ignition.

'Park it near the petrol station in town,' Tenzin told her. 'Its owner will claim it from there.'

Dismay filled her. 'I thought you were going to drive me?'

'I'm sorry. I have to get back.' He half-raised a hand in farewell and turned, about to walk away.

'Wait!'

He paused.

She tried to picture the winding route back to the camp. Would she find her way when she returned? In a rush she realised Dawa Rinpoche had no intention of waiting for her to return with an investigative team. Briefly, she tried to work out what to do, but with no way of communicating with the local police – any police for that matter – she had no choice. She had to return to Tali. She wanted to curse, use a really foul word, but held her tongue, not wanting to swear in front of a monk.

'How will I find my way?'

'Follow the track until you come to a crossroads where you turn right. This track will eventually come to a road, where you branch right again. Stay on this road until you come to the town. It is simple.'

Was it? It hadn't seemed simple when he'd driven her here. She hoped she wasn't going to drive into the middle of nowhere until she ran out of fuel.

'You will be fine,' he assured her.

'You won't move camp?'

'We cannot move Lama Sonam's body for four days.'

She hadn't thought of that and immediately felt cheered. Perhaps she'd been wrong and the group would wait for her return.

Tenzin didn't say goodbye. He simply turned and started walking away. She took a breath, wanting to call out and thank him, not least for saving her life, but the shape of his strong, muscular body vanished into the shadows and she was alone.

*

'Where on earth have you been?' Pete scolded her. 'I know you left a note, but even so. I've been worried sick.'

Pete was drinking tea while Lia tucked into a giant omelette – she was ravenous.

'I need to find a phone,' she said. 'Or drive to get a signal.' She'd already told Pete about Lama Sonam's death, and that she needed to galvanise the police into getting up here as soon as possible.

'There's a phone behind reception.'

Lia devoured the last of her eggs. She pushed back her chair and headed out of the dining room. The second she entered reception, she stopped dead, all instincts bristling.

Two uniformed police officers, both male, both grim-faced, were standing at the desk. To one side stood Myra Kwok. She wore a white padded jacket and matching snow boots. She was smiling at Lia.

'Hello, Supervisor,' she said.

'What are you doing here?' A ringing started in Lia's ears.

'I have a warrant for your arrest.' She nodded at the officers who moved to stand on either side of Lia.

Lia swallowed, her saliva drying up in her mouth. 'I'd like to see it.'

Myra Kwok pulled a sheet of paper from her breast pocket

and came over. Passed it to Lia. Lia saw a procuratorate had approved her arrest. Dread crawled into her lungs. She passed it back.

'You heard what Officer Tan said,' Myra hissed. 'Yet you insisted on continuing this stupid investigation.'

'A man has been killed — shot — in the mountains. If we find the shooter, we may well find the boy's killer.' Lia tried to keep calm, prevent her voice from trembling, but it was almost impossible with the fear riding her blood.

'The simpleton has already confessed.'

'But he's the *wrong man*. Yeshe isn't the Snow Thief. We need to go to the monk's camp where Lama Sonam's body is being kept. I can show you the way.'

Myra Kwok's gaze suddenly fixed on something over Lia's shoulder. 'And who is this?'

Pete stood in the doorway. He looked terrified.

'No one I know,' said Lia, praying Pete would take the hint and flee.

'Please, Supervisor, will you stop being ridiculous,' Myra snapped. 'As if we don't know he's your driver.' She clicked her fingers at the uniforms. 'Arrest him.'

'No, don't.' Dismay rocked Lia. 'Please, he's done nothing wrong.'

'He'll tell us all about your little escapades, won't you, you pathetic Tibetan turd.' Myra went to stand inches from Pete, sneering. 'If you don't give us what we need, we'll take every one of your family and beat them until they die. How do you like the sound of that?'

'I'll co-operate,' Pete said. He was gasping. 'I promise.'

'Good,' Myra purred. 'Now. Let's see where the Supervisor's going to be staying for the night.'

30

To Lia's horror, she was taken to the local lock-up. A single room, the same size as Yeshe's – two metres by three – with a tiny open window, no electricity, no heating. A bucket stood in the corner. No lavatory paper, no water to wash herself, no water to drink. No blanket to help keep her warm during the night. She was already shivering with cold. She may have her padded jacket, hat and gloves, but it was barely above freezing in here.

How was she going to survive this?

With her hands beneath her armpits, she raised herself on tiptoe to peer through the window. Her cell overlooked a narrow rubbish-filled wasteland. Beyond that, she could see part of a muddy street. As she looked, she saw a woman walk past, then another. Lia called out. The women didn't pause. Could they hear? She called again, louder.

The next second her cell door was flung open and a Chinese guard stepped inside. He was holding a wooden stick the size and shape of a cricket bat. Before she could move, he swung it at her. It collided with her upper arm so hard she fell to the ground with a shout, pain whistling, shrieking.

'Make another sound,' he said, 'I'll break your legs.'

Trembling, quaking, she said, 'I've done nothing wrong.'

'That's not what I heard. Traitor.' He walked out of the cell and slammed the door behind him. The sound of the locks being rammed into place made her whimper, begin to cry.

Lia paced her cell until night fell. Nobody came. Nobody brought her anything to drink or eat. She shivered uncontrollably in the cold. She couldn't work out how to keep warm, whether to keep walking, to stand or curl up and huddle in the corner. She ended up doing a mixture of all three. She couldn't sleep. Her bruised arm was throbbing. She kept thinking of the kindness in Lama Sonam's eyes.

She remembered telling him about the boys' deaths, and his face, ineffably sad.

I had a suspicion...

Who had killed him? Why? She had also been shot at. Who wanted her dead? Why?

Her mind went around and around until suddenly she'd see Tashi's bright black eyes, his narrow, intelligent face, but instead of hearing his piping young child's voice, she kept hearing Jian's: Never give up.

She paced to keep her heart pumping, her body temperature up, but she was at a disadvantage. She was city-bred, used to comfortable beds and central heating. She wouldn't last long. Maybe twenty-four hours? She didn't know. Would anyone feed her or bring her water? Already she was incredibly thirsty.

Lia gazed outside. Who knew she was here, aside from Myra Kwok? Did Fang Dongmei know she'd been arrested? What about Commissioner Zhi? Tears seeped from her eyes and she forced them away. She didn't want to lose precious water. She had to survive this.

*

When dawn broke, she was curled in the corner of the cell. She tried to get to her feet, to begin pacing and keep her circulation moving, but her limbs had stiffened and were numb. She felt slightly sick and very tired. The thought that if she fell asleep she might not wake up crossed her mind. Oddly, it didn't trouble her particularly.

When she heard something thud softy against the outside wall of her cell, she thought she'd imagined it.

Another soft thud. Dully, she turned her head to see a fresh dough ball lying on her cell floor. Seconds later, two more joined it. A soft thud indicated the next dough ball had hit the outside wall.

She crawled to the food, but found it difficult to swallow. She was desperately thirsty. She managed to eat a couple of bites out of one of the balls before nausea overcame her. She began to pray someone would come. Even if it was the guard with his club. But nobody came.

She had no idea what time it was when Myra Kwok arrived. It could have been hours, or days.

'I brought you some water,' said the PSB officer.

Lia couldn't unscrew the cap. Her movements were slow and unco-ordinated. Kwok unscrewed it for her, held the bottle to her lips. Lia swallowed slowly.

The PSB officer wrinkled her nose. 'Good grief, you stink.'

Lia didn't have the energy to talk to the woman. She couldn't even wipe her mouth with the back of her hand and had to let the water dribble down her chin. Kwok placed the bottle of water in the corner.

'I want you to know that your driver has confessed.' Kwok's eyes gleamed with satisfaction. 'He's told us every-thing. How you're a Tibetan sympathiser. A member of the TPUM, Tibet People's Uprising Movement. How you came out here to distribute copies of the Dalai Lama's photographs. How you're plotting terrorist activities.'

'Nobody will believe you,' Lia rasped.

Myra Kwok snorted. 'All they have to do is look at you. You're *foreign*. You're *ugly*. You obviously have Tibetan blood in you. We've already started hunting down your relatives. We'll parade them in court. You will be executed for collaborating with an enemy of the state. For being a double agent, a traitor.'

It wasn't until Myra Kwok left that Lia realised she might not make it. She'd stopped shivering. Her thoughts became sluggish. She began to hallucinate. She tried to keep her thoughts sane and real, but soon it became impossible and she sank into the comfort of delusion, dreaming she was in her sleek Shenzhen apartment, preparing Jian's favourite dish, Gongming barbecued goose. The fact that she didn't have a huge pottery stove to cook it in didn't matter, she was flavouring the meat with soy sauce and wine, and searching for some honey. It was warm, mid-summer, and she was going to serve supper on their balcony. Tibet no longer existed for Lia. She was at home, where she belonged, and waiting for the man she loved to come home.

When the cell door opened two hours later and Tan stepped inside, she thought he was Jian.

31

TAN WAS FLYING TO Tali barely an hour after he heard Myra Kwok had arrested Shan and was holding her overnight in some godforsaken jail. He knew he'd only find out what was really going on if he went out there himself. What was Myra Kwok up to? Was she power-building? Using Shan as a springboard for promotion? Fortunately, in the arrest report, Kwok had mentioned the TPUM – Tibet People's Uprising Movement – which he used as an excuse to requisition a helicopter. The government spared no expense as far as anti-terrorism activities went.

What had Shan been doing all the way out there? Tracking down the Snow Thief, of course. It was obvious. She had to be the most obstinate police officer he'd ever known. She was never going to give up. He wondered what he was going to do with her. He'd decide once he'd spoken with her and Zhi, but there was no way he was going to let the simpleton Yeshe go.

The helicopter hit an air pocket, making Tan's stomach swoop and the aircraft slew sideways. Curse Myra Kwok for forcing him into this shit-bucket. One day, he'd make her pay.

Riffling through his briefcase, he brought out the photographs of the dead boys. There were no photographs available of them alive. Few Tibetans owned cameras. What was the point? It wasn't as though they could get them developed at their local yak market.

He glanced outside at the swathes of white, the jagged jumbles of rocks. Thank the heavens Lhasa was relatively civilised. He'd taken the post to prove himself to his superiors and show he could be placed in one of the harshest environments and succeed. He wouldn't be given a second posting as tough as this. He was putting in his time while he was still young, so that when he aged, he'd be in a cushy job in Xian, maybe even Shanghai.

He couldn't let the Supervisor and her obsession with the Snow Thief derail his plans. He couldn't risk being demoted and moved somewhere really awful, like Qinghai. Qinghai was behind Tibet in its rehabilitation, and the flood of Han and Hui Chinese into the area not so comprehensive. This meant the food would be inedible and the living conditions only fit for pigs. Lhasa may feel like the back of beyond, but with the new Special Economic Zone bringing in foreign investors, it was beginning to flourish.

He studied the picture of Pemba Dolma closely. Cute kid, he thought absently, even with the snot caked around his nose and mouth. He wouldn't mind having children. His mind drifted. Would Shan like to have kids? And what about the little girl the CWI had finally caught at the back of his apartment block? They'd laid a trap for her after he'd suggested they leave some food out, but it had taken three staff to capture her. She'd fought like a wildcat, apparently, scratching and biting, but they'd told him this wasn't unexpected. A lot of feral children resented being taken off the streets but after a while, when they made friends in the orphanage, they settled down.

Tan had gone to see Lhamu – that was the girl's name – the following day. Lhamu's hair was thick and shiny, her skin scrubbed clean. She wore a red and yellow smock and leather shoes with a red buckle. She was almost unrecognisable from the filthy, dirt-encrusted child who had gobbled snow.

'Hello,' he said. He ducked down so they were eye to eye.

Lhamu gazed at him. She said shyly, 'Hello.'

'Are you comfortable here? Can I bring you anything?'

She shrugged and looked up at the CWI representative. She didn't speak Mandarin.

'Tell her that if she wants, I will be her benefactor.'

The CWI woman translated. Lhamu looked back at Tan. She said, 'Will you look after my sister too?'

It transpired Lhamu's sister was eighteen months older, and living on the streets. Her name was Dolkar, and both girls had been orphaned a few months ago when their mother had died, from what sounded like a long-standing disease. They couldn't remember their father, but Lhamu said he'd died ages ago. They didn't have any other family.

'Of course I'll look after her,' Tan said. It made no sense to look after one without the other. 'Where can we find her?'

Dolkar didn't scratch or bite when they brought her in, and when Tan visited the following day it was to find both girls as clean as new pins and playing in the dormitory. They greeted him brightly, calling him *Da ge, big brother*, which made him smile.

Now, he pushed the photographs of the dead boys back into his travel bag and spent the remainder of the journey trying to work out how to stop the Supervisor from continuing with the case – threatening her hadn't worked – and somehow get her into his bed.

*

The jail was the usual hell-hole. A freezing, stinking concrete block set to one side of the police station, slap bang in the centre of town. Two armed cops were playing cards in the office. One had his feet on the desk, the other was smoking. Both leaped to their feet when Tan stepped inside and flashed his ID card.

'Sir.' They snapped a salute.

'You're holding Supervisor Shan.'

'Yes, sir.'

'Take me to her.'

'We were told…' the man paused and glanced at his companion. He swallowed. 'Sorry, sir.'

'What were you told?'

'That the prisoner should have no visitors.'

'This is obviously an exception.'

'Yes, sir.'

He'd seen plenty of prisoners during his career and he knew Shan would be filthy and hungry, that her breath would reek and her body stink. He'd been prepared for that, but he wasn't prepared for the way she greeted him.

The second their eyes met, her face lit up. She smiled. A smile filled with such joy, such love and compassion that his heart clenched, his legs went weak. He had an urge to go to her, bury his face in her waist and have her stroke his head.

'Lia.' The word was tugged from him as if he was a fish that had just been hooked; pain mingled with shock.

'Jian.'

'No,' he said, but she didn't seem to hear him. When he dropped to her side she rested her head against his shoulder and closed her eyes. She continued to smile.

'Hold me,' she whispered.

He held her gently. His heart was thundering. He felt dizzy. He said, 'I'm Tan Dao.'

'Take me home.'

*

Tan brought Lia straight to his guest house and laid her in front of the communal hearth. Using a poker, he prodded the coals awake and added more fuel.

Come on! He willed the flames higher. *She's freezing to death for fuck's sake!*

He touched her face. It felt as cold as marble. Her skin had taken on a faintly blue hue. He raced to the kitchen. 'Hot soup!' he demanded. 'Now!'

A Tibetan woman joined him from the kitchen. When she saw Lia's prostrate form, she disappeared briefly and returned with several heavy yak-hair blankets. She gestured at Tan to raise Lia, where she laid two blankets on the floor before gently wrapping the frozen woman in the remainder. She carefully chafed Lia's right hand, blowing on it. Tan took Lia's other hand and did the same.

When the soup arrived, Tan supported Lia's head while the woman spooned it slowly into her mouth. Lia didn't eat much, but the woman seemed satisfied. She helped Lia out of her jacket before making a gesture at Tan's body, another at Lia. She mimed climbing into the blankets and holding Lia against her.

Tan took off his shoes and coat and sweater and clambered beneath the rough blankets and spooned Lia close. She felt so slender, so fragile, that for a moment he couldn't breathe. He felt like weeping. He didn't know why. He continued gently chafing her icy hands, trying to bring back her circulation. The fire built, slowly warming the room.

He felt the temperature beneath the blankets gradually increase. He tucked her hands in front of her chest and covered them with his own. Breathed against the back of her neck. He closed his eyes. Rhythmically stroked her fingers.

Lia, Lia, Lia.

Tan fell asleep with her name still echoing through his mind.

*

Lia awoke to find she was lying in front of a fire. She was hot. She was more than hot. She was *roasting*.

She became aware that a man was holding her in his arms, his breath rolling against her neck in warm waves. He sounded as though he was deeply asleep. He smelled slightly spicy, of cinnamon and ginger.

Disorientated, still befuddled, Lia turned her head. For a second, she couldn't take it in. The man she was sharing a blanket with, *sleeping with*, was Tan Dao.

'Fuck.' She scrambled away from him, pushing him, desperate to get away. 'What the fuck...'

'Lia,' he said. He was blinking blearily.

'Don't call me Lia,' she snapped. Her breathing was tight and she felt queasy. 'What's going on?'

'You had hypothermia.' Tan flung back the blankets and rose. It was the first time she'd seen him without a jacket and she found the sight of his rumpled shirt and bare forearms unduly intimate and oddly unsettling.

'And that gave you the right...the right to, to...' She couldn't say it. The right to embrace me.

'You were dying.'

With awful clarity she remembered the dead chill of the cell. The way her body fell numb, unable to perform the simplest tasks, even to clap her hands.

'I'm OK now.' Her voice was tight.

'Yes.'

His expression was odd. Normally it was as emotional as a slab of rock but today it held something new, something she hadn't seen before. She didn't trust it.

'I helped give you some hot soup.' He made a vague gesture. 'I had to warm you.'

She abruptly became aware of the stench wafting from her clothes. 'I need to wash.'

'Of course.' He straightened.

'My bag.' She looked around as though it might materialise in the room.

'I will have it fetched.'

Lia watched Tan leave. What was going on? How come she wasn't in jail any more? What was Tan doing here? He returned a few seconds later with a Tibetan woman. 'She will show you the washroom,' he said. With that, he vanished.

The water in the bath was barely four inches deep and lukewarm, but it felt beautiful. Her upper arm sported a big black bruise and was sore. Nothing that a couple of painkillers wouldn't fix. Lia lay in the bath and scrubbed every inch of her body as though she could scrub her experiences in jail away. Using a plastic pail, she poured water over her hair and worked the soap into a lather. The water was cool by the time she'd finished, and she was shivering, but she didn't care.

She was alive.

She climbed out of the bath, a little dizzy, legs wobbly. She towelled herself briskly to warm up before burrowing through her bag, which Tan had miraculously deposited outside the bathroom door. If she hadn't known him better, she'd have thought he was almost concerned for her well-being. He obviously had an ulterior motive for her staying alive. Perhaps it had something to do with Myra Kwok?

After downing a couple of painkillers, she walked to the kitchen. She needed some food and to rest. The guest-house owner gave her some hot, fatty soup and bread, and some sweet yak-butter tea. Yesterday Lia had refused the rich, oily drink but now she swallowed every drop, relishing the calories, the slightly rank flavour.

Finally, Lia joined Tan in the communal area, where he was sitting by the fire with a pot of green tea. There were two tea bowls. He gestured that she join him. She sank onto a wooden chair near the hearth. The cup of bitter green tea tasted perfect after the richness of her meal.

'How do you feel?' he asked.

As weak as a kitten, she thought. 'Fine,' she said. Her voice was curt. She didn't want him getting any ideas after their sharing a blanket. Just drinking tea in his proximity felt too personal.

'Strong enough to...'

He broke off at the sound of clattering footsteps. Myra Kwok swept into the room, expression defiant.

'Sit,' Tan commanded. He waved at a wooden stool set to one side.

'I'd rather stand.' Kwok raised her chin. She didn't look at Lia.

'As you prefer.' Tan took a long sip of tea. He said, 'I see a procuratorate approved the arrest of Supervisor Shan.'

'Yes.'

'You are aware the accused has to be questioned within twenty-four hours and her family and work unit notified of the detention—'

'Except in circumstances where notification would hinder the investigation,' Kwok responded quickly.

'Which are?'

'We're tracking down her family. We didn't want to tip them off so they could go into hiding.'

Tan stared. 'Supervisor Shan's mother is in Fuling. Her husband's grandmother is in Lhasa…'

'Her Tibetan family.'

Tan turned his head and looked at Lia. He raised his eyebrows at her.

'I have some English blood, possibly from my grandfather, but I'm Chinese,' Lia said. 'As you know.'

Tan turned back to Myra Kwok. 'Have you done a DNA test on the accused to ascertain her genetic profile?'

Kwok flushed. 'Not yet.'

'I suppose you would have done it on her corpse once she was dead,' Tan said. 'I know how meticulous you are.'

A long silence fell where Tan fixed an icy black gaze on Myra Kwok and Myra Kwok looked as though she was trying not to squirm.

'I shall take over this investigation,' Tan said, 'now that this has been brought to my attention.'

Kwok directed her gaze over her boss's head. Her fists were clenched so tightly her knuckles were like ivory buttons.

'I will see you back in Lhasa,' he said. 'You may go.'

'Sir…' Kwok was hesitant.

'Yes?'

'May I join you in the helicopter back to the city? It will save much time, and—'

'How did you get here?'

'I drove.'

215

'Then you will drive back.' He flicked a hand, dismissing her. Kwok stepped out of the room. She looked as though she wanted to kick something. She slammed the door behind her.

Lia studied Tan. She said, 'Are you having an affair with Myra Kwok?'

Startled, he said, 'No.'

'But you've slept with her.'

'Months ago.' He was dismissive. 'It was terrible. It was like fucking a pork chop.'

To her astonishment, Lia felt a pop of shocked laughter lodge in her throat. It had to be a reaction to nearly dying. She couldn't think of any other reason why she might laugh with Tan.

'She knows she's no good in bed,' Tan confided. 'Which is why she's such a pain in the arse. I wish she'd get a decent vibrator. It might help her temper.'

Lia decided it was time to change the topic. She said, 'You don't believe I'm a Tibetan sympathiser, do you?'

'Don't be stupid.' He gave a snort. 'You've more sense than that.'

'Officer Tan.' Lia became deferential. 'What about Pete, my driver?'

Tan's gaze tightened. 'What about him?'

'He's done nothing wrong.' She tried to keep any anxiety from her voice and remain coolly objective. 'Where is he?'

Tan surveyed her at length. He said quietly, 'You'd like him released?'

'If it's possible.' Hope spiralled. 'Yes, please.'

He jerked his head slightly to the left. A half-nod. 'I will arrange it this afternoon.'

Relief swept through her. 'Thank you.'

He leaned back, resting his elbows on the arms of his chair and steepling his fingers against his chin. 'Now, you must tell me what you were doing up here. I'm sure it wasn't for a holiday.' Humour glimmered in his eyes and for a moment she thought he was teasing her, but she must have misread him.

Lia considered how much to tell him and quickly decided a heavily edited version of the truth would be best. Yeshe's life was, after all, at stake. When she told him Lama Sonam had died, Tan showed not a flicker of interest or emotion, but when she said the lama had shown up at her guest house, he sat upright, his eyes glittering.

'A monk in your room? Why?'

Lia told him about Tenzin driving her through the night, the shots ringing out, Lama Sonam's death. She described her meeting with Dawa Rinpoche, and Tenzin leading her back to the jeep. She left out all references to the Panchen Lama. She didn't know Tan well enough to trust him. Plus, he was such a party man, and hugely ambitious, that he could well approve of what was happening.

'What has all this to do with the Snow Thief?' he asked.

'Everything is interconnected. The man that shot Lama Sonam...Well, he may be the killer.'

'Hmm. Say it *was* him. Why would he kill little boys?'

'I don't know.' She was purposely vague. 'It could have been triggered by all sorts of things.'

Tan rubbed his chin. 'We shall go to their camp later. Interview the lamas and their monks. You can find it again?'

'If we use the helicopter, it shouldn't be a problem.' Lia was confident.

32

THE THREE OF THEM were halfway across the valley floor when Nima heard the distinctive *whap-whap* of a helicopter rotor. They'd been trailing the monks east after crossing the valley, and he guessed they were taking the shortest route to Nyima, the nearest half-decent sized town, and where they'd probably hitch a lift to their next destination. Was there a boy in Nyima waiting to be tested? There were twenty-six boys in all, scattered around the country. Seventeen were now dead. Had one of them been the next Panchen Lama? There was no way to know.

The helicopter's engine note remained steady in the distance. Still, they'd better hide. They couldn't afford to be spotted. He wondered if the female police officer was in the machine. She'd reacted fast to his first shot, but the lama had been slow and he'd managed to pick him off easily.

He'd inspected the monks' camp once they'd moved on, to find the lama's body tucked in a fissure of rock in the mountain. The monks had been unable to bury him properly, or conduct the formal rituals, because they'd had to flee before the police came.

He looked around. They couldn't remain in the open where they'd be as exposed as lumps of coal lying on a white pillow. Through his binoculars he spotted a scrubby plantation to the south – he could just see the tips of the trees. He ordered Rinzen and Sharmar to change direction and head straight for it. He hoped the monks – a good five hours' march ahead of them – wouldn't be spotted. Their group was larger, with ponies and yaks, and would be much more difficult to conceal.

He hoped the trees were growing near a stream. He was

thirsty, and had been all morning. Water had started to be a problem. All their bottles were filled with snow, but due to the temperature being so cold it wasn't melting. They couldn't eat snow. It would chill their vital organs and lower their core body temperatures. They'd die of cold from the inside out.

Nima studied his map as he walked. Were the monks short of water too? If so, they might strike further south, where two rivers met on lower ground.

Another important consideration was where the police would search. By heading south instead of east, the monks were obviously hoping to throw them off. Also, their plans might have to change because of the weather. A storm was brewing. The wind-chill factor would be horrendous. They had to find shelter, out of the wind, but the plateau afforded no cover.

Thwap-thwap.

The sound suddenly seemed to be increasing. Shit. He scanned the sky again with his binoculars, but couldn't see the helicopter. He pushed his way through the snow to speak to his men.

'We have to increase our pace,' he said. 'Hide in those trees.'

They nodded and broke into a shambling jog. Nima brought up the rear.

They were two hundred metres from the scrabble of rocks, brush and low wind-whipped trees when he heard it again.

Thwap-thwap.

This time it was closing in.

'Run!' he yelled. 'Run and hide!'

Both men broke into a gallop.

The area had been generally flat, but now the ground began to gently roll. Undulations were good for concealment. His spirits lifted. They might get away with it.

Thwap-thwap.

The engine noise increased.

He seemed to run for an eternity, the skin across his shoulders tight, waiting for the helicopter to swoop out of the sky, call up reinforcements and grab them, stop their mission. He couldn't have them do that. *They had to find the Panchen Lama.*

Breath hot in his throat, Nima ran as hard as he could, his rifle thumping between his shoulder blades. He reached the tree line last. Ducked beneath a bunch of patchy, leafless branches. Now he was in the plantation, he saw how pathetic the cover was. But it was better than nothing.

'Keep still!' he called.

None of them moved, nobody spoke as the helicopter clattered along the valley. Nima saw it was headed dead east. It was a few hundred metres away. Would they check out the plantation? It appeared to be the only cover around, but from the aircraft's height, the occupants would have a different perspective and might be headed for a forest of trees only they could see from their altitude.

Everybody remained frozen.

Nima released a sigh as the machine vanished over the horizon. They would, he decided, stay where they were until the sun set. Only under cover of darkness would they begin to follow the monks once more.

33

LIA AND TAN SPENT the next day searching for the lamas with no luck. They'd risen at dawn and breakfasted together, Tan grumbling that his rice soup was inedible, the tea revolting, before climbing into the helicopter. The following day Tan borrowed a four-wheel-drive and driver from the local police and together they scouted the area, questioning locals and trying to find any trace of the travelling monks.

Occasionally she'd catch Tan watching her with a strange expression on his face. Once, irritated at his staring, she said, 'What are you looking at?'

He jerked his gaze aside. 'I don't know.' He looked puzzled and slightly confused.

Sometimes, he'd try to make small talk. He asked where she'd like to live, if she wasn't living in Tibet.

Sydney, she thought, but prudence made her say, 'Shenzhen.' She didn't want him to think she was unpatriotic. Talking to Tan was like walking in a minefield but when he asked where she'd like to holiday, she could be more honest.

'Sydney,' she said.

'Why there?' He looked baffled.

'It's called the blue city because the harbour and sky are so blue. Naturally blue. It's similar to Tibet. Even though it's a major city, there's no need for them to fly planes with chemicals to disperse the clouds.'

'A blue city? Really?' Tan looked baffled, which wasn't surprising considering China's skies were always whitish grey.

'The beaches are also beautiful. I think it would be exciting to learn to surf.'

'You can swim?' His eyes widened.

She nodded. Her father had taught her from a young age.

'I'd like to learn to swim,' he said wistfully.

'Why don't you take lessons?'

Humour inched into his eyes. 'I would if you were my teacher.'

Her old persona jabbed through without warning. 'You couldn't pay me enough.'

Instead of being insulted, he'd looked thoughtful. He said, 'Everyone has their price, Lia.'

'And I suppose you know what mine is?' She arched her brows at him.

'Your family and friends. You're intensely loyal. This can be considered a good thing, but it can also work against you.'

She'd felt a jet of unease at the speculative gleam in his eye and hurriedly changed the subject.

On the third day, they took the helicopter out again. This time, they searched all afternoon, widening the area to encompass a dense forest clinging to the sides of a valley in the south.

'Perhaps we should search the forest,' Lia suggested, peering down. 'You could hide a whole village in there and we'd never know.'

Tan had a look. 'It would take a week to drive there, search it effectively, and return.' He turned back to her, eyes sparkling. 'Do you like my company that much?'

For a moment she couldn't look away from the amusement warming his face. Gone was the hard stony PSB officer and in his place was a good-looking man who seemed to want nothing more than to laugh and joke.

He was flirting with her!

'I'm sorry,' she said brittlely. 'But I'm still in love with my husband.'

'But he's...' he started to protest.

'He may be dead —' she rounded on him, almost snarling with fury '— but that doesn't mean I'm looking to jump into bed with someone else.'

Pulse thrumming, she turned her head to continue studying the endless shrouds of snow and bleak grey rocks. What was it with Tan? Ever since he'd freed her from jail, he'd been acting oddly. Perhaps it was because he'd saved her life? Her grandmother, Rong Rong Chang, who told people's fortunes on the city steps of Fuling, once told her that if you saved a person's life, you were responsible for them for ever. When she'd asked why, the old woman had sighed and rolled her rheumy eyes.

'Ayieee! You are a little ignoramus, aren't you? Don't you know anything? When you save a person's life, you alter their *ming*, their destiny. If you intervene with destiny, you must be responsible for it.'

'But what if, say, a fireman saves someone?' Lia asked.

'It's his job.' Chang's response was quick. 'So it's OK for him not to be responsible.'

Lia hoped Tan didn't believe he was responsible for her. The last thing she wanted was to have him hanging around like some sort of strange protector. They didn't speak again, except to direct the pilot, and for no reason that she could see Tan fell into a foul mood that remained until they returned to Tali. The pilot, who hated flying so late – on the edge of darkness – was in a bad mood as well and let them know it.

'It's bloody dangerous,' he grumbled crossly as he lowered the machine to the dirty slush of snow on the edge of town. 'There are no lights, not even a sodding candle. I nearly hit that dog.'

'It's just a dog, for fuck's sake,' Tan snapped.

Wisely, the pilot didn't say any more but concentrated on setting the runners on the ground and switching off the power.

'We fly to Lhasa first thing tomorrow,' Tan told him.

'Eight o'clock,' the pilot said. 'I'm not going before it's light.'

'Can't we have another look in the morning?' asked Lia. 'Dawa Rinpoche said they couldn't move the body for four days. What if I got the direction wrong?'

'You think because he's a monk he didn't lie?' Tan swung a cold black gaze on her. 'They all fucking lie.'

Tan clambered down the metal rungs clamped to the helicopter's fuselage. He didn't wait to see if she followed.

Lia hesitated briefly. The pilot was writing in his log book. She leaned forward, saying, 'Would there be any chance of having a quick look out there tomorrow? Say, head south for a bit?'

'No.'

'He won't know which direction you're going. It all looks the same out there.'

The pilot turned and looked at her. 'If that arsehole gets an inkling I'm not jumping to his every whim, my career is over. Get it?'

Lia clambered out of the chopper, wishing that the system ran on something other than fear and greed. She stepped around two dogs nosing in a pile of rubbish and headed to the guest house she'd stayed in with Pete. It was a fair walk from the lodgings she shared with Tan and, until today, she hadn't had the energy after her ordeal in jail to make the trek to see if her driver was around. Tan had said he'd had Pete released and she wanted to check he hadn't reneged.

The guest house was quiet. Candles glowed in the little reception area. She called, 'Hello? Is anyone there?'

The guest-house manager came out, an iron-haired woman in a choba.

'Is my friend here?' she asked. 'Pete?'

The woman shook her head. 'Pete go Lhasa.'

'When did he leave?'

'Three days ago.' The woman moved behind the desk. Brought out a slip of paper. 'You Lia?'

'Yes, I'm Lia.'

'He leave this.'

Lia opened the note to see it was written in passable English.

It wasn't long, but it made her smile. She could hear his voice as though he was sitting next to her, one hand on the wheel of the Land Cruiser, the other shoving another Abba CD in the player.

I gather I have you to thank for my freedom. I owe you one. I think! If you need a driver another time, don't call me! Just kidding. It's been an adventure.

It was signed simply, *Pete*.

She tucked it into her jacket pocket. She thanked the woman. Although she was relieved that Pete was free, she worried about the consequences. And what about Myra Kwok? She wouldn't have taken Tan's interference lightly. She was probably planning a coup right now.

Back at the guest house she now shared with Tan, Lia slipped on a fleece, tracksuit pants and two pairs of socks, and climbed into bed. She blew out her candle and fell straight to sleep as though anaesthetised.

*

Black, safe warm black. Something was dragging her away from the calm darkness and forcing her to rise into blue, which turned into pale grey. She struggled to dive back into the soothing velvet blackness, but someone was calling her name. Someone was banging on her door.

'Supervisor! Are you all right?'

She struggled awake, unsure where she was or what was happening.

'Lia! Answer me!'

She clutched the blankets to her chest, her senses in threads. Tan? What was he doing outside her bedroom?

'I'm coming in!' he warned.

'No. Wait...' She spoke in a disorientated mumble. She wasn't sure if she was awake or if she was dreaming. The next second his lean shape loomed at her bedside. He was holding a torch. He ducked down by her bed.

'Are you all right?'

'Yes. Fine. I was asleep.'

'I knocked, asking you to dinner, and when you didn't reply...'

'Sorry. Tired.'

'Yes.' His voice turned soft. In the half-light, the planes on his face softened. She could feel the sexual energy rolling off him in waves. She wriggled backwards, wanting to put some distance between them, but came up against the wall.

He reached out a hand, tucked a strand of hair behind her ear. 'You're very beautiful,' he murmured. His hand gently cupped her chin. Nerves quivered across her skin.

'Please,' she said. 'Don't.'

He kept his hand where it was for a few more seconds before withdrawing it.

'Please, go.'

'I'd much rather stay,' he said softly. His gaze travelled from her eyes and came to rest on her lips.

Unbidden, unwanted, a spark of desire rose in her.

Horrified at her body's response, a flash of her old spirit rose. 'I'm not Myra Kwok.'

'No.' His teeth gleamed. 'You're not Myra. You're worth a thousand of her. A million.'

Lia stared.

'Lia,' he said softly. 'Such a pretty name. Goodnight.'

He closed the door gently behind him, but the little click of the latch could have been a gunshot from the way it made her flinch.

She shuddered, praying he hadn't seen her sudden longing for him, his touch. Where had it come from? She hadn't had sex for...what? Two years? That explained her response. Her body was starved not only of affection, but for the release making love afforded. Tan was an attractive man, no doubt about it, but he was also hard, uncompromising and brutal. But then she remembered his gentle approach to Tashi, and the fact he'd talked to a cat, fed it scraps from his breakfast table. He was a conundrum. And an extremely dangerous one, she reminded herself. Getting involved with Tan would be like pairing up with a leopard; she'd spend all her time watching her back and wondering when she was going to be eaten.

*

The journey back to Lhasa was mercifully short. Tan had collected her from her room first thing in the morning to take her to the helicopter. He hadn't mentioned the previous evening. In fact, he hadn't said a word all trip. Now, they were in the rear seat of his staff car and driving past hoardings advertising washing machines, luxury cars and vodka, heading into the city.

'Join me for dinner tonight?' Tan said.

'Where?' She was curious to see if the Sheraton was on offer a second time.

'At my apartment.'

'No,' she said.

'I'm a good cook,' he said.

'No.'

The car swung east off the six-lane highway. They were ten minutes from the office.

'Your friend Mao Ting is a human rights lawyer,' Tan said. A small smile played on his lips. 'He is defending two Falun Gong members. One of them is his sister. I wonder what his local authorities will say when I tell them about his connection to Jian Shan, who was recently executed for being Falun Gong.'

Ice water poured through her veins.

'Are you threatening me?' Her voice was tight.

He turned his head and looked at her. There was an odd light dancing at the back of his eyes, like a lightning shimmer. He said, 'I want you. I think you want me too.'

'You think by threatening my friend I'll jump into bed with you?'

'Would you?' His eyes were bright with curiosity.

She couldn't watch her best friend be arrested like Jian, could she? Thrown into a stinking jail to be executed who knew when? She closed her eyes for a moment.

'No,' she said.

The car began to slow as it made a right turn.

'Lia,' he began, 'surely you can't deny you feel some attraction—'

She turned on him, rage climbing up her throat to heat her cheeks. 'I will not sleep with you. You can arrest all my friends, torture my family if you want, but you cannot force me to fuck you.'

He leaned forward. Spoke to the driver. 'Pull over here. We will walk.'

'Your bags, sir?'

'Drop mine at home and the Supervisor's at the station.'

Lia stood on the pavement facing Tan. Her pulse was jumping, her palms damp.

Never give up.

Tan ran a hand over his face. 'I'm sorry,' he said. 'I have handled this badly. I'm not experienced in this sort of thing. I was just trying to show...I'm not sure...' He stopped. 'What can I do?' he said in a quiet voice. 'What can I say?'

'There's only one thing I want.'

He blinked several times. 'Which is?'

'For you to release Yeshe.'

He opened his mouth, closed it with a snap. For a moment he didn't move or speak, then a speculative look came into his eye. 'And what will you do for this?' he said.

'I won't screw you, if that's what you want. But you'd regain your face.'

'I cannot,' he announced decisively. 'Yeshe is the serial killer.'

'But everyone knows Yeshe isn't the real murderer.' Exasperation rose. 'Come on, Tan. Don't you realise everyone's laughing behind your back? That you're losing face every minute of every day?'

A hint of red flushed his cheekbones.

'Why don't we work on the case together?' she said. 'Track down the monks. Interview them. Find out the truth. Restore your reputation.'

Lorries rumbled past, spraying slush, but Lia didn't notice. Every sense was on Tan.

He opened his mouth again. Cleared his throat.

He said, 'No.'

Lia gave a shrug, then turned and walked away.

34

OFFICIALLY, SHE WAS STILL on holiday, so Lia went to Mrs Lily's and bought a box of steamed *bao*. Mrs Lily had changed her rebellious red streaks in her hair to purple.

'Nice colour,' Lia remarked.

'It's my birthday tomorrow,' Mrs Lily confessed. 'I needed a bit of cheering up.'

After wishing Mrs Lily happy birthday, Lia took the buns to the autopsy suite, two doors away from the police station. She wanted to check whether Hua Ming might give her a lever to help release Yeshe. She hadn't seen the pathologist since they'd flown back from the nomad's camp near Gertse, and she wanted to know what the results of Mingmar's autopsy had revealed.

The fact she was sparring with Tan at the moment gave her a glimmer of confidence that when he discovered she'd seen Hua Ming, he wouldn't punish her. Also, there was the fact Tan had rescued her from jail and probably saved her life by preventing her from sliding into the fourth and final stage of hypothermia. After all that effort, would he really want to see her die in jail alongside Yeshe? Tan might want her, but he wasn't a man to let his feelings get in the way of what he believed was right. He wasn't corrupt, but nor was he controlled by emotion.

The autopsy suite wasn't Lia's favourite place to be, and she was glad she didn't have to gown up and witness some poor soul's body being scalped and cut open so Hua Ming could rummage around before plucking out the organs and weighing them.

'Long time no see.' Hua Ming gobbled two of Mrs Lily's buns straight off. 'Hmmm. Delicious.' He licked his pudgy fingers clean before appraising her. 'Are you trying to bribe me?'

'Absolutely.'

He leaned back in his chair, his white smock strained almost to bursting point. He watched her pacing back and forth across his office.

'For goodness' sake, sit down. woman. You're making me nervous. Where have you been, anyway? I haven't seen you for days. Kwok said you were on holiday but nobody believed her.'

'What did they believe?' She paused her pacing for a moment, curious.

'That you were ferreting around for the Snow Thief.'

She arched her eyebrows mockingly. 'But he's in jail, surely?'

Hua Ming's eyes slid aside. He began picking at his fingernails. 'It's not my fault Tan wanted it done and dusted overnight.'

'You *rang* him. You told him we had a boy killer up there. You knew he wouldn't resist jumping in with both feet.'

'He told me to keep him informed.' Hua Ming wouldn't meet her gaze. 'And when the head of the PSB says that...'

'You could have warned me. We could have had more time, dammit!' She ran a hand through her hair. 'We were gaining the nomads' trust. The fact Mingmar's parents let us have the body proved it.'

'You might think that.' He was reluctant to admit he'd sabotaged her investigation. 'But I'm not sure I agree.'

'Hua Ming.' She put her hands flat on his desk and willed him to look her in the eye. 'Run me through Mingmar's autopsy. Give me a clue to follow, *anything*. I want Yeshe out of jail by the end of the week.'

'I doubt that's going to happen.' He pulled a hangnail free with his teeth. 'Once Tan gets his man...'

'For the umpteenth time, Yeshe is *innocent*.'

The pathologist heaved a sigh. 'Supervisor, you are a like a thorn in my backside. Still, I have to admit you're a very pretty thorn...' He reached for a metal filing cabinet next to his desk and had a rummage, pulled out a file. He withdrew a report and flicked through it. 'You know most of this. Boys found not far from their homes in the dead of night, dressed in what they went to sleep in, barefoot...Oh, not this though: I sent off some samples of the dirt lodged under Mingmar's nails in the hope something comes up, but it's doubtful. There was no sign of a struggle. But I wanted to be thorough.'

'Thank you. What else?'

'I examined every inch of that boy's body. I've photographed every mark, every cut and bruise. The boy knew his killer. He trusted him enough to let the killer stand behind him and put his hands around his head.'

'Show me how it was done.' She sat down. 'Come on.'

Hua Ming hauled himself up and shuffled behind her. He placed his right hand around the left side of her jaw, his left hand cupping the back of her head.

'If I pull my right hand in a long, fluid movement in a circular motion – turning your head to the right – I then use my left hand and arm to stabilise the rotation. The left hand and arm is also pulled, so the movement is to pull both the left and right elbows apart. The spine is severed by the cervical dislocation as the head is rotated beyond ninety degrees, towards one hundred and eighty degrees, therefore facing backwards.'

He dropped his arms. 'Oh, I forgot. I should have...' He fell silent.

'Should have what?' She turned and looked up at him.

He was standing there with a hand over his eyes. 'Ah, shit.'

'What is it?' Alarmed, Lia rose to her feet.

'Something you don't know. When we were at dinner in Gertse...'

Abruptly she recalled him dithering over whether to tell

the group something or not, and when she'd pushed him, he'd clammed up.

'What is it?' she urged. 'I need to know.'

He dropped his hand. His eyes were downcast. 'I should have put my left hand and arm against the right side of your jaw. And put my right hand behind your head. Not the other way around.'

She stared at him.

'Because…I didn't mention…that, er…' He finally looked at her. He was blinking rapidly as though bracing himself for a blow. 'The killer…ahem. Is left-handed.'

'What?'

'He's ah…left-handed.'

She was so astonished she was momentarily silent.

'You never mentioned this before.'

'No.'

'Why not?'

'Because I only had a suspicion, OK? It was only when I got this boy and did a thorough examination…'

Heat flamed her cheeks. 'You weren't thorough with the others?'

'I thought they were fucking *accidents*.' He flung his hands in the air. 'And even then, I was pushed for time. The parents were going nuts, wanting the bodies back. We nearly had a riot once, remember? I had one body for an hour. What am I supposed to do in a fucking hour?'

Although he looked genuinely abject, like a dog about to be kicked, she still would have loved to have slapped him.

'Were they all killed by a left-handed assailant?'

'I think so.'

'You *think so?*' This time her voice rose.

He glanced at the door and made shushing movements with his hands. 'Look, I'm pretty sure, OK? I've looked back on my notes and I'm ninety-nine per cent certain they were all killed by a left-handed assailant.'

'Is Yeshe left-handed?' she asked.

'Only because his right hand has been shattered.'

'When did that happen?'

The pathologist closed his eyes briefly. He looked as though he wished the floor would swallow him. 'After my report.'

'So Tan knows Yeshe is right-handed.'

'Everyone knows.'

Abruptly her mind switched to Lama Sonam. His lighting the match in her guest-house room, leading them to the jeep, driving, changing gear.

He had also been right-handed.

And Tenzin? She couldn't remember. And nor could she remember if any of the other monks or lamas were right- or left-handed.

35

Tan couldn't sleep that night. He kept seeing Lia's smile when he'd stepped into that stinking, reeking cell. The love in her eyes. He kept reminiscing over the way she'd leaned against him and whispered, *hold me.*

But she didn't want him. She hated and feared him. And he couldn't blame her after what he'd said about her friend Ting. He'd been trying to joke, trying to show her how much he desired her, the lengths he'd go to...or had he been joking? He'd threatened so many people over the years to get them to do what he wanted, it almost came as second nature. Today, it had come out all wrong.

Once, he'd found her fear exciting, but not any more. What had happened?

Restless, he moved to the window, looked out over the frost forming on the cars below. He'd played a game with her when they'd had tea in the guest house. Not that she'd known it. He'd orchestrated the conversation specifically to watch the emotions on her face. She could usually hide her emotions pretty well, but after nearly dying in jail she'd been vulnerable, and he'd been able to read her like a book. It had been exhilarating.

When she'd asked about her driver, her face had turned anxious. And when he suggested she might like him released, hope rose like sunshine in her eyes. He had spent a lifetime crushing people's hopes. Many people would have said he enjoyed it, but that wasn't true. He worked for the greater good of the whole, that was all.

He hadn't been able to resist going one step further to see what would happen when he told her he'd release her driver. Her eyes lit up briefly and then she'd let out a breath. A tiny sigh of relief.

He rested his head against the glass. Closed his eyes. He wanted to create more than just a sigh. He'd caught her unguarded jerk of amusement over Myra Kwok's sexual incompetence and he'd felt a laugh start to bubble inside him in immediate response. He wanted to make her laugh out loud…he wanted to bring her joy, make her moan with longing for him, clutch him to her and demand he make love to her, over and over…

Tan spun from the window, grabbing his hair in both hands. What was he thinking?! He must be going mad. She was just a woman, a lowly Supervisor, for fuck's sake! A foreign-looking, stubborn, recalcitrant Supervisor who had been booted out here to teach her a lesson and show any other security personnel what would happen to them if they stepped out of line. He didn't want to get involved with her. She was rebellious, subversive. She'd tried to bribe her boss in Beijing apparently, to get her husband out of jail.

Secretly, Tan admired her for that. He suspected the bribe had gone wrong somehow. He'd heard a rumour that her boss had felt threatened by her and wanted her gone. Had that been it? Or perhaps her boss had wanted to sleep with her and she'd refused? No, that wouldn't be it. She would have slept with a donkey to free her husband. She was loyal, determined and strong-minded. Qualities he appreciated. She was also beautiful, gentle and kind. He'd seen the way she'd talked to the kids in camp. How they'd responded.

Tan shook his head like a dog shaking water from his ears. He wished she'd never been posted out here. He wished she'd stop walking through his head whenever she felt like it. He was going crazy, visualising her every minute of every day, the way she walked, her grace and power.

There was only one thing for it. And that was to have her. Once they'd fucked, he would get over her. There was no way he was releasing the simpleton. Not only would he look stupid for locking up the wrong person, but he didn't want the dry haystack that was Tibet to catch fire should the case become general knowledge.

He went to his computer and looked at the video he'd downloaded from the Australian tourist website. Apparently, it was one of New South Wales' northern beaches, with deep yellow sand and surf crashing and spuming against a deep blue sky. He could hear seagulls and children playing. It looked foreign and strange and compellingly beautiful. He'd never contemplated going abroad for a holiday and now his curiosity was piqued, he delved further. He looked at apartments to rent overlooking the beach, seafood restaurants on the coast. He pictured himself buying Lia a red swimsuit, her smile of pleasure.

Eventually he poured himself a glass of vodka, but didn't drink it. He ended up lying on his bed, fully dressed, and staring at the ceiling. He couldn't shake the look in her eyes when she had thought he was Jian.

Shit.

The realisation was like a blow against his heart.

He wanted her to look at *him* like that.

36

TUESDAY MORNING, DESHI POKED his head around Lia's office door, looking hopeful.

'Can we talk?' he asked.

'Depends what it's about.' She smothered a yawn. She'd spent all day catching up, culminating in a lengthy briefing in the late afternoon. She hadn't realised darkness had fallen. As she stretched, she heard a bone pop somewhere in her lumbar region. She'd spent the last hour or so in front of the computer, absorbed in researching Tibetan Buddhism and the symbiotic relationship between the Dalai Lama, the Karmapa and the Panchen Lama. The more she learned, the more she realised how important the lamas' mission was. No wonder they'd vanished before she and Tan could find them. They were petrified they wouldn't be able to complete their task.

Deshi glanced over his shoulder and stepped inside, leaving the door ajar.

'I heard you were arrested.'

'A mistake,' she said. She didn't want to add any fuel to the already flaming office rumours.

'And Tan released you?'

Lia switched off her computer. Began packing up.

Deshi cleared his throat. She looked up. 'Excuse me,' she said. 'Did you come for something specific?'

For a moment he looked confused, as though he'd expected her to confide in him, but the confusion was hidden quickly, so that anyone else would think they'd imagined it.

'Goldhawk,' he said.

Lia closed her notebook and slid it into her desk drawer. 'Yes?'

'There's nobody I can find using that code name in the

services in Tibet. However, I think I might have found your attacker. One of the monks at the monastery recognised him from my description.'

Lia lifted her eyebrows. Deshi had managed to surprise her.

'If it's the right man,' Deshi said, 'he's from Tashilhunpo Monastery, Xigatsê. His name is Zapa. Zapa means Friday.'

Her mind began to race. From her research, she'd learned that the Tashilhumpo Monastery was the traditional seat of the Panchen Lamas. This confirmed that the attack on her was connected to the travelling lamas, and the dead boys. There was no other explanation.

'Bring Zapa in for questioning,' she commanded.

'I can't. He's returned to Xigatsê.'

'I take it Xigatsê's on the moon?' she said sarcastically, wanting to provoke him into growing a spine. 'Or perhaps you're carsick? Or is it something closer to home, like you don't have the balls to step out of the box and reach for that promotion you've been whining about?'

His lips narrowed into a thin line. He obviously wanted to tell her to get fucked but she suspected he didn't want to risk alienating her.

'They're connected, OK?' She softened her approach and leaned forward. 'My attack and the boy's deaths. Trust me when I say I can't tell you why. Not yet, anyway. But if we can question Zapa, I am certain he will give us the lead we need to the Snow Thief.'

'But it's not my district.'

'So?'

He chewed his lower lip looking discomfited.

'When did you find out that the Snow Thief was left-handed?' she asked.

'Um...' He squinted as he thought. 'Friday? Maybe it was Thursday. We had a good laugh over it, I can tell you.'

'Why?'

He shuffled his feet. 'Because Tan can't admit he's wrong. He even got the guard to break Yeshe's hand to make sure he appears left-handed in court, can you believe it? But we all know he hasn't got the guts to go after the real killer. Not like you.'

'Officer Tan,' she said stiffly, 'is concerned with the bigger picture. He's doing what he believes will keep Tibet on an even keel.'

'He doesn't have to kill an innocent man to do that! He's got the power to—'

'Enough,' Lia snapped. There was no way she was going to start bad-mouthing Tan in front of anyone, let alone a low-grade officer. 'I will not have this sort of talk about a superior officer. Now, if you don't mind, I have a lot to do.'

Deshi pulled a face. He was annoyed she wouldn't side with him. Tough. She watched him walk out, his shoulders stiff. She doubted he'd go to Xigatsê now. Could she sneak over there herself? Track down Zapa? She wanted to know his connection with the search for the Panchen Lama. What had he said? Something about letting Goldhawk do his job... Was Goldhawk helping the lamas, perhaps? Protecting them? Had Zapa been trying to tell her to back off, leave the lamas to finish their mission undisturbed?

I know who is killing the boys.

He'd said that as a ruse to get her out of the police station so he could attack her, but *how* did he know boys were being killed? It wasn't public knowledge. Perhaps he was one of the PSB's spies? Rumour had it that monasteries were riddled with them, taking bribes from the PSB in return for information on any dissenters and possible protests.

She rubbed her forehead. She could feel a headache coming on. She'd slept badly last night despite her exhaustion, worrying about Tan and his threats. She had rung Mao Ting and warned him, but he'd just laughed.

'He can try and disrupt things, but I'm well respected over here.'

'You don't know him. He's cunning and vindictive—'

'And the cops here aren't? Present company excepted, of course,' he added hastily. 'Seriously, Lia, let him do his worst. If it's not him, it'll be someone else. That's what being a human rights lawyer is about. If I wanted a cushy job with no risk I would have become an accountant. Don't sweat it, OK? I'll be fine.'

*

Handbag slung across her chest, Lia left the office and trudged across the square. She gave a wave to Mrs Lily, and another to Mrs Lily's neighbour, Ma Zhaoxu. She was finally getting to know her neighbourhood. Still worried about Ting, Lia didn't have much of an appetite when she arrived home.

'Eat, eat,' Jian's grandmother urged her. 'You're too skinny. You need some fat to keep out the cold.'

Wasn't that the truth. If she'd been as fat as Hua Ming, would she have survived better in jail? She'd told Fang Dongmei everything that had happened. She hadn't left anything out, including Tan trying to force her into sleeping with him. Fang Dongmei had sucked her teeth and shaken her head. When Lia asked if she was still taking food to Yeshe, she drew herself tall. 'Of course.'

'But I thought I told you that Tan forbade it.'

'I have a friend who takes food to him now. And should they be stopped, another of our friends will take her place. And so on.' She flicked a hand dismissively.

After forcing herself to eat something, Lia helped Jian's grandmother wash the dishes. In the past, Fang Dongmei insisted Lia sit and watch TV while she cleared away, which used to make Lia feel strangely rejected, but now they moved companionably around the little kitchen, noisily clanking plates and pans. Lia wondered if their rows had finally ended, or whether Fang Dongmei now simply accepted Lia in her space. She leaned across Jian's grandmother to put a pot in the cupboard, enjoying the sensation of domesticity.

'There is someone who wishes to see you,' Fang Dongmei said. 'May I bring them over?'

'Now? Here?' Lia was startled. They'd never had any guests to their apartment.

Fang Dongmei didn't reply, simply waited for Lia to say yes or no.

'Who are they?' Lia asked.

'I will go and fetch them.'

Lia watched Jian's grandmother pull on her big puffy black coat and snow boots and vanish outside. When she returned half an hour later, the last person Lia expected to be faced with was Yeshe's brother, Anil. Behind him stood a watchful Tibetan girl in a shapeless red anorak. A rucksack was slung over one shoulder. Her name was Dohna. She was, apparently, Anil's interpreter.

'I can't help you,' Lia told Anil. She didn't invite them inside. She wanted to make her position clear from the start.

'What happened to your manners?' snapped Fang Dongmei.

'They fled the instant I was thrown into jail, accused of being a Tibetan sympathiser,' Lia snapped back. 'I will not have Anil or this Tibetan girl in my apartment. What if Myra Kwok is watching us? This is all the evidence she'll need that I'm a member of the TPUM.'

Fang Dongmei muscled Lia aside. 'Your pet PSB officer will protect you—'

'You must be joking. Tan wants to sleep with me, not sabotage his career...' She flung up her hands as Fang Dongmei hustled Anil and Dohna to the sofa. Anil gave her an apologetic look, but Dohna sent Lia an unpleasant sidelong glance, as though she'd caught a whiff of something rotten.

Lia was opening her mouth to demand they leave, but Fang Dongmei jumped in before she could speak.

'He has come a long way,' she hissed. 'I will not have you turn your back on him.'

Lia bit back a curse as Fang Dongmei vanished into the kitchen ostensibly to make tea. Lia stood facing Anil and Dohna who had settled on the sofa. For a long while nobody spoke.

'Please,' Anil said softly. Dohna translated smoothly, her expression unreadable. 'He's my brother. You know he's innocent. Help him.'

'I can't.' Her voice was firm.

Anil's stocky body was stretched forward, elbows on his knees. 'But he will die for something he didn't do.'

Lia remained silent.

'You must protect him,' Anil pleaded. 'You're a good person. We saw that when you were at our camp. You have power as a police officer. Where else can I go?'

'The police station,' Lia said.

'They won't listen!' Anil protested.

It took every ounce of Lia's self-possession not to look away and hold his gaze firmly. 'I'm sorry,' she said.

Anil put his head in his hands.

Come on, Fang Dongmei, Lia willed. Bring the sodding tea, would you? The sooner they drink it, the sooner they can leave.

'I'm sorry too,' said Dohna.

Sorry for *what*? Lia wanted to ask her.

Dohna reached into her rucksack, pulled out a mobile phone, dialled. She had a brief conversation in Tibetan. Lia had no doubt it was about their meeting from the way the girl's eyes flashed continuously between her and Yeshe. Finally, she nodded several times, and hung up. She fixed Lia with a flat black gaze. 'If you won't help us...'

Lia gave the girl a purposely arrogant stare, as though the carpet had just spoken. 'This is between Anil and me.'

'No, it's not,' Dohna retorted. 'This is about our country, our culture, our *rights*. You think you own us. You think you can do what you like to us. You lock us up without charge.

You beat us, torture us, rape us, kill us. You treat us worse than you treat your *dogs*...'

Anil said something, sounding as though he was trying to calm his interpreter, but Dohna overrode him. Her stillness had evaporated and she was a flurry of energy, her dark eyes alive and sparking with fury. 'You have an innocent man in your jail, and yet you stand there as though nothing is happening. Do you really care? I think it's an act because it's in your power to release him but you won't—'

'Releasing Yeshe is certainly not in my power!' Lia said, incensed. 'His case is in the hands of the supreme court!'

'If you won't release him,' Dohna spat, the colour in her face rising, 'then we'll have no choice but to take this to the streets. Tell everyone an innocent man is going to be executed next week. And then tell them there's a killer of little boys on the loose but that the authorities refuse to do anything about it.'

Lia went quite still, quite cold. She would, she thought, kill Fang Dongmei for this, for telling these people about the case.

'Are you serious?'

'Oh yes,' Dohna said impatiently. 'It will be a peaceful protest. We just want to make sure the authorities listen to us.'

Peaceful, my arse.

Lia wanted to tell Dohna to stop being so stupid, that people would get hurt if she went public with what she knew, but she doubted the girl would listen. She had a zealot's gleam in her eye. Dohna wanted to go to war. Lia could feel the heat of righteous anger pouring from her like a river of molten lava.

'OK,' Lia said.

Dohna's mouth opened and closed. The zealot's gleam had been replaced with surprise. 'You'll release Yeshe?'

'I will do everything in my power to prove his innocence, yes.'

This evidently wasn't what Dohna wanted to hear. The

girl tossed her head derisively. 'We want him released by Friday.'

'We?' Lia went and stood over the girl, forcing her to look up. 'Who is this *we* you keep referring to?'

Dohna tried a little too hard to be nonchalant with a shrug and over-widening of her eyes. 'Just me and Anil,' she said with studied carelessness. 'Nobody else.'

Like hell.

Lia had had enough. She stepped back. She said, 'You can go now. And let me continue to do my job.'

'Your job!' Dohna blurted, springing to her feet. 'I was told you were different, but you're the same as the rest of them – corrupt and dishonest, *evil*. You want us wiped off the earth...' She took a shuddering breath. 'You will pay for this, just you see. If Yeshe isn't free on Friday you'll see just how serious we are...'

Anil clambered up. He was speaking urgently. Dohna struggled to regain her equilibrium but Lia could see the effort it took from the sweat forming on the girl's face. He took Dohna's arm. She snatched it away, snapped at him.

'Be quiet,' Lia commanded.

Anil and Dohna fell into a reluctant silence, glancing at one another like a pair of children caught squabbling.

Lia went and opened the front door. 'Goodbye,' she said stiffly.

Dohna made to say something but Lia held up her hand and pointed outside, earning her a burning look laden with hate. Lia closed the door firmly behind them. Ran a hand over her forehead. Her fingers were trembling.

'They've gone?' Fang Dongmei arrived with a tray and pot of tea, some cups. She looked around the room, bewildered.

Lia stepped across the room to stand in front of Jian's grandmother. In a low voice reverberating with anger she said, 'Don't you ever let that girl into my home again.'

37

LIA DIDN'T WAIT UNTIL morning to report Anil and Dohna.
She wanted to grab them before they could start seeding the
city with violent rumours. She guessed Anil had been roped
in alongside the militant Dohna, but she couldn't protect him.
Not when he was endangering national security.

'Where are they living?' she asked Fang Dongmei.

'Why?' The old woman's eyes were suspicious.

'Because I want to send them flowers,' she said sarcastically.

'Swear you won't do them harm.' Fang Dongmei became
alarmed. 'They're good kids. They just want justice for
Yeshe...'

'Dohna's using Yeshe for her own ends. Even you can see
that, surely. Now, tell me where to find them.'

'I thought you'd help them.' Fang Dongmei spread her
hands. 'Come on, Granddaughter. Your reports...You know
it's wrong, having Yeshe executed. Admit it.'

'Tell me where they are,' Lia ground out.

'No.' The old woman's lower lip jutted. 'You'll only have
them locked up.'

'Damn right I will,' Lia hissed. 'You're not protecting two
innocent people. They want war, and if you don't tell me
where they are, I will have to let every security officer know
what's going on. There will be an immediate crackdown,
starting tonight. There will be house-to-house searches,
checking ID papers of all residents, and anyone whose papers
aren't absolutely in order will be arrested. And their arrests
will be *your* responsibility, Fang Dongmei.'

Long silence.

Lia reigned in her temper and tried to soften her tone,
become persuasive. 'But if I get Anil and Dohna into custody

within the next hour or so, nice and quietly, the rest of the population will be spared a security lockdown. We will have the perpetrators in hand. Do you understand? In order to keep the city safe, I have to know *where they are.*'

The old woman's mouth twisted, Lia guessed in disgust.

'No,' she said.

'On your head be it.' Lia slammed the door behind her when she left.

*

Lia went straight to the police station and asked for a pool car. She wanted to drive to Drapchi Prison, Lhasa Prison Number 1, where Yeshe now resided. He was the only person she could think of who might know where his brother might be staying.

'Can't you do this tomorrow?' the desk superintendent asked. He was watching TV behind the counter. You could barely see the screen for cigarette smoke.

'I need to see the prisoner *now*. It's a matter of national security.'

He yawned, stretched out his legs. Gave her a sly smile that ran from her breasts to her waist, then back up again. He didn't make any move towards the car keys lined on hooks on the wall behind him.

Lia pulled out her phone and dialled.

'Yes?' he barked.

'Officer Tan,' she said. 'It's Supervisor Shan. I need your assistance.'

'You do?' Tan sounded surprised.

As soon as she said the words *Officer Tan*, the Superintendent jackknifed to his feet and made panicky motions with his hands.

'Oh. So sorry.' She gave a grim smile. 'The Superintendent here has decided to help me after all.'

'Where are you?' Tan demanded.

'Please, don't trouble yourself, sir,' she said hurriedly. 'Everything is fine now. I just wanted a pool car, that's all.'

'You're at the station?'

'Yes.'

She hung up. Sweat began to collect at her hairline.

Shit, shit. Did I do the right thing telling him where I was? Yes. Tan needs to know what's going on.

'He's on his way,' she told the Superintendent.

He looked as though he might faint. 'Tan's coming here?'

'Yes, you moron.' Lia rolled her eyes at him. 'Now, do I get a car?'

'Hell,' he said. His breathing was coming shallow and short out of his lungs. 'You didn't have to set Tan on me. You know what he's like.' He pulled a bunch of keys from the wall and pushed a book towards her. 'Sign here.'

Both of them flinched when the door opened, letting in a blast of icy air. It wasn't Tan, however, but Fang Dongmei. She was wearing a new pair of red snow boots with fluffy pink fur peeking from the tops. She said, 'I'll tell you where they are.' Her expression was shamefaced.

*

Tan orchestrated the arrests. Once he'd heard Lia's story, he didn't want to risk any cock-ups that might let the two suspects slip through his fingers.

Lia had assumed Anil and Dohna would be staying in or around the Barkhor, but to her relief they were on the eastern side of town, a good twenty-minute drive away. The last thing she wanted was for the entire Tibetan population in Lhasa to wake to the sound of a platoon of aggressive Chinese police arresting two Tibetans at gunpoint.

'How did Anil and Dohna find you?' Lia took Fang Dongmei to one side. Kept her voice low.

'It was through Yeshe.' Jian's grandmother stood with her hands clamped together in front of her.

'I need to know *who* brought you and Dohna together. *Who* wanted to bring me into the frame.'

'I won't tell you that.' Fang Dongmei's eyes glittered rebelliously. 'I'm sorry, I know I made a mistake earlier. I didn't realise Dohna was...well, who she was. She seemed so sweet.'

As sweet as sugared arsenic.

'You don't need to know my friend's name,' Fang Dongmei insisted. 'She's a good woman, one of the best. She meant well.'

As if Lia hadn't heard that a thousand times before.

'Go home,' Lia told her wearily. 'Before Tan realises you're involved. I'll tell him Anil gave me their address, OK?'

Fang Dongmei didn't show that she'd heard. She simply shuffled across the floor and let herself outside.

As a pre-dawn operation to snatch two potential terrorists went, it was pretty much perfect. Two burly police constables smashed open the front door and a team of armed police swarmed inside. Lots of shouting and a couple of screams, but to Lia's relief, not a single shot was fired. She waited in the back of Tan's car until the building was emptied. Half a dozen people, handcuffed and shackled, were bodily hauled out of the front door. Marched to the rear of a police van. Lia climbed outside to study their faces as they passed. Five men, just the one woman. Dohna's face was ashen but her eyes blazed.

'You,' she said. The word was spat as though ejecting poison.

'Yes,' said Lia, chin raised. 'Me.'

Anil didn't look at Lia. He was weeping, tears coursing down his rough reddened cheeks and pooling at the corners of his mouth. He'd tried to do the right thing for his brother, and ended up drawn into the tentacles of something larger, something more perilous. And when the police found a dozen home-made bombs in the house, Lia knew that he wouldn't see his wife again, or his nomadic family. Anil would die in prison.

'Excellent job.' Tan returned, eyes bright, adrenaline still pumping. 'You will be promoted for this. Back to your previous rank. I will make sure of it.' He shook her hand. 'Would you like to interrogate the suspects?'

Lia couldn't think of anything she might bring to the interrogation table. She couldn't help Anil, or the others arrested. And she certainly didn't want to help Dohna who had shamelessly used Anil. She still couldn't believe the girl's stupidity. Had she honestly believed Lia, a Chinese police officer, wouldn't take action to prevent Tibetans demonstrating in the city?

'Would Jenny Wang be available to talk to them?' she asked. Jenny wouldn't be able to prevent any torture ordered by Tan, but she didn't seem to be an overtly cruel woman. Sure, she'd lost her temper that one time, but Lia reckoned the suspects would be better off with Jenny than another, more brutal, officer.

'I will request her,' Tan said.

'Thank you.'

'Do you think this is a single cell, or are there more?' he asked.

'I don't know,' she answered honestly. 'But I'm inclined to believe it's just the one.'

'We'll get the truth from them.' He turned to watch a police officer with a machine gun slung across his chest slam the van door shut on the prisoners. After the man had locked the door, he banged his fist against it. The van pulled out and drove away. Two patrol cars bristling with armed cops fell in behind.

'We need to conduct a house-to-house search of the area.' Tan called for armoured vehicles to block off each end of the street. Requested soldiers armed with machine guns. More armed cops. 'Can I leave you to co-ordinate?' he asked her as the first military trucks began to arrive. 'Perhaps Constable Deshi can help.'

Lia ended up having to work through the rest of the night with Zhang, because, oddly, Deshi was nowhere to be found.

38

CONSTABLE DESHI HAD ARRIVED in Xigatsê the previous day, and was spending his morning at the monastery in the hope of sighting Zapa, the monk who had attacked the Supervisor. He'd asked around yesterday, but nobody seemed to recognise the man's description. He concluded they were protecting Zapa, so there was only one thing for it. Wait the man out.

He wanted to redeem himself in Shan's eyes. The last look she'd given him had been filled with derision. She hadn't thought he'd be up for the job, but here he was. He'd show her he could do it. He'd connected the two boys' deaths in Lhasa. He had the makings to be a good police officer, he was sure of it, and solving this case was the way to start a long, glittering career.

He shifted on his seat. The benches were four inches above the floor, and everyone sat upon them cross-legged. He'd done the same, and found it more comfortable than he'd imagined. Young monks were busy sweeping the floor, filling cups with thick milky tea from huge pots, taking requests and running errands. Candles were lit at the altar and the air was thick with scents of incense and yak butter. Warm, throaty smells that reminded him of tucking up beneath the blankets on a winter's day. Comforting, soothing. The deep thrumming beat of drums pounded alongside the strident, shriller tones of trumpets.

He watched a family arrive to sit in the centre. Apparently, someone had died recently and the service was to pray for peace. Nobody looked at him. He wasn't in uniform. Everyone thought he was a tourist, he guessed, even though it was winter.

Nobody from the station knew he was here. Well, aside from Zhang, who'd told him he was mad, and that if he didn't return by the end of the week, he'd come looking for him. Nice to know he had some kind of back-up. Supervisor Shan didn't like Zhang, he could tell. She didn't much like him either. He couldn't blame her, not after their attempts to undermine her when she'd first arrived. They'd thought she'd be fair game, having been demoted out of Beijing and kicked into Tibet, but she'd been no pushover. He remembered visiting the parents of the dead boy all those months ago. How the father had gone for her, calling her a Chinese whore. He'd been ready to arrest the man but she'd been absolutely firm.

I'm not arresting a man on the day his son has died.

He hadn't thought of it like that. Just heard the man's insults, and gone for his throat. But of course she was right. The father was crazed with grief.

His gaze drifted. Maroon and gold colours were predominant, the walls a profusion of green. Younger monks chanted from books, the older ones didn't bother. They knew the mantras by heart.

Xigatsê was a revelation. It was only a few hours from Lhasa, and had a rapidly expanding modern Chinese town with all the comforts he was used to. He hadn't bothered visiting Xigatsê before, thinking the city would be an uncivilised hole, but as in Lhasa, things had been improved and changed for the better. It was a pretty decent place. He gave a yawn. He'd been sitting here, for what? Two hours now? Gradually, the chants and heavy scents took their toll, and Deshi closed his eyes. Nodded off.

He woke when he felt someone squeeze beside him. The music and chants had softened into a soothing murmur. *Ai Yo*, he was sleepy. Perhaps he'd head for his hotel now, grab some breakfast on the way. He started to uncross his legs.

'Are you looking for me?' a man said.

All the hairs on Deshi's neck rose.

He turned to see the monk who had assaulted Shan. He'd spoken fluent Mandarin.

'Yes.' The word was scratchy and he cleared his throat. The monk looked amused. Deshi forced himself to ask, 'Are you Zapa?'

'Well done. And you're Constable Deshi, aren't you?'

'Yes.'

'Did Shan send you?'

'Yes.'

'Is she going to leave the lamas alone?'

Deshi turned his head to face Zapa with what he hoped was a neutral, steady expression, but inside he was panicking. What lamas?

'I know she has to do her job,' Zapa went on quietly, 'but I would have thought she might do it less keenly, if you see what I mean.'

Since he had no idea what the man was talking about, Deshi opted for silence.

'We've been waiting for this for years.' Zapa flicked a glance at a novice who was pouring tea two rows down. 'Goldhawk and I. *Years*. And we won't have you incompetents fuck it up. OK?'

Deshi swallowed drily. He'd never heard a monk swear before.

'You tell Shan to back off, and leave Goldhawk to do his job. It's nearly over, OK?' Zapa's voice turned fierce. 'We have just eight boys left. Then the system will be irreversibly fucked. Tell that to Shan. And don't leave a single word out.'

With that, the monk made to rise but Deshi put a hand on his arm. Zapa looked at his hand pointedly. Deshi snatched it back.

'What?' Zapa demanded.

Deshi licked his lips. 'I'm sorry. Are you saying you know who is killing the boys?'

Zapa's eyes drilled into Deshi's. 'For fuck's sake. Are you saying you don't?'

Deshi cringed.

'Ah, shit.' The monk pressed his fingers to his eyes. 'I guess that explains it. Why you're crashing around like a wounded fucking buffalo.'

Deshi waited without moving, without saying anything.

'Shan knows, right?' Zapa demanded.

Deshi remembered Shan leaning forward over her desk, her strange amber eyes sparking with conviction. She'd said her attack was connected with the boy's deaths. She'd said: Trust me when I say I can't tell you why.

'Yes,' admitted Deshi. 'She knows.'

The monk was staring off into space. 'And you don't.'

Still Deshi waited for some kind of illumination, but he was too intimidated to speak.

'Goodbye,' said Zapa.

Deshi didn't move as the monk walked out of the temple. He felt as though he'd been punched in the solar plexus. He felt winded, slightly disorientated.

Zapa knew who the Snow Thief was.

Before he could change his mind, Deshi raced after him but when he hit the street, he saw he was too late.

The monk had vanished.

*

Deshi prowled the streets around the monastery until darkness began to fall. Only then did he head to his guest house. He was tired but he barely felt it through his fury with himself. He couldn't believe he'd messed up so badly. He'd lost a prime witness! Just like that! He hoped nobody would find out or he'd never get promoted.

Grabbing a tray of takeaway noodles, he ate as he walked, trying to remember everything Zapa had said.

We have just eight boys left. Then the system will be irreversibly fucked.

What system? He didn't get it. But Shan would. He

guessed he'd better call her and fill her in. Bolting the rest of his noodles, he threw the carton in a bin at the end of the street, narrowly missing a mangy dog lurking for scraps. Deshi brought out his phone and dialled Shan's number, but it was engaged. He left a brief message asking her to call him back.

As he approached his guest house – a neat two-storey building with a yellow and red neon sign flashing *vacancies* above its front door – he rehearsed what he'd say to Shan.

I tracked down Zapa, your attacker. We had quite a chat. He wants the lamas left alone. What lamas? What's going on?

He mustn't give away how much he hated being left out. It made him feel undervalued and stupid and he didn't want her to know that.

Still angry with himself, Deshi strode past his bedroom windows – he was on the ground floor, overlooking the street – and nearly didn't notice that the curtains of his room were drawn. He had left them open this morning. Perhaps the maid had closed them? He walked into reception, his shoes clicking on the tiles. Nobody was around. He peered over the counter, searching for his room key, but the hook it normally hung from was empty. He frowned. It was too late for the cleaner to be servicing his room. Was someone else in there? He flipped open the counter door and was about to step inside to check the key hadn't dropped on to the floor, when a huge dog, some sort of mastiff, materialised from a blanket on the floor and gave a growl.

'Shit.' He spoke out loud, unable to help himself. He hadn't seen the creature lurking in the shadows. It was fucking *huge*. Not only would it feed a family for a month but it would cost a fortune to feed.

'Are you OK?' The guest-house manager, a young guy in his twenties called Andy Ho, appeared.

'I was looking for my key.' Heart still thumping, Deshi gestured at the dog which was blinking at him. 'I didn't realise you had a guard dog.'

Andy grinned. 'Hardly. Sashi's a big softie, but people get scared because of her size.' He opened the counter top and pushed the dog aside with his thigh. 'Let's have a look...Ah, here it is. It's on the wrong hook.'

Later, Deshi found it hard to explain why he acted the way he did. Perhaps it was the drawn curtains and the misplaced key; perhaps his unnerving conversation with Zapa had made him a creature of intuition rather than rationalisation. He didn't take the key. He said, 'Would you mind checking the room for me? Make sure the windows are open? I'm a bit...claustrophobic.'

Unsurprisingly, Andy gave him an odd look. 'Sure,' he said with a shrug.

Deshi waited at the bottom of the corridor and watched Andy put the key in the door and turn it. The man pushed open the door with his shoulder and as he stepped inside, there was a spitting sound and at the same time, the back of Andy's head exploded in a spray of blood and bone. His body collapsed to the floor, his limbs twitching as though he'd been electrocuted.

For a second, Deshi didn't move. He was drenched in horror.

Fuck!

His heart was knocking, his knees weak.

Be quiet! Don't let them know you're here!

Sweat began to pop on his face, along his spine. Carefully, he began to slide his feet backwards. He willed himself not to run, give himself away. If he could just slip around the corner...

At the entrance to his room he caught sight of a brown leather sandal. The edge of a maroon robe.

He'd run out of time.

Deshi turned and tore into reception. He could hear footsteps drumming down the corridor. Drumming after him.

He raced across the tiled floor and opened the front door,

slammed it hard in front of him, then raced back and before he could think, he dived into the darkened recess behind the counter. Immediately he collided with the warm bulk of the mastiff and recoiled, petrified he was going to get bitten, have half his face ripped off, but all the dog did was give a soft groan.

'Sashi,' he whispered, trembling all over, heart knocking. 'Please don't bite me.'

He gave a sob of relief when Sashi's ears relaxed and she shuffled over to make some room for him on her dog-smelly blanket.

Footsteps pounded through reception. The front door was hauled open. Deshi heard it slam shut. He cowered in the shadows, shivering. To his mixed horror and amazement, Sashi put her head in his lap. Gave a sigh. He didn't dare touch her in case she turned on him, but kept quite still.

The front door opened again. A man entered, talking fast, in Mandarin. It was Zapa. Deshi closed his eyes as though by doing so, the monk wouldn't find him hiding in the shadows.

Please don't let him look here. Please, please...

'Yeah, I know I fucked up, OK?' the monk said. 'You don't have to go on about it. Arrange for someone to deal with the manager, would you? He's made a bit of a mess...Yeah. Yeah, I agree. We have to get rid of them both. They know too much, especially Shan. Yeah...set it up like that. An accident, somehow. Yeah, great. We'll be back on track. Not long to go now. Christ, I can't wait to get home. This place is such a dump...'

Zapa's voice faded as he left reception. Deshi didn't dare move in case the monk came back. He didn't have the courage to leave the safety of Sashi's strangely warm bulk. He didn't want to have his head blown off. He didn't want to die.

His heart just about leaped from his chest when a trilling sound echoed through reception.

His phone was ringing.

Oh, God. It was Shan, calling him back...

Desperately, he fumbled the phone out of his pocket and tried to switch it off but his fingers were thick and clumsy. To his horror the ring began to increase in volume. He stabbed the answer button but in his haste he dropped the phone. Shit!

Leave it! Go!

Deshi rocketed from behind the counter and tore across reception. He heard a shout behind him, pounding feet.

He yanked open the door. Pelted down the pavement.

Get off the main drag!

He aimed for the next side street. People stared at him as he tore past. He jinked right and galloped along the next street, ducking immediately left and then right. He was lean and fast, Zapa bulky. He'd be slower. After a while he slowed, listening.

No footsteps pounded behind him.

No Zapa.

But he didn't stop running, not until he nearly collided with a rickshaw driver.

'Hey, what's the rush?' the man asked.

'I have to get to Lhasa,' he panted.

The man sucked his teeth, and gave a dry chuckle. 'It might take a while.'

Deshi hailed a taxi to take him to Lhasa. He didn't care that it would cost a fortune. Before he left, he got the taxi to drop him at a pay phone where he rang the Xigatsê police – thank the gods he had his wallet with him – and told them where to find Andy Ho's body. He assured them he would return to make a report tomorrow, but he had urgent police business in Lhasa that couldn't wait.

Next, he rang Supervisor Shan. He wanted to warn her. What had Zapa said?

We have to get rid of them both. They know too much...

Shan's extension was busy so he rang Zhang, but just as Zhang answered, he spotted Zapa at the end of the street.

His heart just about leaped from his chest.

The monk was walking purposefully, his head turning from side to side. He was looking for Deshi.

Deshi hung up and sprang into the taxi. It was only two hours or so to Lhasa. He could warn the Supervisor when he got there.

39

BACK IN HER OFFICE, Lia began writing up the past twelve hours. Her heart was heavy for Anil, angry at Dohna, and furious with Fang Dongmei for putting her in an untenable position. She felt drained and emotionally wrung out. When her phone rang, she pushed away her computer keyboard and picked it up. 'Supervisor Shan,' she answered. Even she could hear her voice sounded tired.

'Lia,' Tan said.

'Don't call me—'

'We have a situation.' He overrode her. 'A Tibetan man has been shouting slogans supporting the Dalai Lama in the Barkhor. He is protesting outside your house. He's been calling for your death for betraying your Tibetan friends. Apparently over fifty protesters have joined him so far and more are coming. We need to get out there and quash this before it gets out of hand. The Commissioner has been alerted. I will brief everyone in fifteen minutes.'

For a moment Lia thought she'd misheard him. 'The man has been *what*?'

'He's protesting at the arrests made this morning. Apparently the female terrorist, Dohna, is his wife.' A small pause then Tan's voice turned dry. 'You certainly know how to make friends, don't you, Supervisor?'

She put her hand to her head. As if the morning couldn't get any worse!

'Zhang's handing out the riot gear. I'll see you at the briefing.'

He hung up. Lia stared at the phone for a moment. A demonstration outside her *house*? Her pulse jumped. What about Fang Dongmei? Where was she? Was she all right?

Shoving her phone in her handbag, she slung it across her chest and raced to the briefing room, which was already full of police climbing into battle-dress uniform with reinforced knees and elbows, jackboots, padded gloves and riot helmets. Plastic shields followed, handcuffs and super-heavy-duty batons.

She looked around, spotted Zhang. When he caught her eye, he came over.

'Supervisor Shan,' he said, offering his hand. 'Congratulations on your promotion.'

She blinked. She hadn't taken Tan seriously, but he'd obviously kept his word. She was impressed at how fast both Tan and the Commissioner had moved.

'Thank you.' Aware everyone was watching, she shook his hand. It was warm and damp and she had to force herself not to wipe her palm on her trousers afterwards.

'Look.' He dropped his voice and ducked his head conspiratorially. 'About my little jokes. They weren't meant to be anything but fun, you know?' He gave a tentative smile showing his yellow teeth. 'I've always respected you, you know. You're a damn good cop.'

Crawl any further up my rectum and you'll be choking me.

'I need you to come with me to my place,' she told him. 'Watch my back.'

'I can't let you near your property,' he said self-righteously. 'Too dangerous.'

'My grandmother may be there. I've got to check she's all right. I can't wait. Anything could happen.' She paused, looked him in the eye. 'I'll owe you, Zhang.'

His expression cleared as he worked through the opportunities of having a Supervisor First Class in his debt. He called across the room. 'Hey! Bai! Cover for me, will you? I'm going with the Super for a recce.'

He turned back to her. 'Let's get kitted up.'

'No time.' She was already moving for the door. She heard him mutter a curse, but he fell in behind.

Already armoured vehicles and fire trucks were converging on the square. Traffic police had blocked off the surrounding roads. Three Tibetan men were running towards the Barkhor, shouting to each other. As Lia approached, she saw one man bring out a cigarette lighter and try to light a stack of newspapers outside a Chinese shop. Another began kicking a civilian car, denting the panels.

Zhang slowed, making to stop them, but Lia grabbed his arm. 'Later,' she said. She could see a string of smoke coming from the Barkhor. Black smoke, streaming above the rooftops. She ran for the smoke, Zhang hot on her heels, but when she came around the corner and into her street she slowed. An oversized metal drum was outside her house, burning what appeared to be refuse. That explained the smoke. People milled around aimlessly. Lia couldn't see or hear anyone shouting slogans.

'What's going on?' she asked a bystander.

'Don't ask me.' The man shrugged. 'We heard there might be a riot, which is why I closed my shop, but nothing seems to be happening.'

Lia started to walk down the street but stopped when she heard her name being called. To her surprise, she saw Mrs Lily hastening towards her. 'Come away,' she said. 'Your grandmother is with me. She says you mustn't be seen here.'

With Zhang hovering, she allowed Mrs Lily to draw her into a porch a few houses down, where Fang Dongmei stood. The instant she saw Lia, the old woman clasped her against her bosom. It was the first time Jian's grandmother had hugged her and it felt like being enfolded in a duvet that smelled of burned sugar. 'They are out to get you,' she told Lia urgently. 'You must hide.'

Lia scanned the street. She saw a knot of rough-looking men congregate at the burning metal drum. They were dressed in workmen's clothes, dirty jeans and anoraks, boots.

Lia said, 'Tan told me Dohna's husband has been protesting at the arrests made this morning. I've heard he wants me dead.'

The old woman's eyes narrowed. 'Dohna isn't married.'

Zhang stepped forward. He was frowning. 'So who's been calling for the Supervisor's death for betraying her "Tibetan friends"?'

Fang Dongmei ignored him. She grasped Lia's elbow. 'Not anyone we know. We're as puzzled as you are. Most people don't approve of Dohna and her friends. Everyone wants peace, to be left alone without any—'

'I don't like this,' Zhang interrupted. Lia followed his gaze. The men by the burning drum had fanned out across the street and were walking purposefully towards them. Their expressions were intent, concentrated on Lia.

As she watched, the one closest caught her eye. He smiled.

'There she is!' he yelled. He was shouting in Mandarin, pointing. 'Get her, the traitor!'

40

LIA TURNED AND RAN. She heard Zhang say, 'Shit', and then he was pelting after her. She swung right at the next corner and immediately left, ducking and weaving her way through the narrow medieval streets and alleyways.

She pitched down the next street flat out. Her breathing rasped in her throat, hot and raw. Her handbag bounced against her hip.

'Here!' Zhang called. He was pointing up the street in the direction of an alley that led towards the PSB office. Neck and neck they raced along the alley, dodging garbage bags, swerving around pilgrims shuffling along. Behind her she could hear footsteps pounding, the men's shouts.

She was fast, but her pursuers were too. She wasn't shaking them off. Their shouts followed her, their footsteps pounding behind.

Can't outrun them. I have to hide.

Lia dived right again, then doubled back before heading south once more.

'Where are you going?' panted Zhang.

She didn't answer. She heard him breathing hard behind her and his boots thundering on the ground.

Her phone rang in her handbag but she didn't answer it. She couldn't risk dropping her pace.

'We're going in the wrong direction!' Zhang protested.

Past a cluster of stalls, women selling prayer flags, tea cups and silver trinkets, she recognised a string of prayer wheels leading left and down the next side street. She tried to increase her pace.

She jinked left at the corner, raced down the alley. Past the prayer wheels, she saw an open door. 'This way!'

She leaped through the doorway of the Meru Nyingba Monastery. Grabbed Zhang's arm she spun him round. Sweat rolled down his face and he was gasping.

'You keep going,' she ordered. 'Lead them away.'

'You're joking.'

'Do it!'

He jumped back into the alley as though electrified. She didn't wait to see which way he went. She slipped through the temple, trying to control her breathing, bring her heart rate down. The smell of juniper enveloped her, the soft sound of chanting. Candles flickered in the corners. Monks talked in low voices. She couldn't hear any sound of her pursuers. She brushed past several pilgrims, heading for the door at the far end of the temple, where she knew a set of stairs led to the Abbot's quarters. She made her way through a pair of heavy purple curtains, and glanced over her shoulder to check nobody had followed her inside.

Heart still pounding, she climbed the stairs. At the top, she knocked on the door. Silence. She turned the heavy brass knob, stepped inside. The room was empty. A hurricane lamp burned on a desk, casting a pale light across some papers and pens, an open book. She prowled back and forth across the bare boards, her nerves strung tight. Where were her pursuers? Had they chased Zhang? Where were they? Would someone give her away? Someone who'd seen her run inside?

A commotion sounded nearby. Lia went to the door, opened it a crack. She heard someone shouting. The same man who'd yelled in Mandarin, *get her!*

Desperately, Lia looked around but there was nowhere to hide. She was debating whether to leave the room and run again, when she heard footsteps coming up the stairs. Measured steps, not hurried. Maybe two people.

She slipped to stand next to the wall, so that when the door opened, she wouldn't be seen immediately. She heard men's voices outside, talking in Tibetan. Quiet voices, calm. Then they fell quiet. The door opened.

She watched the Abbot step inside. As he turned to close the door, his eyes travelled over her but he didn't blink or give any indication he'd seen her. For a wild, crazy moment she wondered if he'd gone blind. He said something to someone obviously standing outside. The man said something back. The Abbot closed the door and went to his desk. Sat down with his back to her. It was a gesture of supreme trust.

'I won't tell them you're here,' he said.

'Thank you.' Her voice was hoarse.

'Why are they after you?'

'They think I betrayed their friends to the authorities.'

'Did you?' He turned in his seat and looked at her.

'Their friends had bombs. Molotov cocktails.'

'I see.' His face remained impassive.

Suddenly, her legs felt weak. She put a hand on the wall to steady herself.

The Abbot rose, brought over a high-backed wooden chair.

'Thank you.' She sat down. She was trembling.

'You may stay for as long as you like.' The Abbot turned back to his desk and picked up his pen. Began to write. She watched him for a few minutes, allowing herself to regain her equilibrium. Then she withdrew her phone. Dialled. 'Commissioner Zhi,' she said.

'Sorry,' said his assistant, Mary Chow, 'but he's—'

'Get him *now*,' Lia snapped, nervous tension suddenly getting the better of her. 'Or I will report you to the police standards authority and have you demoted to Qinghai and cleaning out jail toilets.'

'There's no need to take that tone,' Mary said tightly. 'He's gone to the bathroom. And no matter how urgent it is, I am *not* going in there after him.'

'I'll wait.'

Eventually, she heard Mary calling to her boss. Zhi picked

up fast. 'What the hell is going on? Someone said there's a mob after you. Are you OK?'

'Yes, I'm OK.'

'Where are you?'

She considered the man's voice shouting, *get her!* and decided a healthy dose of paranoia wouldn't go amiss.

'Somewhere safe,' she said.

'Good. Stay where you are,' he commanded. 'Hang on...' His voice grew muffled as he put a hand over the receiver. She couldn't hear what he was saying. After half a minute, he came back to the phone. 'Sorry, that was Tan. He's doing his nut over these protests...Look, sit tight until we have a security lockdown in place. I'll ring you when it's clear.'

'Thanks.'

She hung up and dialled Zhang, but he didn't answer. She hoped he was OK and hadn't got caught by the men and torn apart. What a mess. At least Fang Dongmei was all right. Thank heavens for Mrs Lily. She tried Zhang again and left a message, asking him to ring her when he could. Finally, she put her phone on vibrate, shoved it back in her pocket and settled to wait.

*

An hour passed. The Abbot continued to write, seemingly absorbed. The only sounds were his pen scratching on paper, the occasional tinkle and ring of temple bells. She resisted the urge to ring the Commissioner to see what was happening. He wouldn't appreciate being nagged. He'd already told her he'd let her know when it was safe for her to come out.

Be patient. Wait.

Her mind drifted to Dohna, who'd started all this. She'd lied about having a husband, but it didn't matter. It made a good story, a *great* story of revenge and retribution. No wonder Tan thought it could start a riot. But where were the fifty people who were supposed to be congregating outside her house? Aside from the burning rubbish bin, there was no evidence of protesters. Everyone had been milling about, both Tibetans and Chinese, seemingly bemused, until the bunch of scruffy thugs turned up. There hadn't been much else going on. Just the three young Tibetan men she and Zhang had seen in the square, getting overexcited.

Her phone chirped, telling her she had a text message. It was Zhang, saying he was back at the station and asking if she was all right. She texted back saying: *I'm safe, am OK.*

She glanced at her watch. Four o'clock. She felt a wave of fatigue roll over her. What with the dawn raid this morning, and then being chased, she was exhausted. Without realising it, she began to doze.

She came awake with a start when she heard footsteps on the stairs. The Abbot paused in his writing. He glanced at her briefly before rising and going to the door. He listened briefly before opening it and stepping out, leaving it ajar.

'Quick!'

The Abbot returned in a rush.

'You must hide!'

He swept to the far end of the room and dropped to his knees. He brought out a small metal hook from beneath his robes and fitted it to an almost invisible ring snugly fitted into the floorboards. To her astonishment, he opened a narrow trapdoor which had been beautifully concealed in the grains of the wood. She would never have spotted it in a million years, even if she'd been told it was there.

'Inside,' he urged. 'No one must know you're here.'

Since he'd hidden her for most of the afternoon without raising the alarm, she decided to trust him. She began to slip down a short ladder but stopped when he put a hand on her arm.

'Do not come out unless I greet you with the name *Hariti* – the protectress of children. This is your code name, the one we use when we talk about you. Do you understand?'

'Hariti,' she repeated.

She slid into a small space containing a single threadbare mattress with a yak-hair blanket folded at its end. As soon as she slunk onto the mattress, the Abbot dropped the trapdoor. Instantly, darkness enveloped her and for a moment, claustrophobia grabbed her lungs. It was like being in a tomb, a coffin...

Sweat sprang. She took a deep breath. Concentrated on the sound of the Abbot's feet walking across the room. The scrape of his chair. A soft cloth rustling as he took his seat. Then she heard the door opening. Footsteps coming inside. It sounded as though there was more than one man. She surmised two, maybe three.

'Where is she?'

The man's tone was calm and collected.

'Who?' The Abbot's voice was perfectly pitched innocence.

'The woman.'

'What woman?'

They were speaking in Mandarin. Why? Was the man Chinese? Or was it to prevent any eavesdropping Tibetans from understanding?

'Stop pissing me off, old man.'

The Abbot's tone was puzzled. 'What makes you think this woman is here?'

'I have my spies,' he said.

Zhang, Lia thought. He was the only person who knew where she'd gone. Her stomach clenched. Or had someone traced her mobile phone? Carefully, not wanting to make a sound, she withdrew her phone from her pocket and switched it off. Sweat prickled her hairline.

'There is no woman here,' the Abbot insisted.

'Shall we check your hidey-hole?' the man said silkily. 'Just in case she crept in there all on her own?'

41

'WHERE'S THE TRAPDOOR?' the man asked.

'There is no trapdoor.'

'Sharmar. Rinzen.' The man clicked his fingers. 'Find it.'

Footsteps began walking slowly across the floor. Lia shrank to the furthest recess of her hiding place, heart hammering, sweat pouring. Her eyes had adjusted to the darkness and she could now see light seeping between tiny cracks in the floorboards.

'Who is she?' asked the Abbot. More innocence.

The man didn't answer.

Lia sat huddled in the corner, arms hugging her knees, and fighting an irresistible urge to scream. She trembled as the footsteps came closer. Would he spot the tiny ring? The hidden shape of the door in the wood?

'It's here, boss.'

'Well, lift it up then.'

There was a scratching sound but the trapdoor remained where it was. 'I need a key or something. Rinzen? You got anything?'

Footsteps, the sound of keys jingling, then metal against wood.

Please, please, she prayed. *Don't let them open it.*

Lia crouched in the darkness. Her pulse was pounding in her ears. Desperately she felt for a weapon, but there was nothing. Just the mattress and the single thin blanket. She gripped her phone in her fist thinking she could always crack it against one of the men's skulls...

A shaft of light beamed into the darkness and the next instant the trapdoor was open. It took a moment for her eyes to adjust from the darkness. She saw a crumple of maroon robe at eye-level. A sandal. A bare brown foot. The foot withdrew.

A man's face peered inside. Tibetan, in his thirties.

'She's here.'

'Bring her out.'

The man began to climb down. He was wiry, not particularly big, but the space was small and awkward, forcing him to expose the lower half of his body.

Lia rose and twisted sideways and lashed out with her right foot, planting her boot squarely in the man's groin.

He went down with a high-pitched whistling squeal, like a pig. She kicked him in the head. He kept groaning, holding his groin. She kicked him again, but then the next man was swarming down the ladder and she tried to attack him but the first man was in the way and the second man was much larger and simply leaned over his fallen comrade and grabbed both her wrists and hauled her bodily up the ladder.

Lia flipped like a stranded fish, kicking out, trying to hurt him, but when he slammed a fist into the side of her head she stopped struggling, momentarily stunned.

'Brother!' The Abbot was standing there looking shocked. 'Please!'

Her ears were ringing, her vision blurred.

The man she'd hit was still moaning. He crawled up the ladder and stood to one side, swaying, still clutching his groin. His skin was the colour of mashed potato.

She studied the three men, all strong and muscular, all in maroon robes. All had shaven heads and wore sandals. 'Who are you?' she managed.

The shortest man came and stood in front of her. 'We ask the questions, OK?'

He reached inside his robe and withdrew a mobile phone. Punched some numbers. Held it to his ear. With a little shock, she saw he was left-handed.

He said into the phone, 'It's me...Yes, it's Nima. I know,

the signal's crap...Yes. We've got her. Yes, she's alive.' He glanced her way. 'No, I've told you before...I'm not killing a police officer...'

Nima pulled the phone from his ear. Even Lia could hear the angry squawks coming from the handpiece.

'Am I right?' He looked at his two men, one of whom nodded, but the man she'd kicked in the groin hesitated for a second, glaring at her, but then he nodded too.

Nima said again into the phone, 'No,' very firmly. Then, 'OK, so send them here...' Long pause while he listened. 'Yes, we'll wait. OK.'

He pushed the phone back into his robe. Looking at Sharmar and Rinzen – she didn't know which man was which – he said, 'The men from the street are being directed here. The ones who fucked up earlier. They'll deal with her.'

'How long?' the man holding her asked.

'It could be a while. The PSB are all over the city. Everyone's finding it hard to move. We just have to hold her until they get here.' He surveyed her thoughtfully. 'I know you've just been doing your job, but have you ever considered you've been doing it a little too well? You've been like a piece of bamboo stuck up our arses.'

Nima stepped close, studying her. He was absorbed.

'You were in the helicopter,' he said. 'But you didn't see us, did you? You may be good, but we're better.'

Her mouth was dry, and she had to work her tongue before she could speak. 'You were travelling with the lamas?' She couldn't remember seeing any of them in the tent.

'You could say that.'

'You followed them?'

'And they never knew we were there. They still don't know, in fact, that we followed them right into the centre of Lhasa.'

Lia blinked. 'I thought they still had more boys to test.'

'They're knackered. Between you and me I'm amazed they

haven't dropped dead by now. They're having a bit of a respite, apparently, before pushing east. With us right behind them, of course.' His eyes gleamed.

She stared. 'You shot Lama Sonam.'

'But I didn't shoot you,' he said. 'We're on the same side, even if you don't know it.'

He looked at his men. 'Good job, heya?'

The two men nodded, absorbed in the praise from their boss. Absorbed in self-congratulation, of a job well done. They seemed to have forgotten they weren't alone.

*

The Abbot moved faster than she thought possible. One second he was standing beside his desk, stick-thin and bent and impossibly ancient, the next he'd sped across the room, flung open the door and plunged outside. He was shouting at the top of his voice, screaming in Tibetan, Lia didn't know what, but it wasn't for long.

Nima spun round and tore outside.

Abruptly, the screams stopped.

Seconds later he returned, dragging the Abbot with him. He had his hands around the Abbot's throat.

'B-brother...' The Abbot's voice was strangled.

From downstairs came shouts. The sound of pounding feet.

Suddenly, the Abbot's body stiffened. His arms flailed and he made a rattling sound deep in his throat. His body went completely limp. He slid slowly to the floor.

Nima stared at the crumpled form of the Abbot. He said, 'I don't fucking believe it.'

More shouts. Feet hammered on the stairs.

The three men looked at one another.

'Let's go,' said Nima.

She thought they might prise open the window and escape through the rooftops, but they simply charged through the door and ran outside. Dressed as monks, they'd slip through the monastery without garnering a second look and although she wanted to run after them, she couldn't leave the Abbot. She raced to his prone form and dropped to his side. He wasn't breathing. She rolled him onto his back, and checked his pulse. Nothing.

Fingers clumsy with haste, she switched on her phone and rang Zhang. Asked him to activate paramedics, an ambulance. Gave him directions. Phone returned to her pocket, she quickly tilted the Abbot's head back, pinched his nose, and started resuscitation. She gave five full breaths fast before checking his pulse.

Nothing.

Monks poured into the room, milling around, excited and noisy with anxiety. She looked up and said, 'Get me a medic! A doctor!'

No time to see if anyone had run to do her bidding. She had to kick-start his heart. She'd never done this for real before. Only in training exercises. She had to find the lower end of his breastbone. Find the midline. I hope this is right, she thought as she placed the heel of her left hand on his chest. Then she interlocked her fingers of both hands and began compressions, counting out loud. He felt incredibly frail beneath her hands and she prayed she wasn't breaking anything, fracturing his ribs, but she couldn't be tentative. She had to be firm or it wouldn't work.

Don't die on me, Abbot!

Fifteen compressions. Two breaths. Fifteen compressions. Two breaths.

After a minute, she checked his pulse.

Nothing.

Come on! Don't give up!

Fifteen compressions. Two breaths.

In the distance, she heard the wail of a siren. Please, let it be the ambulance.

Fifteen compressions. Two breaths.

She only stopped when Zhang burst into the room, the paramedics behind him. Deshi followed.

While the medics worked on the Abbot, she drew Zhang and Deshi aside and told them what had happened.

'Where did you hide?' Zhang asked. He was looking around the room much as she had when she'd first entered.

'I listened outside the door,' she lied. She didn't know if it was instinct that made her lie, or if it was simply because she didn't want the hidey-hole to be made public knowledge, but whatever it was, she didn't feel any guilt over it.

The paramedics rose to their feet. Looked across at them. 'Sorry,' one of them said. 'He's gone.'

*

'Get Hua Ming and his team here,' she told Zhang. 'Lock the monastery doors and make sure no one leaves. Lots of people will have seen the three men. Bring in the murder squad. I want every monk, every novice, questioned.' She wondered if Hua Ming would find the trapdoor. It would certainly show whether his team were as meticulous as he maintained.

Zhang walked outside immediately.

Lia looked at the dead Abbot. Sorrow rose inside her for the man who had protected her, and told her her code name. Hariti, the protectress of children. She rather liked it.

'I need to talk to you,' Deshi whispered. He was hovering by her elbow.

'Not now.' She was curt.

'It's important. Look, I just got back from Xigatsê...'

Her eyes flew to him. 'You did?'

'Yes. I found Zapa. He killed my guest-house manager. There was a dog. It was *huge*. I'm terrified of dogs but it didn't bite me. He tried to kill me...not the dog, Zapa. But Sashi...I rang you but you were busy, and when you rang me back...' His words were tumbling thick and fast, the story disjointed, but Lia stuck to the one thing that alarmed her most.

'Who tried to kill you?'

'Zapa. He had a silencer. He was waiting for me in my room. Andy Ho went in and he shot him. His head was blown away. I saw his brains leaking...'

He was, she realised, close to tears.

'Hey.' Lia caught both his upper arms, squeezed them firmly. Gave him a little shake. 'It's OK. You're safe now.'

Deshi gulped.

'Have you told anyone about this?' she asked. 'Your trip to Xigatsê?'

'I haven't had time. I only got back half an hour ago. Besides, I had to warn you. Zapa wants you dead too.' The young police officer's mouth trembled. 'He wants us both dead. He said we know too much, but I don't know anything. I don't understand what's going on.'

Things had escalated, Lia realised. Warning her off wasn't enough any more. She had to be eliminated.

Lia glanced around the room. The medics were packing up. Zhang was, hopefully, guarding the front door of the monastery and making phone calls.

She drew Deshi into the corner of the room. 'Start from the beginning. From the moment you arrived in Xigatsê. What was the first thing you did?'

'I went to the monastery, looking for Zapa. But nobody seemed to know him. He knew me, though. I was in the temple. I was *asleep*. He came and sat next to me...He swore. I've never heard a monk swear before...'

She let Deshi talk. Gradually he calmed, began to become more coherent. It soon became clear that Zapa hadn't wanted to kill Deshi straight away. Lia guessed Zapa had spoken to someone else after he'd talked to Deshi, who had given the order.

'He said he'd been waiting for this for years. Goldhawk and him. *Years*.' Deshi licked his lips. 'He wanted me to repeat something to you, word for word. I couldn't make any sense of it. I tried, but—'

'Deshi,' she interrupted softly. 'Just tell me what he said.'

'He told me to tell you to back off, and leave Goldhawk to do his job. They have eight boys left. Then the system will be – this is exactly what he said – irreversibly fucked.'

At that moment Lia brought every strand of every piece of knowledge together and fitted them neatly into a single composition. The following rush of goose bumps confirmed the conclusion she'd come to was absolutely right.

Her stomach went hollow. Wō kào. Holy shit. No!

She stared past him, her gaze unfocused as her mind reeled.

'Can you repeat that?' Her voice was scratchy.

Deshi obediently did as she said. He was watching her intently. 'What did he mean?'

Lia put a hand on the wall to steady herself.

Zapa spoke fluent Mandarin. And so had Nima, Rinzen and Sharmar, and the man who'd shouted, Get her, the traitor!

Zapa had said she was being *unpatriotic*.

Nima had said he knew she'd just been doing her job.

She'd bet her last yuan Zapa and Nima weren't Tibetan monks.

They were something far more dangerous. They were Chinese, maybe government, agents.

Zapa and Goldhawk had been waiting for this for years.

Which meant they were agents who had probably been deep undercover. Sleepers, put in place decades ago, to be activated should there be a threat or an opportunity to be had. Zapa's mission was to ensure Goldhawk did his job: to kill every little boy that was a potential reincarnation of the Panchen Lama.

Nima, the left-handed monk, was Goldhawk. He'd followed the lamas, and at each village, each nomadic camp, he'd found every boy that had been tested, and killed him. He'd also killed Lama Sonam.

But he hadn't wanted to kill her, a police officer.

We're on the same side...

For the first time, real fear permeated Lia, making her heart turn cold. Who else was involved? Did the PSB know about the mission? What about Tan and Myra Kwok?

The protesters outside her house had been a smokescreen. They weren't Dohna's family after all, but paid thugs. It was a neat way of disposing her, drawing all eyes away from the travelling lamas to focus on a terrorist cell in the city wreaking vengeance on a police officer they thought of as a traitor.

She could now understand the fervour with which the mission was protected, because if it came out that the Chinese authorities were killing little boys in order to control Tibet's future spiritual leaders, the whole country, the whole *world* would go crazy.

Could she stand aside and let things play out without intervening? No. Did she care? Yes. She didn't want her country torn apart. She didn't want to see the Tibetans, a mainly peaceful and nonviolent people, massacred. She didn't want to see peaceful Hui and Han killed either, but above all, she didn't want another single boy to die. No matter what the reasons, it was wrong. Murder was murder.

'We must go,' she said.

Deshi didn't argue. 'Where?'

'Somewhere safe.' Her mind was already reaching forward, picking up ideas and discarding them just as fast.

'We should tell the Commissioner,' Deshi said.

Another chill. 'Wait here,' she said. She went out of the room and down the stairs, where Zhang was standing sentry.

'Superintendent,' she said. 'Before I rang you to report the Abbot's attack, did you tell anyone where I was?'

Zhang looked surprised. 'No.'

'Not even the Commissioner?'

'No.' He shook his head. 'He was too busy. Why, should I have? You said you were OK...'

'No, you did fine. I just wanted to check, that's all.'

Lia climbed back to Deshi. Was the Commissioner

involved? He'd been reluctant to give credence to Deshi when the constable had linked the two boys' deaths in the Bharkor, and he'd originally agreed with Tan that a serial killer didn't exist. But he'd ordered an autopsy on the second boy...And then sent her to Gertse with full forensic back-up.

How had Nima *known* where she was without tracing her mobile phone?

Better not to trust anybody.

*

She led Deshi out of the monastery and up the alley. Her senses were alive, tingling. She kept a watch for the handful of scruffy thugs, but didn't see anybody. Her street was quiet when she arrived. The bin of burning refuse had been put out. A faint smell of wet ash hung in the air. She let herself into her apartment. Deshi followed. He looked about curiously. 'Cute,' he said.

Lia knocked on Fang Dongmei's door. Immediately it opened.

'*Ai Ya!*' she cried. She wrapped Lia in her arms. 'I was so worried. Those men...' She leaned back and studied Lia from head to toe with a ferocious scowl.

'I'm all right,' Lia assured her.

The old woman grunted then switched her gaze to over Lia's shoulder. Her face instantly became a picture of scorn. 'What's he doing here?'

'He's tangled up in it all. They want to kill him too.'

Fang Dongmei's expression didn't soften.

'He's a friend, Grandmother,' Lia said.

'If you say so.' The old woman remained unconvinced.

'We need somewhere to stay tonight,' Lia said. 'Not here, where they can find us, but elsewhere. Can you help?'

Fang Dongmei fetched her puffy black coat and red booties. 'Come,' she said. 'I know where you can hide.'

42

Tan stared at Superintendent Zhang.

'What do you mean, no one's seen them since?'

Zhang dropped his gaze and shuffled his feet. 'Shan and Deshi left the monastery this afternoon and that's the last I saw of them.'

'You didn't see which way they went?'

'I was inside the monastery doors, making sure nobody left.'

Tan checked his watch for what felt like the hundredth time. Nearly midnight. Anxiety twisted his belly, making him nauseous. Where was she? She'd been hounded by a mob into the monastery, where an Abbot had been murdered, and now she'd vanished, along with Constable Deshi. What was going on? Why hadn't they returned to the station? Why were neither of them at home?

Tan hadn't caught the mobsters, though not from lack of trying. The men had chased Zhang around half the town but luckily Zhang had found his way to the PSB office where Tan had immediately activated just about every officer to hunt the mobsters down. They'd had no luck. It had been like searching for half a dozen weevils in a silo of grain.

He'd checked the monastery, but since the Commissioner seemed to have everything under control, he'd driven across town to question the Tibetan girl, Dohna. Dohna had no husband, not even a boyfriend. She didn't know anything about the man wanting to kill Lia for supposedly betraying her but he could tell she wished she'd thought of it.

Who wanted the Supervisor dead? He couldn't work it out. If it wasn't Dohna, then who was after her? It also appeared they were after Deshi.

What was going on?

'Sir?'

Tan glanced up. He'd forgotten Zhang was there. 'You said Deshi went to Xigatsê?'

'Yes, sir.'

'What was he doing there?'

'He said he was trying to find a monk who had attacked Supervisor Shan. The monk came from the Tashilhunpo Monastery.'

Tan felt his eyes bulge. 'A monk attacked the Supervisor? When was this? Why didn't I know?'

'Deshi didn't say when. And, er...she didn't want it reported, sir.'

Tan ran his hands down his face. Why on earth not? Something treacherous was happening. Instinct told him it had something to do with the Snow Thief, but *what*?

'Tell everyone to keep an eye out for them,' he ordered. 'I want them found. And the second you find them, alert me.'

'Yes, sir.'

Tan watched the Superintendent leave. He'd already notified the CCTV crews. Lia and Deshi couldn't move around in the city without being spotted by one of the hundreds of cameras. Not unless they were disguised. He'd also ordered all their friends to be closely watched. Being reasonably sociable, Deshi had quite a few people he might go and stay with but Lia seemed to have nobody, except the grandmother – who had also disappeared – and Pete, her Tibetan driver, who he'd already put under surveillance.

Tan began to pace. Back and forth, back and forth, like a caged animal. When he'd heard Lia had gone into the Barkhor with just Zhang, and not even wearing a tactical vest, he'd just about had heart failure. And now she'd vanished...

He felt sick and angry. And scared. He'd never worried for anyone before. He didn't like it. He was the one always in control. His world ran according to his rules, his authorisation. It was unimaginable that she might have vanished for ever. That the thugs had got her. That she might be dead.

He tried her mobile phone again. His fingers trembled as he dialled. The same message played. *This phone is switched off. Try again later.*

He continued to pace. Sweat formed on his face. His heart was pounding.

He said her name over and over in his mind.

He prayed.

He had to find her. Anything else was inconceivable.

43

LIA AWOKE TO THE sound of someone calling goodbye. A door closed. She could hear traffic and for a few seconds she didn't know where she was, but then she took in the sunlight slanting across her blanket. She was in Mrs Lily's apartment on the twelfth floor of a block that was identical to the other six blocks on the street. Mass housing with noisy heating and creaking lifts that smelled of fried oil and garlic. Despite being built only three years ago, the concrete was already cracking, paint peeling from its walls.

She lay back on the sofa. She could hear Fang Dongmei snoring from the sofa bed opposite, and Deshi's breathing where he slept on the floor. All three of them were crammed into Mrs Lily's tiny living room. There was only one bedroom, where Mrs Lily and her husband, Duyi, slept. Mrs Lily's real name was Aamina but few people called her that thanks to her stall. Her hair still held a purple streak but her cheerful expression had vanished beneath a look of anxiety at having them to stay.

Lia hadn't wanted to involve Mrs Lily but Fang Dongmei insisted, 'Can you think of anywhere safer?' The block warden – employed to keep an eye on who went in and out – had been busy watching TV and just waved at Mrs Lily, letting them off from signing in. This meant there was no record of them being here, a point which Fang Dongmei laboured.

Lia had relented without any further argument. She'd been exhausted, dead on her feet, and Deshi was similarly tired. Both of them had fallen asleep at the tatty kitchen table after eating. Lia had wanted to tell Deshi and Fang Dongmei that she believed that government agents were killing the boys but at the thought of all the questions they'd ask, she'd run out of energy.

Now, Lia rose and headed to the bathroom. The door didn't fit properly and the hot water was variable. She washed and got dressed. When she came out, Deshi was up. Unshaven, rumple-haired, he was stretching in front of the window. He looked rough. Much like herself, she guessed.

'Hi,' she said.

He turned. 'Hi. Look, we really need to go into the office. Report this...'

'No.'

'I don't understand.'

Last night he'd been exhausted, but now he was rested he was thinking more clearly.

'You only have part of the picture,' she told him. 'Let's have breakfast first.' She was firm. 'Then I'll fill you in.'

After Duyi had gone – Mrs Lily having left before dawn to set up her stall – Lia told Deshi and Fang Dongmei what she thought was happening. She didn't leave anything out. When she finished, there was silence. Deshi opened and closed his mouth. He looked faintly sick. Fang Dongmei didn't move. Just scowled at the linoleum table top.

'What do you make of it, Deshi?' Lia asked.

'It's a breathtaking mission,' he replied carefully, not giving anything he might be thinking away. 'Audacious.'

Lia leaned forward. 'What do you think will happen when the Tibetan people find out that the police, the Chinese authorities, knew what was happening all along, and did nothing? Do you think they'll sit back and welcome our choice of Dalai Lama? I don't think so.'

'They'll have no alternative,' said Deshi.

'Do you really want to be responsible for civil war?' Lia asked.

He raised his head. 'We'll crush them easily.'

Lia took a moment to compose herself. She was aware

of Fang Dongmei, watching them with an air of apprehension.

'You'll be paving the way for hundreds of years of resentment and hatred,' Lia stated. 'Terrorism will grow like a virus. Every Tibetan will become a potential threat. Do you really want to check beneath your car every time you drive it? Check your shopping, your mail, your rice bags? And what about our international reputation?' Lia shook her head. 'Not good, Deshi.'

The young police officer's face stiffened. 'Overseas critics shouldn't judge China by their standards. In my family, if a child doesn't lay his chopsticks down properly, then he's smacked, but in a Western family they're too relaxed about such things. Each family has its own rules and countries are the same.'

Lia actually laughed. 'Oh, my, what will Beijing think when Tibetans start to slaughter innocent Han Chinese by the hundreds? Let's give Constable Deshi a medal for his anti-Western views? I don't think so.'

Long silence.

'What should we do?' Deshi's voice was muted.

Lia wasn't sure. The mission had the stamp of the PSB all over it. She didn't trust Tan, and she certainly didn't trust Myra Kwok. Even Jenny and Commissioner Zhi had question marks over them.

Fang Dongmei rose and left the kitchen. When she came back she had on her coat and was holding her handbag. 'We need to talk to these lamas.' She sent Lia a sharp look. 'You think they're in the city?'

'According to Nima they're having a brief respite here before heading east.'

'I will go and find them. I know who to ask thanks to Yeshe and...' She looked away. 'Anil.''

Lia couldn't think of any reason to stop her. Her brain seemed to have seized up and was unable to think any further.

'Be careful,' she told her.

'Of course.' The old woman looked affronted.

Lia and Deshi spent the morning talking over what they knew, trying to find a way of exposing what was going on without getting themselves killed in the process.

'It depends who knows about it,' Lia said. 'How many people are involved? It could be a dozen, or it could be many more. There were the four mobsters, and then the two monks with Nima, who I assume is Goldhawk. There's Zapa and whoever is running the mission. That's already nine.'

'Not that many,' Deshi said. 'Not for a mission this big.'

'The more people who know about it, the more risk of it being found out.'

Where was Nima now? she wondered. And what about the Panchen Lama, Lobsang Jampo? Lama Sonam had begged her to protect him but how could she do that if she didn't know where he was?

She continued talking with Deshi, but they did little more than go around and around without finding any more answers.

At ten past one, Fang Dongmei returned. She wasn't alone. Tenzin and the five lamas were with her.

44

FANG DONGMEI LED THE lamas inside. Dawa Rinpoche walked across the room to greet Lia. If possible, he was thinner and more fragile than she remembered, with virtually no flesh left on his skull. She wondered at his journey, the toll it had taken, but then she remembered the strength of his grip when he'd held her hands on the mountain, and knew his appearance was deceptive. His face was alight as he greeted her.

'Hariti,' he said warmly. 'You are safe.'

'Yes.'

Behind him crowded the other lamas, craning their necks to see her, and then came the sturdy monk, Tenzin. He crossed the room and held out his hands. He said, 'I'm glad you're safe. I've been worried.'

Touched, she gripped his hands – strong and wide, as warm as freshly baked *man tou* – and thanked him.

The High Abbot called for one of the monks to light some incense, and to make tea, and the atmosphere became relaxed, excitable, almost like a reunion party, but Lia retained her guard. She sat at the far end of the room with her back to the wall and where she could keep an eye on the front door. Tenzin did the same. Unlike the other monks, he didn't relax but remained alert and tense, constantly worrying the prayer beads wrapped around the knuckles of his left hand.

After one of the monks had cleared the cups of tea, Dawa Rinpoche rose to stand before them. His face turned grave. When he began to speak in Tibetan, one of the lamas translated for Lia. 'We have run out of time,' he said. 'The Dalai Lama has been getting weaker and weaker, and we cannot keep his impending death a secret any longer...'

The lama was still translating softy but her mind had frozen. The Dalai Lama was *dying*?

'Obviously our mission is now of the most extreme urgency.' His gaze moved to settle on Lia. 'As we already know, it is only the Panchen Lama who is able to direct the search for the Dalai Lama's reincarnation. We urgently need to find the new Panchen Lama and ensure his safety so that he can start the process of proclaiming the next Dalai Lama.'

A long silence fell.

'Hariti,' said Dawa Rinpoche softly. 'Who is the boy?'

Her mind batted around her skull. Could she finally part with Lama Sonam's secret?

Dawa Rinpoche smiled at her. His eyes were kind. 'Lama Sonam told you who he was, didn't he? You have kept the boy safe, but now it is time for the truth.'

He was right, she realised.

She couldn't keep the name to herself any longer. As she made her decision, there was a certain relief in handing the knowledge over. Of passing the baton of the boy's name to someone else to look after.

'Lobsang Jampo,' she said quietly.

You could have heard a pin drop.

'Jampo?' Tenzin said. He looked disbelieving, almost appalled. 'Lobsang *Jampo*?'

'You know him?' she said.

He opened and closed his mouth, gaping like a fish.

Dawa Rinpoche gave a soft laugh. 'They didn't see eye to eye when they met.'

'Where is he?' Lia demanded. 'Where does he live?'

'Rabang,' said Dawa Rinpoche. He was looking delighted. 'He's a lively boy. Very spiritual, and very intelligent. An interested and enquiring mind. He speaks Mandarin and a little Cantonese, a little English too.' He turned briefly pensive. 'He needs to be nagged about studying. He's very bright but very lazy.'

Lia stared at the lama. He could have described Tashi.

'How strange that we tested his twin,' he remarked quietly, 'but not him. I think it was Lama Sonam's doing. I think he realised who Jampo was, and decided to hide him, keep him safe.'

'What was his twin's name?' asked Lia.

'Pemba Dolma.'

'But Pemba's twin is called Tashi,' she said.

'Good heavens.' Dawa Rinpoche blinked. 'You're right. His name *used* to be Lobsang Jampo until he fell ill at the beginning of the year. His parents didn't know what to do, he was gripped in a terrible fever. They didn't think he'd live. Out of desperation, they went to their Abbot, who re-named him. Jampo means gentle, which didn't truly suit his energetic personality, but Tashi was more appropriate, meaning lucky, auspicious. It seemed to work, as he recovered the following week.'

The Abbot at the Meru Nyingba Monastery had once been called Palden Oshoe, Lia remembered, but when he'd fallen ill, he'd been renamed Tsering Passang.

'Lama Sonam was cautious up to the end,' Dawa Rinpoche mused softly. 'Using Tashi's old name. What a clever tactic.'

His smile faded as his demeanour turned brisk. 'We must go to Tashi immediately. We need to give him a series of tests to affirm his status. Then, if he *is* the Panchen Lama, we must smuggle him out of Tibet. It is a good thing Rabang isn't too far from the Indian border. Perhaps two days' walking. When Tashi is safe in India, he can announce the Dalai Lama's death when it comes, and start the search for his reincarnation.'

'Brother.' Tenzin spoke up. Anxiety etched his features. 'I'm concerned for Tashi. Shall I go ahead to secure his safety?'

'What an excellent idea. But I'd rather you didn't go alone.' Dawa Rinpoche's gaze fell on Lia once more. 'Poor Abbot Passang's death has caused security to be tightened. Perhaps someone in authority would help smooth your way?'

Tenzin looked at Lia. 'That would be a great help.'

'You want me to go to Rabang?' she said, heart sinking.

'Please,' Tenzin entreated her. 'It'll take much less time if you come with me. I could pretend to be your translator.'

She licked her lips nervously. She had to tell them about the spies in their midst. The government agents destroying them from inside out. She ran her eyes over the grave-faced lamas, the gentle-eyed translator. Were there any in the room?

'Look,' she said. 'There's something you don't know.'

Her tone was tense. The room stilled. Everyone looked at her.

She took a breath and released it. 'I believe the boys have been killed by government agents working deep undercover. A man called Zapa, from the Tashilhunpo Monastery in Xigatsê, is one of them. He tried to kill Constable Deshi yesterday.'

All eyes swivelled to Deshi, who looked at the floor, discomfited.

'He wants to kill me too.'

'Yes,' said Dawa Rinpoche. 'We know.'

Her jaw dropped. 'You know about the agents?'

He nodded.

'How long have you known?'

'Since you visited us in the mountains. It didn't take much to work it out.' He smiled.

'Do you know who killed the boys?'

'No.' His eyes sharpened. 'Do you?'

'A man called Nima. He and two men, disguised as monks, followed you as you travelled.'

'And this Nima killed Lama Sonam?'

'Yes.'

'Where is Nima now?'

'I don't know.'

Alarm rose on his features. 'Could he follow us again?'

'We have to be very careful.'

Dawa Rinpoche stood quite still, quite motionless. Finally, he said, 'The sooner you and Tenzin leave, the better. I want Tashi's safety secured. We will follow as soon as we can. This afternoon, I hope.'

As soon as he'd spoken the lamas broke their positions, rising to their feet, rearranging their robes and murmuring. Tenzin came over to Lia. He said, 'We must leave immediately. Do you have a car?'

'No. But I know someone who has one.'

45

WHEN ONE OF THE surveillance officers rang Tan to tell him he'd spotted Supervisor Shan at the tourist office where Pete, her driver, worked, Tan felt as though he'd been stabbed with an electric cattle prod. Even his hair bristled.

'Don't let her out of your sight. I'm on my way.'

He raced out of the office, dialling his driver with one hand, shoving his pistol in its holster with the other. His heart was thumping, his reflexes in overdrive. If she was with her driver, where was she going? Out into the wilderness again? Why? He ran full tilt outside to see his car already waiting. He leaped inside and slammed the door, shouting, 'Drive!'

The car shot forward.

'Siren, sir?'

'No.' He didn't want to bring attention to them unnecessarily. Besides which, he wanted to see Lia alone. Get some answers.

Make sure she's all right.

It didn't take long to drive to the Snowland Rent-a-Car office. He had the car door open even before the car drew to a halt. Springing across the pavement, he pushed open the door. Just three people were inside: Lia and Pete and a muscular monk he didn't recognise. All of them stared at him with horror on their features and fear in their eyes.

Lia looked exhausted. She had dark rings beneath her eyes and she'd lost weight. His chest felt as though it was being crushed. All he wanted was to take her in his arms and stroke her hair, tell her everything would be all right.

'What's going on?' he demanded of Lia. 'Where have you been? We've been going crazy with worry.'

Lia stared past him, blinking rapidly. She went to the door,

looked out. She said, 'Are you alone?' Her voice was apprehensive.

'Aside from my driver, yes. Why?'

'How did you find us?'

'I had this man –' he flicked a finger at Pete, who was
standing motionless and terrified '– put under surveillance in
case you turned up.'

'Call them off.' Her voice was tight.

'Why?'

'Just do it.'

He couldn't see why not. He'd found her, he didn't need
the surveillance team any more. Tan brought out his phone,
dialled. 'Officer Bo? Please stand down and have your
colleague do the same.'

'OK, sir. Standing down now.'

Tan hung up.

Her eyes narrowed suspiciously. 'Why are you alone?'

'You vanished from the murder scene. Disappeared.
There's obviously a good reason why. You feel threatened?'

She didn't answer. She turned to Pete and said, 'Get the
car.' Grabbing a bunch of keys, Pete scurried outside.

'Where are you going?' Tan asked Lia.

'Why should I tell you?'

Her stance was haughty, her gaze bold. His heart flipped.

Because I love you.

He felt a wave of dismay mixed with astonishment. He
loved her. There were no ifs and buts about it. He loved her
to the core of his being, her strange beauty, her strength, her
elegance. How had it happened? He had no idea, but suddenly
his twisting gut, his sleepless nights made sense.

'Because I can protect you,' he said. 'But only if I know
what's going on.'

She considered him at length. 'No,' she said.

He licked his lips. 'Where's Constable Deshi?'

'Somewhere safe.'

Alarm flared inside him. 'What does that mean?'

She didn't respond.

'What is *going on?*' Frustration rang in his voice. 'How can I help if you keep me in the dark? Is it to do with the Snow Thief?'

'How can it be,' she sneered, 'if he's in jail.'

He felt like tearing out his hair. For the first time, he seriously considered releasing the simpleton.

A car drew up outside. Lia walked to the door and opened it. She looked at the monk and said, 'Let's go.'

She was about to step outside but Tan caught her arm. 'Please,' he said.

She snatched her arm free, glaring. 'You want to help?'

'Yes!' It was almost a shout.

'Then let us go unimpeded. And don't tell anyone you've seen us. Not *anyone*. And that includes the Commissioner and Myra Kwok.'

'I don't understand.' He tried to reign in his temper. 'I *need* to know what's going on otherwise I can't safeguard you. Don't you realise?'

For a second, her cool expression softened a fraction. 'Officer Tan, what I'm doing is for the good of our country. That's all you need to know.'

The good of the country? What did she mean?

'Lia,' he pleaded. 'Just tell me...'

He paused when the monk brushed past them. He was carrying a sturdy leather bag. Tan watched the monk put the bag into the rear of the white Land Cruiser. He noticed it was the same vehicle that had been used to take Lia to Tali. Why was she running away with this monk? His mind leaped.

Had she killed the Abbot at the Meru Nyingba Monastery?

Hua Ming had said the man had died from a heart attack. He had some bruising around his neck, as though someone had put their hands around his throat, but he hadn't died of strangulation. Hua Ming had surmised his heart attack had been brought on by shock. If it were known that a police offer had killed the monk, the city would go crazy, even if it had been an accident.

'Will you keep quiet?' she asked him.

He didn't know what to say.

She stepped forward until she stood close. So close he could smell something lemony rising from her, perhaps the scent from soap, or shampoo. She raised a hand and touched his cheek. Her skin was warm, her fingertips as gentle and soft as thistledown. His entire body flushed with heat. He began to tremble.

'If you do,' she said softly, 'I'll make it worth your while.'

She will make love to me in return for my silence.

He took a step back and broke the contact. His arms were stiff at his sides.

'You don't have to do that.' His voice was gruff. 'But I would like it if you had dinner with me when you return.'

'Dinner?' she repeated, puzzled. 'Is that all?'

'Yes.'

She put her head on one side and scrutinised him. Her puzzlement seemed to intensify. 'You won't tell anyone we've left the city?'

'Not even a fucking sparrow, all right?' He ran a hand over his face. 'Look, I don't know what's going on because you won't tell me. But if you killed the Abbot, wouldn't it be better to turn yourself in? I can help you. I can fix things. You know that.'

This time, her mouth slackened. 'You think I killed the Abbot?'

He felt a spurt of irritation. 'Why else are you running away?'

Her eyes flicked past him then back. Back and forth they continued to dart. She was thinking rapidly, evaluating. Finally she said, 'I'm sorry. I can't tell you. I just can't.'

His heart leaped at the tinge of regret in her voice.

She'd softened towards him.

When she made to move to the door, he raised a hand fractionally, wanting to touch her but not daring to. He let it drop to his side.

'CCTV camera teams are looking for you,' he said. 'You'd do well to cover your faces when you leave.'

She stared at him for a moment, disbelief and confusion warring on her face. 'You won't follow me?'

He'd been planning to but now he said, 'Not if you don't want me to.'

'I'll spot you in an instant where we're going. You won't be able to hide.'

So, she was heading into the wilderness once again. Was she going back to Tali? Or Gertse or Rabang? Why?

'Ring me if you need me,' he told her, defeated. 'I want to help.'

She walked outside without looking at him.

Tan stood on the pavement and watched her slip into the Land Cruiser's passenger seat. He didn't think he'd ever felt so dumb or so stupid, but what could he do? Without tying her to a chair and pulling out her fingernails, she wasn't going to share what was going on.

He watched her drive away and only when the vehicle was out of sight did he return to his car. He rang Deshi but the constable had switched off his phone. Tan resolved to keep trying. He wasn't going to give up until he had some answers.

He had to know where Lia was headed.

46

LIA TWISTED IN HER seat and watched Tan dwindle into a dot.
He didn't move. Just watched them go, his posture oddly
deflated. She still couldn't believe he wasn't going to galvanise
the police and the army into chasing after them. She ran over
their conversation, trying to understand what had happened.
She'd offered her body to him, and he'd refused. Incredibly,
he'd asked her to dinner instead. *Dinner!* She couldn't work
out why he seemed to be helping her. Perhaps it was a double
bluff. Perhaps he'd commanded a helicopter to follow them?

Lia kept peering anxiously into the sky, and when no
helicopter appeared and no cars seemed to follow them, she
remembered Rong Rong Chang. After saving her life in Tali,
Tan was obviously convinced he was responsible for her
safety. She gave a grim smile. She couldn't have wished for a
higher-placed or more powerful protector.

As Dawa Rinpoche had said, the city was on tight security,
with machine-gun-armed soldiers on every corner, snipers
on roofs and military trucks and tanks looming on every
street. They'd barely gone two kilometres when Pete pulled
over and brought the car to a stop. The engine was still
running. He said, 'I can't do this.'

Lia closed her eyes. 'It's more important than you will
ever know that we get to Rabang.'

'Not after last time.' His lower lip quivered. 'They were
going to beat my family to death, remember?'

Tenzin climbed out of the car and walked to Pete's door.
He opened it and bodily hauled Pete outside. He said something fast, in Tibetan.

'No, no.' Pete looked at Lia, wild-eyed. 'Don't take my
car. Please, don't. My boss will go beserk.'

Tenzin pushed Pete aside and took up position at the steering wheel. He pushed the automatic gear stick into drive. He didn't look at Pete.

'No!' Pete began to shout but Tenzin gunned the engine, drowning him out. Lia turned in her seat to see Pete standing in the road behind them, still yelling.

'It's for the best,' Tenzin told her.

He was right, but it didn't sit well with her. If she survived, she promised herself she'd make it up to Pete when she got back.

They were stopped a few times on their way out of town, but all Lia did was show them her badge, and they were allowed on their way. On the edge of the city, Lia got Tenzin to head north, hoping to confuse anyone who might be tailing them. Eventually, Tenzin looped back on a rough road and within the hour they were on the way to Xigatsê, their only company being a couple of trucks and the odd bus. They had, Lia thought with a sense of disbelief, made it safely out of the city. Without saying a word, she sank back in her seat and closed her eyes. Within seconds, she was fast asleep.

*

She awoke when they were on the other side of Xigatsê. Night had fallen. Her mouth was furred and she had a crick in her neck. Tenzin climbed outside, letting in a rush of cold air. He walked to the rear of the car. To her surprise, he returned holding a satellite phone which he plugged into the cigarette lighter. He tightened the prayer beads around his knuckes, and dialled without looking at her. When it was answered, he spoke rapidly in Tibetan. When he hung up he said, 'The lamas are just leaving Lhasa.'

She checked her watch to see it was just after eight o'clock. The lamas were five hours behind.

'Do all monks carry sat phones?'

He turned his head aside. 'No. But Dawa Rinpoche thought it prudent.'

'Where did he get it?'

Tenzin rolled his eyes. 'He bought it. Just because we're monks doesn't mean we're technologically backward.'

Leaving the phone lying across the central console, Tenzin continued to drive. He drove fast, and when he tired, let Lia take over the wheel. She hadn't driven for ages and had to take it slower than she liked to start with, but after a while she regained her confidence and pushed harder. They drove through the night, only stopping for comfort rests. There was little conversation, but Lia didn't mind. When she wasn't driving, she lay across the rear seat, catching up on sleep, and Tenzin did the same.

Two days later, late morning, they arrived in Rabang dishevelled and travel-weary. Lia longed for a shower and to wash her hair but after staying here before, knew the best she'd get was an icy bath in the river. As they approached the outskirts of the village, Lia spotted Tashi waving at them from the side of the road. A small white dog sat expectantly at his feet, looking their way. Lia felt the same brush of disquiet that had dogged her throughout the Snow Thief case. It looked as though both boy and dog were waiting for them.

Lia asked Tenzin to pull over beside the boy. Tashi trotted to her side of the car. He was grinning.

'Supervisor!' he said. 'You came back!'

'Yes.' She turned in her seat to indicate Tenzin. 'You've both met before, I believe?'

'Tashi,' said Tenzin cautiously.

'Hello, Tenzin,' Tashi responded cheerfully. 'How is your digestion?'

'A little better.' Tenzin spoke grudgingly.

'I gave him a herbal remedy,' Tashi confided to Lia. 'He was moaning like mad when he was here last .'

Tenzin scowled.

Hoping Tashi's diplomatic skills would improve in the future, Lia quickly moved on. 'Can we give you a lift home?'

she asked the boy. 'We'd like to see your parents. Have a chat.'

Beaming, Tashi slid onto the back seat. When the small white dog tried to follow, Tenzin shooed it away with a sharp command and it dropped back. Tenzin gunned the Land Cruiser down the street. Lia looked in the wing mirror to see the animal desperately running after them.

Tashi kept up an excited chatter as they drove, telling them who had died – a local man called Kalden, and how two days later, his horse also died – and which children had been born and who had argued with who. He was a verbal newspaper, a gossip monger, but there was nothing malicious or salacious in his manner. He simply showed a bright matter-of-fact awareness of his village and obviously took a keen interest in its inhabitants.

'The Abbot says I shouldn't talk so much,' Tashi finally said, and sighed. 'He says I should let you tell me why you're here.'

Tashi was still talking to his dead Abbot? Perhaps he was one of those children who'd wanted an invisible friend, and had chosen the spirit of his beloved Abbot to be his unseen companion. She wasn't any sort of psychologist, but she couldn't think of any other explanation.

She twisted in her seat. Held the boy's gaze. 'We're here to keep you safe until the lamas return. They're not far behind, maybe five hours or so.'

A little corkscrew of concern appeared between his brows. 'They're coming back?'

'Yes. They want to talk to you.'

A wary look crossed his face. 'Like they did Pemba?'

'Yes.'

He nibbled his lip. He didn't say anything, but Lia guessed he was thinking about the fact his twin brother had talked with the lamas and wound up dead hours later.

'We'll protect you, OK?' Lia assured him.

300

Tashi stared outside. He remained silent. Lia was surprised; she'd expected him to bombard her with questions.

The village was busier than she remembered, which she put down to the fact it hadn't snowed recently, making it easier to get around. Smoke drifted from chimneys and children played in the road. Dogs lay outside houses, basking in the fading sunshine. Lia got Tashi to direct Tenzin to his home on the north side of the village and overlooking several rows of stunted apple trees.

Lia climbed out of the car and stretched. The pungently sweet scent of cow manure mingled with the smell of wood smoke. In the distance, rocky peaks pierced the sky like a skeleton's fingers. Once again, she felt a sense of awe at the vastness of the country, the emptiness.

'You like Tibet.' Tashi came and stood next to her. He made it sound like a statement, not a question.

Lia considered the hostile environment, the remoteness of the place and, wanting to be polite, said, 'I'm not sure.'

He gave her a gentle smile. 'Sometimes it takes a while before we see the beauty of something foreign.'

She could see his point, but didn't think it relevant to her. She'd been forced to Tibet, banished to endure its extreme climate. Whether she liked it or not didn't apply.

'Are your parents' home?' Lia asked.

'Mother probably is, but Father won't be back until later. Come inside, have some tea.' He gestured Tenzin towards the front door. 'Please. Make yourself comfortable. You've had a long drive.'

While Tashi's mother poured them bowls of tea from a big charcoal-blackened tea pot, Lia considered the boy. He was a child, with a child's sense of play and the irreverent, but he was also incredibly mature. What child aged six would invite two adults to tea, and with such grace? Whether Tashi was the official Panchen Lama or not didn't matter to Lia. He had such aplomb, such charm, he would fit into such a responsible role easily.

Tashi's home was almost identical to the cottage she'd stayed in when she'd last been here. Same earth-packed floors. Same fire in the middle of the living room, same enormous bed in the corner. She was yawning, wondering where they'd spend the night, when a flash of white caught the corner of her eye and the next second Tashi was running across the room.

'Cherry!'

Tashi skidded to his knees, allowing the little dog to leap into his arms. Tongue lolling, tail wagging furiously, the creature squirmed ecstatically in Tashi's embrace. Lia was wondering how long the boy had owned the dog when she abruptly recalled her late-night conversation with Tashi all those weeks ago, when he'd talked about his brother Pemba's death, and how Pemba's favourite dog, *a little white dog called Cherry*, missed him almost as much as he did.

While Tashi fussed over Cherry, Lia drank more tea. Eventually Tashi's father returned home. The instant he saw them – Lia and Tenzin side-by-side on stools next to the fire – his face froze. Lia saw the effort it took for him to unlock his jaw and release a polite smile. Tashi bounded to his feet and rushed to his father, talking animatedly.

'He's telling him that we're here to look after him until the lamas come,' Tenzin told Lia. 'He's just repeating what you said to him in the car.'

Tashi's father shared a quick look with his wife. Lia rose and went to them. Tenzin followed to translate.

'The lamas want to talk to Tashi?' The father was frowning. 'I don't understand.'

'They missed talking to him last time. They're on their way. They should be here soon, maybe late afternoon. Look, I can understand your concern. After losing Pemba...' She let a small respectful pause fall before continuing. 'We're here to protect Tashi. One of us will stay with him at all times. This means through the night, if necessary.'

Tashi's mother put her hands on her son's shoulders. The boy leaned back and she crossed her arms over his chest and held him close in a lovingly protective gesture. She said, 'Not him.' She jerked her head at Tenzin, who fortunately didn't take offence, but ducked his head in a conciliatory manner.

'I'll stay with Tashi,' Lia agreed. 'Until the lamas arrive.'

47

DAWA RINPOCHE AND TWO High Lamas arrived not long after sunset. One had skin the colour of cinnamon and fingers swollen with arthritis. The other lama's face was pockmarked and he walked with a cane. They looked as ancient as Dawa Rinpoche but, like the Abbot, both had button-bright eyes that were clear and candid.

'We mustn't waste any time,' Dawa Rinpoche told Lia. They were seated in Tashi's front room, his parents standing to one side looking awed and not a little nervous. Tashi, on the other hand, crackled with suppressed energy.

'You want me to do Pemba's test?' he asked brightly.

'We'd like to you to do something similar, yes,' Dawa Rinpoche replied.

'Lama Sonam asked me some questions when you were last here. He told me not to tell anyone. I told Pemba what to say...'

'Yes.' The lama's voice was gentle. 'We know. Which is why we're here.'

Dawa Rinpoche and the two High Lamas then spent the next hour or so talking to Tashi. It was relaxed and informal, and at one point they let him play with Cherry, who had trotted up to Tashi with a piece of rope in her mouth. Finally, Dawa Rinpoche gestured to the cinnamon-skinned lama, who brought out a piece of yellow and red silk cloth, about a yard square, and spread it on the ground. He then placed a variety of objects on the silk, including a hairpin, a pair of battered sunglasses, a splinter of wood, two pebbles and a small hand-carved wooden horse. When he was happy with their positioning, the lama sat back.

'Tashi,' Dawa Rinpoche said quietly. 'We would like you

to choose five objects. Simply touch them in order of your preference. There are over thirty items here. Please consider each carefully. Listen to your instincts, and take your time...'

But Tashi was already kneeling in front of the items, his hand moving across them. He chose the hairpin, a man's glove, what appeared to be a food wrapper and two plain grey pebbles.

A stunned silence fell.

'Are you certain of your choices?' Dawa Rinpoche asked.

Tashi nodded. 'Oh, yes. They're the only ones with the right energy.'

'What energy is that?'

'The same I feel when I pray. It's all around us but it's really intense in these objects.' He frowned. 'I don't know why. I mean why does the hairpin almost *vibrate* with it?'

This time, the silence was alive with excitement.

'It's him!' the crippled lama announced.

'It has to be!' his companion exclaimed.

'Yes,' confirmed Dawa Rinpoche. He was beaming. 'It is him.'

Tashi looked between them. 'What do you mean?'

'These objects used to belong to Gedhun Choekyi Nyima, the Panchen Lama,' Dawa Rinpoche said solemnly. 'The hairpin, for instance, holds a single hair of his. It wasn't the actual hairpin that drew you to it, but the strand of His Holiness's *hair*. The pebbles he kept as a reminder of the sacred Yamdrok-tso Lake. We put two in there as a—'

'Test,' said Tashi decisively. 'You wanted to trick me.'

'Not trick you. Just confirm you are who you are. The fact you have chosen the right objects, and so decisively, shows us how close you are to him.'

'*Used* to belong?' Tashi's eyes widened. 'What do you mean? Doesn't he need them any more?'

Dawa Rinpoche rose to his feet. 'Come,' he said to Tashi. 'Let us walk a while. I will explain.'

As they walked for the door, Dawa Rinpoche glanced at Tenzin and Lia. 'You will follow us, please.'

Lia and Tenzin tagged the old man and boy around the village – a pair of mismatched bodyguards. At one point, Dawa Rinpoche and Tashi sat on a low wall brushed clear of snow, and conducted what appeared to be a heated discussion. Tashi rose and made to leave but when Dawa Rinpoche said something, sank back. He looked defeated, but not for long. Soon they were up again, and walking. By the time they returned to Tashi's home it was dark, and Lia was cold and tired. The lamas insisted on staying the night with Tashi, and insisted Tenzin and Lia stay as well. Lia couldn't blame their caution. They were obviously terrified something might happen to the boy.

'We'll talk with Tashi tomorrow about what's next,' Dawa Rinpoche told Lia. 'And his parents. But we really need to get him to India before word gets out. He's in the greatest of danger.'

'I won't let him out of my sight,' Lia promised.

The lama smiled. 'I know you won't.'

With five extra guests the cottage was cramped, and friends of the family came to help out, bringing extra food and blankets. Lia was glad nobody stayed up late. She was tired, and she curled up with Tashi and the small furry form of Cherry on a mattress shoved into the corner of the main room. She fell asleep almost immediately.

She wasn't sure what woke her. It was pitch dark aside from the faint glow of coals in the fire. She felt apprehensive but didn't know why. She lay there, blinking, and after a while, her eyes grew heavy and her senses dimmed. For some reason, her apprehension grew. She fought to stay awake.

I mustn't fall asleep.

Jian, she thought. I'll think of Jian...he'll help me stay awake, but another man's face filled her mind. She could see every pore, count every glossy hair on his head. Sleek and angular, his eyes were like polished coal. Her emotions rioted. Dislike, contempt and fear warred with the seeds of desire.

Abruptly, she came awake.

Tan Dao. She'd been dreaming of Tan.

She lay there for a few moments, gathering her wits. She could feel Cherry, tucked in the crook of her knees, and hear one of the lamas snoring in the room next door. Inching out her hand, Lia felt for Tashi, wanting to check on the boy without waking him.

Her hand met empty air.

Lia bolted upright, startling Cherry who fell off the mattress with a small grunt.

She felt a second's panic. Where was the boy? She looked wildly around but couldn't see him. Shit. Why hadn't she tied Tashi to her with some string? Handcuffed him to her?

Cherry's fluffy white shape trotted across the room. Her tail was wagging. Lia suddenly made out Tashi's silhouette, stepping outside.

'Tashi!' she hissed.

He ignored her.

'Tashi!'

Nothing.

She scrambled off the mattress, grateful she'd gone to bed fully dressed.

'What is it?' It was Dawa Rinpoche. He sounded alert.

'Tashi's gone outside. I'm going to get him. Wake Tenzin. Tell him.'

Lia grabbed her torch and rammed on her boots. She didn't have time to wake the boy's parents. She had to grab Tashi quickly, and hustle him back inside.

'Lia, wait!' the Abbot called.

She paused in her race across the room. 'What?'

'Your bag. You might need it.'

For fuck's sake! Did he *want* to delay her? She ignored him and bolted outside. She didn't have time to fumble in the dark for something she didn't consider vital.

The village was lit by a half-moon, but the streets were dark and shadowed, and for a moment she couldn't see Tashi anywhere. Then she spotted Cherry's white shape. The dog was bobbing at Tashi's heels. Lia ran after them.

'Tashi!' she called.

He didn't respond.

'Tashi!' This time it was a shout. A couple of dogs barked as she raced past. Cherry glanced over her shoulder briefly, before continuing to follow Tashi. Why hadn't Tashi responded? Was the boy sleepwalking?

He was barely twenty metres away. She increased her pace. She yelled his name again but he didn't appear to hear. She stumbled on the road's uneven surface but didn't slow down. Tashi turned left at the next crossroads. Both he and the dog vanished out of sight.

'Tashi!'

She was aware that lights were coming on along the street and yelled again, hoping to wake the boy up.

Lia pelted for the corner. She swung left around a stone cottage, totally unprepared to run straight into a broad immovable mass of muscle.

'Tenzin,' she gasped. 'What the...'

She staggered back. She saw Tenzin was holding Tashi's wrists in one big fist. The boy looked at Lia, but he wasn't seeing her. His gaze was blank.

Tenzin switched his head to look at something across the street. Lia followed his gaze. Her heart turned cold.

This cannot be happening.

Jenny Wang was standing in front of a Land Cruiser. To one side stood Nima and his two men but they weren't wearing monk's robes any more. They were dressed in black flak jackets and dark trousers tucked into black boots. Nima held a rifle loosely in one hand.

'Back off, Shan,' Jenny called. 'Let Tenzin finish the job.'

Lia stared at Tenzin. He returned her gaze. Regret and sorrow stood in his eyes.

'I'm sorry,' he said.

'Let Tashi go.' Her voice was tight.

He shook his head. 'I can't.'

She forced herself to concentrate on him and not Jenny, who had begun walking towards them.

'You,' Lia said to Tenzin. Horror dribbled through her. 'You're Goldhawk.'

He gave a nod.

'What about Nima?'

'He was my back-up. To cover me. Make sure nobody came into camp to warn the others. Create a diversion if it was needed. Safeguard the mission.'

'You killed all those boys.'

'I was ordered to.'

'Who by?'

'Who do you think?' Jenny slid into Lia's view but Lia didn't take her gaze off Tenzin.

'Why?'

'You know why,' he replied softly. He suddenly looked weary.

Out of the corner of her eye she noted the tell-tale bulge of a pistol holster in Jenny's jacket. Could she reach the weapon? Turn it on Tenzin and get him to free Tashi? She'd be shot before she even got her hands on it.

'But you're not left-handed,' Lia said.

Tenzin's gaze went to the string of prayer beads wrapped around his knuckles. 'I know,' he said.

She said, 'You wear them to remind you.'

Tenzin looked to Jenny, then back to Lia. 'Yes,' he said. 'I didn't want to make a mistake.'

Jenny must have told Tenzin that Lia was looking for a left-handed man. She guessed the person Tenzin had rung on the sat phone earlier was Jenny and that he'd told her where they were headed. Jenny had then no doubt galvanised her troops before requisitioning the helicopter and flying here, landing well away from the village to avoid alerting anyone to their arrival.

Lia glanced at Nima. 'Why did Nima shoot Lama Sonam?'

'We had no choice,' Tenzin said in sudden anguish. 'Lama Sonam told me in the jeep that I wouldn't be reincarnated as anything but something worthless, like a bee or a mosquito. He knew I was the killer.'

'How did he know?'

'He found my sat phone in my bag. When he asked me about it, I made up a story about wanting it for extra security, but he didn't really believe me. And when Lia told him what we were doing...'

Lama Sonam's face appeared in her mind's eye, ineffably sad. I had a suspicion...

'I couldn't have him returning to camp and telling the lamas. *I had to finish the mission.*'

Lia noticed Tenzin was distracted. He had relaxed his grip on Tashi a little, and the boy seemed to be coming awake. He was frowning and blinking, but his gaze was still unfocused and cloudy.

Come on, Tashi. Wake up!

Jenny said, 'You told Nima to kill Lama Sonam?' She sounded surprised.

Tenzin's face contorted. 'Yes.'

He must have used the sat phone, Lia thought. He'd contacted Nima when he'd gone to relieve himself. She looked him up and down, keeping his concentration focused on her, not Tashi. 'You're not Tibetan?'

He shook his head. 'No. My grandfather was Mongolian, which is why my skin's dark. I was already in the army when I was recruited for this mission. Before I left Beijing, I was promoted to Captain. I was thirteen. I was the youngest Captain in the whole country.'

Lia could hear Lama Sonam's voice in her mind, telling her how Tenzin had been found wandering in a snow storm near the Tashilhunpo Monastery. Nobody knew where he'd come from. He couldn't speak. The monks had to teach him everything...it was as though his memory had been erased.

A smile flitted across Tenzin's face. 'My parents were so proud.'

Jenny listened to Tenzin's childhood revelations closely. It seemed to be the first time she'd heard the story. From her surprise earlier, the PSB officer had shown she hadn't known every twist and turn the mission had taken, and the fact she hadn't interrupted them again meant she wanted to learn more, no doubt in order to make sure each phrase she wrote in her reports was accurate in every detail.

'How long have you been undercover?' Lia asked Tenzin.

'Twenty-four years,' he said. He sounded surprised.

'And Zapa?'

'The same.'

Lia watched Tashi's eyes start to uncloud. Confusion began to form on his face.

'How did you lure the boys out?' Lia asked. She wanted to keep Tenzin talking, keep him distracted from Tashi's awakening.

'It wasn't me, I don't have the power.'

His gaze focused on something over her shoulder. Lia saw Dawa Rinpoche approaching.

'Supervisor,' the Abbot said, seemingly genuinely baffled. 'What's going on?'

She stared at Dawa Rinpoche.

The last cog fell into place.

'You're the Snow Thief,' she said.

Dawa Rinpoche stared back.

'You hypnotise the boys and lure them outside, where Tenzin is waiting.'

'Ten out of ten,' Jenny said.

'But you're a *High Abbot*.' Lia didn't drop her gaze.

'And you're a barb in my side.' He shook his head slowly to and fro, as though bemused.

'How many monks are involved?' Lia demanded. 'Is it just you two and Zapa?'

'Don't be ridiculous,' Jenny snorted. 'With the mortality rate out here, do you really think we'd rely on just three agents for this? We started recruiting right across the board the instant the Dalai Lama fled in 1959.'

'Why didn't you kill me on the mountain?' she asked Dawa Rinpoche. 'While you had the chance?'

'Tenzin wouldn't let me.' Dawa Rinpoche's eyes narrowed into slits as he looked at the burly monk. 'He said you were a police officer, doing your job. He considered you to be on the same side.'

As did Nima, Sharma and Rinzen. There was something to be said for professional solidarity, but even so, was it enough to explain why they didn't get rid of her when it would have been so easy to do so on the mountainside?

Lia held Tenzin's eyes. 'Why did you save my life?'

'Lama Sonam...' Tenzin took a shuddering breath. 'He told me if I saved you, safeguarded you, I would be rewarded in my reincarnation. I wouldn't be an ant or mosquito. I would be something magnificent.'

'Don't tell me you believe that shit,'

Jenny interjected.

'He promised,' Tenzin whispered. Torment stood in his eyes.

'Tenzin, you fuckwit,' Jenny snapped. 'If it wasn't for you the Supervisor's corpse would be rotting in the snow, but here she is causing more complications. What do you suggest we do with her?'

The sound of voices came from the adjacent street. Villagers concerned at Lia's shouts were investigating. Jenny checked both ends of the street. 'We've run out of time, Tenzin. Do it now. We don't want any witnesses.'

Before Lia could move, Tenzin put his right hand beneath Tashi's chin and as he began to bring his other hand to the back of the boy's head Lia screamed, 'No!'

She leaped at Tenzin. The force of her movement propelled him backwards and made his grip slip from the boy's neck.

Then someone shouted Tashi's name. Not Jenny. Not Dawa Rinpoche.

Tashi's father.

The last of the clouds left the boy's eyes. He looked straight at Tenzin. Then he looked at Lia. Understanding filled his face. This turned abruptly to terror.

Lia shoved her shoulder into Tenzin with all the force she could muster. It was like pushing against a brick wall but it seemed to work as he suddenly shifted backwards, almost overbalancing, but it wasn't thanks to her. Cherry was biting his ankle, growling furiously. Tenzin's grip on Tashi was now tentative. His attention had been sidetracked to the dog.

Nima and his two men lunged for her but they weren't fast enough.

Lia drew her arm across her body and rammed her elbow into Tenzin's windpipe. Tenzin dropped to his knees, eyes bulging, choking, clutching his throat.

'Tashi!' Lia yelled. *'Run!'*

The boy didn't hesitate. He turned and flew down the street like an arrow released from its bow.

Lia sprinted after him.

Behind her she could hear Cherry's growls and then Jenny. 'Catch them, you idiots!' she shouted.

48

LIA TORE AFTER TASHI. Rather than heading home, the boy ran west, in the opposite direction. The streets were slowly coming alive as people continued to shout. Tashi dodged people as he ran, almost unnoticed. All eyes went to Lia, pounding behind him.

A man stepped in her way, hands raised. Lia didn't stop.

Mustn't lose sight of Tashi.

She hurled herself over a stone wall and tore past a huddle of sheep in one corner, bleating in fright. She could hear Nima and his men thundering behind her. Blood pounded in her ears, the muscles in her legs flexing and tightening, and she stumbled on the frozen, chopped-up ground.

At the bottom of the paddock she saw Tashi scale a wire-meshed fence, as fast as a spider. She'd never make it across in time to see where he went. She was struggling to keep up. He was fast. If she wasn't careful she'd lose him.

Lia looked around, desperate to find a way through the fence, then spotted Cherry wriggling through a gap at the far end. She tore after the dog and, flinging herself to the ground, crawled along the iced earth, rocks and stones digging into her, bruising her hands and knees. She slithered beneath the wire, felt a metal barb catch her sweater and hold her fast. She heaved forward, tearing the wool and yanking herself free.

She found herself in another street, filled with people. Tashi was zigzagging his way round them, Cherry bobbing at his heels. Lia pelted after them.

At the end of the village there was nothing but fields covered in rocks and snow. Tashi didn't seem to notice. He kept running. Lia followed.

Once he reached a low stone wall, Tashi stopped and bent double. Lia did the same. Cold empty silence stretched behind them. They'd lost Nima, at least for the moment.

Lia touched Tashi's shoulder. 'Are you OK?' He put his arms around her waist. He was sobbing. She embraced him. Kissed the top of his head. Relief caught in her throat. Fierce tears rose in her eyes. She brushed them away before Tashi could see. She wanted to remain strong for him. Resolute.

What to do now?

Jenny would have Tashi's home covered. They couldn't return. Nor could they approach the lamas in case they were colluding with Dawa Rinpoche.

'You saved me.' Tashi leaned back so he could look into her face. Tears glistened on his cheeks.

'You saved yourself. You run like the wind. I only just managed to keep up.'

'A man spoke to me.' Tashi's mouth quivered. 'He said Cherry had been hurt outside and needed my help. I got up and went to look for Cherry. He told me where to go. It was strange, like a dream, but it wasn't. I thought it was real, but I was dreaming.'

Dawa Rinpoche had tried to hypnotise her as well. She smiled wryly inside as she recalled the dream she'd had as she'd fallen back to sleep earlier, and realised that the vivid impression of Tan's face and her violent emotional response had prevented her from going under. Without realising it, Tan had probably saved her life.

'I liked Tenzin.' The boy looked bereft. 'He was grumpy, but he was OK.' His face suddenly twisted. 'How could he kill Pemba?'

'He'd been ordered to.'

Tashi looked past Lia towards the village. 'Dawa Rinpoche said all the boys they tested to see if they might be the next Panchen Lama are dead.'

'Yes.'

'All except me.'

'Yes.'

Lia gave a shiver as her sweat began to cool on her skin.

'You're cold,' he said. 'I am too.'

They wore only what they'd slept in. They had no coats, no hats or gloves. Tashi was barefoot.

'We need some warm clothes,' she told Tashi. 'But we can't go anywhere the police might find us.'

Tashi bent and picked up Cherry, who licked his face happily. 'Let's go to my cousin. She'll help.'

*

They returned to the village cautiously. Lamps and fires had been lit. People continued to mill in the streets. Lia saw a soldier walk into one house, another check its garden. Both carried assault rifles over their shoulders.

When had Jenny brought in the army?

The answer was simple: the instant Tenzin had used his satellite phone.

At the next crossroads, Lia stopped Tashi. Told him to wait. Then she crept forward, wanting to check it was clear before committing themselves. To her right, at the far end of the street, she saw Jenny's Land Cruiser and, alongside, a military jeep. Just the one, thank the heavens, which meant a maximum of six army personnel, but with Nima, Rinzen and Sharmar looking for them as well, they couldn't stay here.

They had to leave the village.

Suddenly she saw Jenny appear and talk to the soldier in the garden. He nodded before bringing his weapon from his shoulder and holding it in readiness in front.

Shoot to kill.

Jenny turned her head and looked Lia's way. It was almost as though she could sense her. Lia ducked back and returned to Tashi. She said, 'There are soldiers everywhere. We have to leave now, but we need coats. You need shoes...'

Tashi nodded. He turned and jogged back the way they had come, to the edge of the village. He entered a dark, low-slung stone cottage. No lamps were lit. Lia fumbled her way after him. The remnants of a fire lit a single room in deep greys. It was difficult to make out anything except a sleeping pallet in one corner, where Tashi now stood. She heard him talking in a low voice. A woman answered. Tashi moved around the room, collecting things. He pulled on a pair of strong leather boots, then packed a small rucksack but what with, Lia couldn't see. His movements were quick, economical. He talked all the time with the woman, who remained in bed.

Finally, he came to Lia. Gave her a padded jacket, a pair of gloves and a hat. 'She's called Dechen. She wants to meet you before we go.'

Even though the light was minimal, Lia could see the woman was strikingly attractive, with a delicate chin and high cheekbones. She looked past Lia when she smiled, and from the milky glaze covering her eyes, Lia realised Dechen was blind.

'She says she won't tell anyone we were here,' Tashi told Lia.

'Tell her thank you.'

Dechen reached out a hand and ran it gently over Lia's face. She said something to Tashi.

'She says you're very pretty.'

'So is she.'

Lia went to the door to let them out of the cottage but when she heard strident voices outside, paused. She could hear a man talking in Mandarin.

'Come on, boss. It's just a woman and child, how hard could it be?'

'They're terrorists,' another man snapped.

'You heard what Officer Wang said. They want to create civil war in Tibet. Now, we don't like terrorists, but we like the Paras even less. Wang's bringing them in tomorrow morning, and I'd like us to have found our terrorists before then and disposed of them, nice and tidy, like Wang wants. Everything clear?'

The man said yes, he understood, sir. He sounded galvanised and keen to get to work. Lia knew if one of them saw her or Tashi, they'd shoot them dead. No questions.

'On your way, then.'

Lia shrank back at the sound of metal on leather; an assault rifle being readied.

Where to go? Where could they hide?

They couldn't stay in the village;- if the soldiers didn't find them, the paratroopers would. She pictured the map she'd stuck on her wall weeks ago and considered the nearest village, over a hundred kilometres away. Her mind drifted south, where another village lay much closer. Just forty k's away. The only trouble was that it lay in India.

Tashi will be safe there. But what about me? I don't want to go to India!

She closed her eyes. She suddenly felt like weeping. She had no choice. If she wanted to live, she had to run for the border. If she didn't, Jenny would find her and kill her. Her mind raced ahead, trying to work out what sort of chance they stood.

They couldn't drive. All the roads would be covered. They had to walk. Jenny wouldn't expect that.

The Paras were already on their way. They'd have trackers, helicopters and aeroplanes. They would find them within hours.

They had to leave now.

49

TASHI MOVED LIKE A wraith past the outer stone walls of the village. Cherry pattered silently alongside. Tashi hadn't been surprised when Lia had told him her plan, just sad.

'Will I see my parents again?'

'They can come and visit you in India,' she prevaricated. She didn't want to mention that they were probably already in the hands of Jenny's interrogators, and might be dead by morning.

'Can I bring Cherry?'

Lia couldn't think why not. The dog would help keep his spirits up. 'Sure.'

He had picked up Cherry and held her in his arms as he looked around Dechen's rough cottage. He'd murmured something to the dog, who had twisted in his embrace to lick his face.

'The Dalai Lama had to leave his country,' Tashi said quietly.

'Yes.'

And that was when it hit home that she could never return to China, or Tibet. By helping Tashi to escape, she had become a traitor to the PSB, possibly the government. If they didn't shoot her on sight but caught her alive, she would be thrown into jail and then summarily executed. Even if she turned Tashi over to Jenny, it wouldn't save her.

It was too late.

Fingers trembling, almost tearful, she checked they had enough supplies – some tsampa and water – and then she said simply, 'Let's go.'

Now, she picked up her pace. She wore Dechen's snow boots and the woman's outer jacket made of dense wool. They were headed for a summer hut that Tashi knew, where they would wait out the night before continuing their journey. If they left the hut at dawn, Lia hoped they might reach the border at the end of the same day. That was if they didn't get lost. Dechen had given them what sounded like detailed directions, but without a compass Lia knew the journey was high risk. Tashi insisted he knew most of the way – he'd walked much of the route during the summer months with the sheep – but he hadn't been alone. He'd had his father with him.

I hope I don't die out here.

Lia's spirits rose when Tashi led them unerringly to the summer hut. They arrived just before midnight and for the first time since they'd left Rabang, Lia thought they might stand a chance of walking into India. They didn't dare light a fire, give away their position, so they huddled together for warmth, and tried to sleep. Lia dozed fitfully, imagining herself in Indian police uniform, then begging on the streets, homeless and penniless. Then she pictured herself working as a translator somewhere. After all, she spoke English and Mandarin, surely someone would employ her?

She was deeply asleep when Tashi woke her. It was still dark and she folded her arms around herself, grumbling. She was stiff and cold and hungry. She wanted to go back to sleep, where she didn't have to think, didn't have to face the terror of leaving her country.

'The sun's coming up,' he told her.

As far as Lia was concerned it was still night. But when she poked her head outside into the freezing, bitter air, she saw a strip of pale blue on the horizon. She yawned widely, blinking tears from her eyes. Dawn was barely an hour away.

After drinking some water, she followed Tashi up the mountain, her boots crunching on snow. It was hard work and it didn't take long before her body warmed. She watched the sun creep over the horizon, a slice of lemon, and change the sky's night mantle into a blazing bright blue cape.

She looked over her shoulder, searching for Rabang, but couldn't see it. They'd already walked well out of view. She had to hope the paratroopers hadn't found their tracks yet. Tashi had assured her their tracks would blend in with everyone else's, but Lia wasn't so sure. How many people had walked to the summer hut over the past few days? Several people, apparently, but Lia wasn't sure whether Tashi was just saying that to keep her happy. She couldn't see why anyone would walk two hours through the snow to sit in a cold stone hut. She increased her pace.

As she walked, she ran her mind over the past few weeks. She saw how Jenny had tried to insinuate herself into her confidence from the start while subtly trying to deflect her conviction there was a serial killer.

Perhaps the children overheard something they shouldn't.

Maybe the Tibetans are planning something.

Jenny had dogged her every move as she hunted for the Snow Thief. She'd wanted Lia dead as soon as she realised Lia wasn't going to give up. She'd created the story of Dohna's husband wanting revenge, and then organised the so-called riot outside Lia's house to give the 'mobsters' an excuse to kill her. It had been Jenny who had the means to trace her mobile phone to the Meru Nyingba Monastery and send Nima after her.

They had gone about seven kilometres when she heard the distinctive *thwap-thwap* of a helicopter.

Tashi didn't need to be told to hide. He was already scrambling for a clump of rocks further up the hill. Lia tore after him.

Thwap, thwap.

The machine was travelling fast. It wouldn't be long before it came into view. Perhaps thirty seconds.

Quick! Get out of sight!

Lia ran up the hill, her boots dragging through the snow. It felt as though she was running through wet sand.

Thwap, thwap, thwap.

She could hear the whine of the turbo.

It was closing in!

Legs pumping, she drove herself upwards, her breath like razor blades in her throat.

'Hurry!' Tashi shouted.

She flung herself onto the snow behind a boulder and scrambled to huddle next to Tashi. 'Down,' she said. Obediently Tashi pulled his coat over his head and hunkered beneath it. She did the same. Both their coats were neutral-coloured, tan and grey, and she hoped that from the air, they blended in with the rocks.

Thwap, thwap.

The machine was coming up the valley. Lia held her breath as it approached. The engine was running smoothly, cruising, but then it suddenly changed gear. It slowed.

'Cherry!' Tashi's face appeared next to hers, distraught. 'I forgot Cherry!'

'Leave her,' Lia demanded. 'She's white. They won't see her.'

'But what if—'

'Down,' Lia snapped. 'And don't move unless I tell you to.'

To her relief, Tashi vanished beneath his coat without another word.

She concentrated on the helicopter's engine, which had slowed further. *Ai Ya!* It was coming their way. Slowly, it was inching closer. Had they seen the dog? Or had they simply spotted movement on the mountain and paused to investigate?

Go away! There's nothing here, I swear it!

Suddenly Cherry was upon them, licking and snuffling. Tashi grabbed the dog and shoved it beneath his coat. Neither said anything as the helicopter drifted down, drifted closer.

She could picture the paratroopers and their binoculars, scanning for footprints in the snow. Hunting for any sign of them.

Abruptly, the engine note changed, and it accelerated away. Lia lay in the snow, staring at the sky and feeling as though she'd lost ten years of her life.

*

By 4 p.m. they were at fifteen thousand feet and crossing a narrow, rocky pass when Lia saw a scattering of what looked like dirty white pebbles on the valley floor behind them. Her stomach hollowed. The Paras. They'd followed them.

She looked ahead, along the next valley. The border was no more than four kilometres away. If they pushed themselves, they could make it in under an hour, but the paratroopers would be much faster. They were hard men, extremely fit. They'd catch them up in half the time.

'Tashi.' She pointed the men out.

His face crumpled. 'We won't make it.'

'We might, if we split up.' She looked around. 'You keep going as fast as you can, OK? I'll draw them away.'

Dismay filled his eyes. 'No. They'll kill you.'

Her mouth was dry, her heart pumping. 'We don't have a choice. It's the only way.'

'No,' he said again. He started to cry silently, tears trickling down his cheeks.

'We don't have time.' She was brisk. 'You've got to keep being brave, OK? Keep going until you're safe.'

Lia dug in her trouser pockets. All she had were a few notes and a handful of change, which she passed over. 'Use it to take a taxi or a bus to the nearest village or town. Find the Tibetan quarter, there's bound to be one so close to the border, but swear you'll *get there*.' Her voice reverberated with passion. She didn't want her life wasted.

'I promise.' He tucked her money inside his jacket.

'Now, *go*.'

She began to push him away, but he stopped her. He brought out a simple red cotton necklace. He asked her to duck down and he slipped it over her head, blessing her in Tibetan. Then he turned and broke into a jog, heading for the border, the little dog Cherry running beside him.

Lia immediately turned east. She ran along the ridge, out of sight of the soldiers, for fifteen minutes. Then she checked to see if they were approaching the pass. She waited until they had reached the top of the slope.

Now. Show yourself now.

Her soul shivered inside. Once they saw her, there was no going back. She was dead.

Do I have the courage to do this? Emotion welled, hot and desperate. *I don't want to die!*

The soldiers paused when they came to the rocky pass. One of them began casting around. The tracker. He'd find Tashi's footprints in minutes. And then they'd be after him, hunt him down...

He was just a little boy.

Before she could change her mind, Lia stepped into view. She tried to make it seem as though she'd done it by mistake, pretending to scurry out of sight as though she'd just spotted her pursuers, and it seemed to work, because almost immediately, the entire troupe collected together briefly, then started to jog after her.

Lia ran for her life.

50

LIA TORE ALONG THE ridge, slipping and stumbling on the loose shale before dropping down and heading for a dry river bed that would lead her off the mountain. She hit the snow line at full speed, nearly falling when the snow grabbed her boots, plunging her knee-deep, but she kept going. She was driving herself downhill, arms windmilling, when some snow kicked up in front of her.

They're shooting at me.

Sobbing, gasping for breath, she kept running.

In the distance, she could hear the helicopter approaching. Once it had her in its sights, it would hover above and lead the soldiers straight to her.

Never give up.

She kept running.

The helicopter swooped over the ridge but she didn't pause to look at it, didn't stop.

She skidded around a pile of boulders and plunged down the hillside. A few metres on she fell onto her backside. The helicopter was almost upon her but she still didn't look at it. She hauled herself upright and raced down, down...Past a stunted tree, more boulders. Her breath was rasping, her throat on fire.

When the shot comes, I hope it doesn't hurt. I don't want to know anything about it.

Her boots slipped on rocks, through snow. Sweat beaded her forehead, dripped into her eyes. The helicopter was above her, hovering. She refused to look at it. She came to the lip of a chasm. She had to go around. Head for the ridge on her left. Sweat pouring, she began climbing.

The ridge. Must get to the ridge.

She didn't think about what would happen when she reached it. She just had to get there. That was all she could think of.

The noise of the helicopter filled her head, thundering, roaring. The hillside was steeper than it looked, and towards the top of the ridge, she had to use her hands and knees. She didn't feel the stones cutting and slicing her skin. She heaved herself over the lip of the ridge and that was when she saw them.

A dozen soldiers standing straight in front of her. Each held an assault rifle. Each weapon was trained on her.

She stood panting, sweating. Her knees were trembling but she remained standing.

The helicopter moved away, searching for somewhere to land, she assumed. Did Jenny want to pull the trigger herself?

Lia looked around, but she had nowhere to go. It was over. She tried to summon up Jian's face, but all she could see were the hard, grim faces of the paratroopers – motionless, taut, every sense trained on her.

She was shivering, quaking, sweat pooling at the base of her spine, trickling down her ribs. She thought she might throw up. She wanted to scream, she wanted to weep. She didn't realise she was sobbing.

I don't want to die.

She gave an involuntary whimper when one of the soldiers raised a hand, but it was only to his earpiece. He spoke for a while. He never dropped his gaze from Lia.

The helicopter had landed but its rotors weren't winding down. Still, she wouldn't look at it. She held the paratrooper's gaze. Finally, he stopped talking.

A man called out. The paratrooper glanced to one side, to where the helicopter rested. He relaxed his weapon a fraction. Lia tried to work out if she could use this in some way, but the remaining eleven soldiers were still concentrated on her.

'Sir,' the paratrooper said. His voice carried clearly to her through the icy air.

For the first time since she'd crested the ridge, Lia flicked her eyes away from the soldiers. A man was striding towards them. His face was taut and pale. He barked at the men. His voice was scratchy. The soldiers lowered their weapons. He barked again. This time his voice was stronger. The soldiers flicked on their safety catches, began to relax. One of them turned away. Another joined him. The paratroop leader flicked the man a salute, and then reached inside his combat uniform. He brought out a pack of cigarettes and lit up.

Lia's legs collapsed but Tan was there to catch her.

He said, 'Thank God.'

51

TAN HELD HER HAND as the helicopter rose into the air and turned to fly south-east. Occasionally he'd stroke the inside of her wrist, a gesture she found unbearably intimate, but she let him. He'd saved her life.

She was alive. Tashi was who-knew-where.

They didn't land at Rabang but kept flying, for Lhasa.

'How did you find me?' she asked.

'Constable Deshi. He finally switched on his phone. He told me what was going on. I flew out here immediately.'

'Where's Jenny Wang?'

'Still conducting the operation from Rabang.'

'Does she know what you've done?'

'By now, yes.'

'What will happen?'

Tan didn't answer. He was gazing outside.

'What if Tashi escapes?' she prodded.

He finally looked at her. He said, 'The region will remain stable.'

'But he's the new Panchen Lama. The Tibetans' choice.'

He ran a hand down his face. She saw the bruises beneath his eyes, the way the lines on his brow had deepened. 'If he dies, there will be an uprising. The whole story's out after the fracas in Rabang, Wang throwing her weight around. Every Tibetan is on tenterhooks waiting to hear if the boy has made it, or not. If he has, then things will continue as normal—'

'The authorities will be furious.'

'Will they?' He held her gaze. 'I'm not sure they even knew about this mission.'

'You think it wasn't official?'

His gaze turned inward. 'It's hard to tell, but there's no evidence Beijing were aware of it.'

'Even so, they won't be best pleased...'

'The region is stable,' Tan repeated.

He refused to say any more.

They were halfway to Lhasa when Lia saw another helicopter in the sky, around the same altitude and heading in the same direction. It was the paratroopers' machine and it was flying much faster. It soon overtook them. Lia pointed it out. Tan looked at it for a while, but he didn't say anything.

Eventually they came to the outskirts of the city. Tan brought out his phone and called his driver. Ordered him to meet them at the aerodrome.

When they landed, the paratroopers were already there. They stood by the hangar, assault rifles ready. Lia's stomach clenched when she saw Jenny was with them.

'Tan,' Lia said. Her voice trembled.

'Shhh.' He picked up her hand once more, turned it over. He seemed to be studying her bruises and scrapes. 'When we alight, don't say anything. Not a word. Not to anyone. Not to Deshi, the Commissioner or your grandmother. Not until I tell you.'

'But what if—'

He raised a finger to her lips. 'Shhh. Trust me.'

Her head was spinning. She may not understand what was going on but since he'd saved her life, it made sense to put her trust in him.

Tan climbed down the rungs first. Lia followed, her torn hands painful on the metal. She was conscious of aches beginning to make themselves felt around her body. Jenny came and stood in front of them, an armed man at each shoulder.

'How dare you.' Her voice rang with rage. Her attention was on Tan.

He said, 'Excuse me,' and made to usher Lia past.

'You're both under arrest.'

'You already have the paperwork?' Tan raised his eyebrows. 'Approved by a procuratorate?'

Jenny Wang shifted from foot to foot. Fury poured from her.

'I'll have it by the end of the day.'

'In that case, if you'll excuse us.' Meticulously polite, Tan inclined his head and gestured for Lia to step ahead of him. Pulse jumping, she did as he indicated.

'I wish you'd died in that stinking cell Kwok put you in,' Jenny hissed as she passed. 'You're nothing but a traitor to your country.'

As Tan had ordered, Lia didn't respond. She headed for Tan's car, feeling Jenny's gaze burning between her shoulder blades like a high-powered laser. It was only when she closed the car door behind her that the muscles in her back relaxed.

'What next?' Her mouth was dry.

'You go home and get some rest.'

'But Jenny—'

He held up a hand. 'I will take care of it.'

Did he really have the power to prevent their arrest? Even the highest officials weren't immune to a system which hated subversion, and by letting Tashi go – *actively* helping him to escape – they'd committed an atrocious offence.

Tan dropped her outside her apartment. While his driver waited, he came with her to her front door. He looked at the little Buddha statue, and then at the curved outlines of the Jokhang's roof.

'Do you believe in reincarnation?' he asked.

'I don't know what I believe in.'

'I wonder what we'll be.' He smiled a sad, weary smile. 'I fancy you'll be something beautiful and elegant, like a racehorse. Me...'

'A leopard,' she said.

'You flatter me.'

He studied her for a long time. His eyes travelled over her face as though memorising every detail.

Obscurely, she suddenly felt shy. What could she say to a man who had saved her life?

'Thank you,' she said.

He said, 'Remember, not a word.'

His voice was soft.

'Not a word,' she repeated, nodding.

His eyes crinkled at the corners. 'I think that's the first time you've agreed to do something I've asked without protesting.'

She flushed. 'Sorry.'

The smile remained in his eyes as he turned and walked away. She watched him patter down the steps and climb into his car. He didn't look back.

*

Fang Dongmei clucked around Lia for the rest of the day like an overweight mother hen. She made sure the bath water was hot, that Lia had the best-smelling soaps and gels and the fluffiest, cleanest towels. She helped wash Lia's hair. She told Lia that Deshi had taken a call the day before and that Tan had come to collect him from Mrs Lily's fifteen minutes later. She had been terrified for Lia, convinced Deshi was going to tell Tan everything, but she couldn't stop the young constable from leaving.

'He betrayed us.' Fang Dongmei pulled a sour face.

'It's not about betrayal,' Lia said. 'Deshi's a police officer. He was doing his job. What he thought best for his country.'

She leaned back as Fang Dongmei began to rinse the conditioner from her hair. The only people who'd ever washed her hair for her were her parents, and Jian. And now her grandmother-in-law. Fang Dongmei's hands were surprisingly deft and very gentle. It felt blissful.

'And if Deshi hadn't told Tan,' Lia added, 'I would be dead.'

Fang Dongmei gave a snort. 'Your pet PSB officer.'

'He's no pet.'

After patting her dry, Fang Dongmei applied ointment to Lia's cuts and bruises and then told Lia to go to bed and rest. Obediently, Lia did as she was told. She couldn't think what else she might do. If she went to work she might be arrested. Better enjoy her creature comforts while she could. She picked up a book, but she couldn't read. Every time she heard a noise she couldn't identify, her blood pressure would rocket, convinced Jenny was standing outside waiting to arrest her.

Lia didn't think she would sleep, she was so tense, but exhaustion soon took its toll. She awoke three hours later to hear Fang Dongmei talking. She sounded annoyed. Then she heard a man's voice and she scrambled out of bed, yanked on some clothes and darted into the living room to see Commissioner Zhi standing on the doorstep. Fang Dongmei barred his way.

Lia pushed past her grandmother. 'Commissioner,' she said. Relief ran through her when she saw he was alone.

'Supervisor.'

'Please, come in.'

He went and stood by the TV. He folded his arms. He said, 'Are you all right?'

'Yes, thank you.'

'I need you to tell me what happened out in Rabang.'

Lia hesitated as Tan's words came back to her.

Don't say anything...Not to Deshi, the Commissioner...Not until I tell you.

'I'm very tired, sir. Can't this wait until tomorrow?'

'No, it can't. The whole thing's a mess. Officer Wang is screaming for your arrest. A group of lamas is protesting that the security services tried to kill an innocent little boy. Constable Deshi one minute says you're innocent of any wrongdoing and then says you've been betraying your country.'

'Where is Officer Tan?'

'Tan has been with the procuratorate for over four hours and nobody is allowed to interrupt them.'

Her mind whirled. Was Tan going to pull a rabbit out of his hat for them? Was he powerful enough?

Remember, not a word.

'Sir, I would like to wait until I can speak to Officer Tan.'

The muscles on his face tightened. 'I see.'

Long silence while he looked at her.

'If that's your decision…' He was waiting for her to change her mind.

'I'm sorry, sir.'

'You're suspended until further notice. Contact is forbidden between you and serving officers. Please don't leave the city without notifying the police station.'

'Yes, sir.'

He walked outside without looking at her. Fang Dongmei shut the door behind him.

'I thought you trusted him,' she said.

'I don't trust anyone at the moment,' Lia replied.

Fang Dongmei made them both supper. Fried chicken with ginger and garlic, fresh pak choi and lots of *lau mie*, glutinous rice, which Lia loved. They watched some TV together before Lia succumbed once again to fatigue.

She dreamed she was in Sydney. Next to her stood Tan. His body was tanned and lean, his muscles clearly defined.

He was looking at her expectantly. He was waiting for her to teach him how to swim. Lia awoke with a sense of confusion. She was dreaming of Tan again? In a flurry of limbs she sprang out of bed, wanting to dispel the memory. It was late, past nine, and she automatically reached for her uniform before she remembered.

She'd been suspended.

She decided on jeans and a sweater.

Lia spent the next two days in a strange limbo. Unable to

talk to anyone at the station she had no idea what was happening and had to rely on Fang Dongmei and the gossip she gained from Mrs Lily.

'The city is alive with rumours about Tashi, the new Panchen Lama,' Fang Dongmei reported. 'But nobody knows if he made it to India or not. There's talk of a woman helping him, called Hariti. Nobody knows who she is, or where she might be found. Some say she is a spirit, others think she's a nun.' The old woman's eyes gleamed. 'This is good, heya? That they don't know it's you?'

'I guess so.'

Lia was reluctant to leave the apartment. She wasn't sure why. Perhaps she feared Zapa might return and kill her? Or was it simply that she was responding to an animal instinct and didn't want to move from the safety of her burrow until she was certain it was safe?

On the fourth day, she answered the door to Tan's driver. He gave her a mobile phone. He said, 'He will ring you at eleven o'clock.'

Lia stared at the phone. She'd left her phone, along with her handbag, in Rabang at Tashi's house, both of which were now no doubt sealed and bagged and locked in a police evidence cupboard somewhere. Carefully, she put Tan's phone on top of the TV, and waited.

When it rang, she snatched it up.

'Lia,' he said.

'Yes.'

'The simpleton has been released.'

'Yeshe?'

'Yes.'

'Prove it.'

'He's being processed at the police station. He wants to see you.'

'But I can't go near the police—'

'Wait.'

She heard him say something, and then another man spoke. She gripped the phone hard, her palms slippery.

'Supervisor?' It was the Commissioner.

'Yes.'

'Your suspension has been lifted. Please return to the office immediately. You will debriefed in an hour.'

52

LIA STOOD THERE FOR a second, trying to process what had been said.

'What is it?' Fang Dongmei asked.

'Yeshe's been released.' She quickly told her what she had heard.

'I will come with you to the police station.' Fang Dongmei started for the front door.

'Wait,' Lia said. 'I need to put on my uniform.'

Yeshe burst into tears when they walked into reception. Fang Dongmei went straight to him and pulled him into her arms. It was like watching an oak tree being swallowed by a large black bat. Lia stood to one side, waiting for Yeshe's sobs to lessen. Finally, Fang Dongmei pulled back and tenderly touched Yeshe's shattered cheek. She said, 'I will take you to my friend's place now. She is a nurse. She will look after you.'

Yeshe looked over Fang Dongmei's shoulder at Lia. His mouth worked but nothing came out.

'She'll look after you,' Lia repeated, and although he didn't understand Mandarin, he seemed to realise from their gestures and gentle tones that he was, at last, safe.

Fang Dongmei took Yeshe's arm, and together they shuffled across the room and outside.

When she entered the police station, the desk superintendent stared at her as though he'd never seen her before. 'Welcome back, Supervisor,' he said. 'The committee wants to see you. They're waiting.'

She straightened her tunic. Made sure her hair was tightly tied back. She walked into the room ramrod straight to see just four people sitting behind the table: Commissioner Zhi, Jenny Wang, Constable Deshi and Superintendent Zhang.

She felt a rush of relief when she saw Tan sitting to one side, apart from them. His face was pale but his bearing was erect, his expression alert.

'Sit,' the Commissioner commanded Lia.

Lia took the chair opposite the table and sat with her boots together, her hands in her lap. Her heart was thudding, her fingers tingling.

'Supervisor,' said Zhi. 'Tell us what happened in Rabang.'

Lia shot a look at Tan.

'She didn't know my plan,' Tan said. 'She knew nothing except she was following my orders.'

Lia struggled to keep neutral expression.

'But she tried to protect the boy,' Jenny spoke. 'She tried to help him escape.'

'Only because I ordered her to. I am her superior officer—'

'Not any longer,' Jenny snapped.

'No,' he agreed. 'But she had no choice but to do as I said. She is an exemplary police officer and considering she uncovered who the Snow Thief was, should be rewarded for her efforts.'

He turned an icy black gaze on Jenny. 'As I mentioned to the procuratorate, this wouldn't be the mess it is if my officers had shared what they knew with me all along.'

Silence.

He didn't remove his eyes from Jenny. 'I ordered Supervisor Shan to save the boy and therefore save the entire region from going up in flames.'

'Very high-minded of you,' Jenny sneered. 'But not very patriotic.'

'The Tibetans belong to our country,' Tan said smoothly. 'I had no intention of sitting back and allowing a civil war to start.'

Deshi shifted in his seat. He hadn't met Lia's gaze once, and nor had Zhang.

'So,' said Zhi. He spun his pen in a circle on his desk. 'We have the full story at last. What do you make of it, Supervisor?'

Lia remained stonily silent. She didn't have enough information to speak up with any confidence.

'I thought the mission was brilliant.' Jenny smiled without showing her teeth. 'I wish we'd left Goldhawk and his rogue group of accomplices to finish their job unimpeded. Exterminate the brats and leave the way clear for us to put the right people into positions of power.'

So, Jenny was pretending she had nothing to do with the mission, putting the blame on a rogue group the authorities could deny. Lia held her breath for a moment, trying to decide whether it was time to say something.

'Supervisor?' Zhi arched his eyebrows at her.

Lia finally spoke. 'What made you bring those soldiers to Rabang?' she asked Jenny.

'I received intelligence.' She gave a shrug. 'You know we have spies throughout the monasteries. It was one of these spies who reported what was happening. A monk.'

'His name?' Lia asked. She knew there was no spy. It had been Tenzin who had called her.

'Tsering Norbu. He died two days ago. He was murdered, no doubt by the rogue group who masterminded this mission.'

Lia's breath was taken away at Jenny's brutal audacity. She'd had an innocent monk killed in order to cover her back. Lia didn't know Tsering Norbu but she felt a stab of sorrow for him. Whether he really had been a spy or not was a moot point. The man was dead, giving Jenny carte blanche to stick to her story.

'Also,' Jenny continued, 'you were seen leaving the city. I assumed – correctly, as it turns out – that you were on the trail of the Snow Thief. I was concerned for your safety.'

It was such an obvious lie that everyone in the room looked aside, pretending to busy themselves aligning their papers or readjusting their positions.

Commissioner Zhi cleared his throat. 'I think we've

covered everything?' He looked around but nobody dissented. 'In that case, we're finished here.'

As he began to rise, Lia got to her feet. She began to cross the room toward Tan, but Deshi came around the table fast. He said, 'Not now.' His tone was low and urgent.

She sent Tan a quick look. He was standing by his chair, his black eyes alive on hers.

She'd see him later, she told herself, and thank him in private. She would invite him to dinner, maybe suggest the Sheraton.

He didn't move his gaze from her.

She smiled her thanks to him. A genuine smile of gratitude that she felt glow in her eyes.

He put his fist over his heart. Her breathing faltered at his gesture.

'Supervisor?'

Deshi was hovering anxiously. Lia gave Tan a nod, and followed Deshi outside.

As she walked down the corridor, she stepped aside for two police officers. She didn't see them go into the committee room and handcuff Tan. She didn't see them escort him outside and into a waiting car. When she went home at the end of the day and ate supper with Fang Dongmei, she had no idea Tan was sitting on the floor of a stinking bare-brick cell with nothing to eat and no water to drink.

53

IT WAS FUNNY HOW things turned out, Tan thought. He could be in the same cell where Yeshe had been thrown for all he knew. He wondered what the simpleton was doing and whether Lia and the old hag had taken him in, or if he was already on his way back to his grotty nomadic camp. He didn't feel any remorse for what he'd done to the man. It had been for the greater good, the peace of his country, and if he had his time again he'd do the same.

He paced the cell. It was too cold to lie down, and too cold to sit with bare concrete against your arse and thighs. He breathed shallowly against the reeking air, rich with the stench of unwashed bodies and fear.

He should have known Jenny Wang had been behind the entire episode. She'd been like a spider in the centre of a web, able to scurry here and there without being noticed and trap which flies she wanted, and spare those she didn't. How big an operation it had been nobody knew. Wang wasn't telling, but it appeared to have been contained to under a dozen. Any more, and there would have been leaks.

His mind drifted to his meeting with the Chief Procurator, Chong Gui, a lively man in his sixties with a small yellow mole on his chin from which sprouted three hairs. At first, Chong was sympathetic to Tan's plight and agreed that the safety of the region was paramount. For a while Tan believed he might get away with it. But then Wang stepped in. By letting the new Panchen Lama escape, Tan had committed a monstrous crime. Not that this was ever going to be made public, of course. It was all going to be brushed under the carpet and out of sight.

He heard a low groaning from the cell opposite. His

neighbour was a Tibetan man who'd been arrested for setting fire to his neighbour's house, enraged that his neighbour had been having an affair with his wife. He was, he'd told Tan, usually a devout man, but he'd seen red. Tan could understand his plight completely. If he was married to Lia, he'd kill anyone who laid a finger on her.

Lia's smile came into his mind like sunshine streaming into a darkened room. It wasn't the look of love she'd given him when she'd thought he was her husband, but it had been filled with genuine warmth.

Suddenly, he felt like weeping. He knew he'd chosen this path, to put himself between Lia and Wang and the authorities, but he wished he could have been cleverer and able to think up another plan. But nothing had come to mind. When he'd finally spoken to Deshi and heard the whole messy story, he could have sat back and let Wang do her dirty work. He could have kept himself safe, but he could no more have let Lia die on the mountain than cut out his heart.

He'd always wondered what it might be like to lose someone you loved, and now he knew. He loved passionately and deeply, but it was without hope. Lia could never love him as he wanted. She might grow to like him a little, but she would never smile at him like she'd smiled at her husband.

He'd left her a letter. Handwritten, on the best quality paper. He'd drafted and re-drafted it so many times his hand and fingers had ached. He had tried to pitch the perfect tone – no self-pity, no remorse, nothing that might haunt her later. He wondered if she'd keep it and bring it out to read from time to time. How would she remember him? he wondered. The best he could wish for was that she'd think of him with gratitude.

He looked at his watch. His stomach gave a sickening roll. He tried not to think of what was going to happen tomorrow. Instead, he forced himself to think of Lia, of what might have been.

He closed his eyes and pictured himself sitting on a broad yellow beach looking out to sea. He could hear seagulls and children playing. Lia was on her surfboard, striking out through the waves. He'd surf too, except she hadn't taught him to swim yet. She was wearing the bright red swimsuit he'd bought her that morning. He watched her pass the breakers and lie on her board in the hot sunshine, waiting for the right wave. When she spotted the perfect breaker she rose up on her board in a single fluid movement and then she was arcing along the blue-green roller, surfing for the beach.

Surfing for him.

Tan spent the next twenty-four hours alternately dreaming about Lia, and trying not to weep with fear.

54

LIA DROPPED INTO THE PSB offices the next morning. She wanted to see Tan and thank him properly. He'd stuck his neck out for her and had, amazingly, managed to save her career. She'd spent most of yesterday fielding congratulations on finding the Snow Thief – Tenzin was now in jail and singing to Jenny Wang's hymn sheet, and garnering sympathy for being forced to comply with Tan's subversive plan.

She'd decided to invite Tan to supper in her home. It would be a significant gesture that she knew he'd appreciate. When she'd told Fang Dongmei, however, the old woman had rolled her eyes to the ceiling and muttered something about hell and the devil before saying she'd go and buy pork loin – the most expensive part of the animal. It seemed even Fang Dongmei felt some gratitude to Tan Dao.

The atmosphere in the PSB offices was subdued when she entered. She didn't know the receptionist but the receptionist obviously knew her. The woman was staring at her as though she was a Martian who'd just landed. Was this what happened when you gained notoriety for doing your job?

'Officer Tan,' said Lia. 'Can I see him?'

The receptionist looked as though she was ready to faint. She said, 'No.' She licked her lips. 'He's not here.'

'When will he be back?'

'I don't know.'

Lia looked around, searching for someone she knew, but although the room was busy she didn't recognise anyone. 'Tell him I'd like to see him. I'll be in my office—'

'Well, well. If it isn't Supervisor Shan.'

Lia's heart sank. She turned to see Myra Kwok.

'What are you doing here?' A smirk spread across Kwok's face. 'Oh, let me hedge a guess. You're looking for Tan.'

'Yes.'

'You won't find him here.'

'Where is he?'

Kwok glanced at her watch and gave another smirk. 'Oh, look at the time. Tan has a special appointment at nine o'clock. Only twenty minutes to go.'

All the nerves tightened over Lia's body. 'What do you mean?'

Kwok arched her finely plucked eyebrows into points. 'If you can't work it out, then you're not half the police officer he maintains you are.'

Immediately, Lia knew something was hideously, irrevocably wrong. She glanced at the receptionist, but the woman wouldn't meet her eyes. She would get no answers here. Lia rang Deshi, but it went to answer mode. She tried Zhang to no effect.

Eight forty-one.

Both officers would be at the morning briefing at nine.

What was Tan's special appointment? Dread crawled from her lungs and into her heart. She spun on her heel and ran for the police station. She couldn't afford to wait for a car, or to hail a taxi. It would be quicker on foot – she could cut across the square when she got there.

She pounded along Beijing East Road, the noise of traffic filling her ears. Sounds from the pavement came and went as she ran by. People chattering in Mandarin, bartering, calling out.

Where was Tan?

Her boots felt like clay on her feet. She forced herself harder. A truck belched diesel smoke alongside, making her choke.

Mustn't stop. Must find out what's going on.

She burst into the police station. Looked wildly around.

Two desk superintendents and three people waiting on plastic chairs.

'Deshi,' she gasped. 'Where is he?'

'In the briefing room.'

She ran out of reception. Down the corridor, past Commissioner Zhi's office, the smell of cigarette smoke in the air. She slammed into the briefing room. Two dozen officers swung their heads to look at her. Zhang and Deshi were up front.

'Deshi!' she barked. 'Outside, now!'

He catapulted to his feet and ran into the corridor. She pulled the door shut behind him and hustled him away. She didn't want any eavesdroppers.

'Where's Tan?' she demanded.

'He told me not to tell you.'

'I don't care. *I have to see him.*'

Deshi looked at his watch. Colour leached from his face. 'I can't,' he bleated. 'He made me promise.'

She pushed her face into his. 'If you don't tell me, I will change my report and say you were working with Tan to release Tashi.'

'You wouldn't.' He looked shaken.

'Yes,' she hissed. 'I would.'

'He's, er...' He licked his lips. Took another look at his watch. 'He's in jail. The city jail.'

For a moment she was suspended in disbelief, and then reality crashed in. The authorities couldn't have Tan swanning around Tibet where he might be seen by the Tibetans as some sort of hero. He was an embarrassment, a catastrophe that needed containing. Also, he had to be made an example of, in case another member of the security services decided to take matters into their own hands without telling their superiors.

Were they going to send him away? Post him somewhere even worse than Tibet, like Urumqi?

345

'When's he going?' she said.

'Going where?' Deshi looked confused.

'They're banishing him, right? Somewhere awful, to punish him. Where is it? Some tin-pot town near Mongolia?'

Deshi looked away. His skin turned as grey as pewter.

And that was when Lia knew Tan wasn't being expelled or exiled.

He was going to be executed.

55

WHEN TAN HEARD THEM come for him, he felt the same crushing weight on his chest he'd felt ever since he'd heard the procurator's judgement. He glanced at his wrist, but he no longer had his watch. It didn't matter, because the time had come. He didn't need a time piece to tell him that.

His legs weakened and his breathing faltered. His mouth dried up. He wanted to fall to his knees and sob and howl but he didn't. Instead, he closed his eyes and hauled air into his lungs. He didn't want his officers to hear he'd lost it at the end. He wanted to maintain his dignity right up until the last moment.

He heard the peephole creak.

'On your knees, prisoner, and face away from the door.'

Tan complied. He knew how it went. There was little point in fighting the inevitable. He might give the guards a handful of bruises, but what was the point? He'd only lose his pride and besides, it wasn't the guards' fault. They were just doing their job.

He heard the door open.

'Hands behind your back.'

Tan felt the bite of handcuffs around his wrists. Manacles were placed around his ankles, linked with a short chain.

'Up.'

Tan was glad the guard put a hand beneath his elbow and helped him rise because his knees weren't working properly. He took a couple of shuffling steps and felt some strength return. He said, 'I'm OK.'

One of the guards nodded. There were six of them. He knew they needed that many in case he suddenly went berserk. He'd heard of prisoners breaking guards' limbs, their strength trebled by fear and adrenaline. Today they were taking no chances.

With one guard on either side, two ahead of him, two behind, he shuffled along the corridor. He stumbled once, and felt the guard on his left put his hand beneath his elbow. He flinched aside. 'I'm OK,' he repeated. When they reached the end of the corridor they turned right, then left, walking slowly and steadily through the cold labyrinth until, eventually, they reached the end of another bare-brick corridor, dripping with condensation.

A guard unlocked the heavy wooden door and opened it. The room had no windows. A large sheet of heavy, clear plastic covered the floor.

Tan's blood pressure went into free fall and he knew he was as pale as chalk.

It was the killing room.

He swallowed the moan forming in his throat. He wished he had a faith, something or someone to pray to, but he had nothing. His faith had been his work, his job. He supposed his faith had, in recent weeks, become Lia. He'd told Deshi to make sure she didn't know about today, until it was all over. Her husband had been executed. He didn't want to cause her any more pain than was necessary.

He could feel every brush of fabric on his skin. He could see old bloodstains on the sheet and a grey smear that could have been brain matter.

He tried to swallow but he had no saliva. It was as though he had handfuls of cotton wool balled in his mouth and throat. How long had he got? Seconds now, not minutes. He began to tremble.

'Inside,' said the guard. 'On your knees.'

He stepped inside the room. His legs felt boneless. He collapsed to his knees. His pulse was thudding, roaring in his ears.

Somewhere, he heard a woman's shout. She was shouting non-stop, screaming so hard her voice cracked.

For a moment he thought he was hearing things, but then his brain caught up.

A rush of warmth entered his heart.

She'd come to him.

She cared. She had to, to be here.

He closed his eyes.

'I'm with you!' she yelled. 'Tan, I'm here!'

She was sobbing through her shouts.

'I'll take you to Sydney with me! I'll teach you how to swim!'

She shouted again and suddenly he was no longer in the killing room. He couldn't feel the guard's pistol against the back of his head because he was no longer there. He was sitting on a broad yellow beach looking out to sea. He could hear seagulls and children playing. He was watching Lia leaping onto her board in a single fluid movement and then she was arcing along the blue-green roller, surfing for the beach, surfing for—

56

WHEN TAN DIED, ALL the dislike and mistrust she had harboured for him ceased to be. She saw him as the man he was, deeply patriotic and deeply passionate. He'd been a ruthless man, occasionally brutal and often cruel, but he'd never acted without good reason. It didn't excuse any of his actions, Yeshe still bore the scars, but at least she now understood him.

Nobody would tell her what they did with his body. It could have been sent to his parents, or thrown into the local incinerator, she'd never know. She kept feeling an urge to seek him out, talk with him, ask him why he'd chosen to die for her. Having no grave to visit, she made a little shrine for him in front of the stone Buddha on her balcony, where she lit a candle for him every day.

Do you believe in reincarnation?

She was glad she'd said he'd be a leopard. He'd been pleased, she could tell.

In his death, she'd seen too much of a system that destroyed as much as it created. She couldn't look at Myra Kwok or Jenny Wang. She found it hard to meet Deshi's eye. The rumours surrounding Tan's death would take weeks to die down. She didn't talk about it to anybody. She endured the enquiring looks and gossip like she would the symptoms of a bad cold, knowing they would eventually go away.

Dawa Rinpoche had vanished, who-knew-where. Tenzin, after giving evidence that he'd worked for a rogue group of obsessed and xenophobic Chinese patriots, escaped from jail, never to be seen again. Jenny blamed his escape on his accomplices but Lia guessed she would have transferred Tenzin back to Beijing. If she didn't look after her agents, she wouldn't have any left. Zapa, however, was still in place at the Tashilhunpo Monastery. Lia wondered how many more monks worked for the PSB. What had Jenny said?

We started recruiting right across the board the instant the Dalai Lama fled in 1959.

Which could mean a dozen or ten dozen, she had no way of knowing. Part of her wanted to visit the new Abbot at the Meru Nyingba Monastery and tell him of the spies, but the other part knew she wouldn't. The PSB needed reliable and regular intelligence to keep the region stable. And she was, after all, a police officer who saw the value of such information.

On Saturday she drove to Xigatsê. Booked herself into the Zanglong Hotel. Had dinner with Chen.

'So, you did it,' he said.

'Yes.' She still felt tired from it all.

'Do you think you did the right thing?'

She had no hesitation. 'Yes.'

He nodded. 'I think so too.'

*

She read and reread Tan's letter and although she tried to keep it pristine, it gradually softened beneath her fingers and the middle fold began to wear. It wasn't a long communication. It was purely practical and held no sentimentality, but seeing the bold sweeps of his pen brought her a strange comfort. He'd asked her to visit two little girls at the Children's Welfare Institute and break the news that he was dead. Lia didn't tell them he'd been executed but said he'd died in an accident, and when they heard, both girls cried, and Lia had held them in her arms, shocked at the strength of their emotions.

'But they hardly knew him,' she said to Betty Lu, the director of the institute.

'He visited every day,' Betty Lu said. 'He brought them toys, gifts. He was their benefactor. Besides...' Her face grimaced.

'What?'

'You may not understand this, but they lost their pet dog recently. It was thanks to the dog that Tan Dao discovered them. Tan fed the dog, you see, which, like the girls, was starving.' Betty Lu sighed. 'Tibetans love their dogs. They're like one of the family. Not only have Dolkar and Lhamu lost a friend in the dog, but their elder brother too.'

'May I visit the girls?' Lia asked. 'Maybe bring them home to my apartment occasionally? My grandmother would enjoy seeing them.'

'They would love that.' Betty Lu beamed. 'Where Tan Dao was their brother, you will become their sister.'

Betty Lu went on to tell Lia that the day before he'd died, Tan had settled enough money on the girls to ensure their welfare and education throughout their childhood and beyond. 'He was very generous,' she added.

'Yes,' Lia agreed. 'Very.'

*

A month later, when the sun was low in the evening sky, flaming yellow against the snowy peaks, a novice – no more than eight years old – turned up at her apartment and asked for her to join him at the Meru Nyingba Monastery.

He led her through the Barkhor, busy with pilgrims and market shoppers. Dogs barked and people chattered, creating an energetic atmosphere that vanished the instant she stepped inside the temple. Peace descended, broken only by the murmur of prayers and mantras, the occasional tinkling of a bell. The novice led her to the rich red curtain and pulled it back to let her through. She hesitated.

'It's all right, Hariti,' he said. 'You are quite safe.'

She followed him up the stairs and into the Abbot's room. Nothing appeared to have changed. Same desk in the corner. Same two high-backed chairs. She glanced at the floorboards where she knew the trapdoor lay, but couldn't see any evidence of it. Nor had Hua Ming discovered it, which pleased her.

'Hariti,' said the new Abbot warmly.

He was younger than she expected, perhaps in his fifties. He had a lively, vigorous air that was infectious. She'd barely greeted him when four lamas also entered the room. The same four who had toured Tibet with Dawa Rinpoche. They appeared more animated than she remembered. They had obviously recovered from their gruelling journey.

'They have come together one last time,' the new Abbot stated. He took a seat, but the four lamas remained standing.

'We have splendid news,' the Abbot told her.

Lia found herself holding her breath.

'The young Panchen Lama made it to India. Tashi has arrived in Dharamsala, where the Central Tibetan Administration lies. The Dalai Lama has recognised him as the twelfth Panchen Lama.'

Lia's fingers went to the simple red cotton necklance Tashi had given her, and which she never removed. A rush of relief and pleasure rolled through her.

He smiled. 'His Holiness wishes to give you a gift to show his appreciation of your help.'

Lia began to protest – she didn't need a present from Tashi – but the Abbot stopped her from speaking by holding up a hand.

'It is, he says, the most precious gift he could think of.'

The Abbot gestured at one of the lamas, who crossed the room and opened the door. Lia saw a small white bundle of fur trot inside and look around, slightly bewildered.

'Cherry?' she said.

Immediately the dog turned her head and the next instant she was tearing across the room and jumping up at Lia's knees. She was half-barking, half-whimpering with pleasure. Lia couldn't believe the dog recognised her, but it seemed she did.

Lia bent and picked the dog up. Cherry twisted in her embrace, licking and squirming with delight.

'She is yours,' the Abbot told Lia. He was beaming. 'She will keep you warm when you feel the cold, and she will keep you company when you are lonely.'

When Lia brought Cherry home, Fang Dongmei took one look at the dog and said, 'What's that? It looks like a duster.'

'It's for the girls. A gift from *Da ge*, their big brother.'

Lhamu and Dolkar fell on Cherry with cries of delight. Cherry, in turn, seemed delighted with all the fuss.

Fang Dongmei rolled her eyes. 'Wrong colour dog. Too white. It is no good for soup. No meat on it.'

Lia shot her grandmother a stern look. 'If you even think——'

'OK, OK.' Fang Dongmei flung up her hands in angry surrender. 'But don't forget it's just another mouth to feed.' The old woman grumbled and glowered, but when Lia returned home the following evening, it was to find Cherry curled on Fang Dongmei's lap.

She said dismissively, 'I only let it up to help keep me warm.'

Acknowledgements

FIRSTLY, A SPECIAL THANK you goes to Gary Heads, CEO of Right Nuisance Publishing, for plucking my manuscript from the bottom drawer and publishing it so handsomely. Tibet is a particular passion of mine, having travelled through the country, and bringing this story to a wider audience means more than I can say.

Grateful thanks to Ann Lombardo, for her expert knowledge of Chinese culture as well as the language. Thanks to Susan Opie for a terrific copy-edit, and thanks to Sam Butler and everyone at the Tibet Relief Fund for their invaluable support.

A deep and heartfelt thank you to Steve Ayres who has been a part of this book since its inception. You are my go-to expert on so many things I don't know what I would do without you.

Thanks also to Lisa Foskett, and to Rob Child for such a fantastic cover and a beautiful map.

Lastly, thanks to my mother for introducing me to Tibet when I was a child, and for encouraging me not only to go there, but to respect and cherish it for the magical and spiritual place that it is.

This book is a work of fiction, and some of the locations are entirely fictional, but its background is authentic and the story regrettably plausible. Please bear in mind that I am not an expert on China or Tibet, or Tibetan Buddhism and reincarnation, and that any mistakes made will be mine.